Louisburg Square

LOUISBURG SQUARE

THE MACMILLAN COMPANY
NEW YORK · BOSTON · CHICAGO · DALLAS
ATLANTA · SAN FRANCISCO

MACMILLAN & CO., LIMITED
LONDON · BOMBAY · CALCUTTA
MELBOURNE

THE MACMILLAN CO. OF CANADA, LTD.
TORONTO

No. 8 Louisburg Square

LOUISBURG SQUARE

BY

ROBERT CUTLER

ILLUSTRATED BY
ELISE AMES

New York

THE MACMILLAN COMPANY

1917

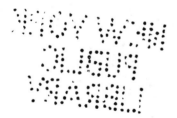

TO

THE MEMORY OF MY MOTHER

"No spring nor summer's beauty hath such grace
As I have seen in one autumnal face."

Brookline 1915-1916

CONTENTS

CONTENTS

LIST OF ILLUSTRATIONS

LOUISBURG SQUARE

LOUISBURG SQUARE

CHAPTER I

AN INTRODUCTION TO EIGHT LOUISBURG SQUARE

MR. SINGLETON SINGLETON, attired in his flowered silk wrapper, reclined at length upon a chintz-covered ottoman and stared passively through the frosted panes of his study window. For a long time he had held himself motionless, with so much unnatural stiffness in his pose and so much unnatural dulness in his eye that he seemed scarcely alive. He was, in fact, a great invalid, a potential paralytic, whose potentiality increased with the passage of years, as if it were a tender flower watered by the curative baths prescribed by his doctors.

But he had not always been a passive, white old man, who spoke only at the rarest intervals, and who lived almost a hermit in his house at 8 Louisburg Square. Once Mr. Singleton Singleton had been the flower of Boston's young men. Educated abroad, he had returned with a reputation for wildness and a large fortune, both guarantees to popularity. The best dancer, the most fluent speaker, possessed of exquisite manners and unlimited means, to mothers eligible, to fathers agreeable, to daughters engrossing, he had early become a lion of society. His exercise was taken in the ball room, his

business transacted over the tea-table; he was to be
the catch of the season.   No lady with a pretty
daughter but kept an eye on his goings and comings;
no father with a doubtful income but took him aside
at the Sarcophagus Club for a chat.   But Mr. Singleton Singleton deftly avoided all the nets spread
to enmesh him and by degrees became a confirmed
bachelor.   Far from necessitating his withdrawal
from the ball-room, his single blessedness served
rather to stimulate his interest in society.   He never
missed a ball; neither waltz nor two-step passed
without his nimble figure gliding through the dancers.
As a cotillion leader he was perfection.   It came to
be a recognised thing that unless Mr. Singleton Singleton led your cotillion, your ball could not really
achieve success.   By the pyrotechnical journals he
was established as the social leader of Boston, and
in that eminent position reigned for a score of years,
alone and undisputed.   Yet despite the tinsel of his
position, despite the hideous unreality of calling
cards and cutaways, there was in him that ability
to love which dignifies humanity.

All men must have their day, however, and Mr.
Singleton Singleton had his.   The hilarious tide of
modern dances surged into the ballroom.   A man
to whom Strauss was perfection, with perhaps a
polka for variety, naturally found ragtime barbaric
and impossible.   In dismay this arbiter of society
forbade the one-step and the maxixe, but the waves
would not listen to Canute.   In a year Mr. Singleton
Singleton was a changed man; and when the cotillion
went out of vogue, at the same time he, too, went out,
for the one thing which he could do supremely well
was no longer the thing to do.   Retiring from the
world of society, he shut himself up in Louisburg

Square, and thereafter the only intimation which Boston had that this once brilliant social light had not entirely gone out, was an occasional glimpse of a long, paralytic figure being driven through the parkway in a victoria.

This is by way of explaining why on this clear, crisp December morning Mr. Singleton Singleton reclined on his chintz-covered ottoman, gazing passively out of the frosty window. He did this simply because there was nothing else for him to do. For years he had sat there every morning on the same chintz-covered ottoman, staring idly out of the same window with unspeculative eyes. He seldom looked at anything in particular. After all, what was the use? He was only waiting; for such people there is no field of vision.

This morning, however, his eye had fallen on the chimney-pot across the way. He frowned at it. It did not offend him that the house should have a chimney-pot, for they were necessary evils; but this particular chimney-pot, the most elevated and salient feature of the Square, was made of green tin. All day long the sun shone upon the innovation. Enhanced by the surrounding snow, its blatant green dazzled offensively, shocking his proprietary interest in the Square — that quaint, semi-impregnable corner of the past which was so very dear to him. Since John Singleton Copley had owned the whole of the west slope of Beacon Hill, some member of his family had always dwelt there. It was in the Copley blood to love Louisburg Square, and Mr. Singleton Singleton was the oldest of the Copley blood. And then it was such a sympathetic place to wait in! With its dying elms, its faded brick houses, its cobble pavement and wrought-iron fence, all now clothed in white by the late snowfall, it seemed like himself to be waiting for Something to come and sweep it away. To feel this similarity was natural. Each step of the march of progress in the Square wounded him. Bad enough to see a convent established at number 21, and be compelled forever to be stared down by its lofty motto — *per augusta ad augusta* —; bad enough to have number 2 turned into a boarding-house for theological students, without the Misses Hepplethwaite across the way — Jane and Joan, whom he had known from their childhood — decorating their chimneys with green tin. From the artistic point of view it offended; regarded as a symbol of progression, it was mortal.

Somewhere in the house buzzed a refined electric bell; the sound came to the invalid's ear as if through rolls of thick velvet.

"Dr. Cary to see you, sir." A servant had quietly entered the room.

As if reluctant to leave off staring out of the window, Mr. Singleton Singleton slowly turned his head, but did not speak. He seldom spoke to his friends, never to his servants.

"He's in a great hurry, sir," the servant went on. "You'll see him, won't you? He's coming up."

There was a quick, light step on the stairs outside, and a little man with steel blue eyes hurried into the room. Dressed in white from top to toe save for a black satin tie, he was a perfect picture of hygienic spick-and-spanness. To the casual observer Dr. Cary scarcely appeared a distinguished surgeon and the recently appointed Chief of the new Longwood Hospital; but if in a crowd of men his stature handicapped him, the incision of his speech and the keen-

ness of his eyes soon betrayed his genius. About
him floated the dry, clean odour of hospitals, which,
when one stood in his presence, made the nostrils
tingle not unpleasantly. With all his spotlessness,
however, it was readily visible from the lines in his
face that he was the busiest man alive. Like all
great leaders he was daily overworked, but loved
and gloried in the stress of life. It suited him exactly to live on a schedule, to have just so much time
for meals, so much for committees, and so much for
correspondence. To live eagerly and zealously is
actually to live.

" Sorry to be rude and not wait, Tony," he cried
even before he reached the room. " I'm in a dreadful hurry. Have a committee at State House on
pure milk at eleven-thirty, so I can only —"

Dr. Cary did not finish what he had begun to say.
It was his custom not to waste time on obvious conclusions. Grasping Mr. Singleton Singleton's listless hand, he drew up a chair and sat down beside
him.

" Well, how are you to-day? " he rattled on, evidently busied only in his conversation, while in reality
making a keen observation of his friend's condition.
" Haven't been in for some time, have I? Thought
I'd better drop in this morning on the way to the
State House. They're trying to lower the milk re-
quirements. Outrageous. . . . Never could see
why you persisted in living up here on this hillside
. . . Let me feel your pulse, will you? . . . It almost breaks the motor every time I come to see you,
and with the snow it's like climbing the Himalayas.
Should think you'd feel as if you were sliding off into
the Charles all the time . . . Good! Pulse bet-

ter. . . . Mt. Vernon St. seems a little more per-
pendicular every time I — what are you pointing at,
Tony?"

Mr. Singleton Singleton's long, pale hand was
stretched out toward a corner of the room.

"Desk?"

The invalid nodded assent.

"What is it? On top? Oh! This envelope
for me? What is it? Shall I open it?"

His friend nodded again.

"Hullo!" cried Dr. Cary in surprise, as he tore
across the envelope. "What's this for? A thousand dollars! You don't owe me a thousand dollars, Tony!"

"Services." At length Mr. Singleton Singleton
spoke; one dull word, accompanied by a ghost of a
smile.

Dr. Cary folded up the cheque and put it back in
the envelope.

"My dear Tony, how many times do I have to
say that I won't take anything from you? Services,
indeed! If we weren't the oldest friends, do you
suppose I'd take the time to come and straighten you
out every so often. Here —"

Mr. Singleton Singleton shook his head, and spoke
again. "Hospital."

"You mean to give it to the Longwood?" Dr.
Cary's eyes snapped with pleasure. "Good! We
always need more free beds. You're most kind,
most kind. You're a blessing to the hospital,
Tony!" The doctor moved to the window.
"Lord! It's a glorious day out! Do you see how
the snow sparkles? You don't miss any day out-
doors?" (Mr. Singleton Singleton shook his
head). "I'm glad to hear it. You ought to find

the sleighing wonderful. . . . Hullo, here's your
goddaughter outside. Beautiful girl, Tony. And
to-day she looks —"

A happy glow came over Mr. Singleton Singleton's face.   Very slowly he arose from his ottoman
and moved to the window with an uncertain, heavy
step, suggesting for all the world, as Dr. Cary took
his arm to help him, a great leviathan being warped
into its dock by a smart little tug.

"There she is. See her? Lean a little this way.
There! She's talking to some one. One of the
Hepplethwaites, I think. Live opposite, don't
they?" The invalid nodding absently, Dr. Cary
rambled on. "Rosalind is a lovely girl. By
George, I wish she were my goddaughter! You
should have married yourself, Tony; then you
wouldn't have had to steal one of your cousin's children like this. I swear I should think Jack would
be jealous, you have her here so much. But I can't
blame you."

Mr. Singleton Singleton beamed in his paralytic
way, as men always do and always will at praise for
what is nearest to their hearts.

"I often tell my son, Ben — you haven't seen
Ben for ages, have you? — I often tell Ben I wish
he'd get to know her. Ben's worse than you were
when you were young. He won't look at a girl;
thinks they're silly things, an entirely different species
from man. I suppose that's because his mother died
when he was so young. He's never known anything
about the other sex at all. Why, Tony, I don't believe he's spoken to a girl in two years. Think of
it! He'll dry into dust at that law office of his with
his investigations and one thing and another. Lord
save us!" he cried suddenly, looking at a clock on

the wall. " I've got two minutes to the State House. Good-bye, Tony. Cheer yourself up, old man. I'll be around next week. . . . Some day I'm going to take that Corot out of the front hall here, I like it so much."

With a merry laugh Dr. Cary pressed his friend's hand, was down the stairs, in his fur coat, out of doors, and into his motor, crying out a " good morning " to Miss Copley, waving to his friend in the window, and bustling away to his milk investigation at eleven thirty. Rosalind Copley passed him at the front door. In a moment she was up the stairs and in her godfather's arms, glowing and out of breath.

" Rose! " he cried, his dull voice almost happy and tender.

" Dear Uncle Sing-Sing! "

She kissed her godfather warmly on both cheeks and sat him gently down on the ottoman. " Uncle Sing-Sing " was the unconventional shortening of Singleton Singleton which she had adopted when a very little girl. Like most such names, it had victoriously weathered the storm of years and maternal disapprobation.

" Why has Dr. Cary been here? You haven't been feeling badly? "

" No, dear." He always made an effort to talk when Rosalind was with him. " Sit down."

She seated herself beside him on the ottoman. Against the dull flowers of his silk wrapper the blue of her eyes and suit was refreshingly clear. There were roses in her cheeks and hands, and the December wind had blown strands of her golden hair out from under her hat. Beside the light grace of her youth his age seemed ponderous.

"It gave me a start to see the doctor coming so early.   He usually visits late in the afternoon."

"On his way to State House."

"Oh!   Did he want anything in particular?"

Mr. Singleton Singleton made a dry sound in his throat, perhaps intended for a laugh.

"Wanted you to marry Ben."

"Ben?"   Rosalind laughed prettily, throwing her head back and bringing her shoulders together. "His son?' He'll never marry any one.   Never looks at a girl.   Why, I've asked him to the house often, but he'll never come.   He scarcely speaks to me."

Across Mr. Singleton Singleton's face flitted an air of relief.

"Why, you dear old Uncle Sing-Sing!" Rosalind laughed again, looking at him out of the corners of her eyes.   "Did you think I wanted to get married?   I don't love any one enough — except you."

Whereat she kissed him again, rearranged his pearl scarf-pin, and declared for taking off her hat.

"No," protested her godfather, "sleigh."

"Soon?"

"Ten minutes."

"Well, I can't stay for long; I have to be at Brimmer House at twelve-thirty.   You'll never guess what I've got to do this afternoon!   I'm going to take ten little Italian imps through the Art Museum!   What do you think of that, Uncle Sing-Sing?"

"Large order."

"I should say it was," replied Rosalind. "They're the best of the class, though, and I've taken them before to lots and lots of places.   I've invited them to have tea at home after the Museum."

Mr. Singleton Singleton made the dry sound again in his throat.

"I know what that means! That mother'll be upset? She is already. You should have heard her telling Paris what to serve for tea; it was as if several crowned heads were coming to 29 Commonwealth. But the children will have a glorious time. I'll invite you to tea, Uncle Sing-Sing," she added merrily. "It's at four o'clock."

"The sleigh is quite ready, sir."

Rosalind smiled a good morning to the servant who made this announcement. Years ago Mr. Singleton Singleton had brought him back from Paris, and now he was a neat old fellow with the face of a bishop and the manners of a cardinal. For years Edouard, for such was his name, had been the cog on which 8 Louisburg Square had moved. Mr. Singleton Singleton had lost his taste for French novels; he had forgotten the French tongue; his love for Paris had faded; everything connected with his stay at the Beaux Arts was changed — everything save Edouard, and the years passed, but he remained still the same.

He now took one of the invalid's arms and Rosalind the other. Between them they steered the old man down the stairway and into his great fur coat. For the more perilous transfer down the icy front steps and into the sleigh, before which two roans were stamping down the snow, the coachman and footman were summoned as auxiliaries. By dint of propping the invalid up here and pushing him on there, they at length hoisted him into the sleigh like a very elegant bag of meal. Rosalind jumped in;

the footman sprang up after the coachman; the whip cracked; the bells jingled pleasantly; and away they went out of the quaint, quiet shyness of Louisburg Square into the noisy brilliancy of the world.

CHAPTER II

EXPLAINING GENERAL WASHINGTON

IT was one of those rare and beautiful afternoons which sometimes come to Boston in December. For once the fallen snow had not changed to slush, and lay clean and sparkling over the city without a trace of the clammy mist which usually succeeds a storm. Everywhere was winter. To the delight of youth and to the disgust of age great drifts of snow clothed and choked the city. Lo! the very heart of Boston was become a polar battle-ground. An army of lop-sided snowmen were over night possessed of the Public Gardens, and the air of the Common lived with volleys of snowballs. The sun was scarcely in the heavens before a dozen adventurous skirmishers had been dragged from the Frog-pond, through which a bold leader, like Ethan Allen of old, had led an icy charge on an imagined Ticonderoga. Even Louisburg Square resounded with the shrill pipings of the children of the district, myriad little creatures, who swarmed in the snow-drifts as if to the temperature born or sought to blow up with their ice-bombs the snowy turbans under which the two little statues at either end of the enclosure staggered. *Chasseurs alpins* indeed, these tiny stormers of Beacon Hill! The houses on Commonwealth Avenue took on a new and livelier aspect; while here and there even a house on Newbury Street, as the sun made myriad reflections on its

snow-covered sides, undertook to sparkle rather
shyly, like an old spinster pleased with a new frock.
All day long the sun had dazzled on the snow, caus-
ing old gentlemen to put on their blue spectacles and
babies in their carriages to hold little mittens before
their eyes; all day long the streets had jingled with
sleighbells, sounding the merrier in the clear, crisp
air. Such air as it was! Air that made you run
down steps you had walked before; that sent the
children out of doors with eager laughter and old
ladies in white caps to the front windows to see them
at play; that mated the tingling blood with every
passing bell; that lent zest to living. A merry day,
a bright day, a clean day, a day which passed too
soon even for those confirmed in winter-hatred.

The sun had just sunk below the building tops,
leaving in the winter's sky the afterglow of a very
bright fire suddenly gone out on a very cold night.
In the gathering gloom a curious little troup marched
down the centre path of Commonwealth Avenue
under the snow-gloved fingers of the deciduous trees.
There were twelve little girls in all, walking two by
two and swinging their clasped hands. Red tam-o'-
shanters and red mittens, clearly gifts, were the uniform wear for the head and hands, but their coats
showed a great disparity in impoverished taste. A
soiled white sheepskin, a blue woollen, a red cotton,
a green Heaven-knows-what with pieces of indescribable fur stuck on here and there, any and every
species of outer garment was in evidence. In winter
the poor must shift as best they can; whatever is
warm must perforce be handsome. Behind this
motley array walked a simply but fashionably
dressed young lady, whose gold hair and fair complexion contrasted with the Latin colouring of the

little girls. It was pretty to see the way in which she marshalled their unruly activity and the skilfullness which she employed in ferrying them across Arlington Street, streaming with automobiles and sleighs. Several men turned their heads to watch her; and a few acquaintances, on the way home from their offices, bowed or cried out a laughing compliment.

At the entrance to the Public Gardens a little clamour arose; for the hundredth time that day the girls were in disagreement. They had squabbled in their Italian dialect over the pictures in the Art Museum; they had marvelled with lustrous and longing eyes before the different cakes at tea; now the question of the route home divided them. Let there be two sides to a question and your Italian will argue and gesticulate till Doomsday. To settle the controversy the young lady shooed the girls through the iron gate of the Gardens, much as one might a brood of chickens.

A few yards before them the equestrian statue of Washington loomed in the darkness on its granite pedestal. In a country notorious for ineffective statuary, the horse and rider, rising grandly in the twilight, dominated with high pride their surroundings. The ghostly outline against the cold, dark sky was oddly decorated with the snow which lay upon the general's hat, his shoulders, saddle, and horse. As the group drew near, the young lady bowed her head respectfully.

" Why you do-a that, lady? " asked a little voice.

" What, Maria? "

" Bend your head, lak sad people? "

" I was bowing to the statue. My father taught me that when I was a little girl and ever since I've done it almost without thinking."

Keenly interested in everything, the little group had stopped to gape up at the huge underside of the horse.

"What ees?" piped up a girl who had been in America scarcely more than a year.

"It's a statue of — why don't you know? Don't any of you know? Bici? Maria? Helena? Look at it!"

"Garibaldi!" decisively answered the little Sicilian who had spoken before.

The others hung back.

"Oh, come! You must know. Look again!"

"Thea da Roosevelt," ventured Maria doubtfully.

"Oh, no, girls, no!" cried the young lady, putting her hands to her ears. "Who was the Father of his Country? Who was the first President of the United States?"

"Abram Lincoll!" chorused half of the group.

"No! Non so!" cried Helena, the oldest of the girls. "I knowa now. It was Georga Washaton. I knowa. He greata, biga man. Live long ago and fighta Spain."

"You've got his name right, Helena, at least. It is George Washington, children. That's a name you all ought to love and respect. Can you all say it? George Washington."

The girls tried it, the syllables sounding strange on Latin tongues; but the little Sicilian, even after she had mastered the name, still had a feeling that this might only be the American way of saying Garibaldi, a suspicion which the ensuing explanation greatly strengthened. The young lady was decidedly at a loss how to give the salient facts about Washington to these little foreigners; to crowd into

a few minutes the story of the cherry tree, the Revolution, the Presidency, and the " first in peace " was
after all no small task.   Little wonder that she
floundered and spoke like a primer, inwardly grateful that only her little girls were listening to her
efforts.   She did not tell it well, she knew, but still
she thought it strange that the children were not
more interested, strange that they stared so avidly
at something directly behind her.   Words which
they usually caught up like pearls from her lips now
seemed to fall unnoticed.   It made the young lady a
little angry.

"— and you must never forget this man.   He was
the truest, finest American we have ever ——"

She could bear that concerted stare no longer.
As she turned quickly about, an exclamation of surprise escaped her; some ten feet off stood a tall young
man with a green bag in his hand, evidently listening to her historical platitudes with the deepest and
most interested attention.

" Mr. Cary! "

" O — I — er —.   Good evening, Miss Copley."

Rosalind felt her face flood with red and was
grateful for the night.   In the ensuing silence the
man moved his feet nervously in the snow.

" I suppose — I suppose it was very rude of me
to — er — listen, but I ——.   I don't know how I
came to —"

" Oh! " remarked Rosalind, coldly.

" I hope you'll — you'll let me apologise."

He came a step nearer.   Holding their breath,
the little girls huddled close together, each one feeling that at last she was seeing how life was lived in
the Upper Ten.   All the inherent romanticism of
the Latin race rounded their young eyes.   Perhaps

had Rosalind and Mr. Cary known that their behaviour was moulding the future conduct of their
spectators they might have performed more gracefully.   As it was, the conversation was largely made
up of a most uncomfortable silence.

"Certainly I shall let you apologise," said Rosalind with decision.   She paused significantly.   "But
I think I ought to punish you."

"I — I suppose you ought."

Cary administered an inward chastisement to himself; here was a pretty mess!   How stupidly careless of him to have listened!   While he wondered
how he might withdraw with the least rudeness,
Rosalind turned over in her mind a fitting method of
reprisal.   She was very angry that any one should
have overheard her kindergarten lecture on Washington.   To be caught would have piqued a saint.

"I know what you shall do.   You shall help me
take the girls back to Brimmer House!"   She almost laughed; surely this was the ideal penance for
a misogynist!

"Brimmer House!"   Cary repeated feebly, chill-
ing at the thought.   He was six feet of bashfulness,
and groaned inwardly.

"Yes!   And I think if I took your arm, it would
be safer — it's so dark and slippery!"

Having thus destroyed the possibility of escape,
she accepted his unwilling arm and bade the children
move on ahead — which they obediently did, though
with faces turned toward herself and Cary.   Never
did Orpheus cast a more interested glance rearward
to Eurydice than the relentless gaze of these twelve
little girls.   They advanced like toy children whose
moveable heads have stuck permanently in the wrong
direction — a posture none too favourable to prog-

ress and very inconvenient for on-coming pedestrians.

"I was surprised; that was it," Cary was saying.
"You see I didn't know that your type of girl did
anything like this."

"Oh! What did you think?"

"Why, I don't know," he replied, falling in the
trap which she had laid for him. "I don't know as
I ever did think very much about it. I guess I
thought you — er — dressed and danced and — er
— went to the theatre."

"Your opinion was not very high."

"No. That's why it was such a surprise to see
you standing there, preaching away like — er —
like anything about Washington."

"Did you hear much of it?"

"Every word," he replied innocently. "I
wouldn't have missed it for anything. Why, it's
changed my views immensely."

So he had heard every word of it! And it had
changed his views immensely! As Rosalind's face
burned with pique, she covenanted with herself for
revenge upon this young scorner of women. But she
spoke as if honey were on her tongue and banter on
her lips.

"I wish you wouldn't talk about me as if I were
being experimented on! It makes me feel cold all
over. When you say in that scientific way that your
views have changed, I feel as if you had just taken
me out of a test tube for examination."

"I'm sorry," said Cary humbly. He wondered
miserably how a man dealt with woman's words, and
fell silent.

When they arrived at Charles Street, he saw her
for the first time clearly under an electric light.
Momentarily her face, framed by her blue fox furs,

stood out in relief. His glance was one of hasty curiosity, but Rosalind, who knew what would follow, stared straight ahead and pretended obliviousness. Cary felt a little thrill of excitement. He looked at her again under the next light, but no longer curiously or scientifically, no longer interested in views; now he looked at her because he felt impelled to. As each light was passed he began to anticipate the next, hoping that it would be brighter and clearer than the last. Having never thought of a girl or looked at one without necessity, he found an odd, mischievous pleasure in stealing these unnatural glances. There was more than novelty in it; he was experiencing the delight of an unreluctant Adam first tasting forbidden fruit. Light succeeded light, and still Rosalind permitted him to cast these sidelong glances. Not until they swung into Brimmer Street did she turn towards him; then their eyes met, and Cary, fairly caught, was not a little moved. Strange that such a thing should stir him, he thought, as he dropped his glance. He did not dare look again; something told him that her eyes were still bent upon him and that she knew that he had been staring at her.

Of his strange uneasiness Rosalind was fully aware. When at length they turned up the dull steps of Brimmer House, she felt certain that she had changed his views much more than he suspected.

CHAPTER III

"WELL, my dear Tony, I only wish you and Jack had been here to see how well-behaved and polite they were! It was a revelation to me. You would have laughed at the naïve way in which they mimicked everything Rose did. She is their idol. When they saw her take lemon with her tea, they all bravely followed suit, although one little girl had been making eyes at the cream from the moment Paris brought it in."

Mrs. Copley was speaking. She sat behind an inlaid walnut table, on which gleamed a silver tea set dating from Colonial days. Though the room was lighted but dimly, the silver shone in the blaze of a wood fire, which flamed opposite her in a cheerful accompaniment to the softly singing kettle. On the dim mantelpiece of veined marble an old-fashioned clock ticked off ponderous seconds. The fire beneath it dominated the large room, dancing on the French walnut panels of the walls and finding an occasional reflection on the rich backs of the books which filled the shelves extending from the floor to the elaborate ceiling. Above the fire-place hung a self-portrait of John Singleton Copley; the red, placid face benevolently smiled about his shadowy and refined surroundings, as if pleased to observe that his descendants were free from the pecuniary difficulties which sometimes had beset him. Below

20

the great, gold-framed portrait, close to the welcome warmth of the fire, the smiling and red-faced John Singleton Copley of the present day sank back into a most comfortable arm-chair of red brocade and warmed his knees.

Although not immediately visible, Mr. Singleton Singleton was also present.   Safe from observation and intrusion, he sat in the embrasure formed by the front window which rounded out towards Commonwealth Avenue.   It was his favourite spot in the house.   Knowing well the strategic value of the place, he had for years ambushed himself behind the book-covered table and the great brocade curtains, hidden from the eye of undesirable callers.   Mrs. Copley had known him to stay there for hours, seeing but unseen.   Whether he listened no one could tell; at least he never spoke, and his taciturnity favoured his place of retirement.   A chosen few were admitted to his secret; but to society in general he was unknown as a visitor at his cousin's house.

"As for Paris," Mrs. Copley went on, "they found him quite inexplicable.   Some of them suspected him of being Rose's father.   To have a man in a dress suit wait on them seemed beyond belief; evidently they considered such a costume fit only for the ultra rich."

"How did Paris like 'em?" asked her husband.

"I heard him tell Albert that they were distressingly poor, but ' as 'ow they be'aved themselves very decorous.' "

Mrs. Copley's rich, warm laugh was entirely harmonic with her surroundings and with herself.   She was renowned in Boston for a beauty which as the years went by seemed rather to increase than to fade. Her hair had turned white before thirty, and most

fortunately for her, since it accentuated the untroubled loveliness which rested in her eyes and
moulded her lips.   Dressed in something black from
the Rue de la Paix and with the Copley pearls about
her neck, she was an object which no one in Boston,
from the most eager débutante to the most lovely
Victorian remnant, could equal.   Mrs. Copley knew
this — not vaingloriously, not spitefully, but as one
knows any incontrovertible fact — and lived accordingly.   Her clothes were the most elegant in Boston;
her jewels the most perfect; her coiffures the most
painstaking.   After all, why not?   Knowing her
talent to be beauty, she determined to put it to good
advantage, and did so with success unquestionable.
As the firelight made shadows in her soft white hair
and danced in each trembling pearl about her neck,
she seemed to be the quintessence of the room's aris-
tocratic beauty.

There sounded a hearty ring at the front-door
bell; footsteps echoed on the marble-flagged hall outside; and a little man with shining eyes and white
hair like Mrs. Copley's popped into the room.

"Hullo, Jack! Beth, my dear!"   Smack!   The
little man's eyes twinkled as he kissed her on the
cheek.   "Lovely as ever!   Tony, how are you?"
This to the invisible Mr. Singleton Singleton, whose
face, like that of an austere and invalid Cheshire Cat,
appeared at his name above a pile of books, and as
soon faded again behind the curtains.

"Maybe this fire isn't good!   There's too much
ice on the front steps; I almost killed myself.
Thank you! Two lumps. Thoughtful   sister!
Lovely creature!"

The little man settled in a chair, slapped his leg,
took his tea, cocked his head on one side like an in-

quisitive bird, and laughed an internal laugh, with
all the expressions of extreme merriment on his face
and none of its boisterousness on his lips.

"Guess where I've been!   You never can!"

"Keith's!" ventured his sister, who knew his
habits.

"The Sarcophagus Club."   This from Mr. Copley who knew his habits better.

"All wrong!   All wrong!   I've been to Mrs.
Thayer's to hear Pierre Rolland, the French editor,
speak.   And in French, too."

"Oh!   I hoped you could tell us about it!"
Mrs. Copley made up a face at him.   She was very
fond of her brother — he formed an excellent subject for her innocent witticisms.

"I can!   Tremendously interesting.   All about
sex!   You should have gone; every one should have
gone; done 'em all good.   I'm a changed man.
Swear I am.   Very brilliant chap, Rolland; brother
of the great tenor, Lucien.   Listen to what happened!   Had a front row seat on the left-hand side
and if Jane and Joan Hepplethwaite didn't see me
there and come and sit down beside me before every
one — on purpose!   They follow me everywhere.
I shall take out my razor and end it all some day.
Really!   Driven to drink and all that, you know.
One is bad enough, but now they're both pursuing
me.   I don't boast, Jack!   It's awful to be attacked
from the rear; a débutante I can withstand, but those
two old —   I don't want to marry; I won't marry!
I'm fifty years old, and I believe in marrying for love.
Love at fifty — where is it?"

Having thus lashed himself into a fury, the little
man drank his tea off at a single draught, set the cup
down with a rattle, and stared darkly into the fire.

"Well, Jo-Jo, you shouldn't be so attractive!
You shouldn't lay yourself out to captivate," reproved his sister.

Her brother was up in a second. "Captivate!
Bah! I set myself out to captivate! Why, I tell
you, Beth, they pursue me! If I didn't live at the
Sarcophagus Club, I believe they'd bring flowers to
my room and call on me."

The front door bell rang again.

"I'll wager that's them; I'll wager anything.
They hunt me, Beth, really! You're a woman and
you know what I mean. What you used to do to
Jack — refined head-hunting, but essentially canni-
balistic."

"The Misses Hepplethwaite."

Amid a subdued chorus of greetings two ladies
swept into the room. They were tall, thin, aristo-
cratic old maids, Joan rather attractive still, but
Jane, the elder, refined to such a degree that, like a
pencil which has been sharpened too much, she
seemed all point and no body.

"I understand," said Mrs. Copley, as she made
tea for the new arrivals, "that you heard Monsieur
Rolland speak at Mrs. Thayer's. My brother was
so pleased to have found some one he knew."

"I am glad," replied Miss Jane Hepplethwaite.
"He occupied by chance the chair next to us. The
lecture was infinitely absorbing; we found it so, did
we not, Joseph?"

For a moment she languished in expectation; then
Mr. Quincy answered sulkily, "Every word he said
was true."

"Very true," echoed the younger sister.

"What was it all about?" asked Mr. Copley.

"I'll tell you, Jack. It was called 'The Third

Sex '— all about our modern women.   Here is the
idea.   One sex, male.   Second sex, female.   Third
sex, female that won't marry.   You know the kind,
Beth!   Think they're superior to men, and won't
touch 'em with a pole.   They are sure men are
vicious creatures, given over to sin and all that kind
of thing."

"Well, don't you think they are partly right?"
asked Miss Jane Hepplethwaite.

Mr. Quincy bubbled with excitement.

"No, my dear Jane, I think man is good; I think
woman is good; I think we are all good.   But as
for the woman who will not marry, I scorn her; I
cast myself in her teeth!   What good is she?
What does she do?   She encumbers the earth.
What is woman's business on earth?   It is to —"

Mrs. Copley thought it time to take the conversation away from her fiery brother.

"My dear Jo-Jo, supposing the girl cannot find
the right man?"

"Oh, there must be plenty of men in the world!"

"Ah, but what if they are not willing?" asked
Miss Joan Hepplethwaite with a pointed glance towards Mr. Quincy, who in sudden confusion fell to
poking the fire.

"And," went on her sister, following up the advantage, "perhaps Monsieur Rolland might have
named a fourth sex: there are men who will not
marry.   Surely women may have their opinion of
them!"

In the midst of his unnecessary reassembling of
the logs, Mr. Quincy almost fell into the flames
himself.

"I think you're quite right, Miss Hepplethwaite,"
Mrs. Copley laughed with a quizzical glance at her

brother, " for the men have the proposing power.
A man may dog any girl's footsteps and make her
love him. But with a girl it's different; she can't
pursue a man."

" Of course not! " simpered Miss Joan.

Mr. Quincy snorted.

" Man proposes, girl disposes."

Having discharged her last bonmot on this topic,
Mrs. Copley changed the subject in full realisation
that the *double entendre* was in imminent danger of
falling through.

" Speaking of Monsieur Rolland, is it true that
his brother, Lucien, is going to sing in the Opera
this year? He must be at least fifty-five! Have
you heard? "

" The incomparable Lucien! Would he were!
We heard him sing once in Paris," replied Miss
Jane Hepplethwaite.

" Glorious! " echoed Miss Joan.

" We met him after a performance and also his
wife, a charming creature. A vicomtesse in her own
name, I believe."

" I know her well," broke in Mr. Quincy.
" Knew her before her marriage. Lovely crea-
ture! Divine! Such eyes and such a figure!
Marie de Nemours was her name. Tony — Mr.
Singleton, you know — and I were at the Beaux
Arts. Jack's family didn't want him to go; they
were afraid he'd fall in love! So he stayed be-
hind and Beth torpedoed him. Lucky devil! "

" You should have stayed, too, Mr. Quincy," said
Miss Hepplethwaite with an assumption of coyness.

" Perhaps," proceeded Mr. Quincy hastily, " but

I didn't.   Poor Jo-Jo!   Wooed the Muses in Paris
and found them cold.   Returning to Boston, discovered that no one wanted him except the bridge-
players at the Sarcophagus Club.   Tony has a goddaughter to comfort him; I only have a lot of un-
paid bills, and they can't be called exactly sooth-
ing!"

"That reminds me," said Miss Hepplethwaite,
rustling in her chair a little closer to Mrs. Copley.
"My sister and I saw your daughter going into
Brimmer House as we were on our way here.   She
is very much interested there, is she not?"

"Dear me, yes," replied Mrs. Copley.   "I had
a dozen little Brimmer Housers here for tea to-
day."

Raising her refined eyebrows a trifle, Miss Hepplethwaite glanced about the room as if expecting
to find traces of the little girls.

"How curious!   My sister Joan once was interested in Brimmer House, it being the most con-
venient charity for her.   One has only to go down
the hill from Louisburg Square and there it is.   But
the infections one is exposed to were so multifarious
that I thought it best for her to relinquish the work.
A month later she had chicken-pox, and I've never
felt quite assured that the germ did not emanate
from some of those Italian children.   They are
most unhealthy creatures; they all inherit disease, I
believe.   I dare say it's in their blood.   Could you
dare to permit them in your house?"

Mr. Quincy, who had been poking the fire, gave
the back log such a blow that it sent forth a shower
of sparks.

"Oh, I trust Rosalind," answered Mrs. Copley.

" She'll come to no harm. She knows more about infections and such things than all the rest of the family put together."

" Certainly does," spoke up Mr. Quincy decidedly. " Only modern girl I've ever seen with a grain of sense. Brought up right. I'm proud of my sister. Excellent mother. Remember Clough's line: ' She that is handy is handsome!' Rose took a cinder out of my eye in no time last Tuesday. Dr. Lloyd couldn't have done it half as well."

" We saw her walking to-night with Benjamin Cary."

" What! The doctor's son? "

Miss Hepplethwaite replied affirmatively. Had her eyes been turned in the right direction, she might have descried a ghostly movement in the brocade curtain by the front window.

" I can't believe it! " cried Mrs. Copley. " Why, he never speaks to girls. Are you sure? Jack, isn't that just like Rose? It's a wonder she doesn't have Edward Everett Hale off his pedestal in the park! "

" Dr. Cary will be so pleased," continued Miss Hepplethwaite. " He said to me weeks ago that his son was worse than a misogynist — that he was a gynophobe."

" That's exactly what he told Mr. Singleton this morning," said Mrs. Copley, " and he repeated it to Rose. Perhaps she's undertaken to cure him in the rôle of an angel of philogyny. She'll do it if any one can."

The door bell rang distinctly again. Mrs. Copley glanced at her blue enamelled watch, a trifle of surpassing beauty suspended by a pearl chain about her neck.

" Since it's after six, that must be Rose herself. She can tell us the whole story."

It was indeed Rosalind, but not alone, for she had brought the unwilling Cary with her.   A brightness pervaded the room at their entrance; it was as if they had caught up the last daylight and now in the darkness gave it off.

Cary was introduced.   Massive and masculine, he bent over the ladies' hands in turn; then took a place by the fire, concealing the old-fashioned clock, which ticked on resentfully behind his back, and even obscuring with his head the silver-buckled shoes of the John Singleton Copley in the portrait.

" Do get warm," urged Rosalind.   " Is there any tea left, Mamma, or shall I ring? I've been perfectly brutal to Mr. Cary.   I walked him all over Brimmer House — even up on the roof playground."

" But — but I wanted to see it; it was most interesting."

" Where did Rosalind discover you to take you on this tour of inspection? " asked Mrs. Copley. " I was sacrificed in midsummer and almost prostrated."

" In the Common," answered Rosalind severely. " Mr. Cary showed such interest in my appearance with the little girls that he couldn't — two lumps, Mr. Cary? "

Cary was unintelligible; he had been afraid Rosalind would betray him before all these people, and blushed as he had not since dancing school days.

" The Common acts as a kind of melting pot in our family," laughed Mr. Copley.   " Once Rose met there a reporter on the *American*, whose camera her Uncle Joseph had the good aim to knock into the Frogpond."

"Did he actually try to photograph you?" gasped the elder Miss Hepplethwaite.

"He did, indeed," replied Rosalind, lifting her tea-cup to her lips.

"How dreadful!"

"Awful!" echoed the younger sister.

"But Uncle Jo-Jo's aim was superb! His volume of Zola went over the fence, too. A little boy fished it out of the water later and I've got it upstairs as a trophy of the chase."

"How magnificently your uncle behaved."

"He didn't hesitate a moment," said Rosalind gaily. "And he wanted to punch the reporter's nose afterwards. I had to catch him!"

"You must be proud to be so well looked after," simpered the younger Miss Hepplethwaite.

Mr. Quincy moved uneasily in his chair. "Well, well, any one would have done the same thing! Jack would. Cary would. Any man would. These reporters don't care what they do nowadays. Take Rose's picture, indeed!"

Mr. Quincy patted his niece's hand affectionately.

"Well, I must say," remarked the elder Miss Hepplethwaite, "that I shall never dare walk in the Common again. The idea! Think of appearing like that in a public journal!"

A smile curled the corners of Mr. Copley's mouth.

"You'd better never go out without an escort, Jane. Take Jo-Jo with you: he's always within hailing distance at the Club. I am sure he'd be delighted."

As Mr. Quincy secretly brandished the poker at

his brother-in-law, the Misses Hepplethwaite murmured something about not troubling him and rose
together. They always rose together, did everything, in fact, in unison, like twin atoms composing
one Hepplethwaite molecule. Joan, to be sure, was
rather the chorus to Jane; she never initiated things
without a reference to her older sister, being the
younger by almost four years. But Jane was a
born leader, while Joan by nature was a clinging
vine.

"Oh, must you go?"

"Yes, we've not got our sleigh and it's rather
late."

"Don't walk through the Common!" laughed
Mr. Copley mischievously. "They might try a
flashlight. Jo-Jo, isn't your motor outside?"

Mr. Quincy's white moustache bristled with indignation as he assented.

"Oh, but we couldn't think —"

"Pleasure, Miss Hepplethwaite, I assure you."
Mr. Quincy spoke shortly. "Stop at the Club for
me and send you on perfectly well. Good-night,
Rose, my love. Good-night, Cary."

Angrily ignoring the amused glances of his sister
and her husband, he popped out of the room in the
Hepplethwaite's train and slammed the front door
after him.

Cary glanced at his watch, doubtful whether his
penance was over. Without being aware of it, he
was beginning to enjoy himself in an odd kind of way.
It pleased him to see Rosalind seated on the arm of
her father's chair and Mrs. Copley at her embroidery on the other side of the fire. He hoped that he
was not intrusive.

"Now that the lovers have departed," said Mrs.

Copley, "tell us what you thought of Brimmer House." ·

"Why, that it was an excellent charity. Your daughter has made me most enthusiastic. I used to suspect these things of being largely shams."

"Shams?" Mrs. Copley looked puzzled.

"So many women take up charity just because they can't afford bridge and aren't strong enough for golf. Of course, there is nothing as fine in this world as real charity, but in my work I come across so many useless uplifters that the sight of your daughter to-day with those little girls was most wonderful. I'm sure they all love her at the House; they ran to meet her."

"You shouldn't say that before me," remarked Rosalind, colouring with pleasure.

Cary was silent; he had just noticed for the first time in his life the matchless glint of firelight on gold hair.

"They all spoil you, don't they!" cried her father playfully.

Mr. Copley's mild jocosity was infectious. Cary began to find himself actually drawn out into conversation, and it pleased him. In the middle of the explanation of a technical point in regard to his last law case — he often wondered afterwards how the subject had come up! — he heard a clock strike and guiltily apologised for having remained so long.

"I do not make many calls, Mrs. Copley."

"You should," she complimented him prettily. "Good night."

"Give my regards to your old man," said Mr. Copley with a genial hand-shake.

Cary bowed. Turning to Rosalind, he spoke in a low voice meant for her ear alone.

" Your punishment, Miss Copley, was — er —"

" Yes? "

" Most — most agreeable."

Rosalind cast a deep, swift glance into his eyes; there are some feminine instincts too strong to be overcome.

" It is more blessed to give than to receive, you know. Good night."

He shook her hand and left the room in a sudden flush of excitement. Going down the front steps he was so busied with estimating judicially what Rosalind had meant by it all, but particularly by her last remark, that he slipped on the ice and narrowly averted a fall. This shook him from his dreams.

" Oh, I suppose it was only common politeness," he mumbled to himself. " She probably says that to every one. Yet —"

He went home to dinner so deeply thoughtful that his father assured him if he did not stop worrying over his work, his digestion would certainly be impaired.

No sooner had he quitted the room than Rosalind hurried to Mr. Singleton Singleton's retreat.

" Come over to the fire, Uncle Sing-Sing."

The invalid shook his head. Drawing her down by him on the sofa, he looked at her gravely.

" Cary," he said. " Told me you didn't know him."

" Oh, dear, old, jealous Uncle Sing-Sing, is that troubling you? " She kissed him prettily. " I'm sorry. I really never saw him before an hour ago — that is, to talk to particularly. I came across him in the park and he was rude without meaning to be so, and I punished him. I shouldn't have done it, I suppose, but when he said that he thought girls of my type did nothing but dance and go to the theatre, I vowed to change his views."

"And you have, dear!" broke in Mrs. Copley from the fireplace.

"Oh, do you think so, Mamma? If you do, I must have."

Long after her godfather had left the house and she had picked up a book to read comfortably on the sofa, her mother's opinion obtruded itself upon Rosalind; and she laid down her book and mused on the reflected flames dancing now high, now low on the richly filled shelves. In such matters Mrs. Copley was a shrewd judge.

CHAPTER IV

CARY BUYS A CHRISTMAS PRESENT

THE memory of the meeting with Rosalind lingered uneasily in Cary's mind for several days before becoming submerged. At first he was keenly affected, and did not find in the established order of his measured and calm life that complete satisfaction to which he was accustomed. Beyond the page of his law book, over his desk, outside of the window, there lay new fields, at which he stared and made brave, strange pictures for his inward eye. When he walked home from the office, he paused in the crisp stillness before the statue of Washington. The few people crunching past on the snowy paths observed him gravely raise his hat; for him the General had taken on a new reverence. He hoped to meet Rosalind again in the Public Gardens, but was not rewarded with even a glimpse. To call at 29 Commonwealth did not occur to him as a solution of his uneasiness. He had never made a voluntary call; in his sedate, dry schedule there was no place for such a thing.

Gradually his work enveloped him. Rosalind was forgotten in the new interest of a building investigation, to a committee on which he had been appointed by the Mayor. In the work there were statistics and facts to be obtained by personal examination; the committee went high and low over the city, delving into unsanitary cellars, creaking up the

broken stairs of rickety apartment houses, scrupulously examining filth-filled alleys, fire-hazards, unsafe roofs, and toppling sheds — so many dangers
and menaces that Cary came to think the city was in
a hopelessly wretched condition. On the day before Christmas he had been asked by the Chairman
of the Committee to examine the cellars of some
miserable, brick lodging-houses in the rear of the
Charles Street Jail. The precinct was mean and
dirty; no snow that ever fluttered down from
Heaven could hide its drab character. Children lit-
tered the narrow streets, making a bedlam of their
poor games.

Cary's request to examine the houses was met with
open suspicion. A cellar may be only a cellar to
Smith, Jones, or Cary; but if one must live in it, it is
a castle, too.

" Cellar? " asked the Italian mistress of the first
house, standing in the doorway with her arms
akimbo. " I no understan'."

Cary pointed to a grimy pane of glass on the level
of the street, behind which a baby squalled.

" I am from the Government," he explained pleasantly, " the mayor. I want to go down and look
about where the baby is."

The black Italian eyes snapped suspiciously.

" Ma babee? What you thinka? "

She turned to another woman, arrived from across
the street, and, while Cary stood patiently by, argued
in Italian with quick gestures of distrust. The conference resulted in a grudging admission of his great
form into the little house, which was filled with a
smell mingling everything cooked there since Novem-
ber's cold weather had closed all the windows for the
last time until spring. As they walked down the

narrow, dark hall, bare of any decoration other than dust, the noxious deadness of the air choked in his throat. By means of a narrow, cramped ladder the two Italian women descended, followed by Cary, scarcely able to squeeze through the small opening. A mud-stained square of glass alone admitted air and light to the room. Pale, dirty sunshine drifted through it, mocking the absence of all comfort with its faded beams. About the room rolled a fetid billow of heat; and in a corner, where a pile of rags was gathered, shrieked a baby. But though most miserable in furnishings, the room had one virtue: it was a degree cleaner than the hallway.

"How many of you live here?" asked Cary, as he accustomed his eyes to the gloom and examined carefully the walls and ceiling.

"Me an' Pietro, ma' man, an' Lucia an' Victor an' Bici an' Tripolita, ma bambina cara!" Catching up the sobbing, little bundle of dirty rags, she pressed it to her half-bare breast.

There was a sound of sleigh bells outside, and of horses trampling the snow near the dirty pane of glass. As Cary bent down to look out, a cracked bell tinkled in the hall above. The baby stopped crying, as if the jangle was a music to its ears.

"It ees Lady; it ees Mees Lady," cried out the Italian women excitedly; and they swarmed up the little ladder, baby and all, leaving Cary, choked with the squalor of the place, to follow them as best he might. When half way up the wretched ladder, the sound of the visitor's voice checked him suddenly; he hesitated in the darkened end of the passage, thrilled and eager. It was Rosalind.

"Merry Christmas, Mrs. Mario," she was saying. "How are you?"

" Ah, wella, dear Lady, wella."

" And Pietro? And the children? Bici's cold?
Does she cough any longer? "

The Italian women were transformed. Their
frowns were exchanged for smiles and friendly ges-
ticulation; their dark eyes sparkled; their nervous
bodies shook excitedly.

" Come ina, dear Lady! Come outa da cold."

" Thank you, I cannot this time. I've only come
to bring Bici her Christmas present, and I have
others to leave. If you'll take it, I'll give you
Maria's now, Mrs. Ferrari."

The other Italian woman smiled and ducked, her
ear-rings bobbing against her yellow cheeks. Fearful that Rosalind depart, yet timid in the sudden re-
awakening of her presence, Cary moved uncertainly
down the little hall. Rosalind was the first to notice
him, and cried out, " Why, Mr. Cary! However
did you happen to get in Mrs. Mario's house? "

He took the extended hand and shook it.

" It's — it's a building committee I'm on. We
have to investigate Boston houses and alleys and
cellars. I've been rather suspected by these ladies.
Couldn't you —? "

Rosalind laughed merrily.

" He's perfectly all right, Mrs. Mario. He's a
good friend of mine."

As Rosalind's hand rested protectingly on his
sleeve for a moment, he sought to estimate correctly
the degree of warmth in her voice. It had not been
at all necessary for her to be so enthusiastic; he
could have imagined a far more cold and common-
place greeting. Perhaps he had made an impression. That same innate pride which ruffles and
fans the peacock's iridescent tail swelled in Cary's

heart, and when Rosalind bade farewell to the women, he turned away with her feeling very strong and pleasingly masterful.

"I'm for Blossom Street next," said Rosalind. "Are you going that way? I've sent the sleigh on ahead."

Although he had no business on Blossom Street, Cary nodded in reply to her question, and they walked along side by side.

"How long have you been at it?" he asked.

"This is my fifth year; I began when I came out. Is it still a source of surprise?"

"Of interest rather." Cary looked at her critically, more at ease. He could not help admiring her dress, a simple but lovely brown, such as is seldom seen in the environs of Blossom Street.

"You have the right idea about clothes," he said ingenuously.

Rosalind looked at him, puzzled.

"I — I mean you don't dress the part of a social worker."

"Why should any one?"

"Lots do. They put on their worst clothes and then try to spread joy."

"I know. They think that they can get closer to the poor that way. As a matter of fact the poor people think they're shamming. I feel perfectly sure that Mrs. Mario likes to see my pretty clothes just as much as me."

"I don't believe that," objected Cary earnestly.

"There is no use in dressing down to people anyway; I learned that at Brimmer House long ago. Our earliest precept was that

'The Colonel's lady and Judy O' Grady
Are sisters under their skins.'"

" Do you give all your girls Christmas presents? "

" Well, it's not much to do," disclaimed Rosalind prettily, " and they appreciate my presents ten times more than any others I give.   It gets to be the best part of Christmas, Mr. Cary.   They give me presents, too.   About this time of year I receive a perfect flood of workbaskets and mottoes which they have made in the House."

" That is a wretched room of Mrs. Mario's. You've been in it? "

" Yes.   Her husband digs sewers, which does not add to the general comfort."

They turned up Blossom Street and passed the great, snow-covered buildings of the Massachusetts General Hospital.   At the genesis of its name this dull street decades ago had ceased to wonder; now dirt-brown snow made the designation seem even more of a mockery than did its flowerless summer.

" You did not come for further punishment," said Rosalind.

" No, I — er — I've been so busy with this work — the very next day I was appointed.   But —"

Cary did not go on, halted by a hopeless inability to phrase the conclusion.   It was in his mind, but not on his tongue, to tell her that he had thought often about their previous meeting.

"— But you've changed your ideas about girls? " Rosalind concluded with a bright look.

" Decidedly, most decidedly."

" A Daniel brought to judgment!   Now that I've done my duty to the entire flock of débutantes, past, present, and future, by enlightening so blind a judge, I shall give him a Christmas compensation.   Your sins are pardoned.   Arise, Daniel, and spread the gospel: you are forgiven."

" Thank you. I — I —"

Running lightly up the front steps of a forbidding apartment of yellow brick, Rosalind turned on the landing. To the open-mouthed Cary she looked impossibly out of place and beautiful in the drab entryway.

" But I warn you, Mr. Cary, to look out for yourself. I'm afraid I have made you into such a dangerously marriageable man that some young girl will seize you, if you're not careful. Perhaps you won't thank me then! Merry Christmas! "

She was gone, leaving Cary on the sidewalk, hat in hand. No one had ever talked to him like that before, and he was astounded to find how much it pleased him. This second meeting, so like the first, so unexpected, so different from all the customary incidents of his life, like the first swept him off his feet. What had she said? A marriageable man? Some young girl would seize him, if he were not careful? Cary suddenly realised that he was standing in the middle of the sidewalk with his hat off — smiling at himself to the unmistakable delight of Rosalind's coachman. He flushed self-consciously, hurriedly replaced his hat, and strode off with his thoughts far, far away from municipal investigations.

As he walked, he whistled. A bold, brave idea had come into his mind, and his long dormant blood ran like sap in springtime. To-morrow was Christmas. Should he not give Rosalind a present? He smiled rather foolishly to himself as he wondered what she would say. And then his father and Aunt Sara — Cary laughed outright at the thought of their surprise. But what could he give her? What do girls like? A sensible, inexperienced man could hardly know what would please a girl.   Then, conscience-stricken at having so soon forgot his lesson, he remembered that he was as of old scanting the intelligence and ability of the other sex.   Still a woman is a woman, he told himself; he could not give her cigars or a bottle of sherry.

In hopes of finding a suggestion he glanced about. His brisk strides had carried him up over Beacon Hill into the more fashionable part of the city, and on his right the show windows of a great florist shop displayed a paradise of flowers.   He stared in for so long a time without being able to make up his mind to enter that one of the clerks opened the door; then there was nothing for it but to go in. He found himself in a sweetly odorous maze of flowers with clerks bustling on all sides.

"Christmas flowers, sir?"

"Yes.   What do you recommend?"

The clerk, of course, recommended everything; pointed out holly here, an azalea there; put a gardenia to Cary's nose; begged him to smell of these violets and of those hyacinths; until Cary in sheer desperation chose a dozen white roses.   He did not care much for flowers, but knew that roses were always appropriate.

"Send them to Miss Rosalind Copley, 29 Commonwealth.   Enclose this and charge it to me."

He gave the man his card.

"Will you write on it, sir?"

Cary took the card back, and absently accepted a pen from the clerk.   What should he write?   What do people write on such occasions?   Three times he wet the pen in ink, vainly searching for some neat phrase which might express his feelings.   If there was one, he could not find it, and after a pause which, he thought, must have made him appear ridiculous in the clerk's eyes, he wrote down nothing but " Merry Christmas."

" Thank you, sir.   They will go to-night.   Merry Christmas, sir."

" Merry Christmas," Cary echoed vaguely.

He walked slowly down Park Street, half wishing he had not sent the flowers after all.   How would she receive them?   Would she not think it very forward in him?   Surely it was a strange thing for him, Benjamin Cary, to be doing!

A clock struck the half hour.   With a shamefaced start he remembered his long established custom of lunching at one o'clock.

CHAPTER V

DEALING CHIEFLY WITH CHRISTMAS

ONCE every year 8 Louisburg Square changed its character. The hushed magnificence which enveloped the invalid disappeared, and that unnatural quiet in which footsteps were not heard and voices fainted into murmurs was supplanted by an anomalous gaiety. On Christmas Eve the very house itself blazed with light. The Romneys in the great drawing-room looked superciliously down upon a Christmas-tree from the Sherborne farm, brilliant with shimmering spangles arranged by Rosalind and Edouard; the dinner-table flamed with candles, myriad reflections of which danced in the silver and glass; in each of the front windows stood twelve, tall Christmas tapers as beacons to the carol singers; in fact, the house on Christmas Eve compared with the house on other nights was as music compared to silence. Light supplanted the customary darkness; laurel wreaths usurped empty spaces on the wall; mistletoe and holly interlaced the banisters in so mischievous a way that no lady could remove her wrap without hazarding a kiss; and, what effected the greatest change, the house was filled with Christmas merry-makers.

The party was strictly a family affair. This night was set apart for the genus Copley to gather together and talk, and if noise and the light chatter of many tongues be evidence of enjoyment, the

Christmas party was invariably a tremendous success. As a result of the bombardment Mr. Singleton Singleton usually spent his Christmas day in bed; but since he considered the celebration a part of his position as the oldest and wealthiest of the Copley blood, each year the invitations went out. No one was omitted. The Copley who drank, he was invited; the queer Singleton, whose wife divorced him because he sometimes preferred to sleep in the bathtub, he was invited; the trying cousin, whose grammatical errors gave her wealthier relatives shivers, she was welcomed; and even the poor Pelhams, who lived in a flat in Chelsea — and that was about all — there was a place for them, too. They all came, rich and poor, proud and humble, old Copleys, young Copleys, bent Copleys, frolicsome Copleys, little children who were very noisy at the far end of the room, but very much awed when near Mr. Singleton Singleton, and their older relations on whom the tall, silent host had to tell the truth a similar effect. They shook his hand on arriving and endeavoured to be polite by making small-talk, but as he never talked and they had nothing to say, they soon chose opportunities to steal off to company more congenial. The party was an institution, and, since they only saw the invalid this one night in the year, they regarded him as a material part of the institution. One cannot converse under such circumstances. It did not hurt their host's feelings in the slightest; he did not care for them. It was merely having them there, the preservation of the old custom, and perhaps a faint regard for this last flickering of his social life, which made the evening bearable. As long as he could sit with Rosalind's hand in his, he cared not a whit who went or came.

As Rosalind concluded her account of meeting Cary that morning, the poor Pelhams arrived. They were always the first to come; in Chelsea, if the invitation read seven o'clock, it meant seven o'clock or no dinner. Abashed by the silence, they hesitated to leave the hall, and Rosalind, on going out to see what had happened, found them there sitting down and engaged in conversation with the second man. Their embarrassment soon thawed under her welcome. The male Pelham, whose hired dress trousers from their singular fulness must have been designed for Falstaffian limbs, even ventured to kiss Rosalind under the mistletoe; and it was in the middle of this operation that her father and mother arrived. The Copley who drank came in at the same time, but, labouring under the misapprehension that he was in the Club, went unobserved up the front stairs and had to be retrieved somewhat later from Mr. Singleton Singleton's bed, on which he had composed himself for sleep. At seven-thirty, the party being fully assembled and the children consumed with hunger and excitement, Edouard with a flourish announced that dinner was served.

Mr. Singleton Singleton took his seat at one end of the great table in silence; Rosalind queened it at the other, excited and glowing. In a noisy endeavour to find their places the guests bumped into each other and apologised and laughed. The ungrammatical cousin admiringly told Mr. Quincy that " she never was set down to such a table, and could he help her find her seat, the candles fluttered her so." This kind office performed, and the Copley who drank being taken out of the rubber tree by Edouard, the dinner went off with a whirl of conversation.

" Joseph, was anything ever more luxuriant than this ? "

" No champagne for John! John! John Copley Ingersoll, not a drop! "

" Land love us! " the ungrammatical cousin whispers confidentially, " I think Milly ought to let him have a drop on Christmas."

" I wouldn't think of using paint! But this is a kind of enamel which Mme. Louise says is beneficial to the skin. So I —"

" By gad, Rose, take my advice, my dear, and never marry but for love. Look at me! I have never married, though I might have had a dozen girls. A little wine, Rose! Merry Christmas and my best wishes! "

" Jo-Jo, are you going to the Fancy Dress Ball? "

" Certainly am! Wouldn't miss it, Beth."

" What's your disguise; true love? " laughs Mr. Copley.

" No, Jack, no. I'm going as a Bashi-Bazouk. How's that? How's that, Lucy? "

" Mercy me, Joseph, I guess you'll be just elegant as a Bash-of-Bazoo. What are they? Somethin' foreign, I suppose? "

" Rose," Mr. Singleton Singleton speaks for the first time and raises his glass.

" A Bashi-Bazouk, Jo-Jo! You can't go as that; you'll look worse than Mr. Tupman in ' Pickwick.' You might as well go as Pavlowa! "

" Well, I did once, Beth."

" Yes, but Mrs. Hereford said you were indecent."

" Rose is going as Sir Galahad."

" I made the costume myself, Uncle Jo-Jo — it's wonderfully put —"

" A merry, merry Christmas to all ! "

Mr. Copley proposes the toast for Mr. Singleton
Singleton and the party rises in happy laughter.
Even the invalid is helped to his feet by Edouard and
lifts his glass with a trembling hand. The children
drink their drop of wine with conscious pride — for
every one has a glass, even Edouard — and the
laughter is general when Ingersoll, despite his wife's
protest, drains off a bumper to Christmas.

" Land of mercy," exclaims the ungrammatical
cousin, who has swallowed perhaps a quarter of a
teaspoonful of wine, " how this champagne does set
me a-flutter. It's the bubbles most likely do it.
Joseph, I don't know when I was to such a party."

" Good for you, Lucy, very good. Expands you,
makes you cheery, you know. Your health, Lucy !
God bless us, your health ! Oh, come, a little more !
Never tell me ! "

" Mrs. Curtis is running the ball. Dr. Cary's
sister, you know."

" And Rosalind is taking up with her nephew ? "
The ungrammatical cousin misses no gossip.

" I met him in the slums to-day, Cousin Lucy."

" Ned, if you eat any more nuts, Santa Claus
won't —"

" Yes, Beth, I've no doubt you saw me with Miss
Hepplethwaite at the Copley Plaza; she lassooed me
in the park. Life's not safe nowadays in public ! "

" You're an old hypocrite, Jo-Jo, I think. Tell
me now, did she say you'd look well as a Bashi-
Bazouk ? " Mrs. Copley laughs till the wonderful
pearls are a-tremble on her more wonderful neck.

" Oooooh ! "

The children rustle in their seats and gasp, and
the Copley who drinks is firmly convinced that he has

seen a serpent belching fire in the air before him; but it is only Edouard with the plum-pudding, a round, odorous affair, dancing with blue brandy flames, and so large that Edouard staggers as he bears it around the table with a proud smile.   It is indeed a triumph of culinary art.   There is no mortal yet born who could refuse such a dish; so it is cut, and in a fair way towards being finished when Edouard comes bustling back with the information that the carol singers are at the other end of the Square.   A hush falls.

> O little town of Bethlehem!
> How still we see thee lie —

Unable to wait to hear more, the children murmur with expectant delight.   Mr. Singleton Singleton rises, and, during the general exodus to the front windows, the house is plunged in darkness.   With only flaming rows of candles in the windows, the company waits and listens in hushed silence as the band of children from afar sing their hymns, cry out " Merry Christmas " and " Good-will," and then move to the next illuminated window.

At length they stand before Mr. Singleton Singleton's house.   The hard splendour of a cold winter's evening so whitens the Square that the electric street-lamps seem consciously ashamed of being lit. In the starlight the little band of singers is vaguely distinguishable.   For the most part it is composed of children in the thickest of coats and mufflers, but there are a few older people carrying lanterns feebly aflame; behind the singers a great crowd of cheerful spectators masses along the wrought-iron fence and fills the Square with shadowy forms.   The singing is clear, sweet, and crisp, piercing the tingling air and lifting each heart to the ever-old and yet ever-new glory of Christmas.

Now the young voices take up Richard Willis's hymn:

> It came upon a midnight clear,
> That glorious song of old,
> From angels bending near the earth,
> To touch their harps of gold:
> " Peace on earth, good-will to men,"
> From heaven's all-gracious King —

Another hymn and yet another, and then the singers move on amid choruses of " Merry Christmas " from within the house and without. The cold air seems warm with cheerful messages. By this time the children are very tired, and the Copley who drinks, excited by the singing, mistakenly assumes that he is at the opera and puts on his top hat to go out between the acts. The guests begin to drift away, singly and in groups. Rosalind stays to the last, and when she finally does say good-night, leaves as the best present of all, a long, affectionate Christmas kiss on her godfather's cheek.

The presents were distributed early next morning in the Copley house with a great deal of that gayness of heart which had always been in Rosalind's family as much a part of Christmas as the actual gifts themselves. Rosalind was mightily surprised to receive the flowers from Benjamin Cary, and stared at the card in silence. Flowers from Philip Brooks, from Francis Wharton, from Frederic Hoyt she took as a matter of course, but flowers from Cary — ! She was pleased, yet at the same time puzzled.

" What's that, Rose? "

"Look, Mamma! Flowers from Ben Cary."

"The idea! What have you done to that young man? Let me see the card. Only ' Merry Christmas '— isn't that typical of the quiet man who says a grain of sand and means the world? His ' Merry Christmas ' is worth a page of Billy Harte ! "

"I know, Mother. I shouldn't have done it ! "

"What?"

"Taken him to Brimmer House. It's all my fault; he never thought of girls before that."

Mrs. Copley looked at the card and laughed.

"The agony of soul the composition of this great thought cost him must have been tremendous."

"But he *was* rude." Rosalind looked quizzically at her mother. "I'm afraid I've done wrong. I — I didn't want him to send me flowers; I only did it to — to humanise him, to give him a shock. I hope he —"

"Oh, well, leave him alone, my dear, and he'll forget. Your father used to give me flowers before we were engaged, but I always had to prompt him."

As she turned the card over in her hand, the melancholy strains of Handel's " Largo " drifted in from a graphophone in the music room.

"Who's playing that on Christmas Day! Jo-Jo? How can you do such a thing? You ought to be merry! Look, Rose."

Beside the phonograph sat Mr. Quincy, a picture of despair.

"What's the matter, Uncle Jo-Jo? You've been blue ever since you came in."

"Blue, my dearest Rose, I'm ultramarine, purple, black! Oh, it's awful! No! Awful is no word for it ! "

"What is it, Jo-Jo?"

"Oh, nothing. Ha — ha! Nothing."

Changing the record to the " Maiden's Prayer," Mr. Quincy gave himself up to a grief which outwardly showed in sundry shakings of the head and heartfelt sighs.

" Tell us, please, Uncle Jo-Jo."

" Rose, never, never trust any one! Listen to me: I'll make your blood run cold. Those da —"

" Jo-Jo! "

"— those Hepplethwaite girls by artful insinuations led me to believe that they were going to give me a Christmas present. Foolish old idiot that I was, I believed them. In retaliation I went and bought 'em books and boxes of flowers, made a regular fool of myself — and now, now no present has come from them! I'm desperate. They'll never let me hear the last of it, you know. ' Oh, those sweet flowers, Joseph! ' ' Oh, that engrossing book! ' Sweet flowers, fiddle-de-dee! Engrossing book, bosh! "

" Whatever will they say at the Club, Jo-Jo? "

Overwhelmed by mock misery, Mr. Quincy opened both doors of the Victrola and put his head as far inside as possible, where he kept it till the end of the " Maiden's Prayer." Then, purged of his grief, he went off with Rosalind to see Mr. Singleton Singleton.

They found the invalid propped up in his great four-posted bed, on the edge of which Rosalind seated herself. After a morning kiss, she displayed Benjamin Cary's card.

" I'm afraid, Uncle Sing-Sing, he's going to fall in love with me." She made up a face of mimic grief.

"Going to!" cried Mr. Quincy. "Has, you mean! Why! I could have told you that the first ever I saw of him. Bull-dog love, you know. Ah! Look out for that kind, Rose, my dear. Put up a dike: it washes it down. Banish it: it knows no exile. It sticketh closer than a barrel of brothers. Mark me! You'll be married in six months, if you're not careful. Take my word for it!"

"You do not like him?"

"Of course not, Uncle Sing-Sing. I only know him out of pique, as it were. But he's all right, you know. I do like him for a change; he is so different from Billy and Phil."

"He's a man. That's what Tony objects to."

"He is a man." There was a trace of enthusiasm in Rosalind's voice. "Billy and Phil aren't."

"They will be some day, my dear, and don't you forget it. Tony and I were flighty once. Fools to-day, fathers to-morrow — and so the world goes. Take Philip Brooks. In ten years — don't laugh, Rose! — he'll be a warden of Trinity Church, and fold up the map of Europe. Earth will cease to have wonders for him; he will not care to know them. But —"

"I don't believe Cary's narrow, if that's what you mean."

"No — no! Perhaps he is, perhaps he isn't. What I say is this: just because an undergraduate wears a club ribbon and prefers Victor Herbert to Victor Hugo, don't you think that he's always going to be a puppy! So many girls marry an older man because he is calm and serious. Don't, Rose! Marry a wild-cat or a polar bear, but don't get taken in by the false gravity of years. Wait till you get the sun and some man mixed up — then jump!"

Rosalind went over to the writing desk and sat down, a smile twisting her lips.

"Never fear, Uncle Jo-Jo! I shan't jump just yet, but I will write and thank him for the flowers. How shall it go? I must be careful! . . . Dear Mr. Cary — I was surprised and delighted . . . (shall I say 'surprised,' Uncle Jo-Jo?) . . . to receive your beautiful roses. They were in perfect condition. Roses are always beautiful, I think, and the loveliness of these, I assure you, is greatly appreciated . . . (I call that neat! I've used it before. Now I'll end it; that's enough, don't you think so, Uncle Sing-Sing? However, shall I say it? Let me see.) . . . I shall hope to see you at the Fancy Dress, where I can really thank you for your thought of me. Sincerely yours, Rosalind Copley. . . . (I think that's awfully good about the Fancy Dress. It ends up with a flourish, you see, and, of course, he won't go)."

"Sure?"

"Sure, Uncle Sing-Sing! And so closes Episode the First."

Benjamin received the letter the next afternoon, and in quite a different mood from that in which it was written. On coming home he turned naturally to the tray on which reposed the day's assortment of mail. Among the letters for him there was one, the fair, precise handwriting of which made his blood suddenly tingle. He had been waiting for it, expecting it. With almost a laugh at the novelty of the thing, he carried the little note to a comfortable sofa in the living-room. Eager to read, yet more eager to prolong the sensation of being alone in a strange land, he smoked a cigarette and like all prosaic men dreamed in the blue smoke which eddied to the lamp. It was ludicrous, yet delightful and disturbing. He had once seen a moving-picture hero ravished by the romance of his cigarette smoke; then the situation had seemed crude and silly, but perhaps he had misjudged it. He opened the envelope and read the lines at first hastily, the second time with increasing care. Having had absolutely no experience with such letters, he was mystified by its sentiments. Was she really pleased or was this but a formal way of saying thank you? The " surprised " disturbed him; evidently she thought him rude, forward, intruding. Yet at the same time she was " delighted " and " enjoyed their beauty." The more Cary endeavoured to form a judicial opinion on this point, the less conclusive he became, and, deeming the evidence on this point insufficient, at length proceeded to examine scrupulously the next line. There the allusion to the " Fancy Dress " puzzled him. Supposedly it was a dance, but when or where he had no idea; fancy dress was not his habiliment. To cap his perplexity she seemed to express a hope of seeing him at this ball, seemed to take it for granted that he would be there. Cary sought to imagine what a Fancy Dress could be like. During his solitary meal the question tortured him till he could bear the uncertainty no longer and determined to smoke his after dinner cigar with his aunt, Mrs. Curtis. To her he unburdened his trouble.

" Aunt Sara, I came to ask you what ' The Fancy Dress ' was."

" It wasn't; it will be a dance on Friday night. It's the regular New Year's Charity Ball that we get up."

" A nice thing, I suppose? "

" The best in the year, Ben, but why? The leopard isn't changing his spots, is he? "

" Why, Aunt Sara, I — I " (Ben flushed as he said it), " I thought I might go this year if I could get invited."

" You go, Ben! You! You're in love; you must be! "

" Oh, Aunt Sara, that's rot. Women do take the most awful leaps to false conclusions! "

" I know, Benjamin," she said shrewdly, " but the farther they leap, the more near right they are."

" Aunt Sara, is that your own? "

" Yes, dear."

" Then it is very clever of you," said Ben ingenuously. " But you didn't leap far enough for me this time! "

" The surprise was too great, dear! I'd as soon expect the Archbishop of Canterbury at the ball as you."

" Could you get him a ticket, if he came? "

" Yes, I certainly could; and I can get you one also, although you've already refused once. I'm running it this year, you see."

" I'm glad of that; you can take care of me."

" All right, my dear. You seem to need it," she added maliciously. " What are you going as? "

" Going as? "

" Why yes, it's in costume, as one might gather from the name."

" Do you expect me to wear a costume? "

Mrs. Curtis nodded.

" Never! My dear aunt, me in a costume? It would be too conspicuous — I'll just wear a dress suit."

" You may if you want to, my dear Ben, but if you

take my advice, you'll wear a costume if only to avoid conspicuousness.   You would probably be the only dress suit there."

Benjamin was aghast.

" Does every one put on a disguise? "

" From the fattest to the thinnest, from the bravest to the most cowardly."

" Then I shall, Aunt Sara!   Can you give me one? I remember you used to have a great many."

Mrs. Curtis surveyed him critically.

" I have it! " she cried, clapping her hands.   " I have it!   Christopher Columbus!   Oh, Ben, you will be stunning in green! "

So Christopher Columbus it was, a glorious, green Christopher Columbus in a slashed silk doublet, painfully aware of the exposure of his legs in green tights, and painfully clumsy in a pair of fifteenth century slippers.

CHAPTER VI

THE FANCY DRESS BALL

IT was a still January night, so cold and brilliant
that the very stars seemed frozen into glittering
immovability in the sky. A bitter wind whispered icily through the streets, eddied about great,
pendant icicles, and stole off to moan in the dark
pockets of the city. There were few people abroad.
A policeman swinging his arms in a calisthenic effort
to warm himself, a miserable passerby whose hurrying feet rang on the sidewalk, a taxicab whirling a
shivering passenger from one haven of warmth to
another — these were the occasional manifestations
of life in a city which took its ease indoors.

Copley Square alone was animated. It was the
night of the Fancy Dress Ball annually held at the
Copley Plaza in behalf of the Indigent Orphans of
Boston. As the invitations openly stated, the ball
was a charity affair, but after the price of the ball-
room, and of the elaborate decorations, and of the
supper, and of the latest thing in bands had been de-
ducted from the receipts, the Indigent Orphans
might well have been justified in feeling that charity
in connection with a social affair of this nature was
more of an excuse than of a cause. But then, of
course, the Indigent Orphans knew nothing about it;
they had never been expected to know anything
about it, and the dance succeeded or failed quite irre-
spective of whether there were any orphans in the

58

Home or not.   The ball had become a social fixture,
dear to our best people — and to the undergraduates
of Harvard University, who comprised the male
dancing population of Boston.   It was dear to our
best people as all fixtures are dear; to the undergraduates it represented the admittance at three dollars a head to as much refreshment as was bad for
them.   As for the débutantes, they held it no sin to .
attend six dances and dinners in one week, provided
one of them was for charity.   And then for one and
all it was such glorious fun to walk about in costume!
What if the charity part did get lost in the shuffle?
The evening was still amusing and magnificent, giving that great body of women who depend on the
society columns of the dailies for their information
on life topics, something to think about, and furnish-
ing the Indigent Orphans pecuniary relief which, if
not too large, was yet not to be scorned.

Motors and carriages thronged about the great
hotel.   Defiant of the cold, the social world was out
in force, and the biting air lived with the cries of in-
furiated cabmen and the insistent racking of electric
horns.   As the guests streamed under the broad
awning, spread from the hotel to the street, the wind
whisked and fluttered their wraps, permitting the
carriage-caller, apparently a living bear-skin, to catch
glimpses now of a harlequin, now of a cardinal, now
of a fairy.

The interior of the Copley Plaza was a pande-
monium of light and music.   As the dancers fluttered past to the ball-room, a crush of people craned
their necks and stared.   These were the hotel guests,
the uninvited, the dwellers in the limbo of bour-
geoisie.   Poor unfortunates!   Even the most unattractive Jewish widow of their number would have

bartered her immortal soul, nay, even her mortal gold, for the entrée of that blazing paradise of society.   But it could not be; and they must dream and envy, they must exchange amenities in their Hinterland, the foyer, and read the details of Mrs. So-and-So's costume in the papers of all the world.

The ball-room streamed with a wild profusion of ribbons and rosettes, flaunting from the massive chandeliers and hiding the upstairs boxes.   Behind a mass of shrubbery in Italian pots blared a celebrated New York band, sixty musicians thumping, shouting, squeaking, swaying, employing every known device, musical or otherwise, to prove the invincible modernity of their art.   Whether it was music or cacophony which penetrated their leafy screen, there was a great deal of it, loud, sweeping, infectious, the bewildering perfume and flashy suppliance of a minute.   Above all arose a ceaseless babel of voices, as bewildering to the ear as the costumes, which displayed every known combination of colour and design, were to the eye.   Even a frenzied Cubist might have hesitated to place his impression of so inextricable a mixture of colour, sound, and motion on hitherto undaunted canvas.   For all the world the five hundred revolving figures resembled an enormous crazy quilt in the act of violent perambulation.   Here a Watteau shepherdess nestled in the arms of Ivan the Terrible; there Cato the Censor attempted the fox-trot with Catherine de Medici; you might have seen a Cardinal waltzing with Mme. du Barry, and Florence Nightingale in the arms of Abdul Hamid.

Above the whirling, swaying, laughing dancers the staid, older ladies, whom the influx of modern steps had not swept onto the dancing floor, sat in their

festooned boxes like minor Olympians, passing judgment behind their jewelled lorgnettes and breathing
deeply under the weight of great ropes of pearls.
Even they were in fancy dress: age hath no ter-
rors for a woman costumed. While they formed
in the front line of the boxes a dazzling array of
Queen Elizabeths, Fairy Queens, queens of all de-
nominations, their heavy and dignified husbands
yawned away the evening behind their backs in talking over the latest bonmot at the Sarcophagus Club.
From their aërial vantage these sexagenarian in-
quisitresses promulgated the autos-da-fé of society.
If Mrs. Lavalle as a nymph was hardly decent, they
had realised it long before the whisper buzzed about
the ball-room; if Mr. Morton's dancing was too
good to be proper, they were the first to take excep-
tion to it. When young Harry Francis tumbled
down the stairs from the champagne punch, it was
quite useless for him to look about for the person
who had tripped him. The dog-collared Junos had
known his father years ago; when the wind was in
that quarter, they could tell falling from being
tripped. Their keen old eyes twinkled over Joseph
Quincy, dancing only with débutantes, ferreted out at
least two engagements, and were perhaps the only
eyes — for the dancers were too busy dancing and
babbling to observe anything — to catch a glimpse
of Sir Galahad quitting the confusion of the great
hall on the arm of Christopher Columbus.

"Now be true to your name," Sir Galahad was
saying "and discover some place where it is quiet.
The noise is deafening here."

Cary led Rosalind to a little room at some distance from the dancing. The perfume, the heat, the
novelty of the night aroused his dusty emotions, and

his heart stretched within him like an awakening Titan.   As they sat upon a sofa, the music came distantly to them, confused with the hum of voices.

"I'm so glad you came.   I think I've never seen you at a dance before."

"I have not been since I left college."

"No?"

"Eight years.   Do you wonder now I could not dance?"

"Hardly.   But you could learn.   You dance as well as Uncle Jo-Jo now."   Rosalind laughed merrily.   "He thinks he dances beautifully, so never tell him what I said.   He must be a trial to the young girls, for he persists in believing that he is as young as he feels, and scorns any one who has been out more than a year.   Even I am *passé!*"

"I caught a glimpse of him.   He ought to look very fierce in that Turkish costume, but somehow he doesn't."

"I'll warrant he spent as much time over it as any lady here spent over hers.   Where did you pick up Columbus?   It suits you."

"Mrs. Curtis chose it for me."

"I made this costume myself," said Rosalind with pride.   "It was a piece work putting these aluminum rings together for the chain mail, I tell you, but its use has warranted the labour.   Almost all my friends have worn it at one time or another."

She stood up and turned about before him, the tunic of chain mail swinging and chinking at her knees.   Scarlet stockings and slippers and a splash of scarlet at the neck, which made a flaming harmony with the honey-gold of her hair, completed the costume.

"You made it yourself? Why! It — it's wonderful!"

"You find new capabilities in girls all the time, don't you?" Rosalind laughed up at him.

"It's — it's the most beautiful costume here!" said Cary stoutly.

"That can hardly be true, but it's nice of you to say so."

"I am sure of it."

"Tell me, Mr. Cary, how did you happen to come to a dance after eight years of monastic life?"

Cary was captivated by the innocence of the question. How should he know that the rosy fingers of the graceful hand on which his eyes rested were twisting him round and round? Lacking both courage to be bold and tongue to be adroit, he stammered in reply.

"I came — er — because your letter — you know you said that you would see me here."

"It's like a moral version of Thaïs!" cried Rosalind merrily. "Athanaël, I apologise for tempting you to quit your monastery. How do you like Alexandria?"

Cary could not banter; neither could he follow happily that feminine celerity of mind which finds in everything in life parallels and analogues to make merry over. It was bewildering to drag Thaïs and whatever name she had applied to him into an ordinary conversation.

"I'm glad I came," he said bluntly.

"Do you think our city wicked? Do you still scorn these maidens who dance and dress, dress and dance? Are their heads empty, their tongues —"

"Oh, please!"

"Well! I've forgotten that. And I'm glad you came. It's been the best part of the dance by far. Look! There goes Uncle Jo-Jo — with a débutante, of course!"

Cary did not see them. The words which came so easily from Rosalind's tongue had made his heart suddenly warm within him.

"How are you going to do it?" he asked ingenuously.

"What?" As Rosalind turned her wide-opened, blue eyes toward him, he lost courage.

"Why in your letter, you know, you also said that you — that you were —"

"Oh! Going to thank you for your present? How thoughtless of me! I think it was awfully kind of you to send them. You may be sure I appreciated them tremendously. Of all my Christmas flowers they were the nicest, because —"

Cary waited in pleasurable suspense.

"Oh, because I knew you wanted to send them. Phil and Bobby feel they have to."

Cary smiled in such content that the consciousness of green tights and mediæval slippers was drowned in its profundity.

"I like Alexandria," he murmured.

"You're on the downward path now for sure!" Rosalind laughed. "Beware of all young Alexandrians who say you look handsome in that costume!"

"I shall be deaf."

"Right! When it comes to ladies' compliments, Mr. Cary, let me advise you. Be like marble to receive and wax to retain, and you'll live happily ever after."

A harlequin, chequered in green and white, appeared at the door.

" Is it time for supper, Freddy? "

" Time! "   The deep brown eyes of the newcomer, tall and graceful in his tight-fitting costume,
sparkled with reproof.   " Aren't you the needle in
the haystack, though, hiding out here!   I should say
it was time."

Cary developed a sudden dislike for the ease and
manner of this young senior at Harvard, and as he
arose stiffly, a conscious feeling that his tights bagged
at the knee possessed him.

" I must go, Mr. Cary," smiled Rosalind, " or
have my head bitten off.   Good-bye."

They ran from the room, Rosalind protesting, the
harlequin indignant, fluttering away like moths to
the ball-room for a last dance before the supper.
Fascinated by the lightness of their youth, yet annoyed that Rosalind so soon disappear with another
man, Cary followed at a distance, and later caught a
glimpse of them gracefully threading their way
through the confused crowd in the ball-room.   For
the first time in his life he regretted his inability to
dance.

As he stood by the doorway, gazing moodily in at
the whirling figures, he felt a hand upon his arm.

" Why — is it?   God bless my soul, it is!   Cary,
how are you? "

Under the fierce black moustachios and jewelled
turban of a Bashi-Bazouk lurked Mr. Quincy.

" Quite lost, sir, I'm afraid."

" Don't blame you a bit!   Not a bit!   I tell
you, Cary, it wasn't like this when Tony Singleton
ran things, eh?   He knew who was who.   Sara
Curtis *aliter visum*, eh? "

" They must all be here."

" Impossible to dance, quite!   I can hardly get

started." Mr. Quincy took a comprehensive survey of the ball-room. "Look at the old girls in the boxes, will you?" he cried irreverently. "Aren't they enjoying it? I wonder whose reputation is going now? Thank the Lord, I have none. Ha-ha! It's a singular thing, Cary, how few old-fashioned low necks one sees to-day."

"Is it?" Cary could not help smiling.

"I assure you. Look at the boxes; not a one!"

Mrs. Lavalle flashed by, a nymph in everything but divinity of birth.

"Not even this Grecian goddess?"

"You have me there. But then she's young, you know, and has a lovely neck! It's quite right, quite the compensation of nature. To age, the dog-collar; to youth — Joe Quincy!"

He was off down the ball-room after Mrs. Lavalle, with his Turkish trousers fluttering behind his short legs, leaving the younger man to affirm his sartorial dictum. As Cary's glance half-amusedly, half-idly traversed the boxes again, it fell upon a magnificent black lace crinoline, framed in the fluttering decorations. An arresting and fascinating sight, this old lace, this white hair, these magnificent pearls, this beauty of middle age which was still young; Cary thought it the most exceptional thing in the room. It gave him a peculiar thrill of pleasure to know that this beautiful figure was the mother of the girl whom he admired so much.

Mrs. Copley was a sensible woman. As well as any person in Boston she was aware of her beauty, of her seemingly perpetual youthfulness; better than any one, she knew that it must never be jeopardised on the dancing floor. There is not a woman living over forty-five who can dance and be exquisite at the same time; a nebula of youth may sparkle about her, yet age is in her sinews.   To be content to watch is but to realise the price of dancing.   Therefore Mrs. Copley held her court in peacefulness, and viewed with interested eyes the heat and kaleidoscopic motion below.   In an idle moment she caught a glimpse of Cary, solitary and silent amidst the excitement, and their eyes meeting, made him a little sign to come and sit beside her.   For all her beauty she was a doting, thoughtful mother.   As Cary moved slowly through the crowd toward her elevated box, she remembered the perturbation of her daughter over his flowers and attention, and hoped to discourage his incipient emotion.

"It cannot be," she thought to herself, "that he is in love yet, but then these steady, quiet fellows are impossible to diagnose.   They boil away inside like Ætna and then explode.   If he does fall in love and Rose does not care for him — well, we'll see!"   Then aloud: "Won't you sit beside me and talk, Mr. Cary?   You didn't seem to be dancing, and I'm so bored with myself up here.   They've gone and left me alone."

Cary sat down in a state of pleasant confusion.

"No, I — I don't dance," he said.   "Not at all."

"Neither do I.   It's more pleasant sitting out, isn't it?"

Cary turned red.

"Your daughter and I —"

"I saw you.   Rose is an inveterate sitter out." Seeing that the little barb on this remark made no impression, she added, "She's out with Frederic Hoyt now.   Do you know him?"

" No. She — she told me he had her for supper."

" My husband and I like him so much. He's just
Rosalind's age — a senior at Harvard — and between ourselves, Mr. Cary, I think Rose fancies him.
Of course, up here I can keep a careful watch on
her ! " She paused to observe the curative effect of
her remarks on Cary, but finding his silence inscrutable renewed the treatment from another quarter. " How do you like Rose's costume ? "

" Perfect, Mrs. Copley ! There is nothing like it
here ! "

" And mine ? " She made a wry face.

" You see how clumsy I am ! But then yours is
different, you know."

" All the difference between Sir Galahad and Mrs.
John Quincy Adams ! "

" But you saw how I was gaping at you ? "

" An open mouth is the subtlest flattery ! Look !
There are Rose and Freddy now. Such a handsome
boy ! He and Rose do look well together, don't
you think so ? "

In Cary's laconic monosyllable there was to a
woman, and especially to a mother, all the evidence
necessary for conviction. Mrs. Copley went off to
supper on her husband's arm firmly convinced that
her cure had been a failure.

Left alone in the box, Cary pushed his seat back
into a corner. To go to the supper-room never occurred to his perplexed brain; he wished to be quiet
and think in the rush of cool air which swept through
the French doors, cleansing and purifying the heavy
silence of the emptied ball-room. After the incessant blaring of the band, the cool calmness was welcome. A problem perplexed him, more intricate and

difficult than those met with in his law practice or on his building committee, a problem intangible and uncertain, of shadowy outlines, a problem projecting the mind far out into impossible spaces.   Cary was too normal to be introspective, but at the same time too sensible not to face an examination and explanation of his state of mind.   What were the simple facts?   A judicial examination of his feelings resulted in the finding that while a month ago he had been a sober, equable young man, devoted to his practice, to his investigations, and to such other activities as befitted a sober, equable life, he now found himself monstrously concerned, even unhappy, simply because a girl whom he scarcely knew was very intimate with a boy whom he had never heard of before.   Cary threw himself back in his chair indignantly.   Brought down to reason, the whole thing was so frankly ridiculous!   Why should these people or their actions, their likes or dislikes, concern him?   Were they a part of his universe?   He summarised the late inconsistencies of his life: he had called on a girl, sent her flowers for Christmas, and had attended a costume ball as Christopher Columbus!   Evidently it was a question of what constitutes one's universe!   Cary smiled a wry smile, because he did not understand; he did not know that earth and water, the dust and dryness of mundane life, are not sufficient materials with which to compose a universe, that without air and fire, the nobler elements of nobler life, our individual planet becomes a dead, cold star.

What should he do?   He sought to devise some plan, to plant a rallying flag; surely there must be some method of destroying this uneasiness of mind. He arose and walked slowly down the corridor.

Could he forget? Could he leave the hotel now and wholly extirpate the memory of Rosalind? Why not? Heretofore determination had been his fiery sword; his will-power, like the pottage of the Benjamin in Genesis, had been five times as much as that of others. If he had set his mind to do anything, that thing was as good as done. Determination had beaten down all opposition; it had succeeded against every adversity. Why should not this will he prided in serve him here? A sudden disgust for his own weakness possessing him, his face assumed an unconscious look of aggression; like a minor Bismarck, he determined to destroy ruthlessly and absolutely this uneasy and alarming tenderness. He was not ready yet; his schedule of life could not at this time permit the blossoming of love. I have the will, he murmured, as he moved down the stairs, I shall have the way, too. But in some matters Cary was twenty-eight years young. He was unaware that he was now dealing with an obstacle entirely novel in its nature, with an adversary stronger than a Yale crew, wilier than a crooked politician, and sharper than both Dodson and Fogg; he was wholly ignorant that to step in even so short a way was to make returning more tedious than going o'er.

On his way to the coat-room he became involved in the general exodus from supper, which choked the corridor with laughing people and rendered progress impossible. Suddenly he was aware that Rosalind and her partner were almost at his elbow. Fearful lest he be seen, he stepped back against the wall in breathless suspense. Yet when she had passed close by him, laughing up at Freddy Hoyt's dark eyes, he felt disappointed and hurt that she had not noticed him, and wished to hear her voice again. He even ran a few feet after them in a spirit of boldness, thinking to speak to her, but lost courage when he realised that he had nothing to say. In a moment the swirling crowd swallowed up the graceful Sir Galahad and her clean-limbed, dark-eyed harlequin. Turning on his heel, Cary stalked angrily away to the coat-room; he had entirely forgotten his fiery sword of determination.

CHAPTER VII

OUT OF THE FRYING-PAN

THE library windows at the back of 8 Louisburg Square commanded a view of the Basin very dear to Rosalind. In her childhood she had learned to love the little room upstairs, where during many a shadowy twilight she had heard her godfather tell stories of their ancestors' sea-captains, grizzled old fellows who came to the high Square with spyglasses in an endeavour to catch sight of some expected ship. There was a romance in the outlook foreign to America. When the sun had dipped from the winter sky, the roof of the houses lower on Beacon Hill formed a gigantic stairway from the frozen river, which stretched like gleaming silver far below them, to the very windows where they sat. Here the curious mysteries of childhood had unrolled themselves; here still she and her godfather often watched the vesperal darkness creep over the city.

" But you haven't seen him since he was a little boy, Uncle Sing-Sing. It's not fair to judge him so harshly. I'm sure after all Dr. Cary has done you might at least give him the benefit of the doubt."

" It's not that, dear."

" Well, never fear for me! I'm well protected now, for Mamma has taken up the cudgels against poor Cary, too. She told me that they sat out together — you see it's in the family! — and that for

Rosalind

my sake she informed him that Freddy Hoyt and I were the next thing to married. It made him furious. I should think it might have! Between Mamma and myself the poor man won't know which way to jump." Rosalind paused a moment. " He's so clean and stern, Uncle Sing-Sing, so very manly and strong! Papa says that he's wonderfully successful, that he has never failed in an undertaking. I can't help admiring him — no girl in America could. I guess it's in us to like big, free men who look as if they could move mountains for a pastime. But say you won't worry any more! I'm not in love with —"

" Not yet," the invalid interrupted.

Rosalind looked thoughtfully out over the river.

" N-o-o. I don't think I ever could be with him — really in love, I mean. Some people strike you that way; they may be the admiration of all the world, but when it comes to loving them, they're too great or too good or too strong for our poor mortal hearts." She laughed. " It's cold-blooded enough, Uncle Sing-Sing, the way you and I go about a thing; it seems like one person reasoning out loud, doesn't it? "

" It is." The invalid appeared amused.

" That's better! I almost coaxed out a smile that time! Do please take Ben like any of my other friends. To have one more doesn't decrease my love of you, dear; it merely leaves less for them to share. You aren't jealous of Billy or Phil or Freddy? "

" No."

" I am fond of them, though; I love them as I do anything that I'm accustomed to, that is always pleasant and kind to me; but they aren't the real

thing yet, and Cary is. He may not be fluent like
Freddy or amusing like Billy, but you feel a superiority in his very hesitancy to speak. And he's very
appreciative, which a girl loves. If you could have
heard him admire my Sir Galahad costume — Pa-
quin might have made it! He went away before
I could see him again, though I looked everywhere.
I suppose it was Mamma's kindness that killed him."

"Mr. Quincy is coming upstairs, sir."

No sooner had Edouard got the words fairly out
of his mouth than the little man bustled into the
room.

"By gad, Rose! Sweetheart!" (patting her
hand and kissing her). "Tony, my boy, good evening. Have I seen you since the ball, Rose? You
were lovely, divine, exquisite!"

"You débutante-killer! You don't get off that
way; you know you wouldn't look at me you were
so busy with the children!"

"On the contrary," Mr. Quincy replied loftily,
"you seemed so busy with Cary that I — well, you
know! Old boy keeps in the background while the
mice are playing. Shows the terrible effect of that
letter you wrote to Cary. He never would have
thought of the ball but for that, never in a dozen
years. Tony, my boy, keep your weather eye out.
You remember what Shakespeare said? 'It's a wise
father that knows his own godchild!' Ah, Rose,
my love?"

"Don't be silly, Uncle Jo-Jo! You're worse
than Mamma!"

"All right, my love. Silence is golden. No one
shall have an inkling of the news until you give the
signal. Only tell me early — by Gad!" Mr.

Quincy's animated face in a twinkling became grave and serious.

"What's happened now?"

"The sight of you, Rose, completely put out of my head what I'd come to tell Tony. Have you seen the *Transcript* to-night?"

The invalid shook his head.

"I wanted to tell you myself so that it might not be too much of a surprise. An old, old friend of ours is dead."

There was a pause, during which Mr. Singleton Singleton leaned forward a little and stared attentively at Mr. Quincy.

"Some one we knew in Paris."

"Paris?" The invalid's lips framed the word.

"Some one you were very fond of. She —"

"Marie?"

Mr. Quincy nodded.

"Who, Uncle Jo-Jo?" demanded Rosalind curiously. She had turned her eyes to Mr. Quincy, and did not see her godfather lean back in the darkness of his cushions, a trifle paler and colder than before.

"Marie de Nemours. You must have heard us speak of her in the past. We knew her when we were at the Beaux Arts; in fact, I introduced Tony to her there. Later she married Rolland. You know, the great tenor."

"I remember the name."

Mr. Quincy looked meditatively at his boots and sighed a long, melancholy sigh.

"Ah, well! Poor, dear creature! To think that she should die, Tony; you used to say, I remember, that she could not grow old. Even your mother couldn't hold a candle to her, Rose."

There was a long silence, filling the dark room with meditative pathos. Touching gently her god-father's hand, Rosalind found it listless.

" I'm sorry, dear," she murmured.

" So am I, Tony. I was sure you'd want to know. Ah, well! There's the first star. I must be off!"

" Shall I go, too, Uncle Sing-Sing?"

The old man nodded slowly. "To-morrow."

" Yes, dear, surely."

Half-way down the stairs with her uncle, she thought she heard her name called.

" You go on down, Uncle Jo-Jo; I'll follow you directly."

She hurried back to the library.

" Did you call me?"

" Miniature in my desk. Bring it here."

In his hand her godfather held a gold key which Rosalind took, and carried to his bedroom. There she found the miniature, gold with a circle of pearls around the painting, lying face-down on the top of a pile of letters in a drawer. On the back an in-scription in a feminine hand inevitably struck her eye. Though the ink had long since faded, she could readily make out two names: Tony — Ma-rie. Wondering, she hurried to her godfather and placed the painting in his white hand.

" Look, Rose."

As she took the little picture to the lingering light at the window, a murmur of admiration es-caped her lips. The lady of the miniature war-ranted all her uncle's praise. The dark, curling hair, the high forehead, the emerald green eyes, the graceful neck, the delicate fineness of the features, these witnessed to an aristocracy of beauty.

"Beautiful?" The old man spoke in a far-off voice.

"Exquisite! So beautiful, that it almost seems impossible that any woman —"

"It is unworthy of her."

"Rose! Rose!" Mr. Quincy's voice called from below. "Do you want me?"

"Coming, Uncle Jo-Jo! Good-night, dearest — or shall I stay?"

"No."

"Thank you for letting me see the picture; it was beautiful."

"You and me."

"I understand — no one else shall know. Good-night, dear."

Rosalind ran lightly down the stairs to rejoin Mr. Quincy.

"At last, Uncle Jo-Jo!"

"One moment! Would you object to exploring the coast first? You know those two harpies, the Hepplethwaites, live directly opposite."

With a merry laugh Rosalind walked down the front steps alone.

"All clear, Uncle Jo-Jo."

His face appeared at the crack of the front door.

"Hush, my dear, hush! No lights in their house?"

"None."

Mr. Quincy slammed the door, took his niece's arm, and hurried up the street.

"A little faster here, Rose, if you please. Just till we get out of range. If you could see the letters they wrote me about those Christmas things! I had to burn them up directly. Think if they ever found out at the Club!"

At the comical expression on her uncle's face, Rosalind laughed louder than ever.

"Hard-hearted girl! Where are your feelings? I believe you'd like to see me married! If so, your joy will never be consummated. Marry for love is my maxim! Never marry for anything but love, my dear Rose, and you'll always be in love. And what is that? Happiness! Laugh you may, Rose, but if you follow my advice, you'll come out right in the end. And now, good-night, my dear; I'm going to run up to the Club for dinner."

Some days later Rosalind found herself seated in the outer office of the Mayor of Boston. It was a large, unprepossessing room, filled with large, unprepossessing chairs, while on the walls hung large engravings of not too prepossessing gentlemen, whom Rosalind took to be the former incumbents of the office. She was by no means alone in her attendance on His Honour's pleasure. Several flabby gentlemen with gold rings and jewelled scarf-pins, expressive of their extreme gentility, conversed earnestly in one corner; opposite them sat three provincial ladies, whose prim, black gloves guarded a petition; in the centre of the room an enormous man with a mountainous wen on his nose, complacently spat into a cuspidor which fortune had placed conveniently near. Of the others, a nondescript dozen were sprinkled about, lolling on the ugly chairs with fragments of dirty newspapers or evil-smelling cigars in their hands, attempting with the vanity of small men to appear important — an undertaking in which they deceived no one, except perhaps themselves. Among this tawdry mess of humanity, this litter of the great pawnshop, politics, Rosalind shone with contrasting serenity.

A stir inside a small door, marked "private," caused sudden silence. The Mayor's secretary swung out into view like the toy bird of a cuckoo-clock, called an Irish name, and mechanically disappeared. As one of the nondescripts moved importantly to answer the summons, Rosalind heard to her surprise Dr. Cary's voice at her elbow.

" Why, Rosalind! What brings you here? "

" It's Brimmer House, Doctor. The Mayor once promised to speak at our fiftieth anniversay and I've come to hold him to his word."

" Fiftieth! Is it that old? "

Rosalind nodded.

" I've been getting his views on the milk question. Like all Irishmen, you know; treat them well and they will treat you well. I am half convinced he's honest."

" Will you get the bill through? "

The doctor shrugged his shoulders.

" You have an appointment, I hope? " he asked, glancing about the room.

" Not exactly. The Mayor told me that any time I dropped in he would be delighted to see me."

" Coming to America doesn't take all the blarney out of them, does it? It would have been better to write him. This place isn't very *de rigeur.*"

" I know; but seeing him personally is the safest way. He can't deny then."

" You've been waiting long? "

Rosalind smiled. " Twenty minutes. It's not half bad with all these curios here."

" Let me help."

" Oh, I couldn't —"

The famous surgeon strode off with the carriage of one who is sure of himself and of his welcome. As the private door closed upon him, Rosalind became the cynosure of eyes, and would have found the insistent scrutiny of the flashy men disquieting had he not in a moment returned.

" I have displaced the buildings committee in your favour," he laughed. " The Mayor will give you a minute."

Rosalind thanked him gratefully.

" Well, I must be off. I'm coming to the Square in a day or so. How is he ? "

" Not so well just lately. I'm a little anxious; in fact, I intended to telephone you to-night."

" So ? " The doctor whipped out his engagement book and fluttered the pages. " Will he be in at five-twenty this afternoon ? I'll come then."

" Hello, Father ! "

Rosalind turned with a smile at the voice, which she recognised as Benjamin's.

" Ben, my boy, you here, too ! I beg your pardon, Rosalind. What ? Do you know each other already ? "

" I should say we did ! " cried Rosalind. " Hasn't he told you ? "

" Not a word ! " Dr. Cary's face was a picture.

" We've known each other for several weeks — and very well, too, haven't we, Mr. Cary ? "

" To think that after all these years Ben should have clandestine relations with a young lady ! Oh, Ben ! "

The son flushed guiltily as he shook Rosalind's hand.

" Father, you're talking perfect rot, you know."

Little Dr. Cary patted his tall son affectionately.

"I realise that, Ben, and I'm mighty glad of the opportunity. It's the best thing you have ever done."

"Why are you here?" asked Benjamin, patiently ignoring his father's efforts to embarrass him.

"I came for Brimmer House, your father for milk, and you —?"

"For my buildings committee."

"I've postponed it. Beauty before business, you know. I've got Flanagan to let Rosalind come first."

"I'm glad to hear it; we can wait."

"I shall only take a minute. Your father's been most kind."

"It's my nature," humorously ran on the great surgeon. "Look at Ben: he's spoiled, quite spoiled by my kindness. He won't confide in his old father any more. That's gratitude for you!"

"Why did you leave the dance so early, Mr. Cary?" asked Rosalind. "I hoped we might have another talk together. It made me feel guilty to drag you there, as you declared I did, just for that little time."

"Never drag —"

"What!" interrupted the doctor in amazement. "Ben at a dance! Oh, this outherods Herod!"

He seemed actually staggered by the news.

"I'll tell no more!" cried Rosalind. "You must get it out of him yourself."

"Ossa on Pelion!" The doctor looked ruefully at his son. "I can't bear it; the suddenness is too much! Good-bye, Rosalind. Good-bye, you marble-hearted fiend!"

With a parting shake of the head at his son he trotted off in his characteristic hurry at the very moment the private secretary announced Rosalind's name.

" I trust you'll come to tea some afternoon," she said to Cary. " I want your views on the ball and on ever so many other things."

" You're very kind."

" You shouldn't make me do all the asking; that's not fair! "

Cary stammered happily. " I should l-love to come. Good-bye, Miss Copley, good-bye! "

Rosalind hurried into the private office, leaving him in open-mouthed bewilderment. It was incongruous to feel sentimental in the outer office of a mayor; yet sentimental Cary indubitably was, standing where Rosalind had shaken him by the hand and staring at the door marked " private." For the first time since the costume ball he felt happy. Since that ill-starred night on which he had rallied to the standard of invincible will-power and determination, a melancholy disinterestednes in his life and affairs had distressed him. The law seemed dry, the Club stupid, the newspapers empty. The more he willed the sun to shine, the more the east wind blew; the more he determined to extirpate Rosalind, the more deeply planted the roots of memory proved to be. Because he was obstinate and strong, he persevered in his attempt, but doggedness, either in winning or destroying love, is at the best a sorry, painful weapon. Now to match his great unhappiness, so small a thing as this meeting with its friendly words, its bright smile and handclasp, had suddenly transformed apathy into happiness. He stood astounded by the rapidity of the change.

Even coming up in the elevator he had been moody
and disgruntled, and now — now even the man with
the wen on his nose seemed a cheery old soul and
the prints of the ex-mayors works of fascinating
interest!

With an amused movement of his broad shoulders
Cary recalled the ratiocinations which had borne
fruit in his determining to forget Rosalind.   In his
present happiness he could laugh at the failure of
his fiery sword.   How hasty and ridiculous had been
his decision!   Yes, he had read the stars wrong,
very wrong, he told himself.   Only to remember how
pleasantly she had asked him to come to tea, to come
and talk on many things, was to confirm his inepti-
tude at reading the stars.   Instead of welcoming
her divine intervention, or so he chose to think of
it in his present happiness, he had insisted on pursuing a distasteful and unhappy course.   Poor blind
mole that he had been!   Let but God vouchsafe him
sight, Cary determined that he would burrow no
longer in the earth!   With his hands deep in his
pockets he walked about the unattractive room and
past the unattractive people.   It was good to see
things straight; it was good to feel again that invincible rightness of life which for so many years
had been his keystone of existence.   When he had
accompanied the rest of the committee into the private office of the Mayor, he thought with a thrill
of pleasure that Rosalind might have occupied the
very chair in which he himself was then sitting.   In
such a temper he could brook no pessimistic views
from his colleagues.

The next afternoon — a dark, cheerless January
day it had been for almost every one except himself — he stopped at 29 Commonwealth Avenue on

the way home from his office. It was a bold step, but Cary was no man to be afraid. Not until he was fairly abreast the bull did its horns look sharp and hard to grasp; then it was too late for retreat, since Paris was speaking his name.

" Oh, I am so glad you came! Mamma, do you remember Mr. Cary? "

" Yes, indeed. Has Rosalind been dragging you through Brimmer House again? "

" No — unfortunately," replied Cary with a heavy attempt at chivalry.

" Much worse, Mamma. We met in a most disreputable place! "

" Oh, Rose! How can you! Do you wonder that my hair is white, Mr. Cary? Tell me the worst. Was it the Charles Street Jail? "

" No. Only the Mayor's office."

" Almost as bad! "

" We had Dr. Cary for a chaperone, Mamma, so it was perfectly proper! "

" Also several ward politicians and an ex-prize fighter."

" I think your father sufficed without them, Mr. Cary." Mrs. Copley smiled as she poured out his tea. " I'm so glad you dropped in; just see how lonely we are! Rosalind was on the point of going to see her godfather for the third time to-day, she found me so boring."

" Is he worse? "

Rosalind shook her head sadly. " I'm afraid he's really not at all well. Your father visited him yesterday and even he seemed a little depressed."

" I'm so sorry."

" Mr. Singleton, you know," explained Mrs. Copley, " is Rose's godfather and perfectly adores her."

" My father has told me."

" When we were children, I used to invite you to my birthday parties in the Square," stated Rosalind with an air of mock reproof.

" I don't remember.   Are you —"

" Of course, not.   You never would come."

Cary endeavoured to embody something clever about the ignorance of youth in his reply, but by the time the answer was framed Mrs. Copley had changed the subject.

" Guess what Rose has been doing with her Italian girls now ! "

" Almost anything would be believable ! "

" Last Saturday matinée she filled our box at the opera with them ! "

" It was ' La Bohême,' and they loved it, Mr. Cary — ever so much more than most of the fat, old —"

" Rose ! "

" All right, Mamma.   But it was wonderful to see their eyes shine and the way they sat forward in their seats.   As for myself, I never enjoyed ' Bohême ' half as much before."

" By the way, Rose, we're dining at seven to-night, remember !   Have you asked any one ?   It's ' Aïda,' you know."

" No, Mamma."

" Will you come with us, Mr. Cary ?   There's only Rose and myself, and I for one should be delighted."

" Why, Mrs. Copley, I —"

" Oh, do come ! " urged Rosalind.   " Have you never heard ' Aïda ' ?   It's glorious.   Mamma and

I are old-fashioned and common enough to prefer
it to Débussy or Rimsky-Korsakov."

Had Rosalind said that she preferred Bergson
to Santayana or Matisse to Van Gogh, it could have
meant no less to Cary than this declaration of faith.
Of these names Débussy perhaps was familiar
though he failed to associate him with anything save
long hair and France. Cary knew that he himself
preferred Blackstone to Kent and, for recreation,
Dickens to Thackeray, but when it came to a question of declaring " Aïda " a vaudeville sketch or a
composer, he had no opinion to offer. Yet at the
same time that he wondered whether Rimsky-what-
ever-it-was ought to be called he or it, he liked to
hear the name come trippingly from Rosalind's
tongue. Like most unmusical men, his attitude towards feminine interest in art was one of amused
tolerance. And then to be talked to after this fashion made him feel not unpleasantly intellectual himself. Protesting that he had always cut a poor figure at opera, he accepted. Indeed, he had been but
once before in his life. Some years past his aunt,
Mrs. Curtis, had inveigled him to a performance of
" La Tosca," his only comment on which had been
a condemnation of the soldiers in the last act for
being unable to keep step.

Cary hurried home and dressed in a state of inward excitement; to one who had become such a
stay-at-home going to the opera with a young lady
was an occasion. As he shaved, he held an intimate
conversation with his lathered image in the mirror.
What a pass the world had come to with himself
attending the opera!

Before the curtain went up he even began to think
that he might like " Aïda " of itself, but in that was

deceived. The succession of scenes, the apparent lack of romance in the immense soprano and the more immense tenor, the long airs which held Rosalind breathless in her seat, proved dull and stupid to him. Yet there was imperishable compensation in sitting close behind Rosalind and feeling a part of her small and intimate world. He was glad and vain that people saw him sitting in the Copley box. When the lights were off, he endured the music in patience, eyeing boldly the smooth curve of Rosalind's neck as it stood out in profile against the brilliant stage; between the acts he listened quietly to her eager enthusiasms and indulgently echoed them. The odours of the gay auditorium drifted upwards, commingling feminine fragrances with the indescribable pungency of white kid gloves; he felt vaguely the eyes of many people fixed upon him, and held himself proudly and well. Out of his element indeed, but, like a captive lion being fed kickshaws in a gilded cage, he found for the moment both sweetmeats and prison altogether too delightful to be roared at.

After the first scene his attention to the opera from perfunctory interest turned to neglect, and he altogether ignored the stage. Far nearer to him than the imitation Nile with its gross Rhadames pouring out his soul in meaningless music his eyes had found a much higher form of art which they could understand. Yet when the great red curtain had finally fallen amidst a splendid burst from the orchestra and a scattering applause from the departing house, Cary would have been the last to deny that the performance had given exquisite pleasure.

CHAPTER VIII

INTO THE FIRE

AS time went by the acquaintanceship of Rosalind and Cary ripened into friendship, and from that into intimacy. Dry and practical as he was, Cary soon learned to count that day lost which Rosalind in some way had not brightened. To be sure, there were very few dark days. He dined often at the Copley house; he sleighed with Rosalind at the Sherborne farm; he went with her twice to the Symphony — although it bored him almost to extinction; he even took tea at 8 Louisburg Square, where Mr. Singleton Singleton with his usual silence dumbfounded him. But he was a distinct success in the family. He held forth on farm implements and model henneries when with Mr. Copley; he talked politics to Mr. Quincy, who had aspirations of an indefinite, but lofty character; he admired Rosalind to Mr. Singleton Singleton and to her mother; and when with Rosalind herself, once his tongue freed from embarrassment, there was a universe before him to explore.

They soon observed themselves alike in many of their tastes and distates. More serious than the majority of her companions, Rosalind found a natural kinship in Cary's seriousness. To hear him talk of his investigations, of the big men he had met and of what they had said and done, was a source of unending interest. She admired his ceaseless activity, his simplicity, and honesty; in his straightforward way of coming right out with a thing there was something clear and clean which made her keenly aware of the rightness of his spirit. He was so much the man, this great, handsome, quiet lawyer, and all her other friends were boys. Yet she never felt toward him as she did toward Philip Brooks or Frederic Hoyt. For them there was in her heart tenderness, the enjoyment of sunshine, of laughter, of flowers, the gay response to the liberty of a child who does not yet understand the black language of this world; but for Cary, older and stronger than herself, though she might admire him greatly and take deep pleasure in his company, there was no tenderness, no sentiment other than interested affection. She never associated him with love. Without him, alone in her room, or with her girls at Brimmer House, she could be perfectly contented; he was no necessity to her happiness. Yet, if it had been a question then of parting with him forever, she would have found in their separation a most sincere sorrow. To her he was more than a friend, yet nothing of a lover; almost heroic in some ways, always admirable, and a most engrossing companion. If she afforded him more and more opportunities for associating with her, it was in ignorance that she was herself feeding a fire whose flames some day might wax unbearably hot.

In Cary's behaviour there was nothing to warn her of the flooding tide of his love. Never a talkative man, he had lived in the belief that to be doubly wise was to obtain the opinion of another rather than to air that which was one's own. Love made him yet more silent. Like a filled bottle, the small mouth of which, when it is overturned, will permit the egress of not a single drop of liquid, so Cary in a company of people could find no words to speak to Rosalind. Few men have suffered more the embarrassments of love, because few men have reached so advanced an age with such inexperience. He had known nothing of girls before his meeting with Rosalind. Love was an unpathed wilderness in which he soon lost his way, yet into which, accounting his own strength superior to all else, he boldly plunged ahead. But calculation and reasoning vanished in the strange beauty of this undiscovered country; far from being disproved, they were ignored, denied admission into a land where behaviour is ruled by the moon which makes men mad, and life and happiness of living abandoned to the uncertain favour of a female heart. At first he had rebelled at the rape of his logic and determination, for no man likes to be deprived of the only compasses which he has known; but once resigned, once he had abandoned resistance he found himself happier. There was a light in the wood after all. In his love he found guidance and inspiration, the incentive to march ceaselessly and doggedly till he should reach that light and stand face to face with Rosalind. Originally employed in crushing out his affection, his determination later embodied itself into love as omnipresent as it was profound. His life no longer was his own, nor could he regard it as such in the fits of abstraction which possessed and held him by his office window. He came to know nothing save loving Rosalind, and his entire, calm, slow spirit bent itself to that love.

Thus January passed into February and February into March. In the train of winter succeeded those grey days when March, not stormy enough to be dubbed lion, yet too ungentle for a lamb's name, drizzled hour after hour from heavy clouds. The much-rained-on inhabitants of Boston began to forget the sun, which appeared, if ever, to shine shamefacedly for a moment at sunset over a city of puddles; they went about their daily work in rubbers and bad tempers.

In time tongues began to wag. Though the sudden attachment of Benjamin to Rosalind was too patent to be good gossip, since the season was dull, a few kindly disposed ladies of inquisitive temperament made much of the matter. An engagement was rumoured. When the report came to Rosalind's ears, she was surprised and good-humoured in laughing it down; but tongues at bridge tables will not be laughed down, and over the cards in the Cavendish Club, where circulated the dark tittle-tattle of other women's business, Rosalind's name was mentioned with glances full of significance. By means of the husbands of these bridge players the news entered the Sarcophagus, and gentlemen of the old school, gazing through their brandy-and-sodas out of the great front windows which looked over the Common, choked at the expression on Mr. Quincy's face when marriage in his family was hinted. " You'll be the next captive, Jo-Jo! " they cried hoarsely, as they rolled about in the great leather chairs. " Joey engaged! Ha-ha! Take your niece's example. Don't be timid! "

Perhaps there was sufficient basis for the rumour. United by many pursuits and inclinations, Rosalind and Benjamin were seen everywhere together. If she found him unappreciative of the higher arts, of paintings which caught her eye and held it fascinated, of music which flooded her with warmth, of poetry which sang so well the things she dimly felt, but never could herself express, if he was hopelessly practical and unromantic, at least he pretended to be nothing else.   He told her frankly that the Symphony made him feel numb with sleep, that the incessant scraping and thumping stupefied him.   Realising with a sense of relief that he did not try to pose as a music lover, like some of her boy friends, she gave up inviting him to go with her. To pretend an admiration for the sake of opinion is to give prima facie evidence of insincerity; Cary with the frankness of an older man pleased her.

Not only were they often together, but sharp eyes often discovered them in the most out of the way places.   Summoned one March morning to the Roxbury police court for over-speeding, Mr. Hereford, in glancing about the dock, caught sight of Rosalind.   She had come to hear Benjamin handle the case of a poor scrubwoman whose husband beat her, a case which he had taken out of kindheartedness.   Rosalind, whose sympathetic heart was much struck by the deed, made a great story out of it for her family; but not half so great as Mr. Hereford's wife devised for the Cavendish Club.   When Rosalind visited the Supreme Court of Massachusetts to hear Benjamin argue before that august assemblage, it was Mrs. Scribble's husband, one of the seniors of Foolscap, Parrypoint, and Scribble, who opposed him.   Throw a pebble in a pond and watch the circular ring of waves spread; in a day the tea-time conversation of three dozen ladies of Beacon Street began with: "*Have* you heard what Mrs. Scribble says?"

But it was not always Rosalind who went to hear

and see Benjamin; he was the constant attendant on the lesser cares of her woman's life. Without his precision and logical arrangement of detail the fiftieth anniversary exercises at Brimmer House could have achieved no such complete success. The afternoon was long memorable to him. Lost in the crowd of guests, he heard her few words in introduction of the captive and smiling Mayor with a queer tremor of nervousness. It was strange to hear her soft voice before so many people, strange and unnatural, like the sudden unveiling of something hitherto hidden. He cast a furtive glance about the room, feeling self-conscious and large among the crowd, but no one had noticed his embarrassment. When she had finished, he was proud of her success and congratulated her warmly on the simplicity of her presence. They walked home together, discussing the future of Brimmer House, a subject constantly before them. He loved nothing better than to be with her as she did whatever work she might have on hand for the House, to watch her interest in her charity, to help and advise her. Here was something at which they could meet on more equal terms. If he could not respond to her enthusiasms over the opera, in the field of practical affairs it was she who must look to him for guidance. And that guidance he gave more happily than anything in his life.

One evening Rosalind was seated at the piano in the drawing room of Eight Louisburg Square, while beside her Mr. Singleton Singleton, sunk back into a deep chair, watched her as she played. The room was peaceful and dark. A lamp near the piano, the light of which enabled Rosalind to read from the music before her, shed a subdued, soft light on her golden hair and created delicate shadows about her bare neck.

"These Chaminade pieces are too fast for my fingers," she laughed at the conclusion of one of the pyrotechnical waltzes. "What shall it be next, Uncle Sing-Sing? It's getting late, almost time for me to go home. What shall we have — the Prelude?"

Her godfather nodding assent, she turned over the music until she came to "Les Preludes" of Frédéric Chopin and opened the little book to the seventeenth. There was reverence in her manner as she began to play, the reverence of any novice attempting a thing well-known and well-loved. She was far from skilled. As the soft sadness of the prelude stole out into the room, there were stumbles in technique; but these occasional errors could not mar the tenderness of the piece, the gentleness, the calm, and the sweetness which she felt in it as she played. Still the delicate refrain called forth a legion of memories; still the insistent booming of the chapel bell blended in harmony with the air. Her eyes shone with the beauty of it; those of her godfather were bright with retrospect.

"Oh! I wish I could play it," she exclaimed in a low voice, when the last deep note of the chapel bell was hushed into silence. "I wish I could really play it."

She slowly covered the piano; the last piece was finished.

"Rose." The invalid spoke softly and tenderly.

She turned to find him holding something in his out-stretched hand.

"Some one I loved once played that." Never before had she heard her godfather speak so calmly. It was the old halting voice, but a voice flooded with shining memories. "This was hers, from me." He opened his clenched hand; in the subdued light a jumble of pearls shone on his palm. "Before she died she sent them back."

Wondering at the words, Rosalind stood beside his chair; to her inward eye came suddenly the picture of the pearl-circled miniature.

"How beautiful they are! I'm sure she loved them."

"She did." The invalid smiled faintly. "Put them on."

Rosalind clasped the pearls behind her neck — a perfect string, not large, but of beautiful colour and faultless gradation.

"There." She tipped the lamp shade so that the light fell full on the soft curve of her throat. "Are they lovely, dear?"

The old man looked at her a long time in silence, so long a time that she thought he had forgotten the present in thinking of the past.

"Take them," he said at length. "Wear them, dearest."

"Oh, godfather! Do you — do you really mean —?" She was troubled with surprise; he had never spoken of his youth and youthful love to her before. "I shall always wear them; I shall always love them."

She kissed his pale forehead gently.

"We two."

"Yes, dear. I shall not tell; I understand."

The entrance of Edouard prevented any further thanks, could she have made them.

" It's your motor, Miss Rosalind, and young Mr. Cary in it."

The invalid looked up suddenly.

" Mr. Cary? " she asked in wonder.

" Yes, miss. He said he found you out at your house."

" I hope there's nothing happened. . . . Good-night, dear godfather. These pearls are the sweetest present you have ever given me; I know how much they mean to you."

She kissed the invalid good-night and quietly went away, leaving him seated by the piano to think of the desperate distance of the past.

" Why, Ben, what brings you here at this time of night? There's nothing wrong, I hope? "

" No, Rose. I have to go away, and I wanted to say good-bye."

The motor rolled slowly down the steep decline of Mt. Vernon Street.

" Going away? When? "

He felt Rosalind turn towards him in the darkness.

" To-morrow morning. I'm going to New Orleans for the office."

" New Orleans! Oh, Ben —"

" It's a legal tangle over a will and I seem to be the only man who can go. Naturally I wanted to say good-bye to you before I left. They told me at your house you were with your godfather."

" Yes. But, Ben, how long will you be gone? "

" A month, I should think, at the least." He said it quietly, but with much feeling. " It will be a long, long time."

" Must you go? I'm so sorry."

" So am I. It will be —"

He did not finish the sentence. In the blank, rather hopeless silence which followed Rosalind began to realise how much of a place he had been filling in her life. The vista of a month without him to advise her in Brimmer House affairs, of a month without his accustomed figure by the fire-place at 29 Commonwealth, of a month without some one more serious than Philip Brooks to talk to, looked more bleak than she had ever thought such a vista could look. In December the absence of any man would not have troubled her in the least; but it was March now, and at the thought of their projected separation she was aware of a crescent sense of loneliness.

"I shall miss you tremendously. We have been so much together lately that it's like having a finger decide to go off to New Orleans to have you leave. Are you sure you'll be a month?"

The question was sweet in Benjamin's ears; under the affection of its tone his love welled up like a fountain which reaches unaccustomed heights when its sources are increased by gentle rains.

"It will surely be a month. Rose, will you — will you write me? A month is such a long time."

It was the hardest speech that he had ever made. The words, which the darkness of the enclosed motor alone made it possible for him to utter, sounded painfully bald on his lips.

"Of course I will, Ben. You must give me your address."

"I'll send it to you when I'm settled there," he replied happily. A wave of content broke over him. "It's awfully kind of you, Rosalind; they will mean so much to me down there."

"It's a little thing to do. If you have time, you must write to me, too, about your progress."

Cary smiled to himself in the darkness; he would have time, plenty of time for such letters.

"Do you realise," asked Rosalind with a laugh, "that we've been stopped before my house for several minutes? I'm sure Edmund will have imagined all sorts of things."

Had Cary been anything but a quiet, reserved, masculine man he would have seized on this opportunity, but, like so many of his fellows, in love he lacked the courage of his convictions. Vaguely sensible of having said not half what the occasion warranted, he handed Rosalind out of the automobile.

"Shall Edmund take you home?"

"Thank you. I think I'll walk for the exercise. It's a beautiful night for once."

Rosalind held out her hand to him. She stood on the first step of her house, where the light of a neighbouring street lamp fell dimly on her furcoat. The gauzy veil which she had flung over her head was partly fallen back, and Benjamin could make out her face in the darkness, smiling into his eyes.

"Good night, Ben. We'll look ahead to the time when you come back. Don't forget to send me your address."

He took her hand. For a moment it lay in his.

"Good-night, Rosalind. Good-bye."

He turned and walked rapidly off into the night without glancing back, though he was sorely tempted. It took determination to leave Rosalind and not steal a last look, but he walked on, turning over in his mind all the happiness which had been compressed into the last three months of their association. It was sad to leave it all, yet his heart sang at her promise to write to him, and he felt that a new relation might arise from it. If he was too phlegmatic to experience the immediate bitterness of this parting, he had at least a keen realisation of the nonsense embodied in the old saying that " parting is such sweet sorrow." Parting is sweet only in the prospect of speedy reunion; his exile was one of thirty days in which no sweetness lay.

CHAPTER IX

WHAT HAPPENED IN AIKEN

TO the genial haven of Aiken, South Carolina, more beneficial medicinally than all the tonics and drugs in the Pharmacopœia, Mr. Singleton Singleton migrated soon after Benjamin Cary's arrival in New Orleans. It is not good for persons of delicate health and great fortune to remain in Boston during March; there is something in the air, something in the rain, something in the mobility of temperature which leads doctors to pack their valuable clients off to the South. Therefore on the sixth consecutive day of storm the establishment of 8 Louisburg Square quitted misty Boston for the invigourating warmth of Carolina, quitted the great, solemn rooms of the old house, on whose panels hung Romneys and Corots, for the simplicity of a little cottage with bare cypress walls, lost among the pine trees. The change was utter and absolute. Instead of a quantity of servants, a large negress cook, a maid, and the omnipresent Edouard; instead of the circumscribed area of city streets, the freshness of the laughing South stretching away on all sides; instead of rain, shrouding the Square in mist, sunshine which sparkled from each blade of grass, from the emerald tip of each pine needle, and from each individual grain of sand; instead of a drab city still in the clutches of winter, a countryside radiant with spring; in short, instead of everything that was discordant, everything that was harmonious and soft.

As usual Rosalind accompanied her godfather; the physicians were far too wise to advocate a change from her presence and affection. During his gradual recuperation she settled into the pleasant laziness of southern days. It was a stupid, comfortable, healthy life, such as even the most active of us for a time finds pleasant — a little riding, a little golf and tennis, an occasional dove drive, a few letters to read and write in the morning.

Of her correspondence Benjamin's letters were the most interesting; they were lawyer-like briefs, written in a firm hand, rather than personal communications. From them she obtained a clear, dispassionate picture of New Orleans, which he found a second Marseilles, an idea of Louisiana's lazy methods of doing business, much information about the case he was investigating, but only faint glimpses of himself. He wrote in his second letter: " I find myself much alone here. It is a relief, though, to think that you are not still in Boston, doing alone all those things which of late we have done together. The picture of you in a new place is pleasanter to look on. Aiken should do you good." Cary had hesitated to send even this scrap of evidence of his oppressive loneliness, but had finally let it remain in the letter. Like all those in love he read into the words the wealth of longing in his heart, and was both eager and fearful that Rosalind value the sentiment at its true worth. But she failed to understand the intensity of his feelings. She found in the words only the affection of one friend for another, such affection as she herself might have meant in like words addressed to him. The love and pain which we write into the letters we make for those we love is never understood as it is written; ink is no true spokesman of the heart, but a lying, weak-kneed, pale translator of divine messages. Yet she was fully aware of the gap Benjamin's absence made in her life, and it was with the keenest pleasure that she obtained a promise from him to stop over in Aiken for a few days on his way home.

A week before he was due to arrive, another and unexpected visitor came to them. Heralded only by a mysterious telegram from Asheville, Mr. Joseph Quincy descended from the northern train one glorious morning, bearing on his face the traces of a sleepless night.

"So you've been in Asheville, Uncle Jo-Jo?" asked Rosalind, when they were slowly driving along the sandy main road.

"I will not deceive you, Rose; I have been in Asheville," he replied with profound decision. "Furthermore, I have been there with the Misses Hepplethwaite; and not only have I been there with the Misses Hepplethwaite, but I have fled from Asheville, if I may use the phrase, *in extremis.*"

"Tell me about it," urged his niece with an admirable effort at seriousness.

"To begin with, I was lured to the place under false pretences. Miss Amy Pearce was to have been there — a lovely young creature! Air and fire! A cousin of the family, I believe."

"A débutante?"

"Last year, but still exquisite. She was not there, of course; the whole thing was a colossal lie."

Mr. Quincy's eyes flamed with righteous indignation.

" But the Misses Hepplethwaite —? "

" Never fear! They were there — the harpies! And they had laid out a systematic schedule to undermine my resolve. I rode with Jane — alone; I drove with Joan — alone; and when she had a headache — bah! headache! — I took Jane on a picnic in the woods — alone. If it was not one, it was the other, but always — alone! " At each repetition of the emphatic word, Mr. Quincy's voice rang with melancholy. " But I was adamant; my heart was as hard as alabaster and as cold as ice. Like Argus, I was all eyes. If I had once weakened, if I had once allowed Jane's superiority to chill me or Joan's blandishments to undermine me, if I had once allowed either of them to get her knife under the oyster-shell —! "

Mr. Quincy threw back his head, and with closed eyes convulsively swallowed several times in demonstration of the passage of a resisting oyster down a greedy throat.

" But what a pearl they would have found in the shell! "

" They are not looking for any pearls," responded Mr. Quincy sagely. " Only women of your age, Rose, who can choose as they go, look for pearls; all the harpy wants is to crack the shell, whether there is an oyster inside or not."

" How did you escape, Uncle Jo-Jo? "

" Ah! That is where my ingenuity came in! While we sat at dinner I had delivered to me a wire saying that Tony was much worse. I clapped my hand to my head, turned pale, and, to make nothing of my strategy, retreated in disorder, but still single." Mr. Quincy smiled in appreciation of his own cleverness.

" But he isn't! He's better than he's been in years! "

"Oh! That's no matter! No matter at all! To make my escape absolute I'm going to sail for Bermuda on Monday."

"Uncle Jo-Jo! Frightened away by a petticoat? "

" You may laugh, my love, because the boot is not on your pretty little foot; but please remember that he. who runs away, lives bachelor another day. Furthermore," he added loftily, " the Governor is to fill a vacancy on his staff, and I do not wish my political opinions — ahem! — to be at all — ahem! — to influence his choice; on the whole it is best not to be present during such a political crisis."

Mr. Quincy was a delightful visitor. At every moment there came to his mind some new intrigue of the Misses Hepplethwaite with which to amuse Rosalind, and his ceaseless and unavailing efforts to compose a bread-and-butter letter of complimentary thanks to these ladies, for whom he appeared to cherish the most consummate antipathy, roused even Mr. Singleton Singleton. One could not but be merry in his company; his mock grief as well as his mock anger were made for mortal delectation.

Benjamin, who arrived some days later, was less amusing a guest, but there was something substantial in his character which Rosalind from the first had loved. Sometimes she had thought of him as a man-mountain. In his presence she had felt that protection which lies in the reposeful shadow of purple hills; in his physical strength she had found that provocative antithesis which attracts all women. If their separation had taught her how much she had come to enjoy his serenity and essential manliness, it had also taught her to look forward to his coming with keen anticipation.

To find even in his first greeting that he was changed was a disagreeable shock. In his absence she had with the deepest satisfaction pictured the renewal of their friendship and the restoration of the old, familiar days and hours. She had gone to meet him at the station with the spirit of affectionate comradeship shining in her eyes; to what end? It takes two people in this world to establish a relation. If the man does not respond in the same manner, it is wasted time for the woman to speak frankly and unaffectedly, to seek an eye which turns from hers. With a sudden discouragement and discontent she realised that there was constraint in his manner; he was no longer the Benjamin of other days, but a changed Benjamin, whose glance followed her about the room with furtive insistence and whose heart concealed something foreign to the serene stability which she had imagined his. As she stood beside him, she was uneasy; mountains are not so pleasant when one discovers them to be volcanic. She was not twenty-three for nothing; there are a thousand little ways in which the manners of a man reveal his heart to a woman. During their continuous association in Boston she had failed to grasp the gradual change in their relations; but now, after a month of separation, it was impossible to meet again as they had parted. Imagination paints our future as we wish it painted. She had imagined Benjamin a friend; to her consummate regret she found him a lover.

"What a pity!" she whispered to her pillow on the night of his arrival. "Are there no sensible men on earth?"

She wanted no lovers; in Benjamin she had never dreamed of finding one.   Boys had been in love with her before, had sentimentalised over her, had written much sound and little reason to win her heart. Of these, some she had tolerated, some she had liked. But Benjamin was not a boy, and he was meant for neither her toleration nor her liking.   To her the very idea of him as a lover was anomalous and ridiculous; as soon should she have conceived the minister of Trinity Church making sheep's-eyes as Benjamin moon-struck and in love.   Here was something very magnificent, very strong, very powerful, suddenly yielding to the common frailty of all men; here was Odysseus deprived again of his wisdom by Calypso and Samson idling in the vale of Sorec.   It was repellent.   Rosalind had thought Benjamin as near the perfect man as one might care to find; she knew that their friendship had turned to dross other association.   But she also knew that, though her heart exalted and admired him as a good, clear man and a brave comrade, it held no love for him.   He had not become a necessity to her life; perhaps an invaluable accessory, but never the necessity which he hoped to make himself.

The knowledge of the change put Rosalind out of conceit with the world, and Benjamin's three days slipped by under a cloud of uneasiness.   There was a lack of adjustment between them, a stiffness, unnatural and unbearable; yet there was no physic for it.   Since going back was not possible, and the constraint between them favoured progress still less, a hollow compromise was struck.   Like puppets they performed their parts with mechanical emptiness. In the morning they rode horseback, threading the sandy roads which wound through odorous pine groves; in the afternoon they played golf at the Country Club, where Benjamin, who had been in college a famous athlete, was the feature of the links.   As he lived, he played — quietly, sternly, precisely, perfectly.   But there was no pleasure in the games; constraint kills all mutual enjoyment. Perhaps unjustly Rosalind grew out of patience with him.   Forgetting that she had paved originally the very path on which he now was walking, she illogically abused him for his steps.   Yet she was not selfish in her accusation; a great friendship is so magnificent and sacred that our poor human fears for its continuance and our sorrows at its end cannot be called selfish without detracting from its quality. Where all mortality is selfish, we call it human; and Rosalind was very human about Benjamin. Since the change in him destroyed not only their friendship, but also its great promise, she was angry and repelled; yet in her heart she cherished him as he had been, and, as they walked to meet his train on the last day of his visit, felt a pang of loneliness.

It was a clear, windy morning with a sky as blue and stainless as if fairy hands had been scrubbing at it with vast, invisible brushes.   The wind, which stirred little whirlwinds of dust from the sandy roads to spend themselves in the fury of their rise, pulled at Rosalind's hair and sent it flying across her face.

"We're early," she said, glancing at her watch. "In this wind you walk fast without noticing it. There's almost a quarter of an hour, and the station's around that corner by the little hill."

They both stopped.   The path had led them by a cedar hedge into a secluded dell which few knew and fewer walked in.

"Let's sit down."

Rosalind followed her own suggestion, but Cary remained standing beside her, looking down earnestly.

"What's been — the matter, Rose?" he asked.

"Matter?"

"Between us, I mean."

She felt suddenly cold, and groped for a word to express the disappointment in her heart.

"I think — you know better than any one, Ben."

"I wonder if you know," he said evenly; then without warning, broke out into fierce, eager speech. The words fell from his lips as if no control could hold them back, scattering, nervous, unbalanced words, words of first and irrepressible freedom. "I love you, Rose, I love you. I know what the matter is; I've known ever since I went to New Orleans, and you must know, too. I love you terribly. Do you understand? Terribly. I cannot go back alone; it is misery. I am changed since last year. Then I did not know, but you have taught me, Rosalind, and I have learned the lesson well!"

He ceased to speak with the suddenness of his beginning. Rosalind found herself staring at a pale blue-bell, the stem of which was crushed beneath his heel, at a loss for words.

"You don't say anything, Rose."

She looked at him for the first time, and with a timid smile on her lips stretched forth her hand. He seized it in his.

"Sit down, Ben. Let's have a talk."

He sat down beside her, his eyes bent fixedly on her face.

"I'm so sorry to see it all go," she said softly.

"Go? What?"

"Our friendship. This winter has been wonderful to me; we've done so many things together and we've found each other so companionable. I've admired and liked you, Ben, and you —"

"I admired and liked you, too, at first, but I couldn't go on like that; it's not human. You can't expect a man to remain just a friend when the world is stupid and empty without a certain woman. A man has to have love; it is inevitable. I need you, Rose; that is all."

Rosalind felt a great desire to be far away from where she was; the little dell was close and narrow, and in the hateful moment which was coming she was to make suffer some one of whom she was very fond.

"And now we can't go back! Ben, you were so different from my other friends; now you're like them. I wish —"

She hesitated. There was nothing for her to say; she realised that it would be added cruelty to speak dull, cold words of regret. Regret is seldom worth the breath that whispers it.

"Rose!" His voice struck pleadingly on her ear. "Can't you say — something?"

"What would you have me say?"

"That you will marry me."

He said it in a firm voice, measuring the syllables with a passionate care.

"Oh, Ben, I can't!"

She jumped up impulsively in almost physical revolt, unwilling to bear the pleading in his voice and eyes. A desire to be alone dominated her, a desire for the freedom of some crowning hill, where the wind might wash about her in clear, cool waves and she might forget the responsibilities and relations of human existence in a communion with the elements.

In the dell she felt enmeshed and burdened; but, woman-like, she spoke tenderly to the man seated at her feet.

"I'm sorry, Ben. I didn't mean to speak like that, but I — I — it was on the impulse. You know how I value you. All this winter I have given you the best in me with pleasure, but that best is not enough to answer your asking. I am afraid that you want more than I can give. It is my limitation, not your fault. It must be in me that I cannot love enough to marry. I have never cared for any man as much as for you, yet for all that I — I cannot marry you. Do you understand?"

She smiled wistfully at him as he arose.

"I can't think now. I can't believe it. Of course, the — the fault must lie in me. . . . And do you mean you never —? It cannot be never?"

Such an appeal is not readily borne; Rosalind's heart softened.

"I don't know that, Ben. Only the gods do. Some day —"

"Then I — may I talk to you again, Rose? I must."

A whistle shrieked imperatively in the distance.

"That's your train."

"Rose, will you try to — think of me?"

His clear, grey eyes held hers for a moment.

"Yes," she replied faintly, "I'll try."

"Until you come to Boston I shall remember that; it will help. Good-bye."

He pressed her hand hard, turned, and ran down the path. Rosalind stood looking after him, recalling the night on which he had come to tell her of his departure for New Orleans. This time he turned back at the curve to wave a last farewell.

" Good-bye, Ben," she called after him.

When the last sound of the train had mingled with the lazy quiet, she slowly retraced her steps to the house. She was angry and disappointed; but whether it was because of her inability to love Benjamin enough to marry him or because she had not told him plainly the whole truth she was at a loss to discover.

CHAPTER X

EXACTED promises are soon broken. Do we but voluntarily make an agreement our sense of honour compels us to its consummation, but a promise made in a moment of weakness or under compulsion is not readily kept. Often after Benjamin had left Aiken, Rosalind regretted the gentleness of her nature which had moved her to extend a deceitful hope. She had promised to try to love him; she had been afraid to face the imminent crisis, and by compromise had hoped to spare the feelings of both herself and him. But her timidity had brought her no comfort. She could not love him; she could not bring herself to think of him as being other than a steadfast friend. He was a man, a creature of noble stuff, of great physical and moral strength, but there was in his nature no single attribute which she could not readily plumb. This was the spring of her discontent. Women are essentially unmechanical. They desire and appreciate those loftier things for which man has no true definition; they are impatient of appearances. If the woman is more religious than the man, it is because she is fascinated by a spirituality which is not to be understood. If she cannot ascribe to him she loves an ideal character, then her love is a poor thing, born of necessity or reason, and will not flourish in the winter-time of life. For Benjamin Rosalind could conceive no higher love, no idyllic passion such as is the promise of all pure, sweet natures; every emotion of his heart, every act of his life was apparent, as offensively definable as any mechanical action. His soul was too clean and clear not to be readily understood; frankly and simply it explained itself, and like a clean, clear lake its bottom was visible to the naked eye.   But if one must live forever on a lake, the mystery of depth in which bottom is unseen and distant as the stars is preferable to the crystal clearness of transparent beauty.

Whether she could love him or no, the promise was obtrusive.   Visions of a day of reckoning troubled her mind, a day when the uncomfortable truth must be imparted to Benjamin, and be so imparted that the question would never rise again.   Knowing that she must tell him, that she must act squarely and not bear him in hand, she could find no words to frame what she must say.   Like all women, she saw the end and not the means, and, as she turned the matter over in her mind, felt more and more that she had become involved in a most uncomfortable tangle.

She was glad to leave Aiken.   If Benjamin had to be faced, she felt it best to face him soon and begin with a clean slate while there was yet chalk with which to write.   Her godfather had preceded her return on some mysterious matter of business, the secret of which both he and her father, who had joined them, obstinately refused to divulge; hence she arrived alone at Back Bay one fine twilight in April, and stepped into the family's open automobile, deluged with that wave of content which is the inevitable accompaniment of the true Bostonian's return.   To any citizen of the world there is no place like home; to the true Bostonian there never has

been and never can be, even in beatific realms, a
place like home.

As the automobile turned the corner by the Cavendish Club to swing into Commonwealth Avenue, a
shabbily dressed old lady with a poke bonnet all
over her head, stepped off the curbing directly in
front of the wheels. With a warning cry the chauffeur threw on the brakes, but it had been too late to
save her, had not a young man standing on the curb
seized her skirts and with intuitive swiftness jerked
the old woman back into his arms amid a confusion
of bonnet and exclamation. The automobile was
brought to a violent stop; the chauffeur (as all chauf-
feurs do on such occasions) glowered and muttered;
and Rosalind, who had nervously stood up, was the
first to speak.

" She's not hurt, I hope? "

As the woman only mumbled to herself in a nervous endeavour to adjust her lop-sided hat, the young
man replied.

" I think not.   It did not even touch her."

He spoke in a low voice with a faint accent which
lent a certain charm and distinction to the few words.
As she murmured that she was glad, Rosalind looked
at him curiously. In the darkness she found him
tall, slender, and well-dressed; and, although his
features were hardly distinguishable, she thought him
decidedly handsome. She thanked him again with
more profusion, and he bowed in return, rather
lower than most Americans do, and removed his hat
as if it were an honour and not a hardship. The
automobile rolled on. As its lights wheeled by, she
caught a glimpse of a pair of clear, green eyes, as-
tonishingly true in colour.

After dinner Rosalind went into the music-room. She knew that Benjamin would come to her and chose to meet him there, alone. When he arrived, she was playing an old French song, *Maman, dites-moi,* and humming the words. With a flutter in her heart she pretended not to be aware of his presence at the door; for a moment she entertained a wild hope that the old order of things might be re-established.

"Aren't you going to speak to me, Rose?"

The old, old remark, half sincere, half false, half bathos, half really pathetic; the old, old appeal to one beloved, but not loving! Rosalind made a poor attempt to cover her pretended ignorance.

"Why, Ben, I — I didn't hear you come in."

"Oh, I thought —"

"Sit down. Here." She pointed out a chair near the piano. "Shall I play some more?"

He did not reply. He had hoped she would not play. Music, especially the music which she liked, he had never understood or cared for. But she was in the mood for it and began the *Chanson Indoue,* a sad, haunting, Russian song, which jarred so uncomfortably in his ear that when she was half through, he arose and laid his hand on her fingers. Drowned in a little discord, the music stopped.

"Benjamin!"

"Rose, please! We — we've got to talk this out."

He walked back to his chair and sat down on the arm.

"Well?"

"You remember, Rose, what you said to me at Aiken?"

" Yes."

He looked keenly at her. " Have you — have you tried? "

" Yes, Ben, I have —"

She meant to tell him the truth, but the impulse failed her. She saw him leaning forward, his eyes yearning for her love, his whole spirit dependent on her lips, and hesitated, frightened.

" And you — you —"

Turning away, tortured and unable to speak, she clasped her hands together in undisguised nervousness.

" Oh, don't ask me, Ben! Please! Why need you? You must not."

" I must, Rose." He drew himself up beside the chair and spoke in a hurried voice. " I cannot wait. I must have some answer. You — you don't understand the torture of my mind. I have thrown everything in the balance, everything worth living for, and you outweigh them — all of them. You know how I live. I know no one well — only you; I have no time nor care for intimate friends. Every bit of my heart is yours, Rose. Tell me, what are you going to do with it? "

She looked mutely at the pattern of the carpet; she had no words in answer.

" That December day was the commencement of it all — by the statue. You remember? You reproved me for my bad manners and took me to Brimmer House; the memory is very clear. You began it; you liked me then. You —"

" I like you now, Ben! "

" And that is — all? " he asked quietly.

" I'm afraid, Ben, that is all."

He sank into the chair and was for a while miserably silent, then laughed coldly.

" Well, I'm a coward. I can't seem to face it. It's all upside down, all wrong . . . You're sure that in time, Rose, sure you couldn't come to marry me ? "

As he leaned forward with his head sadly down, pity overflowed Rosalind's heart and she weakened. She had not forgotten that memorable twilight on which they had met in the Public Gardens; since then she had found cause to blame herself harshly for her behaviour. As he had said, his love was all attributable to the manner in which she had treated him. Knowing that her duty was to destroy all Benjamin's hopes, however it might hurt him at first, she found herself incapable of performing that duty. In recompense for the unhappiness which she had caused, she held out a straw of comfort.

" I cannot say that I am sure, Ben," she ventured in a timid, kind voice. " I don't know. It's hard — can't you see what a hard position I'm placed in ? It makes me feel that I'm a perfect beast. I am so very fond of you that it is terrible to say no "— she hesitated, unwilling to wound, but realising the necessity of frankness —" yet I cannot bring myself to say yes. It may be selfish; it is, I know, but it's human, too. It's human not to take a big chance like that with happiness. I can see how much you care for me: it is wonderful to realise it ! " Her voice was near breaking as she said this, but she strengthened it and went on. " Yet with its beauty, it makes me feel, too, all the more certain that I am right in refusing you. My love, Ben, is too poor beside yours. It is cruel enough when we are friends;

if we were married, it would be unbearable. Do you see what I mean?"

"Yes, I think I see," he answered slowly.

"I can't bear to make you miserable, Ben. If I thought that some day, at some future time I could feel differently — "

"Perhaps you will!"

"Who knows?"

"Rosalind," said Benjamin frankly, "you have known me better than any one. You have known how dependent I am on regularity. It has been at the bottom of all my strength and happiness. All my life has been definite; now it is without any certainty. I do not know if you love me; I do not know if you can love me. It seems I must go on suffering day after day with nothing to fall back on. Can't you do something to help? Is there no word, no promise which you can give to strengthen me? I hate to leave a thing hanging fire. If we could only . . . I'd almost like to finish it all now," he went on rather bitterly. "But if you think there is any chance, I will wait — forever."

"It may be — it is, I'm afraid, a faint chance."

"No matter how slight, when the business is so serious. In time it may grow stronger. It will grow. Such things must happen every day in this world where time so often chooses. Shall we name a day? It will help me, and it will give you an opportunity to decide. Let us make things definite, Rose."

She paused before replying. The commitment to a fixed day repelled her as an attempt to regulate the one thing which should know no regulation; yet at the same time she saw in it a way out. If she had no heart to destroy Benjamin's love now by a single stroke, in the weeks which must elapse before the appointed day arrived there would be many opportunities to discourage his affection. What if the process and period of this attrition be distinctly hard for her? It was a just punishment, falling on her more heavily than on Benjamin. By a variety of means his love might be cooled; by gradual and increasing neglect, by showing herself to him in unpleasant lights, by forcing herself to be not herself. At the cost of their friendship it might be done. But was not their friendship ended now?

"I will, Ben. What day will you choose?"

"Let it not be too near at hand. The first of June?"

"The first of June," she repeated. "Until then, let's try and forget that we're anything but great friends."

He took her hand.

"Thank you, Rose. I will do my best, for you have done yours. . . . Good night."

He went quietly out of the room, leaving her at the piano, staring fixedly at nothing in particular. Had she done her best?

Rosalind had left Boston in the slush and sleet of a vindictive March; she came back to a city bathed in sunshine. As she walked to Louisburg Square the morning after her return, she discovered in the Public Gardens not one robin but a dozen, carolling away with the importance of all harbingers bright promises of spring. There were birds in the Square, too, whispering in its old ear tropical messages; they fluttered from the wrought iron fence to the grass, peering up green and fresh through the stubble of the old year, or sought in the ragged elms, whose tops

were feathering out into a reddish haze, aërial
boudoirs in which to preen their feathers. How
monstrously spick and span the Square appeared!
It seemed as if little hands had dusted each individual cobble-stone, polished each bar of the black
fence, and put the two white statues into the launder-
ing-tub of nature. 'Across the green the houses
smiled like a double row of hibernators recently re-
awakened to find the world a most inviting place.
Rosalind had inherited the Copley affection for the
Square. From her childhood she had found it a
second home, a haven of charm and adventure, in
all seasons to be loved, but especially in spring to be
admired. Who does not think the coming of spring
incomparable? What is wonderful in the country
is the more amazing in the city. That the Invisible
Renovator each April transform the cold, quiet
gloom of this old pocket of the metropolis into the
garden greenness of June was a source of never-end-
ing joy to Rosalind. To see the country reborn at
spring is to see only the material side of the season,
the new crops, the fast-opening buds, the waving hay;
but to see the dull, hard city annually rejuvenated is
to see the most unnecessary and beautiful light prodi-
gally shed in uncongenial grimness.

She mounted the steps of 8 Louisburg Square
with her happiness dancing in her eyes. As the door
yielded without the necessity of ringing, she thought
that she heard the sound of music and listened for a
moment, dumbfounded. Music in 8 Louisburg
Square? Some one playing upon her piano? It
was a thing as unexpected, as impossible to believe
as the wildest range of fancy. Closing the door,
she advanced into the great, formal hall with a silent
step. She recognised the melody as the seventeenth

prelude of Chopin, the favourite of herself and of her godfather. Whoever the player was, the playing was consummately skilful, and her keen ear told her as she listened that years of training and a deep appreciation guided the unknown fingers in the adjoining room. Curiosity impelled her towards the doorway. As the melody swayed softly upward to the commanding note of the prelude, she brushed aside the heavy hangings at the door and looked eagerly in the direction of the piano — straight into the green eyes of the young man who the evening before had rescued the woman from her automobile! His hand was raised for a heavy chord when he caught sight of the figure in the doorway. Rosalind saw him spring to his feet in amazement, leaving the melody to die midway.

"Oh, please finish it!" she cried impulsively.

The young man hesitated; then, with a smile complied.

Rosalind remained standing, framed against the dark hanging like a vibrant figure of light stamped there by the gods. During the completion of the prelude she had an opportunity to examine the stranger, and found him a strikingly handsome figure as he sat before the great piano. Morning sunlight streamed in at a window beside him, glinting on the top of his dark, curly hair, and making the green waves sparkle in his eyes. Though bizarre, his features were undeniably handsome, and the carriage of his thin, graceful body lent distinction to his appearance. What an anomaly was this poetic figure in the staidness of her godfather's house! In apparent oblivion of his surroundings he lingered over the haunting refrain, and not until the prelude was finished did he look again in Rosalind's direction.

The quizzical expression on his face made her smile as she advanced into the room.

"Isn't that prelude wonderful? I try to play it, too, and long to play it well. You —"

"I found the music here," said the young man in the same low voice of the afternoon before.

"It is mine."

The young man raised his eyebrows in surprise.

"You will forgive me for using it? I could not resist the temptation. This prelude is full of memories for me; years ago I heard my mother play it. It was her favourite."

Rosalind gasped involuntarily. She appreciated now the mourning of the young man and his slight accent. In a flash she combined the facts that this prelude was beloved by her godfather and the favourite of this stranger's mother. To solve the riddle of his name was simple.

"You must be a Mr. Rolland!"

With an astonished glance the stranger assented.

"It sounds rather illogical to draw that conclusion, I suppose, but my godfather once told me that this prelude was much loved by Madame Rolland."

"Your godfather?"

"Uncle — Mr. Singleton Singleton. Hasn't he spoken of me to you?"

The young man smiled. Rosalind liked his smile; it fascinated her.

"He is not very — talkative. In a week he has said but little, and not a word of you."

"How like Uncle Sing-Sing! I call him that, although he's only father's second cousin. He's the dearest and most uncommunicative godfather in the world!"

"You must have been surprised to find me here."

"Surprised! I never have had a surprise in my life to compare with that of entering this house and hearing music. I truly expect to see you go up in a cloud of smoke like a genii at any minute!"

"I shan't do that; it's too attractive here."

"You like it then?"

"Like it! I never believed there was anything like this in America. I had always thought it a cauldron of cities and factories, smoking and grinding away. But this — this is a bit of the older, calmer world. I have explored Boston during this last week and I can't tell you how much of beauty and interest I've discovered. Will you show me more?"

"You can probably tell me more about Boston by this time than I can you. It's always the stranger that is the best informed."

"There must be many out of the way pockets, though —"

"I'll try," replied Rosalind. "We'll make a bargain. I'll be your Baedeker, if you'll be my — Orpheus!"

"Agreed!"

"You've come at the best time of year; in a few weeks the country will be glorious. You must come out to the farm."

"Anywhere. And will you introduce me to some people? Your godfather has been most kind, but outside of Edouard and a Mrs. Copley — oh! and Dr. Cary — I have seen no one."

"That's my mother, that Mrs. Copley! I hope you got along well together."

"Splendidly! It worried her that I spoke English so well."

"I don't wonder; you do."

"I went to school at Cheltenham. My grand-mother being American, my mother wanted me to speak her tongue well. Since she could not part with me for America, England was the substi-tute."

"Is Mr. Singleton upstairs?"

"I suppose so; he has not yet come down."

"Do be Orpheus again till he descends! I'll re-pay you some day double-fold."

Mr. Singleton was indeed upstairs. He was sit-ting by a window with almost an expression of eager-ness on his pale face. Edouard, as he adjusted his footstool, was speaking to him.

"They are down by the piano, sir, and it's my opinion, since you ask it, that they've taken quite a fancy to each other."

CHAPTER XI

NEW THOUGHTS FOR OLD

IT was late in the afternoon when Rosalind walked slowly home. A high wind had sprung up which tore at the branches of the trees, making them wave and shiver in the dying light. Head down she struggled along, busily turning over and over in her mind the novelty of a handsome and talented young man in the house of her godfather. In her childhood 8 Louisburg Square had been something of a fairy castle, something of a Golconda where lay concealed innumerable beauties awaiting only an adventurous spirit to discover them. But here was a novelty more diverting than the fourfoot doll which had done everything but talk, until Mr. Quincy endeavoured to endow it with that quality by a mechanical operation involving more ingenuity than technique; here was a surprise more dumbfounding than the tiny dog which had one Christmas popped out of a large plum pudding; here for her entertainment was come to visit the son of the greatest tenor in the world!

Rosalind laughed excitedly to herself. The whistling wind made her thoughts fly fast; it sang by her lips and whirled along in its rough embrace the words she murmured half to herself and half aloud.

"And Uncle Sing-Sing! Why, he couldn't take his eyes off him! There never was anything like it. Calls him Eric, dotes on him, on his music, on his architect's sketches, on everything about him. I'm not in it. My poor efforts at the piano will never be favoured again." She laughed whimsically. "How well he does play; I'm sure there were tears in my eyes over his *Caprice Vienncise*. . . . As a rule I don't like foreigners. There was that nasty cad whom Mrs. Bryce dragged about with her — the Count de Ricrac. I hated the little beast; yet he would kiss my hand and talk about the stars. And after all he turned out to be somebody's valet. Foreigners are always much nicer in their homes. I wonder why? But Mr. Rolland is certainly different. I hope he's going to stay and be ever so interesting with his music; I forgot to ask Uncle Sing-Sing. . . . He said his grandmother was an American. I'm glad of that; it doesn't make him seem so far — I beg your pardon!"

Obsessed with her thoughts, she had collided with two ladies whom the wind was sweeping down Arlington Street.

"Oh! Miss Hepplethwaite, do excuse me! In this wind one cannot see at all."

"How do you do, Rosalind? I hope your trip to Aiken benefited you?"

"Yes, thank you."

"And how is your dear mamma?"

"And your dear papa?" echoed the younger sister.

Even in the whistling wind an indefinable and unruffled primness clung about the two spinsters, and they asked their invariable questions with as much cold interest as if they were all three meeting in the most sedate drawing-room in Boston. Rosalind murmured some reply.

"I haven't seen you for such a long time," went

on the older Miss Hepplethwaite. "You've been with your godfather, I suppose?"

"Yes. He came home before me."

"We are most curious, my dear Rosalind, to discover who the very handsome young man is that calls on your godfather. Joan and I have observed him entering the house several times. He is not a cousin —?"

"Oh, no," said Rosalind, "not a member of the family at all. He is the son of Lucien Rolland — the tenor, you know. His mother was a great friend of my godfather, and at her death she expressed a wish that her son come to America. He is a most —" In the excitement of her interest in the stranger it was on Rosalind's lips to say "charming young man," but remembering the ears, eyes, and tongues before her she concluded — "beautiful pianist. He played for us to-day."

"Is that his profession?"

"No." Rosalind scented cold disapproval in the question. "He is an architect, and a very excellent one, too. My godfather told me that he won the Grand Prix at the Beaux Arts two years running."

"The French are so clever! Their *esprit* is remarkable."

"And their *élan!*" added Miss Joan, not to be outdone.

"His grandmother was an American. He speaks English perfectly, with just a shade of accent."

"He must be very diverting. I am afraid that I shall have to keep an eye on my sister; Joan is so impressionable."

"Oh, Jane, how can you?" The younger Miss Hepplethwaite simulated coyness with the full benefit of forty years' experience.

"And your poor dear uncle, Mr. Quincy! He was so worried over your godfather at Asheville that it was pitiful to behold. We tried to comfort him. When he departed for Bermuda, he sent us a sweet present."

"Too thoughtful of him," murmured Miss Joan.

"And a cable. Do you think the Governor will really appoint him? Mr. Hereford endeavoured to induce Joan to believe that the Governor's staff had no political importance, but after what Jos — Mr. Quincy has said, we understand fully its responsibilities. He was quite justified in leaving at such a time."

"It was imperative," said Miss Joan.

"I am certain it was," Rosalind assured them, remembering with an inward smile the more cogent reason for her uncle's departure.

The wind had become so boisterous that the Misses Hepplethwaite, having acquired that information necessary for the concoction of a little scandal, took their leave, begging Rosalind some day to bring the stranger to talk French with them. As Rosalind watched the wind blow them across the street, lady-like even with their skirts fluttering about their knees, a sense of their pitiful inutility came over her. If they had only married, they might have made decent enough wives; in a crowd of modern married women they would have passed muster. But they had waited too long and too carefully. They had ignored opportunity's knock, because it had not been loud and distinct; now every moment their ear was at the door to detect the faintest scratching. As she turned towards home, Rosalind told herself that, God willing, such a fate would never be hers.

Hearing a murmur of many voices at tea in the living-room, she went quietly up to her own chamber, a pretty blue and white room, companionably quiet. She removed her hat, smoothed her golden hair in front of the mirror, and then wandered to her desk and sat down, still busy with her thoughts. How pleasant it was to sit in her comfortable arm-chair and think of the walk which she had taken with Eric Rolland along the Esplanade! His typically French nature had amused and charmed her. The French in their happiness and sorrow are children, in their courage giants, in their talent geniuses, in their sympathy angels. The remembrance of the walk called to her mind a promise to take him to a concert of Schumann-Heink's the next afternoon. As she reached for a pencil to note down the engagement, her eye fell upon her calendar, a loose-leaf affair with a separate page for each day of the year. On going to bed the night before she had left it turned over to June 1st; written on that page in large bold letters: ANSWER BEN!

Rosalind stiffened in her chair. The day long she had not thought of Cary. Engrossed by the stranger from across the sea, she had lost sight of her troubles in his happy usurpation, and had drawn idle fancies strangely at variance with an attempt to return Benjamin's love. When Damocles observed a blade trembling above him upon a single thread, he took no pleasure in the banquet which Dionysius had spread for his consumption; so Rosalind's fond imaginings soon lost their charm with the vexing promise to Benjamin staring her in the eye. She arose and walked pettishly about the room, injured and confined. How foolish to have made that agreement with Benjamin in contradiction to her

first impulse! She would not consent to be forced
into anything by a man; however masterful he might
be, Benjamin could not compel her to love him.   In
aggrieved revolt she forgot that without her own
encouragement he would never have entered into her
life, that for all his concern she would have been
as free as the libertine air.   A low knock at the
door interrupted her petulant walk.   It was Paris.

"It's Mr. Cary, Miss Rosalind.   I'll tell him
you'll be down, shan't I?"

Still annoyed, Rosalind exclaimed, "No, Paris,
stop!   Tell him I've — I've a headache; I'm not
coming down."

She turned away toward the windows.

"Yes, miss.   I'm sorry you're not well."

When Paris was gone, she was angrier with herself than she had been with Benjamin.   She had no
headache; this was nothing more or less than the behaviour of a spoiled child, and if she disliked one
thing more than another, it was the petty selfishness
of life.   Pricked by an excellent conscience, she
opened the door and hurried down the hall to the
stairs, on which she intercepted Paris and left him,
gasping at the suddenness of her change in health,
with a glorious tidbit for pantry gossip.

There were some dozen people in the drawing-
room.   She caught sight of Benjamin pinioned in
his chair by a lady whose fantastical garb and disar-
rayed ringlets declared her to be one of those intellectual females whom society lionises and — in secret
— laughs at.   From such captivity she rescued him
with a graceful facility which was the admiration of
Benjamin and the confounding of his blue-stocking
interlocutor.

"She was telling me about the soul," he mur-

mured weakly, as Rosalind led him into the quiet
music room, "about the soul, and Maeterlinck, and
silence. There was a lot about silence, I remember,
and its beauty."

"You know how a python mesmerises a rabbit?
When I dragged you away, you were in the last
hypnotic stage."

"Thanks a thousand times for the rescue. I
thought I saw you come in, so I —"

"I have been at — at the Square all day."

"Did you find Mr. Singleton Singleton well?"

"About the same. The day — passed quickly."

Rosalind let slip an opportunity to tell Benjamin
about Eric Rolland. A month earlier she would
have instantly related the whole story to him, but
now she was glad to postpone the moment.

"How does it seem to get back to the office, Ben?
Have you finished your New Orleans business?"

"I'm afraid not. I may have to go back soon
— very soon."

Rosalind started involuntarily.

"I'm sorry," she said. The words sounded con-
victionless to her, and she repeated them in another
tone. "I'm sorry. How soon?"

"In a week or so; and it will take another month,
too, I'm afraid."

Rosalind received this piece of news, so painful
for Benjamin to relate, with a criminal sense of inward happiness. She forced herself to murmur,
"Really?"

"In one way," he went on, "it will be a good
thing. You will be absolutely free to decide for
yourself. From New Orleans my influence can be
but small and by June first you ought to know as defi-
nitely as — as I do now, where we stand."

In dangerous waters so soon! Rosalind walked nervously to the fire-place, crying to herself, " Oh, Ben, Ben, why must you always bring it up? " Aloud, however, she assented. " Yes, it will be fairer." After an uncomfortable pause, during which the wind rattled in the chimney, she added, " Listen to the wind. I wish you could have seen it blow the Hepplethwaites across Arlington Street ! "

After all, there is nothing like the weather! The gentle rain of Heaven which falls upon the just and the unjust has watered many a backward conversation and brought it to full growth. Far from being the infirmity of talk, the weather is often its strength and guide. As Rosalind's friend of friends, Camilla Cabot, often told her: there is nothing like a rainstorm to dampen sophomoric effusions, and the mere mention of wind will blow Byron and all his verses into the next county. With Benjamin the well-worn ruse succeeded; he turned to his law.

" It seems good to be at my desk again. I like to work methodically as you know; in the South business is transacted according to the thermometer."

" You mustn't work yourself to death, Ben. I know how ambitious you are."

She spoke kindly and softly, as she had often spoken in the past, suddenly moved by a wave of tenderness. Perhaps Benjamin noticed a subtle change in her tone, for he glanced towards her as if pleased by her words.

" Thank you, Rose. Ambition isn't worth a continental without health to back it up. That's why I lay so much value in method. Regularity spells health."

Rosalind shrugged her shoulders. His desire to

standardise everything had long been a contentious subject between them.

"I don't believe any great man was ever regular!"

"How about Edison and John Marshall? How about —"

"I don't mean that kind. Look at Shelley or Dr. Johnson — or Maeterlinck," she added with a laugh. "Do you suppose they were regular? Bah! Don't be a dry-as-dust, Ben! Trollope was your perfect machine. What of him? However the world is amused by what he wrote, it knows exactly where to put him."

Benjamin, who did *not* know exactly where to put him, resigned literature to irregularity with a wave of the hand.

"I wasn't thinking of literary men — they may live as they please. I was thinking of great practical men, men of affairs. If I am to succeed in politics, let us say, I must have method; for who ever heard of a famous statesman who was not the soul of system?"

"Daniel Webster!" cried Rosalind triumphantly. "He never could get up until ten in the morning and then it was usually to drink whiskey. 'It is a small college, but there are those who love it,'" she quoted gaily. "Now what? Now where are you?"

Benjamin smiled with such infuriating indulgence that she suddenly wondered if he ever thought of her as "little woman," a term of endearment which she despised. His paternal condescension seemed sometimes to betray what might be a mental application of the term.

"Well, never mind; we won't argue about it until I can array more facts on my side. You women al-

ways have the faculty of dragging in exceptions or
long-haired literary men to win a victory.   By the
way, to-morrow afternoon Father is to show me
certain parts of the Longwood Hospital in great
detail on a legal question.   You have long wanted
the opportunity to see it all; won't you come?
Father would love to have you."

"I'm so sorry, Ben.   To-morrow is the Schumann-Heink concert and I've promised to go with
some one."

In past days the projected trip to the Longwood,
then newly completed, had been a source of mutual
anticipation; if the opportunity came, nothing could
deter them.   Yet now Benjamin found Rosalind
with a ready excuse.

"You couldn't give up the concert, I suppose?"
he asked rather stiffly.

"I'm afraid not, Ben.   It's a — well, I couldn't."

Being in no mood to introduce a troublesome
third party, Rosalind let slip a second opportunity to
speak of Eric Rolland.   To herself she declared
that things being as unhappy as they were, that
bridge she would not cross until she came to it.

"I'm — awfully sorry."

Benjamin rolled all his unhappiness into this little,
halting sentence.   Like all men new at love — or
old, for that matter — he intensified this minor refusal, probably perfectly reasonable, and suffered as
regards not the true object but its magnified image.
But almost immediately his manner changed; he became solicitous, appealing.

"Forgive me, Rose," he said with humble in-
genuousness, "I did not mean to speak like that:
it was not playing the game to you.   I forgot, for a
minute; you'll forgive me?"

It was hard to nod and say yes, when conscience mocked within. For what need she forgive him? For letting her see that there was a love in his heart which knew no master? For a rare, God-sent impulse proudly to array before the world his firstling thought untarnished by mortal reconsidering? She turned away, as if his love were a blank abyss before her feet.

"Do not think me brutal or unsympathetic —" Her hands flew forward to disclaim. "No, listen, Rose. I would not have you marry me without affection: that would be a sin. The world is too unhappy now that ever we forget our duty." He spoke with the ingrained rectitude of a Puritanic ancestry as fine as that of Rosalind herself, with that inflexible excellence of morals which bends backward in its walk through life. "I do not ask for such a pledge; you know that. I only pray that love come in your heart, that you try; and you do try, I know, because I understand your strength and beauty. It is I who forget."

Rosalind was not aware that he had quitted the room until she heard his firm step ring upon the flagstones in the hall. A conflict of impulse and emotion shook her body.

"Ben," she called; and in the same moment snapped close her lips, her hands pressed over them, her eyes wide. Had he heard? With her whole body she listened. . . . The footsteps still sounded, fainter and more faint. With a sudden, half-ashamed relief she crumpled back into her arm-chair. After all, there was nothing to tell him yet, she reassured herself; it was better that he go and she look into the fire and think on — Orpheus.

CHAPTER XII

THE concert was a great success. Half of the enjoyment derived from music lies in sharing it with a congenial mind. To the amateur sympathetic response is everything, and Rosalind, after a legion of youthful escorts who took music only on sufferance, found the keenest delight in a companion who understood and adored that which she found moving. Each song to Eric was definitive of some mood; and thanks to a long schooling in music, he could readily interpret and explain what Rosalind only felt. Between the songs the conversation turned on his celebrated father. To Eric he was a demigod. The memory of the tenor's early triumphs, when, a boy of ten, Eric had stood in the wings to hear whole theatres rise in tempestuous acclamation, lingered in his mind and threw about his father as if it were real the artificial glamour of the stage. As a father, he had never existed. A man singing now at the Covent Garden, now in Buenos Ayres, and the next month in Berlin is ever more of a luxury than a parent to his child. To the son's mind the father was always the resplendent Duke in " Rigoletto," glittering with jewels, or Rhadames on his triumphal car, a station in which even ugly tenors appeared to advantage and one in which his father had been strikingly handsome. Upon these stories of triumph Rosalind fed till her imagination could almost picture the La Scala in a delirium of excitement; she felt that at last she had met with some one to whom she might confide her appreciations and yearnings.

Woman cannot be understood; there are two parts to her which play hide-and-seek for domination. One part requires strength, muscles, physique, and worships a Hercules, though his head be filled with bran and his feet be clay; the other sets eyes upon the soul and stares till blindness comes, infatuated by some shred of genius discovered in an effeminate ass. If the woman marries the Colossus, she despises the sterility of his soul; if she marries the man who understands her heart, she despises the sterility of his body. Whatever happens, the part which has not conquered makes life miserable for the part which has, and at forty the giant's wife has an affair with a dream-eyed poet, whose own wife in turn is playing golf in the mountains with the champion of three states. Fine women do not go to these extremes. Rosalind had always found Benjamin insufficient, had known from the first that her heart required more love than was his to give. When his foot went to sleep during Melba's singing of Tosti's " Good-bye, Summer," she suddenly realised that at forty he would be unbearable. How different it was with Eric! She glanced at him, leaning forward with intense interest in the matchless voice, and smiled a contented smile. Comparisons are never odious to the one who makes them.

When the concert was over, they walked back in the soft light of late afternoon to 29 Commonwealth Avenue, where Mrs. Copley was sitting with Rosalind's young brother, Jack, just returned from St. Matthew's for the April holidays. He was one

of the familiar type which our best boarding-schools,
furnished with the right material, can and do turn
out in large quantities: attractive, clean, high-
tempered, and obstinately opposed to the cultiva-
tion of his mind.   For his scholastic deficiencies
Mrs. Copley blamed the school, Mr. Copley the
boy, and Jack himself the whole ridiculous educa-
tional system, which he chose to characterise as
" bughouse."

"How was Jack's report?" asked Rosalind, when
her young brother had disappeared.

Mrs. Copley made a grimace.

"Don't speak of reports, dear.   Your father's
been lecturing me all the afternoon about them —
me, mind you.   Now he's gone off to the Club
completely exhausted, leaving Jack not yet spoken
to.   The mind has study pains just as the body has
growing pains; the latter are painful to the son,
the former to the parents.   I'm glad you've come,
Mr. Rolland, for I need to be soothed.   You'll
play to me, won't you?   Rosalind has said so much
about you that ever since yesterday I have been on
the *qui vive.*"

Rosalind's face burned self-consciously as Eric
turned towards her: she felt it impossible to face
his gaze.

"She has been most kind to mention me.   I
hoped she would."

With a bright glance he followed Rosalind into
the music room.

"Will you stay with me?"

She smiled in reply, and sat where she might
stare at him unobserved, the momentary wave of
strange unrest ebbing from her.   He ran over a
few of Schumann-Heink's songs with a deft, sure

touch, then essayed something more pretentious. In the midst of a dashing French waltz voices from the drawing-room halted his fingers.

"Oh, don't stop!" cried out Mrs. Copley. "It's so improving for Ben and my husband! Please go on."

"You must meet my father. You haven't yet, have you?"

Rosalind saw an excellent opportunity to bring Benjamin and Eric Rolland together, and though she shrank from the meeting, realised its necessity. During the last two days her position had been too false and too perilous for maintenance. It was far better that she introduce Eric to Benjamin than malicious tongues perform that office.

In a moment the meeting was over. As Benjamin measured the stranger's slender figure and eager, mobile face, she could see that her choice of the concert instead of the visit to the Longwood Hospital rankled in his mind. It was plain that he was hurt and plain that he wished her to know. For a moment the situation was strained; then Mrs. Copley came to the rescue. Better than any woman in Boston she knew how to combat such a moment.

"I'm done with Russian literature, Jack," she said, picking up a book from the table beside her with a wry face. "If you want to please me, never give me a Russian novel again."

"Why, Mrs. Copley?" asked Eric with a quizzical look.

"Oh, they are so unpleasant!" Mrs. Copley shrugged her pretty shoulders. "My idea of Russian literature is a composite picture of any number of consumptive death-beds. And they always die under the most revolting circumstances. As for the characters, no one would ever want to know them; they are all unclean, unmoral, and unscrupulous."

"There are lots of people in the world like them."

"But why write about such people? What is the use? It's too depressing." Mrs. Copley shook her head till the lamplight danced in the pearls about her neck. "If they'd only wash up their heroes and let them die pleasantly! I'm sure it does nobody good to read such books."

"Hasn't it done you good already without your knowing it?"

"I can't see how." Mrs. Copley looked in a delightfully puzzled way at the young Frenchman.

"Why, it's made you angry against such conditions in books, and that's the next thing to being roused against such conditions in real life."

Mrs. Copley's eyebrows were still arched. A person who regards literature as confectionery to be sampled and consumed like candied comfits in leisure hours, readily fails to grasp any personal relation with a dirty peasant in a Russian novel.

"He's right, Mother. I'm sure that such books do a world of good. If our friends would only read them, perhaps Chambers Street wouldn't look as it does on a hot day in summer, crammed with dirty and pitiful babies. They're as thick as flies, aren't they, Ben?"

"Indeed, yes."

"And you know about them, Miss Copley?" Eric asked with surprised interest.

"Know about them?" broke in her father from over the *Transcript*. "Rosalind is one of our best little social reformers!"

"Jack, stop! You know you're prouder than any one of what she has done at Brimmer House."

"Don't you think I look interested in such things?" asked Rosalind.

"Perhaps you do." Eric looked boldly at her. "At first I didn't think you did; you are so —"

"Don't!" interrupted Rosalind gaily. "Don't throw my femininity in my face! I believe every man in this world thinks that a girl must have the appearance of a prize-fighter to delve into anything more than bonbons and styles. You one and all condemn us to be butterflies."

Is not woman perverse, uncertain, hard to please? When Benjamin cast blundering aspersions upon the feminine world, Rosalind thought it necessary to her honour to punish him; but the same condemnation from Eric's lips brought forth no more than a gay provocation to further condemning. Circumstances do indeed alter cases.

"I suppose it's because the average man prefers the eater of bonbons to the social worker," laughed Eric, "and hopes to find, almost without knowing it, the old Victorian type in every girl he meets. No one can see a butterfly without wanting to catch it — but it is not so pretty at home under glass. I'm glad you are interested in the poor."

"They all adore her, Mr. Rolland. I've even had some of her girls here to tea!"

Mrs. Copley smiled a benignant, disarming smile. Behold her concession to poverty; was she not abreast of the new movement?

"Her girls?"

"From Brimmer House, Mamma means. That's the charity at which I've helped for four years."

" I should like to see it.   Will you take me some time ? "

" With pleasure.   I'll even make you play for them.   I impress all my men friends into the service; Benjamin has been my trusty financial aide for months."

A sop for Cerberus.   But Cerberus was in no mood for such trifles and glowered at the words. Benjamin arose stiffly from his chair; Brimmer House had been one of the closest ties between himself and Rosalind, something peculiarly intimate; who was this stranger invading the hallowed ground of their friendship?   He went home, jealous, resentful, unhappy.   No matter how small the provocation, a man in love can find tears in the eyes of angels and spots as big as his head upon the sun. Everything to the lover is wrong until proved right; everything goes under penalty of suspicion until absolved by a kiss.

But with Rosalind how different!   As she sat down after dinner to write a long overdue letter to Camilla Cabot, the sole repository of her thoughts, she was resplendently joyous.   Enchanted by Eric, she was also happy that her cowardice was conquered, that she and Benjamin had come to an agreement by means of which, with a little skill on her part, a not too unpleasant adjustment of their relations might be effected.   Thanks to her high spirits, the letter was written in the most flippant and sprightly of tones.

Friday, April 12th.

Dearest Cammy:

I really don't deserve the bushel of ungenteel adjectives your last letter dumped on me.   Wait until you hear what has happened, my darling Cam, before you bite because I didn't write. Skipping lightly from poetry to the Bible, I have walked through the Valley of the Shadow — and even still my path is umbrageous. Which is all by way of saying that your old Samson has gone and done it!

It happened at Aiken, my lovely Cammy, when the sun was peeping through the singing pines. And it came that sudden: PLOSH! Just like that! A first class chance to be the Governor's wife! You said when you departed for Panama with my best Thomasine jabot — as I later discovered! — that Ben would some day be the First Gent. in Mass., you know. But I disregarded gubernatorial attraction, and can still sign " Ever thine " to thee.

Poor Ben has taken it terribly hard. (I know, but there's no one else to say it!) Our friendship is all gone packing, and the situation now is AWFUL! Cammy love, he won't take " no "! And I, being as you know a sweet, affectionate, loving creature, cannot be brutal with him. So we've set a Doomsday — June 1st. You must return, dear, and help dust up the room after the battle is over.

Life is not all thistles and cabbages, though. Loveliest Cam, *eine bluhende Rose ist in meinen Garten gekommen!* It's my perverse nature to write in German, for he's a French rose, come a-visiting Uncle Sing-Sing. Conceive me *abattue, aplatie, émue* — and everything like that — on entering the Square and finding an adorable young demi-god at the piano! At least he looked like that in the morning sunlight. He plays *comme un inspiré.* Look up hero in the dictionary. Tall, slender, graceful, dark, curly-haired, green-eyed — oh, so green, Cammy, dear! — well dressed — hold that pose, please! Doesn't that sound like a six-best-seller? I call him very handsome; his face is bizarre, I suppose, but so interesting and mobile. (Pit-pat! pit-pat! My heart beating, Cammy.)

Are you jealous? Ben is! But wait till *you* see him! No-o-o! You might turn abductress. At present we are artistically flighty; perhaps from the style of this epistle you will gather that I am a trifle aërial, but you have told me you liked it.

Anges en ciel
Mangent de miel.
Miel, ta louange;
Je suis ton ange!

Rose.

P.S.   His name is Eric Rolland; the son of the tenor, Lucien.   Glamour, you say?

P.P.S.   Cam!   They've got a new Club in town.   I'm going to-morrow.   They have a Bible talk in the morning from Dr. Snuffle; in the afternoon they play bridge.   That's preparedness against the Evil One, ain't it?

Lastly, lovely Cammy, he's an architect.   *Do* you suppose he designs love in a cottage?

CHAPTER XIII

WHAT PATRICIA THOUGHT

THE sprightly mood in which Rosalind had composed her letter to the admiring and excellent Camilla continued on the day following. She arose with a song in her heart and descended to breakfast with it on her lips, returning Jack's shyly affectionate embrace with a kiss of splendid dimensions. To fill her cup brimful, the family readily acceded to her postponement of the annual spring removal to the Sherborne farm, thus leaving her an additional week in town to spend in cultivating her newest and most alluring interest.

With far more gaiety than was her wont, she set off with her mother for the Bridge and Bible Club, which on this day met at the magnificent residence of Mrs. Preble. One could not call it a house. A house suggests home and the fireside, something to leave and return to, something to cherish almost as a friend; but this was nothing more nor less than a magnificent residence. Mrs. Preble accorded with the popular conception of a social leader. An imported product, she had gone in for everything which she felt sure might galvanise Boston: monkeys, suffrage, professional dancers, Arabian footmen — why not a Bridge and Bible Club? The idea had come to her from New York; they were doing it there. Before this dazzling novelty, even though the Biblical morning scarcely appealed to her, Mrs. Preble lost interest in her effort to provide the babies of the North End with pure milk. Here was a pursuit far worthier of her attention; and she gave it with the fatuous eagerness of all those ultra-fashionables who, lacking the brains to entertain themselves, must spend their time in entertaining others. Lo, the Bridge and Bible Club waxed as is the way of fat weeds! On this morning all the smart ladies of the town were assembled in Mrs. Preble's ballroom, gorgeously dressed and bearing a treasury of jewels. Rosalind swept her eyes over the " flock "— as Dr. Snuffle, from a coign of vantage under a Nattier depicting a bathing nymph, unctuously called them — and wondered with a smile why they had all come. Her mother, she knew, spoke of Mrs. Preble with a pretty shrug. Had they come, like herself, out of curiosity? Surprises in Boston society usually emanated from one source, Mrs. Preble; and the *beau monde*, though it often wondered if she were not going a little too far, invariably went with her.

Dr. Snuffle exuded a diluted account of Ruth and Boaz. It was a pretty subject, pretty in other days and pretty now by contrast; he told them so, but apart from that ventured nothing constructive, except a hope that each one would carry away the lesson of faith and love. When he had finished, Rosalind could see women right and left carrying away the lesson. Some of them carried it into the library for a smoke; others carried it to the butler and one of the Arabian footmen, who were serving cocktails in the music-room; but most of the women carried their faith and love into the dining-room and thus strengthened fell upon the luncheon.

Rosalind could plainly see that the talk had benefited them all.   They spoke in hushed voices of the
subject and the preacher.   One woman, though she
remembered having heard the story before, expressed over a plate of chicken salad her agreeable
willingness to hear it again just for the sake of the
moral; another found Boas cold; a third thought
Ruth forward; but all agreed that Dr. Snuffle had
told the story in a charming way — and wondered
how soon the bridge would begin after luncheon.
To Rosalind the whole affair was delightfully engrossing.   It was such a stupendous sham!   She was
sensible enough to realise the ludicrous side of the
gathering at the same time that she deprecated its
essential wrong.   To Mrs. Copley it was only another breach made by Mrs. Preble in convention;
her daughter saw also the breach in society's strength
before the world.   A Bridge and Bible Club, indeed!   Plague take the twentieth century for its
terrible gift to our poor mortal world, its naïve and
impudently ingenuous manner of doing wrong.

"Hello, Rosey!   Have a cocktail?"

Rosalind turned with a pleasant shake of her
head.   She had seen too much of the bitterer life
at Brimmer House to be shocked by such a jarring
note, and could be Roman enough in Rome, however she inwardly disapproved of that city's manners.

"Why, Patsy Canfield!   Wherever have you
come from?"

Patricia Canfield, whose hands Rosalind would
have seized, but that she bore a glass in each, was
a dark-eyed brunette, considered by most mothers
dangerously beautiful and by most sons beautifully
dangerous.   Though her family was as old as any

in Massachusetts, Patricia and her parents were not highly regarded in the community. Some said that the family was too old. Patricia's father had committed suicide; her mother's residence abroad was explained in polite conversation by that phrase of phrases, " for her health." For years Patricia and Rosalind had gone to school together, but, though they had seen much of each other all their lives, Rosalind had never fully made up her mind whether she liked her friend or not. Miss Canfield had the attractions common to youth and cleverness, being beautiful and, superficially at least, the last word in reckless modernity. Like the last word in anything, she engrossed the attention of friends and enemies alike. Cubism is to-day the thing in art; and you will find the most high-waisted devotee of pre-Raphaelitism that ever worshipped Burne-Jones lingering for hours in front of the " Nude Coming Down Stairs." The world is ever progressive. If it were not, people would take as little interest in the last word as they do in any fixed thing. It is because the last word of to-day is the revered idol of to-morrow that people regard it with a fearful interest, fascinated by its prophetic character. For Rosalind there was too much of Helen in Patricia to trust, and too much of Cassandra to understand.

" I've come from Paris within a week. Been over with Mat. There! " (as she drank one cocktail). " Religion makes me thirsty! Do I look dreadfully wicked, Rosey? "

" You haven't changed much anyway, Pat! "

" Change? Age cannot wither, nor custom stale my infinite — my infinite infinity! Sure you don't want this, dear? " She pointed to the second cock-

Patricia

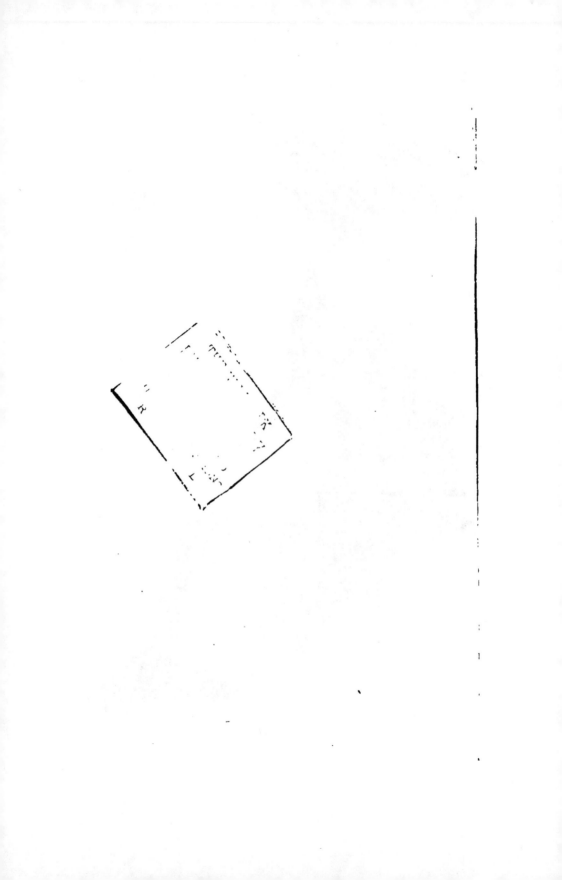

tail. " No, of course not!   What shall I do with
it?" she asked in a general way.

" Do with it, Patty?" called Mrs. Preble, as she
swept imperially by on a tour of inspection.   " Drink
it, child!"

Patricia Canfield smilingly complied.

" One can't be rude, Rosey!   To such a hostess,
too!" she whispered, catching Rosalind by the arm.
" Let's go in to lunch together, dear.   It's months
since I've seen you, and we must talk, talk, talk!
Ain't I wicked, Rosey?"

She let slip a provocative smile, such as she had
often employed in the past to reduce Harvard undergraduates who fancied themselves in love to a
state of utter imbecility.

" Patsy, who were you before you were Cleopatra?"

" Priscilla Alden mustn't flatter!   What luck!
Here's a table for two."

They sat down amidst the bustle and chattering of
the crowded room.

" Now, Pat, tell me all about it.   What have you
been up to?"

" First, Rosey, is the Ogress here?"

" You mean my Cammy, I suppose.   She'd give it
to you for the way you've behaved to-day, Pat!
But I'm too good-tempered.   No, the Ogress is off
doing Panama with her papa."

Patricia Canfield made up a face.

" With all respect for our angelic school friend,
I'm glad.   You'll never guess what I've been doing
this winter!   I've been keeping pigs in Pau!   Oh,
I'm the bucolic, I am!   Barbara Frietchie and Maud
Muller all in one.   How does it go —' Up from
the meadows fresh with corn '?   Mat and I had

the darlingest farm at Pau! Look at my figger,
Rosey: haying! My complexion: gardening! And
the pigs: my dear girl, I could bring up ten babies
now! They're nothing like a litter of piglets, I'll
warrant."

"I suppose you've thrown over a dozen dukes!"

"There's no telling, Rosey. How's your god-
pa?"

"He's the same. We went to Aiken again."

"So? And the Square is lively as ever, I suppose?"

"Lively, Patty! We've got a 'young Frencher'
there, as Alfie calls him."

"Not with Sing-Song?"

"Patty!" Rosalind shook her head in comic reproof. "Eric Rolland's his name. Did you ever
meet him — the tenor's son?"

"Eric! Not Eric?"

"You have met him, Pat?"

"Met him? I came over on the boat with him!
Met him? Oh, Rosey! One of those slow French
liners and a moon for nine nights."

Rosalind sat up very straight in her chair and
grew red. She was glad Patricia was looking out
of the window.

"Don't he play well, dear?" she went on reminis-
cently. "I tell you he gave me quite a flutter. You
must take me to see him. I'm a desperate case of
Eric or erotic or something."

Miss Canfield laughed and to Rosalind's relief
turned the subject of conversation, dashing off in
a brilliant extravagance upon a poor farmer's son
who had fallen in love with her in a hayfield at
Pau.

"The trouble was that a little village girl adored

him.   They were engaged or something, and I guess his parents regarded me as a second Carmen.   They even came one Sunday to plead with Mat.   Will you believe it, Rosey, they asked Mat to interfere for her poor dead husband's sake? *Imaginez!* Mat flew into such a passion that even I was alarmed at the size of her vocabulary and the quantity of her breath.   Andrea Sebastien was his name and he was handsome enough for the whole of it. There's a lot in a name, dear; you look rosy, you know, and every time I see Camilla I think of Fanny Burney and all those other stupids.   I do wish Mrs. Preble would hurry.   Apologies aside, Rosey, I'm dying for cards and cash.   I'm going to play against Mrs. Gloucester, and if I don't get some lingerie out of the old dear, why, I shall have to go without and add Lady Godiva to my other accomplishments!"

After the ladies had sat down to bridge and Rosalind had excused herself from what Mrs. Preble predicted would be the fun, she walked down the Avenue to her godfather's house, turning over in her mind what her old friend had said.   The matter of Patricia's having crossed on the same liner with Eric Rolland was an occurrence of concern to her.   While, as she told herself, she was no more than much interested in the young Frenchman, she knew Patricia well enough to regard their acquaintanceship as a troublesome element in certain little plans which she had been shaping.   To some ways of thinking nine days is a short space, scarcely more than a week; but in that time Patricia was capable of both subjugating and devastating a male heart. Rosalind herself had known Eric but for three days.

She earnestly wished that he had not met Patricia. Yet at the same time that she felt a little shocked, she could not but remember that Patricia was one of her own oldest friends. Whether she approved of her behaviour was apart from the question. She had successively adored, fought, and tolerated Patricia; why should not others? No, she certainly could not blame Eric in her mind for knowing her, even for liking her. Did he like her? Thanks to her absorption in this insoluble question she unobservantly walked directly into an oncoming perambulator, the propelling power of which was gazing across the road with unfeigned admiration at a friend in the police. Probably there had been on the French liner no other attractive people; probably Eric had played for Patricia often and she had heaped adulation on him; probably they had sat out on the top deck in the moonlight, discussing those unfathomable subjects which seem inseparably connected with sea voyages. If this were true — and it did not take long for Rosalind, building on Patricia's flighty remarks, to believe that it was — why then, the sooner she abandoned a course of intimacy with Eric for one of civility the better. But in matters of love decisions based on reason are soon broken. She entered 8 Louisburg Square to meet Eric, with his fine hand extended to take hers, saying, "I have been waiting for you; I thought you had forgotten."

Resolutionary firmness vanished; the thickest fog melts under the beneficent radiance of the sun.

"Not I. Even the Bridge and Bible Club couldn't efface that appointment. Where's Uncle Sing-Sing? I must tell him all about it."

Together they went up to the invalid's study,

where he lay on his ottoman, watching aërial fingers at work upon his beloved Square in the interests of a new and softer season. He turned his head to see them enter, and there was longing in his eyes. He cared, as we have seen, for almost no one. Indeed, one might have said that all the love the human heart is capable of yearned in his breast for these two fair young creatures, standing side by side in the premature gloom of his front room.

"Godfather," ventured Rosalind, after an account of the party from which Patricia was tactfully omitted, "we ought to launch Mr. Rolland —"

"Eric," interrupted Mr. Singleton Singleton slowly.

"What?"

"Eric," he repeated.

"Oh, please do, Miss Copley. Please call me —"

"Rosalind!" the invalid interrupted again.

It was Rosalind's turn to cry out this time. She and Eric looked at each other and burst out laughing.

"Listen, Uncle Sing-Sing! We must launch Eric in Boston society!"

"You speak of me as if I were a man-o'-war!"

"I'm sure you are much more interesting than one; see if Boston doesn't think so. Now, Uncle Sing-Sing, I should imagine a very little dinner in the Square would be the best thing."

"Must we?" Mr. Singleton Singleton appealed rather sadly to Rosalind. What was he thinking of behind those wan eyes? Society had taken young Rosalind from him on the eve of her début; perhaps he had hoped to keep this new source of joy all to himself.

" We mustn't be selfish, dear. I have thought of April the twentieth."

" So soon? "

" We mustn't lock poor Eric up as if he were a criminal or a monk. Of course, he wants to see and meet a few people; even you and I prove a bore after a while."

" Not at all. I —"

" April twentieth is fixed for your public appearance," she interrupted with a laugh. " You mustn't look a gift début in the mouth. You're agreeable, Uncle Sing-Sing? "

The invalid nodded.

" Who will be invited? " asked Eric, affecting great timidity. " May I know? "

" Leave the guests to me," replied Rosalind, " and I'll surprise you both."

The list had been in her mind all day. To write the invitations was a small matter — Benjamin and Dr. Cary, Mr. and Mrs. Veneerable, Mrs. Montgomery Longfellow, Justice Pauncher, Mr. Swelfront, the world-famous architect, for Eric's particular benefit, and several people to fill in. When the invitations were all written, Rosalind meditatively bit the end of the penholder. How about Patricia Canfield? She had deliberately passed over her name, but on consideration wondered if a greater wisdom did not lie in inviting her troublesome friend. The only way to ascertain the true relations of two people is to bring them together; here lay an excellent opportunity for observation. Valuing the sharpness of Patricia's tongue and knowing that her omission would inevitably lead to embarrassing inuendoes, she tore up the note to Pauline Peabody, and wrote as follows, suiting her style to Patricia's well known humour.

Dear Cleopatra:
  Dinner at the Square — April twentieth.   A foreign gentleman to be entertained; has no title, but good looks and genius.   Eight o'clock.
  Your Rose and Sing-Sing need you!
  P. S.   Pigs not allowed on the premises.— R.

The week which intervened before the dinner was a memorable one.   According to their original agreement Rosalind turned Baedeker for Eric's benefit, and found her personally conducted tours an infinite pleasure.   Together they journeyed everywhere, to every historic landmark, to every nook of interest or curiosity, and especially to any towns where Eric could observe examples of Colonial architecture.   Salem and Newburyport were ransacked until his notebooks were filled with rough sketches of relics of simpler days.   Americans no longer build homes; they build factories, sky-scrapers, houses, to be sure, but the art of building homes vanished with the art of living in them.

Particularly memorable was one glorious day spent in the country.   They had automobiled out to a famous mansion near Lancaster in the early morning, a fascinating old house, typical of the finest Colonial spirit.   Before it Eric soon fell a-sketching with eager zeal, while Rosalind, stretched at full length on the grass under the shade of her gay cretonne parasol, pretended an absorption in Verhaeren's poems.   The grass was soft and warm from the morning sun and as it stirred against her breast, she enjoyed a delicious sense of relaxation.   Above the house swept the graceful branches of elms, moving an intricate tracery of shadow as the breeze, which still bore in its dash a trace of the season gone before, gently moved them to and fro.   From the corner of her eye she caught a glimpse of Eric, so close that it was possible to touch him with the silver tip of her parasol.   The book dropped from her hands; in this radiance she smelt the kerosene of its nocturnal composition.   How little poetry has been written which can be read with respect and pleasure out of doors in April!   Rosalind turned lazily upon her side, lowering the parasol that the sun might fall upon her face.   There was a great stillness everywhere; the countryside slept like a child.   Far away a silent hill swelled in a brilliant outline against the sky.   It was as if the concentrated essence of the most inspired of seasons had been poured forth with a lavish hand, as if before its adolescent beauty nature and all things productive of sound were hushed in a perfect concord of silence.   Being one to whom out of doors is dear, Rosalind felt the inexpressible beauty of this morning rise resistless in her heart. She sat up and stretched her arms out in the streaming sunlight.

"Oh, Eric, I can't read this poetry!   It's all around me now so much fairer than mortal hands can write it.   Those old elms as they droop over the house are like tired guardians.   Don't you love them?   Just see the green of those meadows, the aquamarine of that little lake, and far off the deep blue of those hills!   Doesn't it make you want to sing?   I feel like crying out that this is the best and most beautiful world ever created!"

Eric looked up from his sketchbook.

"No, not cry out."   He cast his eyes reflectively

over the country side. " Rather fall on my knees
and thank God for it all! What might not a Corot
or a Constable feel now. And here I am paltering
away with these dry architect's sketches. Let's climb
the hill, Rose."

" Yes, yes! We can see even more from
there! "

Together they climbed the hill, struggling side
by side over fences and bending under hedges,
breathing fast in the eagerness of the ascent. At
length they stood upon the summit. The panorama
spread out at their feet in a wealth of dimpling
meadows and swelling hills made them exclaim in
unison.

" How grand it is! " Rosalind murmured.
" And yet," she continued after a pause, " it is
simple. Other hills are twenty times as magnificent
as these and other fields twenty times as rich. Yet
spring can make this seem unparalleled."

" America is so big! " said Eric. " Look how
it stretches away on all sides! In France the horizon seems the end of the world; here the horizon
promises only more grandeur. Sometimes America
is ragged and ugly, but it is always great."

" This is the America we love. I wish it could
all be spread out over the vile city! "

" That would only cover up its wickedness."

" In time the roots would grow downward. Oh,
Eric, I adore this. I should have been born a milk-
maid. I am at home with nature as you are; I feel
it is a neighbour, a friend."

" ' *Les ombres, les eaux, et l'art champêtre avaient
composé une harmonie si simple qu'elle paraissait
conduite selon le rythme de la flûte à trois notes,
taillée dans le roseau palustre,*' " Eric quoted.

" What is that ? "

" D'Annunzio, I think.   It has always stayed in my memory."

" How quiet it is!   We might be in Mars or Venus and be no more alone.   There is no one to hear us, no one to care."

A pause fell between them; words were empty, as is the wind in a blue sky.   For the first time in her life Rosalind felt that deep communion of spirit which is so rare in mortal worlds.   They stood for a while in the clear morning with heads high, silent and thoughtful, made akin by the subtleties of like and dislike; then turned and slowly moved down the slope, still silent.   They were almost afraid to speak.   There had been more than a vision of nature in the panorama on which they turned their backs, and they could find no words to express that which at first mortality can never understand.

The day of the dinner arrived.   After a week in which she had been thrown continually with Eric to the exclusion of every one else, Rosalind could not regard the event without concern.   It was worse than casting a pearl before swine; it was casting a pearl before a connoisseur in jewellery, an action naturally repellent to any woman in her senses.   All women are protectionist at heart; there is not a one of them who in the matter of the opposite sex believes in the open-door policy.   Rosalind began to wish that she had not been so rash in her launching of Eric on the social sea.   Never a week in her life had passed more happily than the one just finished.   Nothing had been amiss; she had found Eric as lovable as he was handsome and as interesting as he was gifted.   Attracted to him primarily by

his great personal charm and beauty, she later found
in his naïveté, in his warmth of heart, and in his
kindred interests and ambitions the causes for much
more than mere attraction.   Love had come to her
quickly, with the superb suddenness of the first note
in a symphony.   When it had once begun to vibrate,
that note swelled into a diapason that flooded her
whole life with music.

There were two things to trouble her.   Having
assured Benjamin that she could never love any one
greatly, she now found her life impregnated with a
mighty adoration.   Far from being concerned over
this contradiction, she found it rather delightful than
otherwise; but Benjamin's unhappiness did hurt.
Her regard for Eric soon made itself apparent to
his ready watchfulness.   One does not need to explain such things to a man who loves; there are a
thousand thousand unconscious mannerisms, affecta-
tions, glances, words, expressions, all of which betray what is supposedly concealed.   Explanation
surely boggles such a business; tacit revelation is the
more sure — and the more painful.   In the midst of
her happiness Rosalind felt Benjamin's grief as one
is aware of the prick of a thorn hidden under a profusion of roses.   A second thorn was Patricia Canfield.   Rosalind had not told Eric of their meeting;
she had pushed her old friend as far out of her mind
as possible.   But it was of no use to submerge
Patricia in her thoughts; as if made of cork, she
bobbed to the surface, a perpetual bogey.   Having
consistently recoiled from probing the matter in her
heart, Rosalind felt, as she sat waiting for the guests
to arrive that Friday evening, that she would have
been far better off to have made up her mind to the
matter long ago and introduced Eric and Patricia be-

fore things had gone so far with herself. But what was done, was done; and her business this night was to use a very bright pair of eyes and a very sharp pair of ears to the best advantage.

The guests were politely late, except Dr. Cary and Patricia. By reason of living life on a schedule the great surgeon was never late on any occasion, and arrived at eight precise. But Patricia, who in her whole life had never been on time for anything, was the last to arrive. As she moved across the room to speak to Mr. Singleton Singleton, she was the observed of all observers. She always was the last arrival at a dinner party, and, since truisms are never spiteful on pretty lips, her friends agreed that she staged her entrances well. Even Rosalind could not fail to admire her dark beauty; it was as irresistible as her dress, the latest importation from Paris, which must have given even to that city a fillip of excitement. If Patricia was generous in displaying her neck and shoulders, however, she felt assured that the most exacting judge who ever sat in judgment had no license to cavil. If men craned their necks, it was a success; if ladies gasped, it was a triumph. As she swept across the room with graceful and sinuous assurance, she courted ogling from one sex and indignation from the other — and, since she aroused both, was pleased beyond words.

Fixing her eyes on Eric, Rosalind noted the surprise on his face at Patricia's entrance immediately transformed into the most winning smile imaginable. As she saw them shaking hands and observed Patricia behaving in a way calculated to reduce the most catholic-minded man in the world to an idolatrous state, she doubly doubted the wisdom of her invitation.   Her glance followed them to a corner, where they fell into a most earnest talk.   From the fatuous smile on Eric's face, it was apparent that Patricia, past mistress in the manipulation of that most deadly instrument, the trowel, was engaged in laying it on very thick.   Tactically Rosalind had made a mistake.   So be it!   It was her fault, and no regret, however heartfelt, could put spilt milk back in the pitcher.   With this sound conclusion, she took Mr. Swelfront's arm and went in to dinner.   Eric and Patricia she had seated opposite; Benjamin was two places off; she herself sat between Dr. Cary and Mr. Swelfront, whose large head bore on it fewer hairs than might be counted on the fingers of both hands. Its sheen in the candle-light fascinated Rosalind; she felt sure that it would have made an excellent material on which to design architectural masterpieces. But while she imaginatively traced cupolas and palaces and town houses on her famous guest's head, she was busied ocularly in watching Eric and Patricia and verbally in praising the architectural capacities of him she watched.   Even in the midst of his struggle with the asparagus, Mr. Swelfront was politely interested and promised to give Eric what poor information and introduction lay within his power; at which Rosalind felt well pleased with herself, for a word from Mr. Swelfront was sufficient to make sealed doors fly wide.   His name was the Open Sesame of American architecture.

Yet she was far from easy in her mind.   It was bad enough to have Benjamin two seats away with his reproving eyes continually upon her without the added torture of Eric and Patricia speaking French in an undertone across the table.   What were they saying? Patricia was animated, eager, impulsive as ever, filled with the reckless unconcern of to-day. These might be commonplaces which she murmured to Eric, leaning close to him, warm and beautiful. If they were, why need Eric dart so smiling a glance at his companion? Why need he seem so tender in his demeanour; why dilate upon Patricia, seemingly regardless of the lady on his right? And even commonplaces, spoken in French, seem much more deep and wicked!

For a moment Eric's eyes turned upon herself. She had sought to attract his attention, but now averted her gaze, losing completely a valuable dictum of Mr. Swelfront regarding the architecture of ancient Smyrna. Why had she looked away? To rectify a conscious mistake, she glanced boldly across the table, but Eric was again talking animatedly to his companion. Patricia never turned her eyes away; if one gazed at her, she returned the look with rich interest.

In this fashion Rosalind sat through the entire dinner, observing every move of Eric and Patricia to the tune of Mr. Swelfront's drone, an occupation far more trying than diverting. When the ladies had left the gentlemen and retired to the drawing-room, Patricia flew to her side.

"Rosey, you're a dear to put me next to Eric. I had a perfect time."

"You seemed to, Pat," Rosalind assented a bit coldly. She did not wish to discuss Eric with Patricia; any association of the two was distasteful to her. But curiosity got the better of her proud reserve. "You and he seem to have become well enough acquainted on the boat."

"Acquainted, Rosey! Do you know what I think?"

"No one does, Pat."

"I think that if I gave that young man half a chance, he'd propose to me. I do, indeed!"

CHAPTER XIV

A CONVERSATION IN THE SQUARE

THE remark of Patricia's with which the last chapter closed caused Rosalind much unhappiness. Though it acted as a confirmation of her fears in its seeming assurance that her love was hopeless, it did not in the least alleviate the pangs of that feeling. Some time before the dinner she had found herself deeply in love with Eric. Together they had spent a week of quiet beauty with no one to interfere in their friendship, and Rosalind had dimly hoped that thus alone, the world forgetting, they might struggle side by side up sunlit hills or investigate sequestered crannies of life in an unending succession of blissful days. She had come to regard Eric, if not as her own property, still as a being peculiarly allied by circumstance to her and to her alone. In a single evening this was changed; in a single evening Virginie found that there were other maidens upon their exotic island against whose blandishing eyes Paul was not proof. When the dinner had broken up and Rosalind was being whirled home in her automobile, she dramatically assured herself that never again could her relations with Eric — or with any other man — be what they had been. She had learned her lesson, and it had changed her mightily. In her sorrow, half petulant, half sincere, she renounced men. Yet in the very moment of her renunciation, her heart echoed the

falseness of this abandonment by an insistent recapit-
ulation of her happiness and its downfall. She
knew not what to think. Those that become the
plaything of jealousy seldom recognise their peril in
its incipient state.

As she lay in her bed unable to sleep, Patricia
haunted her thoughts. Once again her old friend,
the source of many girlish tears in her school days,
was at the bottom of her unhappiness. Yet she
could blame no one. Patricia was her friend; she
herself had invited her; on her own volition she had
risked incurring this unhappiness. Yes, and she was
glad that she had done so, she protested to herself,
very glad! It was better to know Eric's state of
mind than to become involved in a hopeless love.
But was it better? Should she not have been happy,
if Patricia had never come between them? She
might never have known; she and Eric might have
become happily engaged and married. Yet there
are post-marital infelicities more bitter still than
lovers' quarrels. What if Patricia might have had
some power to fascinate Eric after their marriage?
There would have lain the cruelest gall. Shatter the
heart and age may mend its fracture; but shatter
the hearth and no agency, divine or mortal, can
rekindle the fire which has once gone out. Eric's
behaviour, if nothing else, justified Patricia's invitation. "What a piece of work is a man! How
noble in reason! How infinite in faculty"— and
how prodigal in love! For a pretty smile and a
pretty amenity he will think himself rich as any ma-
harajah of Orient empire. The meanest man in
love is a poet, with knowledge to profess and understand the harmony of spheres — and only too ready
on the slightest provocation to fancy that he hears

that silver-sounding music in the voice of every
woman who flatters him with her favour.   Because
man is an egotist, woman leads him by the nose; because he is fatuous, he thinks it is his nose which is
leading woman.   Alas for Eric!   Rosalind had
thought him made of some finer stuff, " in action like
an angel, in apprehension like a god "; she found him
after all a mortal, and like so many others of his
kind, a victim to Patricia's wiles.   She had seen
other young men taken captive in like manner with
considerable amusement, but the substitution of the
individual case for the general was far from diverting.

In a moment of pique she had given Benjamin
a promise to play golf on the next afternoon, half in
anger with Eric, half in a reproof quite unintelligible
to him.   For the moment the promise had raised her
pride and she held her head high in queenly dis-
regard of what another might do.

To Benjamin her promise was like manna.   His
mind was not the complex organ of a woman in love,
nor could it understand the mutations of her heart.
Dark things to him were black; light things trooped
in the category of white.   The multifarious inter-
mediate shades which lend colour and fineness to
exquisite temperaments were entirely lost to his mat-
ter-of-fact comprehension.   To a man who knows
but the sun, the world by night is a dark place indeed.
Only the finer eyes may see the stars.

Making resolutions when one is in love is like
throwing into the air directly above one's head a
large stone and waiting for it to descend.   For a
time the thrower is disembarrassed of his weight,
but the longer he stands where he is the more rapidly

increases the unpleasant imminence of the rock's return; for a moment the lover's resolution clears the mind and makes valiant the will, but the longer he who makes it remains in love the weaker becomes the resolve. The same divine gravity which governs the rock governs the lover's resolution; in either case the dependency upon human volition is nil. What lover but resolves a dozen excellences in the sobriety of morning only to forget them in the madness of eve? Who has not put in his bedside prayers renunciations of some fickle heart and waked in the full sunlight of morning to find courage sufficient for still another day's devotion? A lover's pledge shall survive the promised end, but a lover's resolution is too gossamer in web to hold a gnat to duty. Thus with Rosalind. Having resolved to hold aloof from Eric, having fallen to sleep in a drowsy declaration to herself that he must come to her if they were ever to meet again, she found in the morning wiser counsel. *Perhaps* he would not understand; *perhaps* he might never come. The Jeanne d'Arc which is in all women rose within her. It mattered not that she bitterly doubted to herself the possibility of meeting him again as if nothing had occurred: the battle is to the adventurous. She put on her hat, and excitedly sallied forth into the sunshine.

Mr. Rolland, so Edouard informed her, was out walking, but would soon return. Though she had regarded meeting him with a nervous hesitation, she went up to her godfather, disappointed and cast down that Eric was not in the house.

" Uncle Sing-Sing," she asked, after an affectionate kiss, " did the party tire you too much? "

" No, dear. No. Am I pale? "

Despite a certain novel brilliancy of eye and what

seemed to be a real desire to speak, she thought the
invalid more pallid and wasted than ever, the lack
of colour made all the more evident by the lustre in
those eyes that for so long a time had been dull.

"Only tired, dear heart," Rosalind lied glibly.
"Was it cruel in me?   There was Eric, you know;
he was having, I suppose, rather a stuffy time with
no one but me of his own age to see and talk to."

"I don't believe it."   Her godfather smiled tenderly.

"It was natural that he should want to meet people.   I dragged a promise from Mr. Swelfront to
take him under his wing.   You should have heard
me advertise him during dinner; he'll never have a
better press-agent."

"I hope not."

"Thanks, dear.   Why are great men bores?
Mr. Swelfront's bonmots dated back to the Mycen-
æan Age!   I was dying to recommend him my hair
tonic — it worked miracles with Papa.   We passed
the time of day discussing Greek temples.   I followed him closely through the Acropolis, but when
we forded the Hellespont and moved towards Baby-
lon the conversation turned into a monologue punc-
tured by asparagus.   His appetite saved me from
an untimely end."

"Why Patricia?" asked the invalid irrelevantly.

"Patricia?"   Rosalind repeated vaguely with a
little flush in each cheek.   "Oh, I — I thought she
— she might amuse Eric.   He met her on the boat,
you know."

"She did."

"Did amuse him?"   Rosalind looked away.
"Yes, she has a way with men.   Eric — Eric —"

"Do you like him?"

They had not discussed the visitor in many words before.   For once in her life Rosalind found it strange and hard to answer her godfather, found actual embarrassment in the question of her habitual confidant.

"I never loved Ben, godfather.   You know that. But with Eric — well, it's nothing like Ben.   Eric is —"

She broke off.   A black cat prowled about the grass-plot in the Square on the watch for birds. With her hand clasped tight in her godfather's, Rosalind stared at the marauder.

"I am glad, Rose."

"I thought you would be, dear, when I saw how fond you were of him.   I might well be the jealous one this time!"

There was a pause between them.   The cat had ambushed itself behind the little statue of Columbus with malicious intentions on a fat robin, greedily eyeing the turf.

"Eric is so like his mother."

"Yes.   He makes one think of her miniature."

"And it is her voice, too."

"Who would not love him?"   Her enthusiasm bubbled over restraint.   "Surely he is handsome and talented and sympathetic; and more, too, I know. And he has a poise to his head that American men lack.   Do you know what I mean?   A woman always looks to see how a man carries himself."

In a sortie the cat failed to capture its prey, which flew to the wrought iron fence with indignant chattering.

"Is he happy here?"

"I — I think so, Uncle Sing-Sing.   Of course. Why not?"   As she turned her eyes to her godfather's face, she wondered if Eric had found her companionship dull. "Has he said anything?"

"No. Must be stupid with me."

"He does not need many people to make him happy. With his books and music he is content. How beautifully he plays! I suppose he inherits his talent from his father."

"I think not," the invalid returned in a low voice.

"Why, his father —"

"Let's not talk of his father."

The sharp note in the dull voice surprised Rosalind into silence. What was hidden in this lavender romance to bring so marked a change in her godfather's manner? Without glancing at him she fell into a reverie. Outside a lumbering spaniel had driven the black cat into one of the ragged old elms, at the foot of which he was yelping himself inside out. From its refuge the cat regarded her tormentor with delicious unconcern.

The arrival of Edouard cut short both Rosalind's reconstruction of a romantic past for her godfather and her observation of further developments in the warfare on the green. With the assistance of a footman, Edouard towed the invalid to his bedroom for a rest, leaving Rosalind to walk down stairs, undetermined what to do. Though eager to see Eric, she felt so aggrieved by his absence that she determined to leave without meeting him. Pride reasserted itself. She walked slowly to the door; then, a wave of resentment sweeping over her, suddenly ran down the steps. Ten paces off Eric came striding towards her.

"Not going?" he cried out.

Rosalind bit her lip.

"I was," she replied doubtfully.

"But you're not now? Oh, please don't go away!" he appealed.   To Rosalind he looked radiant and beautiful in the soft sunshine of the Square, like some exotic plant in an old manor garden.   She smiled.   "That's better.   I hoped I'd find you here. Let's get over the fence; it's too beautiful to go indoors.   We can sit down on the grass and talk."

In a moment she found herself being helped over the old iron fence, a suspicion of white petticoat and pretty ankle fluttering for a moment in the face of the staid old Square.   Discouraged by the eminence of the cat's vantage, the noisy spaniel had trotted off in search of more accessible worlds to conquer, leaving the green in peaceful quiet.   Rosalind seated herself with her back against one of the elms.

"I have been down by the river, reading," Eric explained, stretching himself full length on the warm grass beside her, his face raised on his palms. When Rosalind looked down, she found his brow wrinkled and his green eyes upturned.

"What?" she asked, catching up the book. "Oscar Wilde!"

"Yes: 'Lady Windermere's Fan.'   It is a most entertaining thing.   I could not lay it down till I had finished it, and so almost missed you."

"There is one magnificent line in it.   How does it go?   'All of us —'"

"It is the very one that struck me!   I turned the page.   'We are all in the gutter, but some of us are looking at the stars!'"

"It makes him worth while — just that one line. You will be interested, Eric: my Chief at Brimmer House used to quote it inverted."

"Inverted?"

"Yes.   She said it gave the idea of charity.

' We are all in the stars, but some of us are looking at the gutter.' "

" But we aren't ! "

" Oh, yes, Eric. She meant we all have our ideals and aspirations, no matter how poor or miserable, but some of us, though we do live in our stars, look down at those really suffering in the gutter."

" I see . . . Rose, do you often think about such things ? "

" Often? No, not often, but sometimes I do. Why ? "

" I don't know. So few girls do now — and men, too, for that matter."

" I don't believe girls in other times thought of them any more, Eric."

" Perhaps. Still I sometimes think it would be a good thing if a great flood or a plague or a war were to devastate this world. Then more people would look in the gutter. If this world were wracked with suffering, people wouldn't seek Jesus Christ so much for their own sakes; they would seek Him for others."

" Of course we're unchristian now; religion is no longer the mode. But surely you're not going to advocate a war! What can be more unchristian? Two wrongs, you know —"

" What can be more unchristian? Why, the way most of us live to-day! That thing at Mrs. Preble's is a trifle, a small instance of what I mean. To be slain in an honourable cause is far more Christian than to attend that mockery! "

" I went, Eric. Am I unchristian? "

" I wish you had not gone. Why did you go? "

Rosalind paused before replying, literally astounded. To see Eric ride the high moral horse, to have his serious reproofs for her sins come flooding in her brain, there to mix with the torrent of reproach she felt towards him on account of Patricia, left her helpless. Could he know Patricia's ways and yet reproach herself? Surely his conversation with her friend the night before had borne no outward semblance of reproof. Did he tolerate Patricia's sins with a smile to find hers reprehensible with a serious mien? She flushed. Surely he was not making sport of her? No, these were earnest eyes, so earnest that she found them embarrassing, and forgot her anger in an attempt to justify herself before them.

"I — I went because I was curious. You do not think the less of me? You did not think I went because I approved of such a thing?"

"I was sure you did not, but then — who can be sure of anything? I am not sure of myself!"

"Why, Eric, I did not know you were so puritanical! You surely do not appear so."

"Who isn't puritanical in theory?"

"No one except the devil!"

"And you never thought me him? Why, I am infinitely puritanical. As much as you are, Rose. I was quite noted for my views in Cheltenham."

"Really? Your views?"

"Just so. That's the trouble, though. I have the best intentions in the world. I am most charitable; it puts me in tears to see little children suffer, to hear the cries of poverty and want. If you were to tell me that by giving the money for a new suit of clothes I could save a baby's life, and were to name to me the baby, I would go without the suit gladly. But I don't go without the suit; I am always well-dressed. Nobody names the baby; so I go on buying new suits in spite of a vague knowledge of the power of the money which I spend for them. My intentions are good, and I have a kind heart. I am religious; I am charitable; I am willing to serve."

" Then what troubles you, Eric? "

" I hardly know. I suppose it's that a good deal of all this is in my head and not actuality. These are my ' views.' Then,. of course, I'm poor. My father is recklessly extravagant. If he earns a fortune, he spends it all. Why shouldn't he? It's his. My dear mother left only a little. But for your godfather's kindness this visit would have been impossible."

" I had not known."

" *Maman* told me to come: so I came."

" I am glad you did, Eric."

" Are you? So am I, *tout à fait bien aise.*"

" Except when you worry over your intentions? " Rosalind asked with the shadow of a smile. She scarcely knew what prompted her to make so pointless a remark. Eric had fathomed her eyes as he asked the question, and had raised himself till his face was yet closer to hers.

" Ah, my intentions, my poor, abused intentions! " He let himself sprawl back with unconscious grace upon the grass. " They have no more spine than myself now; or shall we call it dormant spine? " He laughed, enchantingly Rosalind thought, and the sun was bright on his teeth. He might have been a latter-day Cephalus resting from the chase, garbed in the uncouth habiliments of a century which destroys all beauty save that which it chooses to petrify in museums. " I feel those intentions, Rose. When I walk through a miserable, ugly district like your West End, I feel that it is I who am the blot on the landscape, however poor it may be. What right have I to walk in my smart clothes before these over-crowded, wretched homes? I do it at times to prove that I am not a coward, but truly I feel like running away."

" I doubt if the poor notice you."

" That makes it worse; the struggle then is all with myself. I tell you, Rose, some day I shall throw a paving stone at some of these smug, self-satisfied, well-fed men and women who motor complacently through the sad streets of big cities. *Canaille* they call the poor, too! I'd like to *canaille* them! A paving stone in their stodgy faces would be more benefit than a dozen beauty parlours."

" Why, what an excitable person you are! You never have told me, Eric, of your interest in socialism."

" It is the interest of any man who thinks he is put in the world for more than eating and sleeping. If I do not talk about my intentions, none the less I have them."

" I believe you, Eric."

" I knew you would. We understand each other. If we aren't better than other people, we at least realise that we should try to be; we realise that we should put into life the very best, if we are to take out the very best. Life should be lived at concert pitch. I should like to live mine so."

" Mr. Eric! " It was Edouard who spoke. He stood, politely deprecatory, on the other side of the fence. " I beg pardon, Miss Rosalind. It's Miss Canfield on the telephone, sir." (A sudden stiffness laid hold upon Rosalind at the name.) " She says she has the two seats in the front row, and wants you to call for her at Mrs. Preble's house, sir."

"Please thank her, and tell her that I shall be there at one o'clock. Thank you, Edouard. Now I say that's awfully kind of her," he went on, turning to Rosalind. "Put herself to no end of trouble to get seats to this play. She's a most vivacious, attractive girl."

With such terrible suddenness was the subject changed. O, heavy declension! Here was Zeus become a bull, a prince become a prentice, a discourser upon the moral profundities of socialism and temperament become the admirer of a pretty face and a flippant tongue. To man the contiguity of Christian morality and a Patricia represents nothing shocking; but to woman, in whom high exaltations dominate both during and after the period of stress, a lofty subject unless loftily completed is poppycock. Rosalind found the change in theme unbearable. As much as she disliked Patricia, she disliked Eric's precedent moralising more. She longed to ask him whether he thought Patricia unchristian. Bah! His "concert pitch" was sham! At the moment he spoke the phrase, no doubt his mind was contemplating the afternoon at the theatre with Patricia. Rosalind bit her lip and arose; *she* should not detain him.

"You have known her before, Rose?"

"I went to school with her."

"You were lucky then." Rosalind felt her cheeks burn. "We came over on the same boat, and I have never been so entertained. She seems characteristically French."

"Her mother lives in France for her health." In an attempt to read a vicious meaning into the last three words Rosalind's sweet voice failed signally. "She was born and bred in Boston."

"But she is certainly different from Boston girls," laughed the unconscious Eric, as he helped Rosalind over the fence. "Must you go back now?"

"Yes." She spoke jerkily. She felt an emotion which, if her intuition taught her to diagnose, it did not teach her also to combat. "I hope — you enjoy — the play. Good-bye."

She turned and almost ran out of the Square with Eric's last words afire in her ears: "she is certainly different from Boston girls." Yes, thank God, Rosalind cried passionately to herself, Patricia certainly was different. With what a smile he had said it, with what a meaning! Yet the moment before he had been gazing in her face with such intensity that his life might have hung upon her lips. This was her paragon of virtues and excellence! This was the prodigy trumpeted forth to Mr. Swelfront! This was her fond-imagined tutelary genius! An automobile flashed by in misty outlines; the bricks at her feet were confused and blinding; and in her eyes unbidden tears screwed themselves over her eyelids and glistened on her lashes. Petty incidents often reveal great truths. This little conversation in the Square told Rosalind of the immensity of her love. If a stream of water is dashed suddenly into a vase which can well accommodate its volume, the violence of its entrance may often shatter the vessel. As she panted home, Rosalind felt the agony of misprized love breaking her heart.

Going to her room, she sat down moodily at the desk. Her excitability had worn off; now was left the gloom of consideration.

"Rose!" Jack's voice called outside her door.

"Ben Cary's come in his car about some golf with you. What shall I say?"

Golf? With Benjamin? In this state of mind? A shadowy smile at the absurdity of the suggestion curled her lips. If there was one thing in the world she could not do, would not do, had not the heart to attempt doing, it was to see Benjamin in her present desolate condition. Yet even as her lips formed the refusal of the invitation, her demeanour changed. A fire came in her eye; a firmness sat upon her lip. Defiant and scornful of her wound and of the person who had inflicted it, she arose.

"Tell Ben that I'm coming right down. I'll play golf with him — certainly!"

CHAPTER XV

A RUMOUR

THE weather, that divine panacea free and common to us all, cannot be denied its power. There is no man so wearisomely tugged with fortune but the sunshine of April cannot thrill him to the midriff. And thank God for it! Thank God that what is forever in our sight, the opening eyelids of morning, the arboreal verdure, the starclustered firmament, the unmeasured dance of waves, thank God that all of these rain influence while the great Potter turns his wheel above our mortal clay. It makes us feel the nearness and omnipresence of God.

Thus it was with Rosalind, her heart strings snarled into a very knot of Gordius, when out flamed the vernal sun, a divine Alexander, with one sharp-edged ray to split and solve all difference. As we have seen, her decision to accompany Benjamin had been made in the heroic strain. A violent grief must be combated by a violent cure — a doctrine akin to that mediæval homeopathy which prescribed to the chronic neurasthenic physic of a sour and melancholy hue. Yet while it was almost pain to face Benjamin at first, once the inertia of repugnance overcome, things went better than Rosalind had looked for. One cannot for long be dramatic unless one is to the manner born. Having entered Benjamin's automobile whispering to herself that she would be

brave, that no one should know how sad she felt,
that if Eric could be heartless to her, she could be
heartless to him, Rosalind found herself drifting in
the grateful sunshine from an heroic to a tender
mood.

As for Benjamin, his joy was childlike and unforgettable. His long sojourn under swarthy Sirius
was ended; even the great sun himself now seemed a
beneficent planet. The purest, greatest joys are all
unreasoned: to weigh and measure happiness is to
destroy its bloom. Benjamin had no idea of the
why of Rosalind's acceptance of his invitation. A
murrain on whys! Was she not side by his side,
hand by his hand? Reasons and past unhappiness
were lost in the train of the pleasurable moments
which were passing. If he had been jealous of Eric
in his unyielding, overpowering fashion, in the present moment of opportunity and felicity his jealousy
was forgotten in the song of his heart.

Oftener than not we dislike or feel constraint for
those that love us more than we do them. Unless
love is at an equilibrium, the balances perforce must
hang askew. Yet there are moments when we melt
to those importunate friends, moments when we are
generous, not for love, but merely for the sake of being generous. Such a moment is frequently one in
which we endure sorrow in ourselves and are thus
purged to a gentle kindness towards others. Rosalind wanted to stretch out her hand, touch Benjamin,
and whisper a word of sympathy; but the mortal
wall of reserve belied her sensibility, and she kept
silent. To find a friend's happiness sadly pleasant is
one thing; to phrase it another.

There were few people on the links; the green was
practically free for their speed or leisure. Though

Rosalind could not swing into the game, her partner was in such fettle that even the lackadaisical eyes of the caddies shone with benignancy. It was a delight to watch the joy and skill of his swing, and Rosalind with her healthy love of out-of-doors found that the time passed far faster than an hour earlier she would have deemed possible. Through the match Benjamin was the soul of patient, kind devotion, hovering like a giant guardian by her side, and she found his attention restful and healing.

The stroke of the day was his drive on the seventeenth hole. The ball seemed to soar interminably into the sunlight, a white sparkle above the distant green, beyond which it fell among thorns and long grass. In an attempt to make a shot comparatively respectable in length, Rosalind pulled her ball into a thick-clustered clump of diminutive oaks on the left. Sending the caddies ahead to find Cary's ball, she and Benjamin disappeared among the trees in search of hers. There was a hot beauty about the place. The dead brown leaves of the oaks, through which the sunlight fell in great splashes, seemed to radiate heat into the dry, almost dusty, air. High above them the derisive caw of a hoarse-throated crow floated down through fathoms of space. They stirred among the underbrush, now side by side, now separated by trees, now bending beneath low-sweeping branches. Rosalind raised her hand to her head: it was unbearably close. In the same moment strong arms went round her from behind and she heard Benjamin's voice huskily murmuring in her ear.

"Rose, let's not wait! Why not now? Let's not wait till June."

She had never been so touched before, and the

first, fierce contact with the brute earth which occasionally upheaves itself in the best of men momentarily stunned her. Then struggling greatly with her small strength, she sought release.

"Ben!" she demanded breathlessly. "What are you doing?"

"Doing?" he hurried on, bending his head close to her tossing hair. "I'm being happy, Rose. I'm a man, and I've suffered terribly. I'm doing the necessary, the natural thing." His voice was big in her ear. "I'm asking you to marry me now, not to wait till June to decide."

Still Rosalind struggled, though she could scarcely move. The blood rushed through her heart till the beats seemed to trip one over the other; her brain was filled with the ungovernable desire for freedom. This embrace, unwished and unreceived, created in her only a feeling of repellence.

"Don't struggle, Rose. I can hold you safe. You are safer with me than with any one else."

She was quiet at last; she fluttered no more against her imprisonment.

"I had thought so, Benjamin. Are you mad?"

Of a sudden she was free, uncertain of her footing after such impetuous support. She shivered slightly. Still close by her, Benjamin was leaning against a tree, one hand covering his face, the other clenched by his side. A great wave of pity came over her. Indignant as she was, she now felt no repugnance nor any desire to punish the man who had offended. Had this happened before the sense of her own desolation had possessed her, she would have quitted him in just anger without a word; but now she saw in the plucking of his hand at his shirt the nervous pain of a sorrow kin to hers. A scale

had fallen from her eyes. The anger and sympathy
of the happy are too often mere phylacteries, mere
emblems and forms. They matter not! Only
those who have also suffered can understand grief.
Now that she comprehended, she could no more increase his sorrow than she could pierce him with
a sword. Be worthy of a grief and it makes you
tender; it teaches you to subtract from the unhappiness of others. Rosalind stretched forth her hand
and gently touched the bare, muscle-ribbed forearm.

"Ben —"

His arm dropped in his evident amazement at
finding her still standing near him.

"Forgive me . . ." His voice choked in his
throat. "I was — a cad . . . I couldn't help myself. It was a rotten thing to do."

"You shouldn't have done it, Ben. It hurts me.
Some day it will hurt me more; it will kill me for
you."

She was thinking of the mountain again. Here
had been the most dangerous eruption of all! Yet
in her sympathy she gave him only this simple re-
buke.

People who permit their hearts to govern their
heads sometimes find that they have no longer heads
to govern. In giving her passionate heart to Both-
well, Mary Queen of Scots incidentally gave her
head to Elizabeth. No doubt she was aware of the
capital penalty for her weakness, as Rosalind was
aware in this moment that her long-sought opportunity to break forever with Benjamin had knocked
and not been heard. The chance to dismiss the importunate suitor had come and had not been accepted.
Thus it is ever with best laid plans which brains devise! The heart forces them all to gang agley, and

does so with conscious pride.   If Rosalind later rebuked herself for soft-heartedness, at the moment
when repudiation was possible she rather prized herself on the generous kindness of her heart.   She had
suffered; another should not.   But in acting the
friend to Benjamin in the little, she acted the enemy
to him in the great.   Kind as it was not to break his
back suddenly at this moment, it was cowardly to
renew again the opportunities for what she had felt
convinced was a hopeless love.

" Then you will . . . forgive me ? "
Rosalind was silent.   Her hair was like so much
spun gold in a patch of sunshine: to the breathless
Cary she was loveliness incarnate.

" Yes, because I know, Ben, that you are sincere.
I have no heart to be angry with you as I should be,
but you have been wrong, terribly wrong.   And you
know it. So we are friends again."

With bowed head Benjamin took his punishment.
Shame for the rashness which he had exhibited could
not but soon rise from his clear nature.   Self-reproach bears a more bitter sting than scorpions.
To the condemnation of parent or friend we turn
the ear of one who reserves an ulterior judgment,
but from the condemnation of oneself there is no
court of appeal.   Since man is to himself sufficient,
his own judgment supplants in mortal life the Word
of God.   If a man have light within his own clear
breast, earth is his Paradise; but the consciousness
of wrong-doing stirring in his heart makes the world
a dungeon.   Benjamin condemned himself bitterly
and turned to go, his brain in tumult.   It seemed as
if something had withered while he held Rosalind
in his arms, something which in fancy had been imagined sanctified and which in actuality was pitifully

mortal. The first touch and pressure of her body had been dreamt on tremblingly; he had thought of it as the implicit papist does of his first vision of the *Casa Sante*. His love was his religion, and this was to be a culmination of his worship. But alas for human nature! He had in his fierce, rough embrace desecrated his shrine, hurled down from the gleaming altar monstrance, pyx, and crucifix, made gross and rude the most tender and beautiful of moments. Self-shamed and self-unpitied, he strode away.

"Where are you going?"

It was Rosalind's voice. Benjamin stopped. Like Adam, banished by Michael out of Eden, but catching at straws of comfort in the kind archangel's words, Benjamin at this unexpected question recovered his scattered spirits.

"I hardly know," he repeated lamely. "I — hardly know."

"You aren't going to leave me here like this, Ben?"

"I thought you wanted me to go," he dumbly replied.

In his contrition there was that which could not be withstood. He seemed afraid to move or speak lest he commit some further blunder in her sight, and remained uncertainly, half faced about. Rosalind stretched out her hands to him.

"Not at all. I wanted you to take me home."

He hurried to her and took her hands in his. For a moment they stood in a pool of sunlight under the serene sky.

"But mind! We're to forget this, Ben!"

He pressed her hands reverently.

"I'll mind," he answered obediently, and together they trudged off to his automobile.

When they arrived at 29 Commonwealth, they found Mrs. Copley in the clutches of the ungrammatical cousin.

"Don't she look healthy!" exclaimed that lady, rapturously holding up both her hands. "My dear Rosalind, those cheeks are just like — just like —"

"Roses?" suggested Benjamin with a gallantry unusual in him.

"Ah, that's it! Mr. Cary knows, I'm sure."

"How was your golf?" interrupted Mrs. Copley coolly. Cousin Lucy was tolerated only so long as she behaved well. Since the accompaniment of the airy inflection of her last remark with an unfathomable glance in Cary's direction hardly fell within the category of good comportment, Mrs. Copley, at once the Lachesis and Atropos of her garrulous cousin's thread of discourse, cut short the conversation.

For the second time Cary rose handsomely to the occasion. "Rosalind won, Mrs. Copley, as usual!"

But Cousin Lucy refused to be counted out: a woman with a piece of gossip is unsnubable. She hitched her chair toward Rosalind with alluring friendliness.

"I was just telling your mother, Rose, the terrible accident that happened to your Cousin Arthur Copley. He's burst an artery in his neck. I understand it happened while he was playing whist — the excitement and all, I suppose, was responsible. I know my poor father used to say cards were provokers of strife. He was a bit of a Baptist in his way, Mr. Cary." She favoured Benjamin with a benignant smile. "Not a big man by any means, but a powerful talker. Hell-fire was his favourite line." She shook her head despondently. "He couldn't abear games, not because they were wicked, but because they gave others sinful dependence on things not of the spirit. I'm not like that. You know, I reckon Arthur's thing came from drink," she whispered eagerly to Rosalind.

" Cousin Lucy ! "

" It's the truth, my dear: I'm no tale-bearer."

At this moment the Misses Hepplethwaite were announced. Mrs. Copley sighed. A call from the Hepplethwaites was at the best trying, but with the added complication of the ungrammatical cousin, who like all poor relations became excessively effusive to be thought genteel, the event was one which she could regard only in the light of a penance for some sin.

" We have been driving in the park," remarked the elder sister, icily seating herself. " It was so beautiful we felt it as much a duty as a pleasure to come and relate to you our enjoyment."

" Exquisite ! " murmured the younger sister.

" Isn't it ? " broke in Cousin Lucy affably. " You must drive out to Franklin Park some day and see the elephants."

Miss Jane Hepplethwaite favoured Cousin Lucy with a glance of indifferent interest, as if she were a rather unattractive specimen of an uncultivated age; Miss Joan started in her chair at her words.

" How is your dear husband ? " asked the former of Mrs. Copley.

" And your dear godfather ? " added her sister, turning to Rosalind with a dazed look.

The formulæ of polite conversation never abandoned the Misses Hepplethwaite. Despite the shock of Cousin Lucy they could still like twin automata go through the motions of talking. But even

the conventional field of health was unsafe. Observing her redoubtable cousin about to relate the
tragic tale of Mr. Arthur Copley's accident, Mrs.
Copley was again forced to exercise her right of
closure.

"City life seems to agree with us all. Rosalind
won't hear of our moving to Sherborne just now."
(Rosalind coloured as she felt Benjamin's eyes upon
her, wondering if he knew the reason for her desire.) "But I do hope she'll let us go before May.
Jack worries over the garden day and night."

"You'll not migrate before the Pearce wedding, I
presume?" said Miss Jane.

"You must stay for that," murmured Miss Joan.

"Amy Pearce and Philip Brooks!" laughed Rose.
"Think, Mother, an old beau of mine!"

Here was a chance for Cousin Lucy.

"What are you going to wear, Miss Hepplethwaite?" Despite the rattle of Mrs. Copley's tea-
cup Cousin Lucy held the floor. "My white dresses
are all shrunk by washing; you wouldn't believe how
they shrink on me! I've a green velvet that's
awfully sweet, but a *leetle* bit tight," she confided in
a low voice, "about the hips. You know how I
mean! Girls our age do have trouble with their
hips somehow!"

At this open reference to the feminine anatomy
the Misses Hepplethwaite shuddered. If that celebrated Queen of Spain had no legs, for the purposes
of polite conversation she was also hipless. But
Lucy would have tripped innocently on, had not the
entrance of Freddy Hoyt cut short a further revelation. By the time the stir of introduction was over
Cousin Lucy had lost the thread of her idea, and
Mrs. Copley was spinning a new and safer line.

"Have you any news, Jane? Of engagements, I mean. Your speaking of the Pearce wedding made me think of it."

"Only concerning what we hoped you might enlighten us."

"We hoped you might," echoed Miss Joan.

"Me?" Mrs. Copley arched her eyebrows prettily.

"Oh, not Rosalind!" Miss Hepplethwaite gave one the impression of being amused. "But a friend of hers — Eric Rolland."

"That attractive young foreigner," supplemented her sister.

"We see him so often in the Square."

"So often."

"To whom is he supposed to be engaged?" asked Mrs. Copley. "It's rather quick work, isn't it? He's not been here but a month."

"Oh! He became acquainted with the lady on the steamer — Patricia Canfield."

"Eric and Patty engaged! Rose, dear, do you hear this?"

Rosalind had heard it all. From the first suspicious word to the last whisper of the rumour, each syllable had struck like a stone against her heart. She had listened with painful eagerness. What did these people know? Until this moment she had heard the rumour only in her own breast; now it was on the lips of the world.

"I hear it, Mamma," she said in a low voice.

"Not that handsome *garsong!*" exclaimed Cousin Lucy with a deliberate display of high school French which made Mrs. Copley shudder.

"*I* thought," ventured Freddy Hoyt, laying a

tremendous emphasis on the pronoun, "*I* thought to have heard other news of him."

" Yes? "   Rosalind looked into his laughing brown eyes.   " What? "

She knew he meant herself, but boldly faced him.

" I said I wouldn't tell!   But then Rose must know, Miss Hepplethwaite."   He turned to the elder sister.   " Her intimacy with this foreign interloper has long been a thorn in my side.   You see, as a callow freshman I swore to be faithful *à l'outrance;* so for one, I hope it's true!   Thus perish all my rivals! "

He laughed again, but Rosalind had not the heart this time to look into his boyish face.   She was grateful for Benjamin's silence.

" Is it true, Rosalind dear? " asked Miss Jane ingratiatingly.

" We hate to press you," pressed the younger sister.

" I don't know.   They haven't told me."

Rosalind spoke coldly, as who should say that the business was not hers either for interest or participation.   But just under the rim of her control surged an intemperate desire to shake these two prim icicles till by the very friction of their motion they dissolved.

" They'd make a lovely couple," ventured the ungrammatical cousin, " so dark, both of 'em!   Do you suppose there is anything in the attraction of like to like?   I met an albino lady once.   She was never married, perhaps because she couldn't find an albino man.   Funny thing; their eyes are reddish, like rabbits.   Creepy, I call it."

Freddy Hoyt choked into his tea-cup, **and even**

Benjamin's stern lips had a humorous expression about them.

" I have heard Mr. Rolland was completely fascinated by her on the boat," ventured Miss Hepplethwaite.

" So romantic ! "

" I can't think who told you," said Rosalind, endeavouring to veil under an ill-maintained indifference her passionate eagerness to ascertain the source of the information.

" I really forget ! "

" Just a rumour." Miss Jane smiled sweetly.

" We saw them at the Copley Plaza just now on our way here."

" Going to tea, we supposed."

" Then there may be something in it." Mrs. Copley shook her lovely head doubtfully. " I had not known they were acquainted; Rose didn't tell me."

Rosalind had arisen and moved aimlessly to the shadows by the windows. As he followed her, Benjamin could not see her face, but from the pathetic slope of her shoulders he gathered something of her unhappiness. It was a hard moment for him. How might he offer sympathy on this subject, the very downfall of his rival? Yet there is a sorrow which supersedes all personal emotion; it is the pain of those beloved. Her wounds were more precious than his own. With some divine intuition guiding his heavy heart, he understood how best he might help her.

" Good-bye, Rosalind," he said in a low voice. " You have been kind to me to-day."

" Thank you, Ben."

When he was gone, Rosalind went slowly up the stairs to her room. It seemed as if with each step there was an incalculable weight to be lifted, as if a mighty, vague depression flowed through her body, numbing its muscles and interdicting their function. The pipe of rumour, " blown by surmises, jealousies, conjectures," plays a tune easily accredited by two ears, the one most eager for its music, the other most dreading its note. For Rosalind this piece of news had blotted out the sun, and she could cry with blind Samson, " O dark, dark, dark, amid the blaze of noon!" Rumour is painted with many tongues; the whisper of each had found an ear in her saddened heart.

She went to her desk and took the little calendar in her hand. June 1st: ANSWER BEN! How should she answer him with Eric become a vital part of her daily happiness? Oh! Had these last days been a dream? Should she awake soon, unable to finish this song so beautifully begun?

CHAPTER XVI

WHICH CULMINATES IN A SECOND LETTER TO CAMILLA

THERE are a thousand homes in Boston, dwelt in by the nicest people imaginable, which are painfully alike. Alike in their calm propriety; alike in their Victorian homeliness; alike in their chastening influence upon the young. The children grow up to their homes; nothing grows down to them. Even if they do not walk about the streets reading Emerson, they alone are the losers by such abstention, for the world at large is convinced that they do. At a tender age the boys are whisked off to boarding-school, where they are cast into an excellent mould and turned out six or seven years later in varying degrees of completion. The girls remain at home, sometimes beautiful, often inconsequential, and usually idle ornaments.

After a year of this ornamental stage — though even during the winter of her début she had discovered Dostoievzki and Brieux to parental alarm — Rosalind had decided to be useful. It shocked her mother; it hurt her father; it displeased her godfather. Among the lists of subscribers to charity the name of Copley had led all the rest; but to work, actually to work, in Brimmer House! Collectively and individually the family shook its head. But Rosalind's determination won the day, and within a year — lo and behold! Mrs. Copley had

entertained a carefully selected group of Rosalind's
little girls at the house; Mr. Copley was telling
stories about her at the Sarcophagus Club; and even
her godfather acknowledged to be pleased with her
success.

People are hungry for life in proportion to the
courage which they bring into it, and Rosalind was
brave. She had not wanted to live as does the average, the conventional girl. Perhaps she did not
court the storm and stress of existence; yet at the
same time she was unafraid before it, and could regard its possible incursion upon her virginal serenity
with the pleasurable thrill of a novice in oriental
travel who hears by night the far-off shriek of the
monsoon on Arafura Sea. Life is very sweet; no
wonder that it be human nature to desire the utmost
of it. In Eric she had found what she believed
to be the reason of her existence, and had been
mightily stirred. What she had endeavoured to find
in Benjamin, affining qualities in Eric had showered
upon her. Even in so short a time he had taught her
to see the world in a grain of sand, to find eternity
in a second. Life had not been lived entirely on
the hilltops, it is true: to scale the loftiest mountain, the lowest valley must be tread. But with a
cloud by day and a pillar of fire by night the path
mattered not: the goal was all.

It was different now. Rosalind sat at her desk
in Brimmer House, leaning back in the chair and
biting her pen-holder, her mind filled with the rumour heard yesterday from the Misses Hepplethwaite. A feeling came over her that both ame-
thyst mountain and purple valley had vanished away,
that nothing now was left but the endless, humdrum
flatlands of life. She set herself to write.

" . . . . Antonio is worse than when he first came to the class-room, and I really begin to think his is a case for the House of Correction . . ."

The pen trailed off the page in an inky hen-track. Little words that Eric had said tumbled through her brain, scraps of sentences, music that tinkled in a past harmony, a glint of sunlight on his dark hair. Was it all to go, this beautiful universe? " A sorrow's crown of sorrow is remembering happier things."   She thought of all those trivialities, so incomprehensibly dear, which had made her life rich of late; she thought how warm and precious past hours had been; and her tears, like those of the Recording Angel upon Uncle Toby's great oath, dropped one by one upon the page, blotting the sins of Antonio from all legibility.   There were not many tears, but the few were bitter, and left her as miserable as before they had been shed.   Incapable of work she jumped up, put on her hat, and moved irresolutely to the door.   A magnetism stronger than her pride was drawing her towards the Square. As she climbed up the hill she whispered that she was going to see her godfather and no one else, but she was painfully conscious of falseness to herself in the thought.

Despite a few pale streaks of sunlight which still filtered slowly into the Square the place was gloomy and chill, with an angry wind whistling in the chimney-tops and rattling a loosened shutter with imperious rage.   Aristides and Columbus, cold little statues, looked across the enclosure at each other in dejected misery; up above, the wind shredded the limbs of the ragged old elms.   Rosalind shivered. Yesterday morning it had been warm enough to sit in the enclosure with Eric; to-day — she doubted if she might now sit anywhere with him! And yet her heart filled with but one desire: to know what he was about, to see him, to hear his voice, to observe close by his hand, though unobserved. Acting on some impulse, she stepped across the road and, pressed close to the old iron fence, looked in at the spot where together they had been the morning before. There was so much loveliness in the remembrance that she forgot to turn away. On the darkened grass she could see Eric's slender figure flung back with a laugh; the sun was still dazzling on his face; the nearness of his body still stirred her blood. Like an enchanted pilgrim, she stood gazing in through the bars as if a Garden of Armida lay beyond and not a dark, shy old square.

"I have been watching you from the window, Rose. Have you lost something?"

With electric surprise Eric's voice aroused her from her reverie. She could not look at him, so overwhelmingly she felt his presence.

"Yes, Eric. I have lost something," she truthfully answered in a voice so low that the wind caught and swept it away from her lips.

"What?"

There was nothing to say, nothing that she could reply which would be truth.

"My — my purse! It must have dropped yesterday morning, as we sat here. You remember?"

"Let me look!"

He was over the fence in a moment. Rosalind watched his slim figure vault through the half light in a confusion of admiration, self-reproach, and anger.

"Don't trouble, Eric!" She blushed as he

groped about the grass. "It's only a trifle after
all."

"It doesn't seem to be here anyway," he called.
Then he came close to the fence on his side.
"Where have you been? I have waited all the
morning about the house."

Rosalind's heart leaped up as he spoke, and she
felt the skin upon her scalp tighten and tingle.

"Have you — really?" she asked with suddenly
bright eyes.

"Of course. Did you forget?"

Something, she knew not what, made her think of
Patricia and she bit her lip, angry at his deceit.

"Yes — that is, no. I've spent most of the day
at Brimmer House." Her voice was coldly polite.
"There's much work for me."

"I wish I could help. Couldn't I?"

Rosalind looked sharply at him. Another day
the solicitude in his voice would have warmed her
heart; now she was tempted in her anger to be cyni-
cal. He help her? Was this a game of buff he
was playing and was she the blindman? Through
the bars of the old fence she could see the breeze
ruffling his curly hair and flooding his cheeks with
colour; in his eyes there was the clear coolness of
high winds on high hills.

"You allowed Cary to help you. You called him
your financial aide. Why not ask me?"

"I will ask you, Eric." She met his eyes seri-
ously.

"Thank you." He was very close now; the same
breath of wind that played about his head stirred also
about her before it flung itself to Heaven. "You
are not angry with me, Rosalind? Tell me!"

"Angry?" She grasped tightly the bars of the old fence, overwhelmed with a feeling that she had somehow betrayed her jealousy, and said the easiest thing, the first thing that came into her mind. "What do you mean, Eric?"

"Lately it has seemed that I displeased you. I have wondered why to myself. Perhaps I have been wrong in my conclusions. . . . I thought you liked me." He paused. Rosalind, tremulous and with bent head, could say nothing. "You seemed to take a fancy to me at first. Perhaps it was only kindness: every one has been so kind. I hope I have not offended you? How have I? Rose?" Still no reply. The joy of the moment stifled her and she felt her jealous conviction, built upon rumour, like an evil spirit before the exorcising charm fade at his words. "I do so want all people to like me. My mother was sweet to every one, simply because she said it was easier to be pleasant than disagreeable. I have inherited the manner from her, and it makes one seem false, I suppose. If I see a person, I desire that person to like me. And I try to make every one want me, though I don't care perhaps at all for them. It's a selfish thing, I suppose."

"Did you try with me, Eric?" asked Rosalind timorously.

"I hardly had an opportunity. I — that sounds conceited enough, doesn't it? I meant we seemed to like each other so well that endeavour wasn't necessary."

"Not at all necessary."

It was dark now. Rosalind smiled to herself. From the moment when first she had discovered him at the piano to the present instant, love had seemed to her inevitable.

"If you are not angry, then I am most pleased. It means a great deal to me. . . . And now before we both get pneumonia in this tearing wind, let's go in to godfather!"

Eric had mounted the fence and stood a moment above her silhouetted against the angry sky with arms outstretched. So might Mercury have poised in flight upon a heaven-kissing hill. But the footing was too precarious and the rushing wind unbalanced him; he twisted, caught at the air, and fell to the street with a cry. At the misstep Rosalind had stretched out her arms to steady his position, and as he fell his foot struck her, spinning her back against the fence.

"Eric! Are you hurt?"

For a moment she stared sickly at the figure on the cobblestones, her heart cold in her breast.

"Eric! Eric! What has happened? Are you hurt, dear Eric? Answer me!"

Dropping to her knees beside him, she caught his hand as it moved about his head. He lay upon his side, and she endeavoured to support his shoulders and raise him from the cold ground. His lids were heavy as if with sleep.

"I must — have stumbled," he murmured in a faint, dazed voice. "It's my head; it hit the iron fence. I'll be all right now. Nothing broken. I'll be all right."

"I'm so sorry," she cried with a break in her voice, as with her support he arose unsteadily. "It must hurt dreadfully, Eric."

"I'm dizzy." He tottered on his feet. "Give me your arm, Rose. Stupid of me — fall."

She slipped her arm through his, looking up in
the pale, drawn face. At the first step he reeled,
like to fall again from his faintness, and with quick
pity and strength she put her arms about him. For
a moment they stood thus in the stormy twilight,
his weight thrown heavily upon her, his face de-
clining with the weariness of pain toward her face;
then, with an effort, he took another step, halting
and weak, another and another, and so on up the
stairs and into the house. The weight was precious
in Rosalind's arms. Perhaps it was only a step
across the street to the sofa in the drawing-room:
such steps are rare, invaluable measures, quite unknown to linear scales. There was an eternal mag-
nitude about that minute which defied all temporal
calculation. To help in a moment of pain, to feel
a dazed head heavy upon the shoulder, to clasp about
the waist, to touch with light fingers the temples —
in these small services is the lover's great reward of
love.

The slightest accident to one beloved is infinitely
magnified. Charity we measure by our incomes, but
sympathy by our hearts. Had Eric been Horatius,
fresh from washing his wounds in hurrying Tiber,
he could not have received a more lavish yet sincere bestowal of fuss and affection. He reclined
upon a sofa, cushioned, cologned, and comforted,
a moral Don Juan revived and restored by a west-
ern Haidée. Mr. Singleton Singleton would have
called a doctor, but Eric balked at that. A man
likes to be made much of if he has only pricked his
thumb, but even though he be dying he will not
summon a doctor. Love is the best physician; it
is the one infallible cure-all of immedicable woes.
Though Asclepios brought Hippolytus back to life,

he could not have prescribed comfort for a bump on the head; but Rosalind's cool fingers at Eric's temples were like ministers of peace, in a hot and aching world. At dinner Eric was the focus of attention. Sitting beside him, Rosalind could not eat; one never eats in the presence of a person much loved or much respected. Between the excitement of the heart and the stimulation of the nervous system the conductive usefulness of the alimentary canal is reduced to a minimum which holds only ambrosia palatable. Who could be so oblivious as to eat with a garden of roses blooming in the heart?

After Eric had been put unwillingly to bed, Rosalind sat down at the desk in the small library upstairs, her eyes still brilliant with happy excitement. She felt a desire to laugh and a desire to cry, and in her mood of exaltation took up a pen to write to her friend, Camilla. The deathless joy of friends is this: wherever they may be, whatever their estate, they represent a sympathetic and intimate audience before which the cloak and subleties of life may be stripped off and the confidence of strong love remain.

April 22d.

Dearest Camilla:

As a hors d'œuvre Uncle Sing-Sing sends you his love. I send you mine, dear Cam, too, and I wish with all my heart you were here this minute. What a talk we could have! But you aren't, so I take my pen in hand (like the country lover) hoping you are still the same. I'm not. I'm involved in a drayma.

The curtain goes up, disclosing to view a beautiful, young, society girl, right centre, in tears. (That's me.) Centre stage, handsome foreigner with ice-green eyes and air of divine *insouciance*. (That's HIM, Cammy!) Left centre, dark woman of vampire beauty, dangerous temperament, and Gallic moral code. (That is — you've guessed it, Cam! Patricia!)

Everything you have ever said about P. C., I now endorse, Camilla. Anything you ever can say will "when found, be made note on." Is this music to you? It's ten thousand trumpets out of tune to me, dearest. What makes it all the worse is this: *I* warped those trumpets. *I* brought Patricia and Eric into contact, *moi!*

You know, my sweet Cammy, how said Patricia can act! Well, she tried out all of those and a cargo of new allurements on Eric, and within Jack Robinson my fairy prince was a god in chains. Since that moment the sun has risen in the west, my ears have burned, and I have dreamed of walking under ladders. (Also I have been attacked on the golf links by a tall, handsome friend of yours. You remember what Samson did to the lion? — But I'm not going to tell you that secret. It wouldn't be fair to Samson.)

But dearest Cammy, you mustn't be jealous when I tell you what glorious times Eric and I have had together! Oh! to walk on air and contemplate the sun! And I have done it. *Ah! ces beaux jours de bonheur indicible!* I have felt a joy that has passed all my belief, Camilla. And now? I don't know anything, *m'amie!* I don't know whether he likes me or not. It's torturing to live this way. To-night I'm almost very sure I'm *grand' chose* in his life; to-morrow — *qui sait?* As for jealousy! My dear Camilla, I'm positively ochre; Leontes out-Leontesed! But how can I help it? Two suns cannot revolve in the same sphere: Patricia Canfield and I cannot both be Venus! As for my pride, Cammy dear, I've not two penny's worth left.

Oh, Camilla, you understand me, I know. Other friends have not been like us. Then lend me now your love. I have yearned for Eric, put him before everything in the world. To me he has not been what he is, what you might think him, but something inhumanly beautiful. I have set him on a pedestal of crystal; I have put him in my prayers — all in so short a time! You think it is a passing craze perhaps? No, Cammy! It is very deep in my

soul. There are some moments when you can feel a revelation: with Eric such a moment has come to me. I could
strike Heaven dumb with hyperbole, so changed am I,
but — tears, idle tears! *Ça ne vaut rien!*

When you come back you'll be dearer to me than ever —
and be in at the death!

Patience on a monument,
Your adoring Rose.

P. S. Allegra Tompkins' new free verse poems are just
out. You'll be interested in this parody Eric and I — in
one of our HAPPY MOMENTS — have concocted.
Mamma says it's much more sense than the original. Eric
calls it

" A Temperamental Temperance Tour de Force."

> Of late of thy wine of love
> Much have I drunk.
> Gushing and ebbing in my red heart,
> Tide upon tide has clutched and passioned
> For something there.
>
> Now am I full of broken bottles,
> Chipped, ruddy glass, amber beer bottles,
> Splinters that tear and scream.
> Why, having drunk up all the wine,
> Did I drink, too, the bottles?
> My parched soul, unslaked,
> Shrieked for that more which you had not;
> So of your love I swallowed the shell,
> Hideously indigestible . . .
>
> I was thirsty, so thirsty!

CHAPTER XVII

MISFORTUNES NEVER COME SINGLY

BETWEEN Eric's accident and the wedding of Amy Pearce to Philip Brooks there lay in Rosalind's life an interregnum. The days filed by in a dull succession, strangely devoid of the initial glamour of being passionately in love. It was as if before the full sense of her deeper emotion could be appreciated an adjustment of spiritual values must be made. Rosalind was puzzled, and came to regard herself with mistrust. At times she felt almost repugnance for her love. In moments of bright sunshine and gay laughter she entertained those torturing, mortal misgivings and half-doubts as to the possibility of eternal devotion. So new and swift in its conquest, could this passion endure the infinite weaving of years? To one assured of reciprocal love the future is a land of jasper and of gold, glowing with celestial roses; but Rosalind enjoyed no surety of affection, and so with unscaled sight could see in all its grey reality the cold, hard road that stretches up to the gleaming hill where man and Maker meet. Yet far more often a sense of all that which was now hers swept over her in a torrent of reproach that such doubts could find entertainment in her breast. When she awoke in the vast silence of the night to find a square of moonlight nicely painted on the floor, the firm belief in Eric as the quintessential of her life possessed her, tossing and turning its mortal casing in an ecstasy of loneliness. Moved by this sudden influx of feeling, she would steal to the window to watch the stars like armies of eyes march silently across the heavens, and find in each twinkling radiancy a cold distance that struck into her heart. In the daytime, too, the sense of being alone came over her. In little country groves the wind sang unearthly melodies, faint echoings of something which had never been; in city streets she found associations rich with past remembrances; and the dulness of mundane associations contrasted vividly with the omnipresent spirit of her love.

One afternoon she unexpectedly came across Patricia Canfield, standing on the steps of Violet Lee's house. For a moment Rosalind was embarrassed, but her friend with the characteristic flutter and bustle of all beautiful women who live life as if it were a foot-race, flew down the steps to embrace her.

"Hullo, Rosey-ro!" Patricia always kissed on the lips for sincerity's sake. "Where are you going, dear? Do come in and see Vi's olive-branch!"

Rosalind paused uncertainly.

"I suppose I — all right, Pat."

"I'm crazy to see it. I adore babies — they're so puddeny. Vi is perfectly mad over hers; sits it up on the bed beside her and cries, 'Now when you grow up, you and I are going to be bess, 'ittle, quiet fre'n's.' Let me see," mused Patricia maliciously. "Do you remember said Violet in the ante-baby days? They had to put the lights out to get her home! Now she's that demure and maternal I feel actually rebuked in her sight!"

They slipped into the house.

" It must be a relief for Hugh."

" Yes.   I suppose you think marriage would be good for me, too, Ro-ro? "   Rosalind coloured abruptly.   " I've thought so lately.   A couple of babies might make me into a Penelope or a Lucretia."

" What's the child's name? "

" That I'm thinking of kidnapping, dear? "   Patricia wilfully misunderstood the question with facile stupidity.   " Never mind — but you know him."

" Really? "

Rosalind was glad when they reached Violet's boudoir; fencing with Patricia about Eric was a particularly disagreeable occupation.

" Hullo, Vi.   I've brought Rosey with me.   Where is the blessing? "

Rosalind kissed the mother and knelt down beside the baby.

" May I take it up, Violet?   What a splendid child! "

Mrs. Lee, nodding assent, Rosalind raised the baby to her breast with a skill taught by long experience at Brimmer House.   The little bundle of blankets was quiet in her arms.

" Look, Violet!   She's smiling at me."   Rosalind lifted to her lips one of the little hands, its rosy fingers crisping in the first exercise of strength.

" Want to hold it, Patricia? "

Miss Canfield was sitting by the window, where she could look out upon the street.

" Heavens, no! " she replied with marked declension of interest in infantile welfare.   " I might drop it.   Don't be offended, Vi!   This is a Paris dress anyway, and if you don't know just how to handle the little things, they're liable to forget themselves.

Look! There's Hatty Mason: shall we have a bridge? I'm dying for cards."

Rosalind excused herself and, putting down the baby, bid Mrs. Lee good-bye.

"I only just dropped in, Violet."

"Ta-ta, Rosey," called Patricia from the window. "Is he going to the wedding to-morrow?"

"Who?" asked Rosalind, firmly meeting her friend's half-mocking, half-inquisitive stare.

"Eric, of course! Did you think I meant the baby?"

Rosalind bit her lip.

"I don't know," she replied truthfully. Eric had gone into the country on a sketching trip and had not defined the day of his return.

"Don't fence, Rose," laughed Mrs. Lee from her reclining chair. "You're with friends!"

Rosalind was standing at the door.

"I really don't know, Patricia. He didn't tell me. Good-bye, Violet."

As she ran down the stairs, her face burned to hear Patricia's laugh floating after her. It is not pleasant to know that your friends are dissecting you with an amused smile behind your back. Sharper than all the blades of Damascus is the tongue which wags malice against an old friend.

On the next morning her answer to Patricia would have been different, for she received a telegram from Eric declaring his intention to return at noon and go to the wedding. With this in her thoughts Rosalind sat in Trinity Church, staring about on all sides. The dingy interior was impregnated with the perfume of the roses which decorated the altar and wreathed about little columns guarding the length of the aisle. But if Eric was there, he was not to be

seen in the crowd of fine dresses and dark cutaways
which filled the pews.   Rosalind leaned back in disappointment.   What a circus our world of to-day
makes of a wedding!   What an opportunity it af-
fords garrulous women to sate that curiosity of theirs
which damned mother Eve!   What a perfect carni-
val of barbaric impudence is all this frilling and fur-
belowing and staring at two inoffensive human be-
ings — strangers, more often than not — who are
for the moment standing close by God!   Clack-
clack-clack go the ladies' tongues, intruding their
scandal-mongering upon the magnificent thunder and
drone of the organ.   The men in the audience —
what else, indeed? — yawn and cough; the minister
and the best man behind the altar settle the account
— in gold pieces and not human teeth or bright
stones, for this is not Madagascar, though it appear
like it — and the trembling protagonists march away
from the presence of God, grateful that what should
be most divine in life is quickly over.   Marriages
are certainly not made on earth!   Were it not better
done to stand in a rain of apple blossoms from an
age-old branch, sole separation from the Lord's high
Heaven, and speak the simple words before a simple
man than endure all the tinsel and trumpeting of a
marriage in a crowded church?

Rosalind was glad when the ceremony was over;
marriage was too close to her own heart to be a
visual pleasure.   Still there was no sign of Eric.
Despite ceaseless burrowing in the tight-packed press
at the reception, her efforts were unrewarded.   With
a sense of disappointment she mounted the stairs to
retake her wrap, but passed absent-mindedly from
the hall into a chamber opposite the improvised coat-
room.   It was a cosy little place, overlooking the

Basin, a place on the gay chintzes of which the sun fell brightly. Not until she was well inside the door did she realise her mistake. At the same time she experienced that curious sense of being not alone in a room. A glance towards the window confirmed her subconscious feelings; a man had risen from beside a woman on the chintz-covered sofa.

"I — beg your pardon," stammered Rosalind. Then as she recognised the person: "Why — why, Eric!"

He stood framed in the dazzling window; afar behind him shimmered the river in the warm midday sun, reflecting from its glittering bosom light that shone about his head in a soft aureole. He was on the point of speaking when the lady on the sofa turned about, and Rosalind found herself looking into the eyes of Patricia.

"Hullo, Rosey! So you've found the only quiet spot here, too?"

Rosalind felt that her face must be exceedingly pale.

"I beg your pardon," she said at length in a splendid effort to keep her tones even.

"Don't mention it, Rosey," ran on Patricia pointedly. "How d'you ever find us? Sit down, dear, on the sofa. Eric's no end of pretty speeches today. He's been dazzling me with 'em."

Rosalind repressed a great desire to do something mad and unheard of, abruptly turned, and quitted the room and the house.

Wise and long-suffering La Rochefoucauld! When he proclaimed to the world that nothing is more natural or more fallacious than to persuade ourselves that we are beloved, he voiced a terrible warning to all sensitive people. Do these folk but

care for a person ever so little, they can interpret
any word or any action in some way intimately
favourable to themselves; they look into the sun of
love and are struck blind to the truth.   Yet could
Argus, with all his eyes, have withstood its light?
Surely it had tricked Rosalind like a veritable Friar
Rush, hobgoblin flame which dances on and ever on
in the darkness.   Through vicissitudes of doubt and
error, she had at last concluded that there was a relation between herself and Eric which was both peculiar and sincere.   On the receipt of his telegram
this very morning of the wedding, she had anew resolved that every opportunity for a felicitous conclusion lay before her.   And now — now she felt
assured that he had been but playing with her!
Nothing can raise so resentful a passion in the human
breast as the knowledge that what to us is most
sacred and profound is undervalued by another.
To Eric her existence must be negligible.   Torturing herself with the thought that he and Patricia
were undoubtedly laughing together now over her
white face and patent sorrow, she strode angrily
along the Esplanade.   Plainly the world was out
of joint: there was no beauty in this day.   The wind
bore only dust to her; the river's surface irritated
with its perpetual sheen; and the gaiety of the children playing about her made the more vivid her
unhappiness.   There was but one way to deal with
the horrible tangle.   No hesitating, no attempts to
unravel the skein — enough of her pride and life
had already been spent in that effort: one swift, sharp
stroke, and it was over!   Rather than share a corner
of the heart she loved, she would live a loathsome
thing, as Othello would have been a toad sucking in
the vapours of a dungeon rather than have lived with

Quietly she closed the little book . . .

Desdemona false. She must be free; all possibility of reciprocal love must be abandoned and with it her own mighty passion. A person of courage, Rosalind told herself, would end it now. It matters not to have half-seen beatitude, if the consummate sight is denied. In questions of the soul that materialistic doctrine of the half loaf, propagated by the stout Hanoverian, has no place. Love knows no halves: it is a beauty indivisible.

The afternoon was endless and miserable. At tea-time Rosalind vanished from the house to avoid the influx of callers; and dinner was such a tiresome, vapourish affair, that she escaped as soon as politeness allowed, and, protesting a headache, wandered alone into the music-room and gave herself over to melancholy. A chair before the fire inviting, she sank into its cushions; in each curling finger of flame she found a memory. That would not do. She picked up a book, one of those gorgeous trifles which with jade and jasper figurettes litter the tables of the rich, and aimlessly fluttered the pages.

> " Go from me. Yet I feel that I shall stand
> Henceforward in thy shadow. Nevermore
> Alone upon the threshold of my door
> Of individual life, I shall command
> The uses of my soul, nor lift my hand
> Serenely in the sunshine as before —"

Quietly she closed the little book with a trembling lip. Had she not stood in Eric's shadow? Had she not felt the unforgettable influence? Oh, Elizabeth Barrett, by that one gold string set trembling under thy touch how hast thou awaked a responsive chord in every breast of youth! As she put down the " Sonnets," her hand fell upon " Gil Blas," and she turned its pages with a sense of relief. Always the roguery of La Sage, had made her laugh, and now she trusted in his power.

> *" Ay de mi! un ano felice*
> *Parece un soplo ligero,*
> *Fero sui dicha un instante*
> *Es un siglo te tormento."*

She let the book fall to the floor. " Alas! a year of pleasure passes like a fleeting breeze; but a moment of misfortune seems an age of pain! " No comfort anywhere. She strayed about the room, restless, almost afraid, at last to sit moodily before the piano. As her fingers trailed over the keys, she struck by accident a chord in a waltz by Edouard Schütt, " À La Bien-Aimée," a favourite with Eric and one which she had learned to play from him. She drifted into the swinging, irresistible melody, her body alive with harmonic echoes. Each note pulled and stretched the strings of her heart. Through her half-closed eyes she seemed to see a graceful figure at a piano with head thrown back and fingers flying.

A step sounded in the hall outside. Absorbed in her own reflection, Rosalind had been subconsciously aware of the opening of the front door some time past; now a sudden wild hope crowned her heart. At last Eric was come and they could re-establish the glorious quality of life!

" Benjamin! "

It was a dizzy height to drop from. Relaxed in every nerve and muscle, Rosalind turned away to hide the profundity of her disappointment. A sudden hope at the best, it was come and gone like a tardy lightning gleam after a storm.

" Rose, you are not ill? "

Half-turned from him, she shook her head slowly. She was not what he would call ill.

"Your mother said —" He did not finish his sentence, but stood looking at her. There was a pause and she dully wondered why he had come.

"Rose, are you happy?"

She looked quickly at him, erect, handsome, a solid foundation of society. Yet how small he seemed to her! Nothing about him save his physical mass in this moment created in her the impression of size. He was a child.

"No," she answered truthfully, "I am not happy."

"Nor am I. Is there any good in it? Couldn't we combine — and — and make one happy out of two sads?"

Rosalind shook her head slowly.

"Why not, dear? I could give you everything. I could make you happy. There is nothing you could desire that I wouldn't slave to win for you. Everything would be yours."

"Not everything."

"Yes, Rose. Dear —"

"I couldn't give everything to you, Ben."

"Oh! It doesn't matter. Just you — to be with you, hear you, see you — that is what I want. A touch of your hand, a look, the feeling of your arm in mine — I do not ask for more."

"Some day you would."

"No — no. You don't understand, Rose." He spoke with the typical pride of man, the superior sex. "You can't understand the — the — how much I love you."

"I can't, Ben?" Rosalind smiled pathetically. "I can understand perfectly."

"Perhaps you can: I'm sorry. But it should make you understand everything then."

He was close by her now. In the soft light of the room he seemed to loom up beside her tired body in preposterous dimensions.

"Why have you come to-night?"

"Because, dear Rosalind, I am leaving for the South. It's that New Orleans case I told you about. When I learned I should have to go again, I — I rather liked it, but now I don't see how I can go without a word from you. It's too much for me."

"You promised to wait till June first; you named the day."

"I know. I know."

"Now you are continually forgetting. Why do you do so? Do you think it will help you?"

"No. But I can't avoid it, Rose. Think! I am going away for a month, probably more. At the earliest I cannot get back before the last of May. Leave you for a month! It seems a — a devil of a time."

"So you must really go again?" Rosalind asked in a feeble effort to frame some reply.

"How lonely I shall be! Bad enough last trip; think how much worse it will be now. If I only thought I had some — if only you loved me, Rose! Then I could bear it. You will forget me in my absence; other friends will occupy your time and thoughts. And I — thousands of miles away."

"Poor, dear boy!"

She said it softly, touching his arm as she spoke. It was as if the remark, so innocently meant, so sweetly said, had ignited a fuse in his heart. Overwhelmed by her closeness and the gentle touch of her hand, he suddenly flung his arms about her. This time Rosalind did not struggle; quiet, cold, neither willing nor unwilling, limp against his body, she endured the mightiness of his embrace.

"Say it again, Rose! Oh, say it again! Those words are sweet. God knows I need some sweetness. Can't you love me, Rose? Won't you try? Think what it means! Where can you find another to adore you as I do? You are my world, dearest; I'd chuck up everything for you. Come, Rose! Speak to me! You don't try to get away this time? You could not escape. It is better for you always to stay like this, I know. Am I cruel? I don't think I am. Will you let me kiss you, Rose? One kiss? Before I go for a long time?"

He would have kissed her whether she willed or not, for resistance was impossible, when of a sudden the noise of some one in the hall caught his ear. Freeing her, he turned quickly, breathless and ashamed; there was no one there. Swept by the tempest, Rosalind sank dispiritedly into a chair. She felt neither great indignation nor sorrow. We are all of us human: even in the midst of this passionate embrace she had been able to think of nothing but her own woe. In her passivity lay the sign of defeat. Had Eric loved her, no struggle she could have made would have been omitted. Now it did not matter.

"Will you say — good-bye, Rosalind?"

She roused herself with an effort.

"Why not? Good-bye, Ben!"

"You understand. I — I couldn't help it —"

"I forgive you."

"Good-bye, dearest Rose. Try — try to — don't forget June first! Good-bye!"

Long after he had left the room, Rosalind sat

quiet in her chair by the dying fire, thinking of nothing in particular. Her brain was dulled. Images of thought flitted like shadows through her mind, but they were meaningless, whirling, distorted. Chaos was come again.

Finally she arose and went into the other room. The sorrow of her disillusionment robbing from her the tenor of years, she was like a little child, wide-eyed and gentle in its early grief.

" Good-night, Mamma."

" Why, where's Eric? " Mrs. Copley looked up from her embroidery with surprise.

" Eric? " Rosalind repeated vaguely as if she did not understand.

" Haven't you seen him? He came about an hour ago." Mrs. Copley bent her lovely head to examine the infinitesimal emerald watch pendant about her neck. " He seemed so particular about seeing you that I sent him to the music-room."

" You mean that — that he was here this evening? "

" Yes. A little before Benjamin came to say good-night to us. We thought he was there with you all this time. Haven't you seen him? "

Rosalind shook her head, but she was not thinking of her mother's question. With bitter faithfulness she recalled the picture of herself in Benjamin's arms, the sound without the door, and her sudden release. The shaking of her head was a pathetic recognition in her own mind that at last was come the culminating misfortune.

CHAPTER XVIII

A SHORT CHAPTER BUT AN IMPORTANT ONE

"ERIC, go to my desk."
In obedience to Mr. Singleton Singleton's wish the young man moved from his side.
"The drawer on the left. . . . Bring it here." The invalid's eyes followed with a tender regard the movements of this companion who was doing so much to make bearable his dull watch in the store-house of years. Lifting from the drawer a pearl-circled miniature, he spoke again.

"Look, Eric. Your mother."

The young man took in his hand the little picture and, carrying it to the window, gazed at it long and steadfastly. The wound of his mother's death was still unhealed. Again those images which cluster round the child's love winged in unending sequence through his mind; again the realisation that she was a soul in bliss caused his throat to tighten.

"When I die, that shall be yours. She gave it to me; you will treasure it."

"I thank you, sir," said Eric mechanically, like one whose mind voyages in unknown spheres. His eyes rested darkly on the shining jewels, yet seemed not to see them.

"Did she ever speak of me?" asked the old man.

"Sometimes to me, Godfather." (He had fallen into the way of calling the invalid by that name.) "More often when I was a little child and — just lately. She thought so much of you. How it would please her to know your kindness to me and my happiness here!" The sunlight, streaming in through the window, made shadows on Eric's down-turned face. "She does know, I am sure. I feel her sometimes . . . close beside me."

The invalid stretched out his thin arm. The white hand, reaching the square of light which fell through the window, trembled slowly.

"I loved her, Eric."

"Tell me, Godfather." The young man's voice was more than tender; some thrill of kinship haunted it.

"No. It's gone. . . . She was married and I — young, at the Beaux Arts. . . . Like you." He smiled wanly.

"I had not known that — that she was married to father then."

"Yes. He was away much, singing."

"He always was. Poor mother! She never saw much of him. I scarcely knew him when I was little. Then the glamour of the thing was a source of pride; but now that mother's gone" (he paused before continuing) "I wish I'd had a more human father. I am — almost alone. . . . Mother and I were such comrades."

"My dear boy!" In the invalid's tones sounded a deep affection. As he bent his eyes on Eric's fine features, his own youth rang back across the years like the faint echoing of a far distant sound.

"Godfather, were they happy together?" The old man's hand moved across the arm of his ottoman. "You must have known."

"Why?"

"I scarcely know. Father always seemed intensely devoted and mother — mother loved him, too. Not as much as he loved her, I think. Somehow, though . . . I scarcely know what I mean, but there seemed something missing in their life. Yet I could not say what it was. I suppose it was father's career which kept him apart so much."

Mr. Singleton Singleton did not make any remark.

"Eric," he said at length. "Don't make your life like mine . . . ruined."

"But you couldn't help your sickness, sir."

"Not that. . . . Loneliness, Eric. Loneliness. At night — by day." There was a longer pause. With the painful introspection of all invalids the old man was making a sad summation of his life; his companion waited, wordless when words were of no avail. Mr. Singleton broke the silence first. "Love some one, boy; keep that some one."

The young man gazed over the graded housetops to where the Basin dazzled.

"I did love some one, sir," he answered slowly. "But I think I found out in time. I thought she loved me, too. She had been more my ideal of womanhood than any one I had ever seen — except my mother. But just before I — I lost myself, I found out by chance that some one else. . . . You see, I happened to see her in his arms." Eric shook his head with a sad smile at the world outside, a smile which seemed to dismiss an infinite amount of potential beauty from life. "The memory is very fresh — now."

"My dream always was . . . you and Rosalind," innocently volunteered Mr. Singleton Singleton.

Eric wheeled about, his face alive with swift surprise.

" Rosalind! "

The old man nodded.

" Why! It — it was Rosalind I —"

He broke off in amazement.

" You — you — mean? " The old man moved on the sofa eagerly.

" I had begun to love Rose; I was on the verge of great happiness; and then — then — I found her, as I said, in another man's arms! So I've had to give it up. . . . She does not love me. Why should she? She will marry some Boston man, some fine, noble, stup — but never mind! . . . Yet, Godfather, she really seemed to love me. I —"

" She — she — she —"

Mr. Singleton Singleton half rose in his chair, his hand outstretched, the eagerness for the perfection of his ideal starting in his eyes. Suddenly the words murmured, turned into unrelated sounds upon his pale lips. His dull eyes dilated; he had become in an instant deathly white. He wavered uncertainly on his feet, then dropped to the floor with a gulping sound and sprawled there, voiceless, motionless, senseless. The long dreaded stroke had come.

With a horrified cry Eric leaped to his side. Exerting his strength to the utmost, he dragged the stilled body to the ottoman, noting that the pulse still kept up an uncertain beating. In answer to his furious pressure of the bell the servants streamed upstairs and stood in helpless consternation, while he, overwhelmed by the suddenness of the catastrophe, remained standing by the invalid, clasping the limp hand. Edouard alone retained his wits. With faithful tears in his eyes he hurried to the telephone, making the necessary calls with so much despatch that as he arose from his chair, Dr. Chick, the nearest physician, was heard knocking at the door.

Dr. Ebenezer Chick had the appearance of a fretful humming bird, and was one of those practitioners who derive their practice from this sole recommendation: their propinquity to the house in a case of emergency. Standing beside the ottoman in a fluster of excitement, he felt of the invalid's pulse and stared helplessly at his watch, as if he hoped to find in its vacuous face the information which no internal agency could furnish him.

"It's very serious," he ventured nervously. "Oh, very! I really think — I mean I scarcely know what to say. This pulse is very bad! Put him to bed! He can't stay like this, you know. Oh! it's very serious, very! There's the nurse, thank Heaven!"

Fluttering to the window, Dr. Chick looked out and shook his head with indecisive weakness. In an agony of doubt Eric followed him.

"Do you think he — he will live?"

Under the supervision of the nurse the invalid was carried from the room to his bed. Only his laboured breathing testified that the air of life still stirred within him.

"I could hardly say. Perhaps; perhaps not. In some cases, yes; in some cases, no. If I gave him a week, he might die to-morrow; if I gave him to-morrow, he might live for a year. It's a touch and go thing, sir."

Dr. Cary's arrival put an end to such torturing insufficiency. As the little surgeon sprang up the stairs, two at a time, a new feeling seemed to walk through the house. At last was come authority, if

not in the malady particular to Mr. Singleton Singleton, most certainly in the highest practice of the art
of medicine.   Followed by Eric and Chick, Dr. Cary
approached the bedside of his old friend.   There
was in his bearing that which struck into the hearts
of his companions confident respect for what he
would say.   In such a moment a great doctor is
figured in the mind as can no other mortal ever be;
he seems a medium between life and death, a translator of a divine message, one about whose head the
pentecostal flames have danced.   Even Dr. Chick,
swollen with the importance of being the associate
of the most famous surgeon in America, hung like
Eric on the newcomer's lips.   After a careful examination of the white, still figure, Dr. Cary addressed them.

" I wouldn't give him a week to live.   It's over
this time . . . Poor Tony! "

Eric, who had been so recently in the presence of
death, stepped back, his heart full of swift-grown
grief.   Was he to lose also this newest and kindest
friend?

" Chick," said Dr. Cary, turning from the bed,
" will you stay by Mr. Singleton from now on?
There's little to be done, but I want you to see to
that little yourself.   Make him as comfortable as
possible.   You have treated parallel cases? "   (Dr.
Chick nodded importantly.)   " Aphasia, you see.
Complete shock.   Paralysis on right side.   Er —
ah — with your permission I will associate Sir
Chadby Leigh in the case with us."   (Dr. Chick almost gasped: the great Leigh, his associate!)   " I
am to meet him in conference this afternoon.   He, if
any one, will know what to do.   How fortunate he

is on this side just now. By the way, Rolland, where's Rosalind? Has she been told?"

Privileged by long service, Edouard answered in his stead. "She was out, sir. She's expected back at any moment."

"Tell her gently, Rolland. You know what he means to her."

Eric nodded.

"I'll call her up again myself," he said, flushing. "The surprise of it all made me forget."

A warm current of sympathy sped through his body. When he saw that the doctors were engaged in earnest discussion, he hurried to the telephone and called the Copleys' house, his heart touched to the quick. Above all things he desired at that moment to make her feel his compassion.

"Yes; who is it?" answered Rosalind, after what seemed an interminable time.

"Eric."

"Oh!" A staccato exclamation came distantly to him, tinged with an indefinable antagonism.

"Are you — coming to the Square to-day?" He fumbled for words, uncertain how to speak.

"No — that is — I —"

"I wondered. You see your — your godfather — he's not — quite well."

"What do you mean? What has happened?" The voice was changed now; the tones sounded painfully expectant.

"Why, Rosalind, he's — he's — we've had to put him to bed and get the doctor. I think you had —"

"Is it very serious? Oh, Eric! How did it happen?"

Without waiting for his reply, Rosalind flung

down the receiver. It did not take her long to reach the Square. As she mounted the stairs, all hope seemed to drop from her. The automobiles of the two doctors, the pale face of the servant who admitted her, the silent nurse, the already increased oppression in the house's atmosphere, made her keenly aware of impending tragedy. At the time she entered his room the invalid had in no way recovered from the shock. Inert, blank in mind, unable to speak, he lay upon his great four-posted bed, unconscious as the coverlet itself of the tears which flowed from Rosalind's eyes. Nor had he mended from the shock when at twilight with bending head she trailed down the stairway.

Eric came forward to meet her.

" Any change? "

" None."

She shook her head. As together they entered the great drawing-room, she found a pathetic comfort in being with Eric in her grief. If he had been bitterly unkind, nevertheless to him she had given her most inspired love. Her godfather had been almost a part of her, the guardian of her youthful secrets, in her young womanhood the greatest bond between herself and Eric. In the moment of this bond's loosening, it was sweet to be with that which it had formerly grappled to her heart.

" You were with him? " she asked at length.

" Yes. We were together in the upstairs library."

" If I had only been here! Now he may never speak again, may never know me any more. And I was not here! "

" It was very unexpected. We were talking together and suddenly — ! "

" How did it happen? What were you talking about ? "

Eric felt a colour surge into his face. The sudden remembrance of the scene, of all that had been said swept across him as he stood halting for words. " Why ! We — we were talking about — you ! "

CHAPTER XIX

THE SUN GOES DOWN IN LOUISBURG SQUARE

SIR CHADBY LEIGH invariably wore a dark blue cutaway with a gardenia in the buttonhole. As a rule his face was red, and his lips were pursed into a magisterial frown which well became a man of his position in the medical world; but whether his face was red or white and whether he frowned or smiled, the gardenia nestled odorously on the lapel of his coat. Only once had the wax-like boutonnière been forgotten: on that day he had been summoned in the same hour to the bedsides of two Princes of the Blood. In such a crisis even an Englishman forgets what is customary.

The morning following Mr. Singleton Singleton's shock there was a conference in the great drawing-room of 8 Louisburg Square. While Sir Chadby stood grandly in a corner by a window, Dr. Cary walked to and fro near him and Dr. Chick gazed at the great man with unqualified approbation.

"It is your definite opinion then that there is no chance?" Dr. Cary asked with the air of a man who is determined to take the reply as final.

The baronet looked thoughtfully at his gardenia. "None," he answered.

Dr. Chick shook his head as if he had suspected this all along and had only waited until now to confirm his impression. "You have seen a worse case, though?" he queried.

226

Sir Chadby coughed impressively.

"Perhaps. Our patient's stroke recalls that of Prince George, whom I had the honour to attend last year. You recall his illness, I have no doubt."

Dr. Ebenezer Chick nervously assented. Though he had never heard of Prince George, it gave him a peculiar thrill of pride to talk with a baronet about the symptoms of a prince.

"How many days do you give him?" asked Dr. Cary, emerging from his meditation.

"Four. Not more than five at the most."

"I am not particularly up in this field, Leigh. He will talk again?"

"Probably. I think, I am almost sure that the aphasia will disappear a little before death. It happens in sixty per cent of the cases. Then, if he regains consciousness, he may speak coherently." Sir Chadby paused to snuff up the sensuous odour of his little flower. "Is there anything further, Cary?"

"I think not."

"Then I must run along. Since I am leaving for Montreal to-night after the conference, I shan't see *him* again." He looked upward significantly. They had moved into the hall and Sir Chadby was putting on his top hat. "By the way, Cary," he asked in an appropriately delicate voice, "to whom shall I send the — er — note?"

"To me."

"Right! I shall see you at the conference."

The door closed behind the baronet and the two doctors returned to the drawing-room.

"A very great man!" exclaimed Dr. Chick. "Dear me, how interesting! Did you hear him refer to Prince George? I've no doubt he's on inti-

mate terms with half the peerage of England.   How
fortunate that he was here! "

" Fortunate? " queried the other coldly..   " I do
not see that he has helped us or could have.   Bah! "
Dr. Cary turned his back on the discomfited practi-
tioner.   " I wanted help, not confirmation.   But
there's nothing to be done: it's all over."

Without looking round again, he quitted the room
and went upstairs; after which Dr. Chick returned to
his little house in Lime Street and told his wife the
first version of a story destined to become famous in
his small circle: namely, how Sir Chadby Leigh,
Bart., had asked his (Ebenezer Chick, M.D.'s) advice about a certain Prince George, whose other titles
medical tact forbade the narrator ever to disclose.

Rosalind had waited in the library upstairs for the
conclusion of the conference.   As the little surgeon
entered the room, the expression in his eyes betrayed the truth.

" Oh, Dr. Cary! "

He gently took her hand in his.

" It has to come, Rosalind.   That's the only way
of thinking about it."

A faintness filled Rosalind's body; she was pale
and dumb before this first great deprivation.

" And is it — must it —"

" Leigh said there was no chance."

" And you? "

" He must know."

She sat down slowly, trying to think out what had
happened, to appreciate what she was to lose.

" Will he — ever know us — again? "

" I think so — and speak, too.   Leigh seemed
sure on that point."

" I am glad," she murmured simply.

Dr. Cary placed his hand kindly on her shoulder.

" I know what you are losing, Rosalind. I was about his oldest friend, I suppose."

After the surgeon had gone, Rosalind sat still in her chair. At first grief is impossible to realise. Though her godfather had been for the last five years an invalid, she had never associated him in her mind with mortality. In the flowering of her womanhood he still remained the dominant figure of earlier days, of the time when from him blessings and presents flowed. The happy impressions of childhood are those which linger longest: that is why in the chill of age we remember our mothers as young and beautiful. As she sat by the window Rosalind sought to make compatible in her mind the pale, rigid figure in the next room and the remembered godfather of her youth. Yet tears did not come. Until the sufferer's breath ceases to fluctuate in his breast, death remains to the anxious watcher as a possible but not a probable occurrence. So strong are the bonds of mortality with us.

With the next days came understanding. Terrible days they were, filled with watching and waiting by day and night, with hoping where there was no possibility of hope, with praying where the negation of the prayer was gone before. There was about the house a stillness which rendered spoken words louder and more pointless than at all other times, and Rosalind and Eric, though continually together now, said but little to each other. At first she had found his presence an embarrassment. Mindful of her shattered hopes, it seemed an added strain to have him by her, tacitly sympathetic. This feeling soon passed away. As the days dragged by, the sole comfort in her hours of ceaseless watching

by the invalid's bed was the presence and accordant
sorrow of Eric.   Together they sat side by side in
the panelled bed-chamber; together they saw the
morning sun swim hotly through the vacant sky; together they watched its softer light, shadowed by
clouds, sweetly glowing in the old Square; together
they experienced the calm sadness of the finished day
and silent saw the stars creep out.   Through the
unending passage of hours the invalid lay motionless.   Sun, moon, stars stirred across the sky and
still he rested in oblivion.   Very rarely Rosalind
went out, but occasionally it was necessary to breathe
air freed from the attendant presence of death.   At
such a time Dr. Cary or her mother or father would
take the place by the window, that when the invalid
awoke for the last time he might not look upon an
unknown face.

To the world outside, the sickness of the old man
was of no interest.   Even the yellow journals
seemed to have forgotten him who in other days had
furnished them with such abundant social copy.
When a figure in society abandons the customary
cane with evening dress or grows sidewhiskers, the
world is accordingly thrilled; but when he dies, he
dies alone.   Only the intimate circle, those who
could remember five years back to the time when
his name had been a Sesame, were solicitous.
Among the latter, his neighbours, the Misses Hepplethwaite sent flowers, and called several times at
29 Commonwealth, but whether because of real
sympathy for their old neighbour or because of that
curiosity which is the inseparable attribute of all
spinsters, Mrs. Copley declared herself at a loss to
decide.

May Day came.   In the afternoon Eric and

Rosalind quitted the house, leaving Mr. Copley by
the window in the invalid's room.   Upon the Square
slept the calm, sapphire glow of afternoon; only to
live in such air was peacefulness.   They wandered
to the Esplanade, where the sunlight burned in golden
bars upon the river's breast.   There a ragged child
offered fragrant mayflowers for sale, hawking the
blossoms timidly among the stream of slow-moving
passers-by.   Struck by her appearance, Eric gener-
ously purchased the whole of her stock, which made
even then but a moderate bouquet.

   " The first flowers of the year," said Rosalind.
" Thank you.   How sweet they smell ! "

   Raising the pink sprays to her face she breathed
in their fragrance.   This was Eric's first gift.   She
stole a glance at him, gazing abstractedly across the
bright river.   How little the thought and the giving stirred him, how much her !   A crowd of pathetic
desires eddied in her heart as she thought of those
dull, sad times to come when memories of her godfather would swarm back and find her alone without
the comfort of Eric's presence.   As she turned impulsively away, she felt assured that the inevitable
accompaniment of her godfather's death would be
her separation from this beloved companion; and
the assurance made her grief intolerable.   But Eric,
however deeply abstracted, observed her turn away.
Attributing the movement to her sorrow for her
godfather, he cast about for some object of interest
with which to divert her attention.   An eight-oared
crew came swinging through the still water towards
them, the paddles gleaming in the sunlight.

   " Look ! " he cried, pointing to the approaching
shell.   " How graceful that is !   Who are they, I
wonder ? "

She turned her eyes to the river again.   They had stopped by the iron railing and were standing where the river slowly lapped about the stone embankment.

" Some Harvard crew, I suppose," she answered listlessly.   In her heart arose a sudden bitterness that such irrelevancies could hold place with Eric.

" Rose."

" Yes? "

" I wish I could — make you think of something else."

Rosalind started.   What had she been thinking of?

" Thank you, Eric.   You can; you always do." She said it far more gratefully and truthfully than he could understand.   A sudden desire to empty her heart took possession of her as she looked up in his face, tender in sympathy.   " Just now you have made me think of something else."

" What? "

Rosalind thrilled with a new courage to speak. The glistening river, the sun-bright air, the soft placidity of the Basin contrasted with the rumble of the haze-veiled city, everything that was beautiful and fair in the midst of the ugly town seemed to tell her that the moment to speak had come.

" I was wondering where — you would go after — after it was all over."

She felt his eyes upon her.

" I have wondered, too," he replied with a reminiscent slowness.   " Back to Paris, I suppose."

" What a long way off that is," said Rosalind wistfully.

" A whole ocean's breadth."

There was a pause, broken by the staccato cries

of the coxswain of the fast receding crew.

"And you will be glad to go back, Eric?"

"Glad because it is to France; sorry because it means leaving you all."

Rosalind looked hard at the dark, turgid water in the shadow at their feet. Whom did he include in that little word?

"I shall come and see you some day in Paris, Eric."

"Do you mean it?"

"We'll be old then." Rosalind's voice was soft. "And we can talk about old times and never care."

"That will never be," said Eric earnestly.

"You mean —"

"I shall always remember these days as something to care very much about."

"And I, too." She glanced at her companion and was filled with a sudden boldness to speak further. "I am so glad you are here now. I have not told you, but — you understand."

"If I could help you — and him — by it, I'd stay here forever."

Rosalind's fingers played excitedly on the railing. If only he might be made to understand! If only he could truly mean these words!

"When you go back — it — it will be —! How shall I get along without you, Eric? It will be quite unbearable!"

She looked wistfully in his face.

"My home seems really here — now. It is good of you to say these things, Rose."

"I mean them," she went on in a low voice. "Our friendship is a great deal of what is worth while to me."

" I shall remember that always. Rose —"

" Miss Rose! Miss Rose! Come back quick, if you please! Mr. Singleton's speaking! "

With a startling suddenness the imminent beauty was dispelled. At the very instant when her desires seemed about to be fulfilled the faithful Edouard, his eyes staring with haste and excitement, burst upon them. No dreams more! No gazing at the shimmering river! With a single motion Rosalind and Eric turned and sped up the Esplanade towards Beacon Hill.

Mr. John Singleton Copley had taken Rosalind's place by the window. Sitting rather uncomfortably in his chair, he now and then cast a glance at the bed across the room. He was not a sentimental man, nor a particularly sensitive one. Perhaps he loved his wife and children considerably more than most rich husbands, but beyond that his affections were hardly profound or far-reaching. Mr. Singleton Singleton and he were second cousins, which of itself in Boston usually meant no more than that all our best people are in some manner connected. But closer ties had bound them. Not only were they the two oldest members of the great Copley family, but Mr. Singleton was his daughter's godfather and had in fact seemed in his younger days almost his own brother.

Mr. Copley was thinking of all this as he sat rather uncomfortably in his chair. He had tried to read at first, but one cannot read at such a time anything but words. Therefore, taking off his glasses very slowly, he resigned himself to thought. He had been fond of his cousin. Mr. Copley remembered the pleasures which they had shared together.

From knickerbockers they had been playmates — at school, at college, in later life; they had been in the same clubs, known the same circle; they had travelled together, lived together — yes, he had been fond of his cousin. He nodded his head a great many times and then, remembering, looked at the bed furtively. The room was utterly quiet: *he* could not notice. Mr. Copley felt suddenly very old. Looking at the pale, rigid figure across the room, it seemed that he himself was probably paler and less supple than he imagined. Death. What happened to people when they died? What would happen to his cousin? What would happen to himself? Mr. Copley stirred uneasily in his chair; up to the present time these questions had not troubled his mind to any great extent. He looked through the window at the warm, swimming sky. Was there anything behind that blue canopy? Then he remembered that it was not a canopy at all, but ever more and more infinite space. Where was God in this blueness? A little bird swooped down in a flutter of wings upon the window ledge outside. As Mr. Copley stared at it, it came into his mind that God loved even the birds and would suffer no harm to them. Then certainly his cousin would be cared for; there was reasoning in that. Mr. Copley did not say prayers; like so many men, his churchgoing was limited to unpleasant winter Sundays. By no means agnostic, he was of the modern type to whom religion is a rod with which to frighten children rather than a staff on which men and women may lean. He had always considered religion illogical — when he did consider it. Yet now he found in it reason which made him feel more at his ease. Still it was not comfortable sitting in that panelled cham-

ber with the inscrutable enigma, death, at hand.
Even the very outside world itself looked different
from the windows of such a room. The clouds
which now and then stole before the sun cast their
big, ruthless shadows over the Square like foreboding messengers; yet when the sun itself shone, it
seemed cruel and hard in contrast with the painfulness in the house.

Mr. Copley's mind drifted in a gradual transition
from death to life, from life to his life, from his
life to what he had done with his life that morning,
from that to his farm, where he had been all day
before coming to town.   There his thoughts rested.
He loved his farm with the pride of a child possessed of a magnificent toy, with the intensity of man
who is too rich to work, yet too refined to do nothing.   He thought of his asparagus and his beets, of
the Angora goats and the thirty-two Jerseys, of the
new hotbeds which he had himself designed.   A
pleasant channel this: let the mind run free!   Let it
wander through the great pine groves and the beanfields and the odorous meadow with the little foals
in it!   Let it traverse all the earthly beauty which
it prized!

In the midst of an apple-orchard, Mr. Copley
suddenly started, his hands gripping the arms of his
chair.   A faint-whispered sound had come to him.
With a scarcely perceptible circle of sweat upon his
brow, he turned uneasily in his chair.

" Jack! "

Again! The room was darker now, and Mr.
Copley, straining his eyes, could see no motion in the
figure on the bed. What was it? He had heard a
voice. Rising softly, he walked to the bedside.
Then he saw that he had not been mistaken; for all

its blue-veined pallor there was life and light in the face of his cousin.

"Tony!" he cried gently. "I'll get the nurse, old man."

"Stop!" The voice, though faint, was deep, with curious, whispering overtones. The lips scarcely moved to form the sound.

Reading in his cousin's eyes a desire, Mr. Copley came close to him and sat in a chair by his pillow.

"Yes, Tony?"

"Jack." With painful slowness, halting, seeking breath to form each syllable, the voice struggled on. "Listen . . . secret . . . you . . . should . . . know . . . E . . . E . . . E-ric . . . is . . . my . . . son."

As the invalid's breathing became thick, the voice ceased. Mr. Copley, who had been listening with his head inclined, sat bolt upright in his chair. His face was red, his eyes wide; on his knees his hands spread out in astonishment.

"S — s — son?" he stuttered.

The invalid breathed the word again. Mr. Copley stared at him with the most profound amazement. Eric Rolland! This handsome young boy whom Rosalind admired!

"You — mean — not Rolland's son?"

"Marie . . . and . . . I."

"Does he know?"

"No . . . one . . . knows . . . except . . . Rolland."

"I see," Mr. Copley said, although he did not see at all. There was a pause, during which the invalid's stertorous breathing quieted somewhat.

"Help him . . . Jack. . . . My son. . . . Where's . . Rose?"

Mr. Copley roused himself.

"I sent her out with Eric to get the air for a moment. They've scarcely stirred from this room in four days."

When Édouard had been despatched to search for them, the invalid closed his eyes, and save for the movements of the nurses, the familiar stillness was renewed. Dumbfounded by what he had heard, Mr. Copley remained sitting in his chair. To a person of his conservative temperament the disclosure was decidedly upsetting; he was nearly shocked. Whatever would his wife say? And what must he do in regard to Rosalind, especially if she really loved Eric and wanted to marry him? Mr. Copley frowned. That would hardly do. He shook his head a great number of times, casting an occasional, dubious glance at the sharp, pinched profile in the bed. This second chair was proving far less comfortable than the first.

Twilight stole into Louisburg Square. A glow of sunshine still lingered on the housetops, but the day was done. Silence brooded in the ragged elms and the old houses; the very air of Heaven itself seemed heavy with quiet.

Inside the panelled chamber of Number 8 a little day was ending, too. About the bed the family grouped in painful helplessness, with eyes looking their sober last upon the sunken face on the pillow. Rosalind held one of the old man's hands; close by her stood Eric. The old eyes were fixed on them, but the voice was stilled. A calmness lay upon the pale lips which defied all earthly tribulation. Then the glow vanished from the housetops and death, with the silent sweep of a great cloud fleeting across the face of Heaven, entered the room and possessed the body of the old man.

Turning, Rosalind left the chamber to be alone. With aimless steps she went to the library, and there at the window stood looking over the Basin stretched out far below, about which the lights of the Esplanade shone like a chaplet of jewels. Her thoughts in dulness, she remained there for a long time without moving. The night was come; it rose up from the earth on all sides until only the zenith of Heaven was bright. Tears trembled in her eyes. She turned from the window and found Eric beside her in the darkness.

CHAPTER XX

SOME LETTERS, AN ENGAGEMENT, AND A TELEGRAM

TIME passed heavily enough for Rosalind during the first weeks after her godfather's death. It was not so much that her grief was unbearable; rather it seemed that she had lost from her life an integral part. In some ways her godfather had been to her more of an institution than a personality. To suffer such a loss is to endure a broad and general sorrow.

The weeks were not lacking in occupation to force her thoughts into other channels. There were numberless letters to be read and answered — gloomy labour, indeed. If it is hard to write a letter of condolence, it is much harder to reply to one. To overdo sympathy is a common fault; to repress exhibiting in reply the wealth of one's sorrow without falling into phrases so worn as to be revolting is incomparably difficult. Two of the letters at least differed from the usual tenor of sympathy. One was written from New Oreans very late at night and sent by quick delivery; it arrived the day after the funeral.

May 3rd.

Dear Rosalind:

I have just heard of your godfather's death. Was it very sudden? I had not known he was worse. You understand how sorry I am. I know well you loved him a very great deal. If there is anything I can do, any way in

240

which I can help you, be sure that it is my sincerest aim in life. I have been at work eleven hours to-day and can scarcely think; to-morrow I shall write to you again. But take my deepest sympathy to-night. Yours, BEN.

Being so very like its author, the letter struck Rosalind's heart. Brief, dry, unaffectionate — yet with what infinite pains conceived! As she pictured him writing it, his great hand enveloping the pen-holder, his brows knit in the struggle between his legal vocabulary and the kind but for him inexpressible sentiments in his heart, there were grateful tears in her eyes.

The other letter, which arrived a week later, bore on its envelope, across which scurried a violet superscription, a New York postmark. Olfactory inspection betrayed a perfume. After turning the letter over curiously for some time, Rosalind suddenly realised that it came from Patricia.

RITZ HOTEL, May twelfth.

Oh, Rosey-Rosey-Rosey, I'm a million times sorry, dearest. Just up from the country, been playing divine polo on the Island, when Florrie told me about your godfather. I hadn't heard before. You aren't still mad with me, Rosey? Old songs are the best.

I don't know what to say and Florrie is calling me to stop. I'm staying with her here. And busy! Darling, I'm in the high speed from morning on; and Florrie's bed hour is something we don't speak about.

Cheer up, Rosey. Look at the sun and the shadows fall behind.

Your old — PATSY.

P.S. There are some exquisite mourning things at Cécile's! Can't I get you some? I love to shop and haven't a cent. If I can do anything for you, write me here. I'm going to stay with Florrie as long as I can before going

to Washington, but she drives me *insensée* within a week.
I wish you could *hear* her dance — actually!! And she says
the most awful things about her friends, too. So long,
darling —   P. C.

With a sad smile twisting her lips Rosalind laid
aside the odorous note. Who but Patricia would
express sympathy so? Who but she so incoherently
mix frankness with hyperbole? Of late Rosalind
had forgotten her old friend; to have her thus
brought to mind was both bitter and amusing.

The Copley family had migrated to the country
at the invalid's death, and there Eric had joined
them. Sherborne in mid-May is not to be withstood. A grave serenity stole into Rosalind's heart,
a sweet calmness which tempered sorrow and made
her in her mourning doubly beautiful. Furthermore her untroubled association with Eric brought
great happiness and comfort. To gallop side by
side along hedged country paths, the turf of which,
untracked by many feet, sprang beneath the speed-
ing hoofs; to walk through the shadows of unde-
ciduous groves, where still the cool, damp air of
night clung undispelled by sunlight about the mossy
trunks of pines; to stand upon the crest of some steep
hill and gaze about the gentle panorama spread below, far fairer in the clear light of the early-risen
sun than in the majestic dazzling of noon — these
comprised the simple and lasting joys of life. At
such times Rosalind's sorrow seemed a cloudy background, and in the absorption of present loveliness
she let a solace wind into her heart. After all,
with Eric by her side, life was hers. The essential
though often unconscious desire of all mortals is not

for some one they can be loved by, but for some one whom they can love.

The day on which Patricia's letter arrived marked another departure of Eric, this time in the train of Mr. Swelfront to a great architectural congress in Philadelphia. The invitation was such a golden opportunity for Eric's advancement that Rosalind bravely swallowed her disappointment and smiled on his departure. In sorrow one is doubly generous to those one really loves.

And so he went away and she was left to ride alone. Often in the days which followed the memory of his voice sang strongly in her heart. She could not pass a certain tree, gnarled with age and battered by the winds, which stood upon the summit of a smooth-browed hill, without remembering how they had sat together on its mossy roots and Eric had told her of his boyhood. She had loved the story. Each small, elfin trick of youth, half laughingly revealed, was dear to her. She conjured up bright pictures of his boyhood friends, feeling a strange jealousy that she had been nothing to him then, unknown and unknowing. They had passed each other in strange lands, dwelt at one time in the same city; they must have walked upon the same street, gone to the same theatre perhaps in those past days of Paris, and yet never knew it. That he had had a life apart from hers seemed fit subject for jealousy. As for these friends of whose love he spoke so brightly, they did not approximate her devotion, she told herself, while she begged to hear more. And by a silver brook that wound slenderly through a meadowland, observed only by the beady eyes of a pale-throated shrew-mouse, he had told her of a Parisian girl, Mélanie, the queen of his youthful heart. At his words she had stopped suddenly, her hand upon his arm. Who was this Mélanie? Was she pretty? Was she of his age? She had laughed in relief to find the haunting name a mere memory. But ever as she wandered by the brooklet's side it murmured " Mélanie, Mélanie " in her ear, as swift Hebrus once lisped out " Eurydice." And then there was an arbour by the house, where in the warm night before his going they had stood together. The moon had moved, but motionless they remained. Shyly Eric had talked of great ambitions, of what he hoped to do. Loving ambition in a man, she gloried to find him so possessed of it. His breath had been upon her cheek, his hand near hers where it fingered a rose-leaf on the trellis; and she had stifled with yearning and felt her heart melt.

The death of Mr. Quincy's old friend brought him back from his refuge in Bermuda for a visit at Sherborne, where as usual he proved to Rosalind a great diversion. Finding himself the chief executor of Mr. Singleton's great estate, he plunged into his duties with his customary zeal and assumption of importance. The buoyant child surviving in his manhood found great gratification in his novel industry. It was his delight to carry sheaves of paper about with him, to lay them down and finger them, to put on his eye-glasses or twiddle them on a chain, and to introduce an occasional " whereas " or " *de minimis non curat lex* " into his polite conversation. The very mention of Messrs. Foolscap, Parrypoint, and Scribble, to whom he referred as " his solicitors," caused him to swell with importance. In short, for a man who had never done any business, he soon learned to adopt to perfection the airs and attributes of the legal profession.

One noon Rosalind strolled slowly up to the house from the gardens which she loved so well, her arms filled with early flowers. A striped awning flaunted over the trim shrubbery on the terrace above her. It was a lazy, lovely day; already the murmuring hush of afternoon dreamed upon the air. Drooping above the old-fashioned house, a huge elm seemed to expand in the pleasant warmth and in its hazy branches fluttered the restless wings of little birds. Under the awning, where Mrs. Copley sat in a white garden chair, were also her brother and husband.

"Why, Uncle Jo-Jo," cried Rosalind, "what's brought you out of town so early to-day?"

"It's happened!" cried her mother with a laugh.

"What?"

"The Governor —"

"You mean?"

"I'm a general now!" replied her uncle simply.

"I don't believe it! Tell me the whole story."

"I'm still rather nervous," began Mr. Quincy. "You see I was at Foolscap's with the will, when a telephone message — ahem! — came for me. It was the Governor's secretary. You can fancy it made quite an impression in the office. Appointment at ten-thirty. Down I went to the State House in a taxicab. Ante-room crowded; nothing to me! In I walk, cynosure of all eyes. The Governor was — ahem! — delightful, reassuring, confidential. We chatted for a few moments on political matters and our views were singularly coincident." Expressing this coincidence with a sweeping gesture, Mr. Quincy blandly proceeded. "He asked me in a few simple words. ' Quincy,' he said, ' will you serve on my Staff?' What could I say? ' Your Excellency,' I replied, ' I will — and with pleasure!' ' You will be a general,' he went on. ' You may have your tailor make your uniform. That's the most important part!' he added — jokingly, of course! We shook hands and I left him. General Joseph Quincy. Rather neat, Rose? I went directly to the Sarcophagus Club. Quite a day's work!"

"Oh! Uncle Jo-Jo, I do congratulate you. Think of being a general! Does the uniform have lots of gold braid? I'm dying to see it!"

"It's coming out on Saturday. We'll try it on then, by Jove!"

On Saturday afternoon the uniform did indeed arrive. To struggle into it Mr. Quincy retired to the upper regions, where by a cunning contrivance involving a cheval glass and a bureau mirror he was enabled to adjust the shining garment to a nicety. Some half an hour later he strutted back to the terrace, smothered in epaulettes and gold cord, every inch a general. Mingled exclamations burst from the family.

"Jo-Jo!"

"You look like the Brazilian Ambassador!"

"Or the carriage-opener at the Opera!" added Mr. Copley.

"Joseph and the coat of many colours!"

"I think I look thin in it," remarked the little man in a voice which courted assent. He set about revolving like a *mannequin*, stretching out his arms so that the family could view him on all sides. Engrossed by these unmilitary antics, all failed to observe the approach of two ladies over the lawn. In the middle of his fourth revolution, Mr. Quincy caught sight of them. With a horrified cry he stopped short, his face a picture of dismay. It was too late to flee: like a true general he must face the guns.

"I hope," ventured Miss Hepplethwaite (for it was she and her sister), "we are not in the way."

"Not at all." Mrs. Copley struggled with a laugh. "Do sit down and have some tea."

"It's Uncle Joseph's new uniform," explained Rosalind to the younger sister. "You've heard?"

"Yes, indeed."

"We came partly in hopes of seeing your brother, Elizabeth, and felicitating him on his honours."

The two sisters favoured the new general, ablaze with embarrassment for once, with congratulatory glances.

"You're very kind, I'm sure," said Mrs. Copley. "Aren't they, Jo-Jo?"

Mr. Quincy assented with deep feeling.

"I like the uniform," said the younger sister, glancing through her lorgnette.

"It might be more chaste," remarked the elder.

Mr. Quincy squirmed under this double inspection.

"Chaste, ma'am?" he fumed. "You talk about me as if I were a ballet girl."

The Misses Hepplethwaite were shocked and rustled in their chairs, but the trend of the conversation was diverted. Relieved of their inquisitorial glances, Mr. Quincy permitted himself to be flattered. After a time he even ventured out in the sunset light to examine the garden with the younger

sister.   Their return was long delayed.   The shadows lengthened, faded, vanished; twilight crept
across the fields and smothered them in darkness.
The ragged outline of trees loomed against the evening sky, a suffused green on the horizon, like light
shining through clear ocean depths, but mounting
to dark sapphire at the zenith.   Just above the tree-
tops sailed the crescent moon in company with the
great, bright evening star, first wanderers in the
celestial darkness.   After the tea things had been
removed, the conversation despite Mrs. Copley's
noble efforts lagged.   The quick-darting flight of
bats across the lower sky marked the inception of
night.   A train whistle hooted in the distance; near
at hand a premature cricket shrilled.   But the general and his companions still lingered in the garden.

" Something must have happened," ventured the
elder sister nervously.

Something had happened, but none of the four
under the awning knew of its nature until after the
Misses Hepplethwaite had been sent home in the
Renault, and Mr. Quincy, still in his uniform, was
smoking with great puffs a very long and very black
cigar.

" Jo-Jo, don't fidget so! " reproved his sister,
as the little man picked up a book for the tenth time
since coffee and laid it aside.   " You've been like
this for hours.   You haven't got anything on your
mind, have you? You haven't committed any
crime?   Look at him, Jack! "

" No crime, Beth, no."

" Well, do behave like a Christian then!   Say
something."

" Why doesn't Rose get married? " asked Mr.
Quincy with sudden irrelevance.

Rosalind bent her eyes over the paper which she was reading as if engrossed in some passage.

"Why doesn't she get married?" Mr. Quincy repeated in a louder voice.

"Is that what you're nervous about?" asked his sister.

"No, but I believe in marriage. It's a good thing! Early and often!"

"You haven't practised that yourself. It's never too late, you know."

"You're right!" Mr. Quincy took an enormous puff at his cigar.

"Well, why don't you do it, Jo-Jo? You're only fifty-five."

"I'm not yet fifty!" responded the general with indignation.

"It doesn't matter. You just get married and stop talking to Rose about it."

"Perhaps I shall," said Mr. Quincy, picking up the book for the eleventh time. "I believe in devotion. None of your love at first sight for me, but love that weathers time and storms. Perhaps I shall get married."

"Nnnnnever!" said his sister with emphasis.

"Perhaps I'm engaged now."

"Tosh, Jo-Jo."

"Very well, I —"

"You weren't engaged yesterday."

"No, but that — ahem! — doesn't signify that I mayn't be — ahem! — to-day!"

Suddenly Mrs. Copley clapped her hands together, her pretty mouth round as an o. On her lips trembled delicious laughter.

"Do you mean, Jo-Jo, that after all you've said about Joan Hepplethwaite you're —"

"I never said anything about her!"

"Uncle Jo-Jo! Not in the garden?"

"In his uniform, too," cried Mr. Copley.

"Oh, Jo-Jo, you poor lamb!" Mrs. Copley ran to her brother, put her arms about his neck and kissed him squarely on the lips. "No sooner a general than captured!"

"What did you say?" asked Mr. Copley.

"Don't be silly!" said Mr. Quincy with some heat. "There, there, Beth! You'd better sit down now! Can't a man get engaged without his whole family biting him?"

"I never thought you'd have the courage, Jo-Jo!"

"I don't believe he did," laughed Mr. Copley. "She did it for him."

"She did not!" expostulated Mr. Quincy. "Nothing of the kind! We were out among the nasturtiums and it — it sort of came over me. It was a lonely life; there's no love in the Sarcophagus Club. Time I settled down."

"I hope you'll be very happy, Uncle Jo-Jo."

"Thank you, Rose, love. One member of the family can speak pleasantly, I'm glad to see." Mr. Quincy looked defiance at his sister. "I shall be very happy, very. I intend to be master in my house. No foolishness. This marriage is built on true love. I have served, like Jacob, seven years for Rachel —"

"Be careful you don't get Leah instead!" broke in Mrs. Copley.

Her brother favoured her with an indignant glance.

"My seven years have passed as so many days; now, having tested my affection, assured of its strength, I fold my wife to my bosom. There has been no haste; I have been firm and have refused to let my heart run off with me. I must admit," said Mr. Quincy modestly, " that Joan needed persuasion and yielded only to the arguments of common sense. I was masterful — one has to be a man with women. But that is all forgotten now, and she has begged me never to remember that she once hesitated to accept me."

Recalling how her uncle had sought to avoid the Misses Hepplethwaites, how he had fled even to Bermuda to escape his prospective bride, and now how he sought to persuade himself that it was he after all who had brought about the match, Rosalind could not refrain from bursting into laughter.

" What's the matter? " asked her uncle suspiciously.

" I was only thinking of Bermuda," innocently answered Rosalind.

" That was a test," replied the general very severely. " Knowing that she was young and impressionable, I thought it might be unfair to ask her without trial. But I could not bear it; I came home and conquered."

Rosalind contented herself with an " Oh! " and went upstairs to dream of her uncle and Miss Hepplethwaite settling down to light housekeeping in the Sarcophagus Club. To their establishment the presence of the future Mrs. Q.'s elder sister added that something more which marital felicity seldom countenances. The tragic conclusion of the dream was a vision of her uncle wandering about the streets of Boston in search of his former masterfulness and wailing out the plaintive cry of Io, " *Eleleu, oh, Eleleu!* "

On the next morning Rosalind received a letter from Eric. It was the first time that any written word had passed between them. With a great sudden warmth in her body she pressed the little envelope to her lips, scanned it eagerly, turned it over, followed the tracery of the ink, examined the postmark, made as much of the innocent paper as if it had been the manual of every gift and virtue in the world. The music of fantastic melodies rose irresistibly in her heart and smothered her. A desire for the free air of Heaven, for some quiet, sunny spot hallowed by silence and far from possible interruption sweeping over her, she hurried from the house. Across the smooth, green lawn she sped, through the trim hedge that marked its confines, into the first pasture, over a moss-grown fence, and so through the second pasture. At the brook she stopped; still it whispered " Mélanie " in a rustling cadence. A lovely spot, but here interruptions might disturb the perfect silence she desired. With a reassuring glance at the letter she traversed the meadow, lying like a garment of soft Oriental stuff in the morning light. So gentle was the sun it seemed to soothe the tired world and make a harmony with Heaven. As she walked slowly along, head erect, heart singing, listening to the airy voices of the wind which syllable a language well understood if but the heart be right, an early bobolink flew up from the grass with his rich, bubbling melody, and she laughed aloud for the joy of the song.

Rosalind penetrated almost to the distant river before her quest was ended. Upon a rise of ground, a kind of knoll, she at length descried the place of places most perfect to her mind. An old sycamore stretched its knotted fingers above her in the sunlight; about its roots the grass was of imperishable green and warm from lying in the early sun. It was on this knoll that a constellation of wild narcissus scattered its delicate perfume to the winds. Quickly mounting the little rise, she seated herself at the foot of the great tree in silent admiration. To see this beauty in a moment so ecstatic was too see a double beauty. From the starry narcissus at her feet to the white, distant spire of a country church the world smiled up at her. Fascinated and tremulous, she deftly opened the letter so as not to injure the envelope, and read eagerly.

May nineteenth.

Dear Rosalind:

You will be glad to know I have had a most interesting time. The Congress, like all congresses, was a magnificent failure, but I have met a great many distinguished men and heard endless speeches. My being a kind of equerry for Mr. Swelfront has spread the opinion that at the least I am a member of the Institut de France. That is delightful. I will tell you all about it when I get back.

Philadelphia is unexciting. It is not as quaint as Boston or as monstrous as New York, but I find the women very pretty. The tinge of southern accent delights me. Yesterday the Congress ended with every one talked out. I went to Havre de Grace for the horse races. I used to visit Longchamps and Auteuil a great deal when I was younger, and once made eight hundred francs. I do not think Americans care for horses any more than the French. In America you go to bet; in France you go to look at the latest fashions.

I am sorry I have not written earlier, but my letters are not good and I have been busy every minute. Did you expect me to return directly after the Congress? I am eager to stay here longer as there is much to see. I shall telegraph when I decide. Here I have discovered Harry Farr, who was at the Beaux Arts with me. Over there he was the laziest boy in the atelier and the gayest on the boulevard. Marriage has changed all that. Now he is only gay at the office. He says that he spends all his time being lazy with the baby. His wife is lovely — Susie Harte, perhaps you know her? It makes me want to get married myself!

I received a letter from my father yesterday. He is at his villa in Cadenabbia and wants to know when I am sailing. I wrote him that I had not made up my mind. Perhaps it will be necessary for him to come over and take me back by force. I have become very much attached to Boston; I feel at home there. I even have that feeling for Beacon Street which all Bostonians entertain, and when you begin to love streets, it's a serious matter! Then you have been so wonderful to me! I have never thanked you; I cannot; but with every bit of my heart I feel your sweetness. It is not easy to come among strangers and so soon find a home. It will be a thousand times harder to leave after having found it. We have been very close, you and I, Rosalind. Since Mr. Singleton's death our friendship has seemed even more intimate. Do you remember our walk along the Esplanade that afternoon? It has lingered in my memory. Some day I hope we may finish that conversation. I trust you are not lonely at Sherborne now. I know you will not be, though, for you have no end of friends to amuse you. I am almost alone here, and I think of you.

I hear bells striking two o'clock. From where I write I can look out across the still city. How bare and quiet it is in the smokeless air! The vast thing seems asleep. *Me voilà bien fatigué; je vous souhaite, Rose, bon soir et rien que des beaux rêves.*

Votre ami —
ERIC.

There was a tear in each of Rosalind's eyes as she slowly laid the letter in her lap; the world had become too beautiful to look upon. She thought that she had never read so sweet, so diverting a letter. To contrast it with Benjamin's was natural; and this made her laugh softly as she pressed the paper to her lips. It was hers, this wonderful letter, hers to be treasured, hers to be re-read in the vastness of night, hers to be a bulwark against future doubts. With an overflowing heart she threw herself back upon the warm grass, so that the narcissuses danced above her golden hair on their slender stems. A while she contemplated the sun through half-closed lids as it flamed behind the branches of the sycamore, mastered by the supreme calmness which one feels after work well done or when one has at last arrived at some long-dreamed-of resting-place. She was ready to cry with Faust to the fleeting moment: *"Verweile doch, du bist so schön!"*

It was hard to quit painting thought-pictures, but at length she arose and slowly made her way back to the house. To leave the shining knoll with its starry-white flowers and vivid green seemed a departure from Paradise. One by one the beauties dropped away. As she stepped into the house, the dust and tedium of the world again were with her.

" A telegram, Miss Rose."

She felt in her heart that it was from Eric, and moved to a window.

> Gone to Washington. Buildings and
> Patricia. Will write.   Eric.

For a moment she did not appreciate the words. Then she remembered that Patricia had written of visiting Washington, and, marvelling at the effront-

ery of the thing, read the telegram again. Hot
anger rushed into her heart and in a swift revul-
sion she flung Eric's letter defiantly into a waste-
basket. Could such a change be possible? She
felt insulted, made sport of; her ecstatic dreams
of the moment before now seemed mockery. The
telegram in a thousand fragments followed the letter. Throwing herself in a chair, she stared moodily at a man in dirty blue dragging a hose across
the lawn; when he tripped in its serpentine coils,
she laughed resentfully. How indifferent and
cross-grained the world had become! The birds
outside the window chattered out of tune and their
notes mixed on the air with sounds of subdued but
cross words. Irritated that another be angry, she
flung her hands to her ears. We are all alike in
our disappointments; since we must vent our spleen
on something, it is as provoking to have those about
us angry as happy. At odds with herself and with
the world, Rosalind pushed aside her chair and
strode away. At the door she paused with cloudy
brow. Then, half indignant at her own weakness,
she returned and bent over the partly-filled waste-
basket.

CHAPTER XXI

CULMINATION

"THAT will finish the business as far as you and Mr. Quincy are concerned. I obtained his final signature yesterday."

Mr. Foolscap was speaking. Shuffling all the papers on his desk together as one shuffles a pack of cards, he glanced over his eyeglasses with a suggestion of relief. The senior member of Foolscap, Parrypoint, and Scribble had a fat face, in colour and texture so much like calfskin that it might have been bound uniform with any of the legal volumes which crammed the deep shelves of his office. With both their stolidity and their conservative colouring, it was a good face behind which to obscure much knowledge and all emotion. Faces are sometimes fortunes. To be Prime Minister of England the Duke of Newcastle was once willing to ape the manners and looks of a stupid fop; but to be the most fashionable and successful lawyer in Boston Mr. Foolscap had only to ape himself. Behind his impenetrable countenance he might evolve the most profound thoughts, yet pass in the eye of the world for a know-nothing.

Mr. Copley and Mr. Quincy had been appointed executors of Mr. Singleton Singleton's will. Knowing that alone they could do nothing and together less, they had agreed that if the estate was ever to be executed Foolscap had better execute it. So execute it Foolscap did, while Mr. Copley, who never on any account dabbled in business, signed one or two necessary papers and his brother-in-law created a great deal of smoke out of his duties, though precious little fire.   In consequence of this Mr. Quincy was continually getting the smoke in his own eyes and in those of every one else concerned. However amusing in the Sarcophagus Club beside a sea-coal blaze, he was not a success by the legal fireside.   Almost   a   breath   of   relief,   therefore, stirred on Mr. Foolscap's lips as he spoke the foregoing words.

"The estate, when everything is finally settled, will be almost two millions, then?"

"More, Mr. Copley, more.   Your daughter has a rare inheritance."

"You say it is all hers, apart from the annuity to Rolland?"

"Absolutely."

Mr. Copley looked absently out of the opened window.   A great deal of money!   The rumble and roar of the city swelled up through the opened windows and broke against the fat calfskin volumes.

"What about illegitimacy?" Mr. Copley asked, his brow suddenly wrinkled.

Mr. Foolscap bumped his knee against the desk.

"Did you —?   Did I —?"

Mr. Copley's red face turned a shade redder. He had not meant to phrase the question in such a way, but it had slipped out of his thought into speech in all its baldness.

"A-hum!"   He arose brusquely from his chair and moved to the window.

"You startled me.   I thought you said — illegitimacy."

" I did."

Silence. As he stood looking down upon the noisy street, Mr. Copley felt uneasy and vaguely dissatisfied with himself: Foolscap never spoke inadvertently.

" Will Mr. Quincy be married soon? " The lawyer broke a silence becoming painfully long; he had no intention of making so valuable a client uncomfortable.

" I dare say. He doesn't know where he is! Perfectly depraved over his clothes and things." Mr. Copley moved to the door. " I think he finds getting married even more diverting than being executor. Fickle, I call it. Good-bye."

Deep in thought, he descended the steps of the law office. His slip of the tongue some minutes before testified to what had been his mind's chief activity since Mr. Singleton Singleton's death. The secret revealed to him at that time had been more than a piece of information; as we have seen, the surprise had been both unpleasant and shocking. Mr. Copley was not a prude by any means. At the Sarcophagus Club any designation rather than that might have been applied — and where, if not at a man's club, is one to learn his true character? It was not so much that he was outraged from the social point of view. Men of his position in the world, with great wealth and no application, long before they are forty lose their sense of social propriety; it turns with their hair. Where the sword thrust home was that this indelicacy had occurred in his own particular circle. Such things ought never to happen in so well regulated a family. His prominent, kindly eyes bulged in his head as he strove to

imagine the colours with which scandalous tongues
might decorate the tale.

And not only this misfortune, but his daughter
had fallen in love, as far as he had been able to ascertain, with the disturbing element himself! The
more Mr. Copley considered the matter, the less
soluble the quandary appeared. It was not a thing
to tell his wife; even if it were his right to repeat
the secret, it would cause her endless worry. If
Rosalind knew, it might destroy her happiness for
ever; as for Eric, it would certainly cast a cloud
over his whole life. Like a kind husband, he had
no desire to disturb his wife; no more did he feel
it his duty to impart to Eric such destructive information, especially since his own father had always kept it from him. For the fiftieth time Mr.
Copley came to the conclusion that there was not a
soul to whom he could unburden his puzzling knowledge. After all, he assured himself, since the dog
was soundly asleep, there could be no reason for
waking him. Eric was committing no crime; if
Rosalind chose to marry him, there was no real
objection to it. He was attractive, sincere, evidently exceedingly clever and talented. What more
could be asked? Mr. Copley's private knowledge
was of the kind that is often employed as a weapon,
but some weapons do as well upon the topmost shelf
as elsewhere. Feeling this to be the case, Mr. Copley shook his head decidedly and permitted a stew-
ard of the Sarcophagus Club to prepare him a cocktail. Parental interference never yet benefited
love.

Like father, like daughter. For every thought
relating to Eric which her father entertained Rosalind had a parallel and many, many more. By day

she read him in the chapters of her heart; he flamed
in sunsets; he scattered across the sky in flying
clouds; and if there were " books in the running
brooks, sermons in stones," there was for her his
spirit in everything. The few and far-off sounds
which break the boundless quiet of the country night
are vague and sad: little wonder that they brought
tears to her eyes as she contrasted the richness of
her love with the poverty of his return. And all
because of Patricia! Hotly Rosalind pressed her
lips together; Patricia was unworthy of him, unworthy to speak to him, and yet he tolerated her,
visited her, liked her — even he! In an ecstasy
of unhappiness she would slip from her bed and
steal down the long hall to the room which had
been his. The moonlight streamed in on the bed,
a square of white softness. Breathless she stood,
almost able to visualise his fine features and dark,
curling hair upon the pillow. And now — ended
and forgotten with him! She passed through the
moonlight to the window, where the clear trilling
of the tree-toads, like vibrations of silver thread,
came to her ear with a fine insistence. In winter
the stars seem to hang upon the trees and the sky
is close, chill, and near; but in May they shimmer,
myriads of them, almost lost in distance. And this
was sad, too.

In the days which followed Eric's letter proved
of some comfort. At times believing it, she warmed
in her heart to beautiful possibilities; at others,
marking a mockery in each line, she tossed it from
her disdainfully. It was but kindness all. Patricia the whole time had been Eric's love; his regard for herself could be interpreted only in terms
of his gratitude to Mr. Singleton. Kindness!

Kindness! Mortifying counterfeit of love — she had come to hate that word!

On the thirtieth of May, Rosalind paid one of her frequent visits to the Square. She went often, for there was much to do, endless reading of dusty papers and the wandering through of an infinity of drawers. To know it all was hers added to the interest and love which she had always felt for the old house. The majesty of summer reigned in the Square, all the still, sweet calmness of full afternoon decorating its shy beauty. Brick is a blank, harsh colour in other places; but on such a day, in such a worldless spot, the red of the houses was but a pleasant glow of light. Yet one could not say that light was anywhere. Long, silent shadows of the housetops and the trees drifted indistinguishably into areas of brightness. The two white statues shone gently at either end of the green like twins of ivory; a placid glow lingered in the hazy tops of the old elms and mirrored in the upper windows of the higher houses; but nowhere was there light and light alone. The soft shadows that become old age lingered in the sun's own shining.

Slowly Rosalind drew near the house. It was a day for slow steps and memory, a day on which no power of will could keep the mind from reverting to the past. There are such days for all of us. Thinking of the first wonder of her love, she half-unconsciously approached the iron fence. Here Eric had come to her, standing in this same spot on a gusty evening in the last of April. He would not come now — that was changed! In the passage of one little month she had understood and lost the mystery of living. To dream of the stress

of love is enevitable; to experience it, divine; to
lose it, ineffably melancholy. There was something
hot in her breast as she touched the iron fence; once
there had been no more than its blackened bars between them. Rosalind struck them with her hand
— one is always dramatic in one's memories.
White clover, faintly tipped with pink, dotted the
grass where she and Eric had sat, and its odour rose
delicately on the afternoon air. As she looked
wistfully in at the blossoms, a cry escaped her lips:
almost at her feet, so close was it growing to the
wrought-iron fence, a four-leafed clover had caught
her eye. Stretching her hand through the bars, she
plucked it and stood awhile silent. There are times
when one can well afford to be superstitious. She
placed the green leaves carefully in her handkerchief and with a sigh entered the house — her house.

As yet she had not recovered from the strange-
ness that had come over the rooms. A house not
lived in is easily recognisable; it is like a man without a religion. Everything may be in perfect order, the rooms magnificent, dusted and swept, filled
with every conceivable comfort, and yet! — there
is a materialism, a deadness about the place which
reveals itself instantly on examination. No attention of servants can dispell this pervadant emptiness. Wandering through the rooms, Rosalind felt
deeply the sentiment which can exist for purely in-
animate things. There were the brocade curtains
in the great drawing-room; framed in their folds,
she had observed Eric at the piano for the first
time. Romney's portrait of " An English Gentleman " catching her attention, she recollected how
her godfather had lifted her as a baby in his arms
to kiss the picture. That had been a favoured ac-

complishment of her childhood; but to this day the worldly eyes of the young swaggerer still fascinated her.   As she turned away, the afternoon light gleamed upon the piano and she went to it.   Finding her book of Chopin's Preludes still opened on the rack, she essayed a few notes, but found the emotion of music too strong to bear.   When soft voices die, music becomes impossibly sad.

Slowly she mounted the stairs and passed to the little library.   A sheaf of letters lay by the window where she had left them the morning before. Seating herself near the table on which they were scattered, she picked up the topmost envelope and took out an old letter written in grey, faded ink from Paris in her godfather's youth.   Half amusedly she marked the filial politeness of past generations; their respect seemed cold and distant. This letter to his mother contained an account of his life in the atelier, of his progress in French, and quaint little sketches of people whom he was meeting.   "Yesterday we drove in a cabriolet to Saint Cloud.   The President was having a fête there.   Joseph introduced me to one of the most beautiful women that I have ever met, a Mme. Rolland.   A vicomtesse in her own right, she lately married the tenor who created the great furore last spring.   Rolland, they say, is very respectable, yet I think she regrets the match already.   The most perfect green eyes and luxuriant black hair.   I am to meet her again at dinner at the de Freycinets' to-night."

Rosalind's eyes had almost drifted over this passage before she appreciated its context.   This was Eric's mother!   She closely scanned the passage again and her blood, mounting to her temples,

throbbed in excitement. The past was alive, opening to her now. Eagerly she finished this letter
and devoured all those bound in the same packet,
feeling that this must be a part of her own life
which had been hidden from her. She read with
the interest of a wide-eyed discoverer. At first the
mentions of Mme. Rolland were voluminous; her
hair, her eyes, her dresses, her bonmots, her sweetness, drives in the park, parties at the Gallifets',
at the Opera, at the Waddingtons', filled the pages.
Yet as the note grew more intense, the reflections
on Marie dwindled. Letters passed in which she
was not mentioned, and there was never more than
a line in the others — a strong, burning line which
made Rosalind thrill with the fierceness of the feeling steeped in it. It was as if a great passion were
being condensed and compressed into an impossibly
small area. " Marie and I spent Sunday at Saint
Cloud again. We walked in the park where Joseph first introduced us. Oh, madam! Saint
Cloud is divine! " . . . " Monsieur Rolland sang
in ' Lucia di Lammermoor ' to-night. His voice is
exquisite and he acts with great elegance; he sings
always to his wife, but sang chiefly to me to-night,
as I sat in the front of her box." . . . " Marie has
been ill. I cannot bear that she suffer." . . .
(And this from the last letter:) " I would you
might meet Marie, dear madam; we speak together
of you."

This was all! The thread was broken here.
Rosalind remembered that Mr. Singleton's father
had fallen suddenly ill, that the son had sped back
to Boston, and, so she understood, had never left
that city again. As the faded envelopes slipped to
the floor, Rosalind was tremulous, almost frightened

before these flowers of the past. Outside the sun with salmon and gold was tinting the haze-blue of the sky, and far over the shining Basin the spires and chimneys of Cambridge gleamed with yellow. What had happened to this romance of her godfather? Why had he never again left Boston? Why had his life been first one of social diversion, full of the eager pursuit of pleasure, and then in his years of illness one of hermitage?

Puzzled, interested, saddened, Rosalind, her chin on her hand, stared across the housetops of the murmuring city. There was a mystery in these letters which evoked all the sympathy and romance of her young heart. The salmon changed to pink in the higher heavens; the gold fled eastward. Dominant and huge, the red orange sun rolled upon the horizon. Time fled, unheeded, unwelcomed, ignored; and in its flight, over the diminùendo of the city's vague hum, chords of music stole to Rosalind's ears. At first the sounds seemed only imaginary creations of harmony; but the strain persisted. Of a sudden she was standing erect, trembling a little. The Seventeenth Prelude of Frédéric Chopin! She almost stumbled in her trepidation. A delicate gloom had stolen through the library, increasing the eerie effect of music in a house where only she could play. For a moment genuine fright conquered her; the gentleness of the touch below befitted ghostly fingers! Stealing from the room, she tiptoed to the banisters, where softly the melody sang upwards. Then from the nuance of the playing she knew it to be Eric. Suddenly faint with surprise, anticipation, hope, she leaned against the wall. A picture stirring at her touch, she clenched her hands and listened. He had not heard. The emotion of the

moment entered into her body and swept it clear of
earthly dust. With glistening eyes and pulsing blood
she stole down the stairs; the supreme moment of
her life was at hand, and before its reign the history
and time of ages fell away and left the world to her
alone.

The last deep monotone of the prelude united
with silence. In the folds of the brocade curtains
Rosalind stared, as long before, towards the piano.
About her the room was darkening, but enough
brightness fell through the window to place the
player in bold relief, to reveal his poise and subtle
carriage at the same time that it denied his features.
The curve and suppleness of his back was marked
by a pencil of light.

" Eric! "

At the sound of her voice, unexpected and unnatural, the figure at the piano sprang to its feet.

" Why, who — Rosalind! "

She came towards him into the area of light.
Her shining eyes gained new beauty as they stared.

" I did not know you were in the house. You
startled me." Smilingly Eric took her hand.

" And you startled me, too."

" Did you just come in? "

" No. I have been upstairs all this afternoon. I
thought it must be a spirit, when you began playing
my prelude — our prelude," she corrected with a
smile.

" I found it open on the rack." His fingers
stirred aimlessly across the white keys. " It made
me think — of you."

Rosalind's heart leaped within her in the greatness
of her desire to speak, but she could find no utterance
for the words which tumbled through her brain. A

chill permeated her body, delicious, sudden, dominant. She turned her head aside and traced with a nervous forefinger the letters of Eric's name upon the piano's cover.

"I came back, Rose."

"Why?" she asked with a sudden courage. "You did not let me know."

"I wanted to surprise you."

"You have, indeed."

"I had no idea that you would be here so late. I came on the chance."

"I have been reading some letters of godfather's. They were — about your mother."

"May I read them, too?"

Rosalind did not answer for a moment.

"Did you know, Eric, that they had loved each other?"

"I guessed."

"These letters are from godfather to his own mother. There are only hints in them; some things you don't speak of to a mother."

Eric murmured a reply. Rosalind had never told her mother of her love for Eric; she had never even intimated it.

"Tell me!" she demanded suddenly. "Was Washington — amusing? Did you like it? What did you do?" She sought to be guileless, but the ugly shadow of Patricia had stolen into her mind and her questions seemed conscious and false. Patricia was the one thing destructive to the quietude of life; with her explained time might run through the roughest day and all would be well. Yet Rosalind could not approach the subject directly, bereft by delicacy of words.

"Let us not talk of cities, now, Rose."

"What, then? Of the people you saw there?"

"I stayed with Patricia's aunt."

Fencing is a dangerous game, yet Rosalind persevered in it.

"Where did you find Patsy? Was she in Philadelphia?" she asked with apparent indifference.

"No; she wrote to me."

"Did you go to Mt. Vernon?"

"I made some sketches of it. It certainly is the most inspiring thing that I have seen in America! I think it as nearly the perfect type as one can find. You Americans must love it. Why, there were a hundred songbirds on the lawn and below us the Potomac gleamed and turned in the sunshine. Beautiful? Every bit of it! I will show you my sketches."

"I shall love to see them." She wondered if Patricia had been with him and had watched him at work. What did Patricia know of the beauty and worth of his drawings? Little, pricking devils goaded her to ask, "Did — Patsy like them?"

Eric's eyes rested on her.

"You seem mightily interested in Patricia," he said softly. "I thought you did not like her."

Rosalind was fairly caught.

"She is an old friend of mine," she murmured.

"Old friends are not always the best, are they?"

She turned her eyes to his face as they stood by the window in the fading light. Surely the double meaning which she found in these words he had not placed there intentionally?

"No, Eric, not always."

"Let's forget about Patricia! There is a happier and more interesting subject to discuss."

"What?" Suddenly she felt a clear, untram-

meled happiness encircle her. In this renunciation
of Patricia, this careless, trifling valuation of her
worth, there was a free release from jealousy.

"Ourselves." She trembled at such a union.
"What have you been doing in my absence, Rose?
How has the time passed?"

"Slowly enough. It has been dull and quiet and
lonely. I did not know that I should miss you so.
Your letter helped cheer me up — thank you for it.
Look! A four-leafed clover! I found it this afternoon — out under the elms."

She showed him the little leaves, nodding towards
the Square.

"It should bring you luck," he said, holding it to
the light.

"I hope it will. That's why I picked it."

"Hasn't Cary come back?"

"Cary? Benjamin? I had forgotten him!"

She sank down on the sofa by the window. Benjamin's name sounded out of tune, discouraging, and
dull in the midst of her nervous happiness, and the
remembrance that in two days she must give her answer to him again showed its Gorgon head. Where
was he? In his last letter he had written of returning Thursday. Perhaps at this very moment he was
in Boston or at Sherborne. She fell into uncomfortable silence.

"He seemed a fine man."

"Yes," assented Rosalind vaguely. Then, half
to herself, half intentioning: "Poor Benjamin!"

While the afterglow of sunset yet brightened the
lower heavens, on high a few pale stars were visible
and the room in which they sat was become almost
wholly dark. Eric stood beside the window, where
still there was light enough to trace the slenderness

Eric stood beside the window . . .

of his body. For a moment his face was turned
from Rosalind; and the dark hair on the top of his
head glinted dully in the window which framed him
before her. When he turned toward her again, his
voice was gentle.

"Do you remember our walk along the Esplanade?"

Rosalind nodded.

"There was a conversation then we never
finished."

"You wrote me —"

"Rosalind, shall you still miss me when I go back
to France? Shall you want me here?"

"Yes, Eric."

"Is there not some one else who —" He broke
off, thinking of the evening when he had seen her in
Benjamin Cary's arms.

"No one."

Eric bent forward.

"Cary?"

Rosalind, too, remembered that sad evening; a
flush mounted to her cheeks, but her eyes did not fall
from his face. She was drinking from the cup of
eternal happiness.

"No, not Ben. No one," she replied in a firm
voice.

"Rosalind — Rose, will you listen while I tell you
something? I came here, a stranger, and saw you
— do you remember the night I caught up the old
woman from before your machine? I do. I met
you; we were always together at first. You seemed
to like me, to want me with you." In divine suspense, Rosalind clutched among the cushions on the
sofa. "I did not feel I had a right to care for you
— and then your godfather told me that he had

wanted you and me to — but I thought you loved some one else! And so I went away and tried to amuse myself. I couldn't, Rose." He had moved to the sofa. His hand was close by hers; he almost touched her dress as he stood, bending to see her eyes. When he spoke again, his voice was softer still, a mere breath trembling in her ear. "I missed you. Why, Rose? Because I loved you. I seemed to find you in everything beautiful and wonderful I saw. When I sat at Mt. Vernon with my sketchbook, I saw you in its loveliness. I thought how you would enjoy it; I drew for you. And what shall I do if I must return to Paris? In a dusty atelier I shall have no hope to find you. All my spirit shall be gone. I have learned from you to do things with a new meaning; your approval is all the value of achievement. I have no one to be alive for in Paris."

His head bowed above her.

"Eric," she murmured.

She could say only this, for her throat was dry. Taking his hand which touched hers warmly on the cushion, she pressed it hard, as if she sought to translate all her love and her desire into this one touch. Of a sudden a magnificent torrent seemed to break upon her. Eric was half-kneeling, his arms flung round her, his face beside hers. His lips brushed her cheek as the words tumbled out, and she felt his hair against her temples, and the warmth of his blood dancing in his face. A mighty thrill invaded all her body; her pulses raced in the nearness of his heart to hers.

"Rose, I love you! I love you! Life and happiness are ours — we'll share them with no one. You do want me, dearest? Oh, my Rose, my Rose!"

He had drawn her to her feet and his arms were about her now, so powerful that Rosalind marvelled at his strength. Together they stood in the deathless moment of embrace, their hearts stirring in tumult and their lips in the darkness meeting in culmination.

CHAPTER XXII

DEAD NARCISSUS

"DINNER is ready, madam."

Mrs. Copley laid down her neatly-folded *Transcript*.

"Has Miss Rose come in?"

"No, madam. Not yet."

"We'll wait a while, Paris. It's only just seven-thirty."

She picked up the paper again, but thought better of it before she had actually begun to read.

"Jack!" she called.

A masculine sound, intended to denote pre-occupation and a great unwillingness to be disturbed, came from the adjoining study, where Mr. Copley perused with devotional solemnity his copy of the *Transcript*.

"Rose is not yet at home, dear."

Another sound.

"I hope nothing's happened. It's not like her to be late, is it?"

To this Mr. Copley vouchsafed no answer. His wife sighed, looked at her wrist watch, and, as she did so, caught a reflection of herself in a neighbouring mirror. For a moment that wooden expression, peculiar to every one when looking into a glass, moulded her features. The inspection was momentary, unintentional, but pleasing; she rather fancied

274

herself in horn spectacles, the large kind with great owlish lenses, the dark frames of which against the white of her hair were engagingly scholastic and added to her beauty a provoking air of erudition. Since the reputation for intellectuality in a society which devotes its time to other matters depends a great deal upon appearances, Mrs. Copley often passed for a modern Mme. de Rambouillet — a resemblance which, from the physical side at least, would have pleased *la grande Arthènice*.

A suggestion of day faded in through the opened windows to combat vaguely the lamplight and lingered with refreshing calm about the subdued greys and silvers of the room. A simple room, for simplicity is the requisite of coolness, and the house was intended for the incipient heat of May and June. Indeed, the simplicity to some seemed studied. There were no paintings; only a few of Turner's water-colours with an occasional Sargent for the sake of balance. The ornaments were on a similar plane of simplicity; two vases of lapis lazuli, filled with tall, shadowy larkspur; a figurine of Mrs. Copley by Prince Troubetzkoy; some Chinese porcelains; nothing, in short, pretentious or arresting. It was a country house, the " Sherborne farm," and at any cost Mrs. Copley sought to preserve its character. To her it seemed that flowers should suffice for decoration and blossoms filled the room: blue larkspur in vases, white rosebuds floating in a great circular dish, and the occasional glow of marigolds defying darkness in the corners. On the air loitered the perfume of heliotrope.

In the centre of this loveliness sat Mrs. Copley, rare, untrammeled, exquisite to the tips of her fingers. In warm weather, when only the family was present, she affected a cerulean blue — scarcely a dress, yet every detail of its apparent incoherence represented the ardour and grace of Parisian design. Embodying all the witchery of feminine apparel, a veil of chiffon fell in soft blue lines from her white shoulders to her golden-slippered feet, while underneath shimmered a silver bodice. About her neck drifted a scarf of hazy pink, like a little cloud at sunrise making the blue sky immortal, and on the taper fingers which for a moment pressed against her hair glowed a great sapphire. It was Fragonard in the twentieth century! Boucher dressed à la mode! Watteau with the evening *Transcript!*

" Jack! "

A cricket chirred insistently outside the window, but Mr. Copley, steeped in editorial wisdom, kept silence.

" Please call up the Square, dear. The telephone is right at your elbow. I can't think where Rose is."

Mr. Copley groaned irritably.

" Please, Jack."

There were sounds of a disgruntled man putting aside what he considered his legitimate field of endeavour for the evening — namely, his paper — and taking up that most useful and most condemned of all instruments, the telephone. In the prolonged and vexing parley with central which followed, Mr. Copley soon lost his temper and Mrs. Copley her interest.

" Well? " she asked, when her husband at length appeared.

" She's at the Square."

" What happened? Machine break? "

Mr. Copley's back was turned and he did not answer.

" My dear Jack, you'll not find any odour in those marigolds; not even if you sniff yourself black in the face. What did she say? "

" Nothing particular. These are fine larkspurs."

" Yes. I picked them this afternoon. She's coming home to-night? "

" Oh, yes. She'll be —"

Begun with pretended conclusiveness, Mr. Copley's sentence did not conclude.

" What's, keeping her, Jack? Do say something! "

" Why, it's — it's Eric."

" Eric? Where did he come from? "

" He's just back, she said. They're coming home together."

Mr. Copley looked hard at his wife.

" Eric Rolland! " she murmured surprisedly. Her pretty mouth was framed to ask a question when Paris with a cough announced dinner.

After the meal Mr. and Mrs. Copley sat together in their restful drawing-room, the one smoking and the other reading. Somehow Mr. Copley's cigar did not draw well and his wife's book failed to hold her attention. When her husband arose to throw his cigar away, Mrs. Copley, looking up for the fiftieth time since dinner, found his eyes were upon her and smiled indulgently.

" Well, Jack? "

They had been happy together — and how difficult it is for the rich, since they have no aspirations, no struggles, no bread to share with one another, to be happy in marriage! To share diversions and luxuries is indeed comfortable, but to share bread is divine. Over caviare there can be no real sympathy or appreciation; with corned beef and cabbage there must be comradeship or nothing. Any day in the year a dinner of herbs makes for love. Yet despite these disadvantages — disadvantages which nevertheless are the universal goal — the marriage of Mr. and Mrs. Copley had been a great success, and her indulgent smile comprised their years of affluent happiness.

"Beth, I have been thinking."

"About Rose?"

"Um." Mr. Copley chose another cigar from a silver box with affectionate care.

"Do you think she loves Eric?"

"I thought — wasn't she fond of Cary?"

Mrs. Copley shook her head. "Not in love, though, Jack. Benjamin is one of those St. Bernard people, don't you know? No girl can adore a St. Bernard: it takes up too much space."

"Don't see it! I thought girls liked the big, red-blooded kind. He was a wonderful athlete — captain of the crew his year. And then he's a good lawyer, I imagine. I'm not saying he's emotional or anything like that."

"You mean like Eric?"

"Well, don't you think Eric is a little —"

"Of course, he is flighty, Jack, especially for America. I didn't take to that sort when I was young, did I?"

Mr. Copley puffed at his cigar with a self-satisfied smile; this one went well.

"Hardly. I used to play the flute, though."

"But I never held it against you." They both laughed. "I tell you what I think, Jack. I think that Rosalind is head over heels this time."

" She never says anything."

" They never do. Nobody else's opinion is of any use at such a time — not even a mother's."

" She sounded over the telephone as if dinner were too material a think to speak of. She said they'd forgotten it — and laughed."

" Really? "

Mr. Copley nodded several times.

" What do you think? "

" Everything," replied his wife with a pretty gesture. " And I don't see but that it will make a very happy marriage. I'm sure Tony would have wanted it. In fact, it's a wonder he didn't speak of it in his will. Did he ever say anything to you about Eric? "

Arising precipitately, Mr. Copley walked to the mantelpiece, where he stood with his back to his wife. Within him his secret whirled about like a dervish. After so many years of absolute confidence, it was hard beyond belief to keep to himself any piece of information.

" Oh, yes. Of course. Some things."

" What, for instance? "

Mr. Copley put his cigar between his lips for an artificial dike.

" He — er —"

After all, she ought to know! She was as much Rosalind's mother as he was her father. If she felt so assured that Rosalind and Eric were in love and meant to marry, it was plainly his duty to inform her of any details concerning the proposed son-in-law of which he was cognisant. Yet he made a last effort to hold the oozing secret back, hoping she would enquire no further.

" Just about Eric's family."

" They were all right, weren't they? What did he say, Jack? I should hate to have Rose marry into a bad inheritance —"

" Not that! "

" Foreigners are so different from us. Of course, Eric has a great deal of American blood in him."

" Indeed he has! "

" His grandmother, you know, was a New York girl. What is the tenor like? Did Tony talk of him? "

" No."

" I don't care particularly to have Rose marry a singer's son." Mrs. Copley pulled the pink scarf about her neck with a relic of primness in her manner. " But then —"

It was too much for flesh and blood to bear! That wicked babbler of Rome spoke true when he wrote, " *Citius flammas mortales ore tenebunt quam secreta tegant.*" The secret fairly sparkled in Mr. Copley's red face.

" Hang it —" (What would she say?) " I've got to tell you, Beth! Rolland isn't Eric's father! "

" What? "

" It's true. Tony told me."

" Who is, then? "

Mr. Copley looked hard at the grey ash on the end of his cigar.

" Tony was," he answered in a disarming voice.

" Jack! "

Mrs. Copley arose from her chair and swept to her husband, the colour mounting to her cheeks in waves.

" Tony? Tony Eric's father? "

" It's true, dear."

" Oh! Jack! " Mrs. Copley's voice was subdued,

shocked, disappointed. " I'm glad I didn't know while he was alive."

There was a pause, during which Mr. Copley drew a pattern on the soft grey carpet with the toe of his slipper and Mrs. Copley watched him.

" And the mother? " she asked at length.

" Madame Rolland."

" Oh! In our family, Jack! "

" I know, dear. Tony told me just before you came, on the day that he died. He left me Eric to look after."

Mrs. Copley was not paying attention; to her the maternal point of view was dominant.

" I do not see how Tony could expect, could desire Rose to marry a — Why! Jack! It's dreadful! How can the boy himself want to marry Rose, if he really loves her, knowing what he is? "

Mr. Copley took her hand in sudden alarm.

" Listen, Beth! He doesn't know! You must understand that! Only Rolland and you and I know. It would ruin Eric's life, if he found out."

" It will ruin Rose's, if he doesn't, won't it? "

" I can't see why. No one shall ever know."

" Oh! the secret is bound to get out. They always do."

" It isn't fair to ruin the boy's life."

" You're standing up for him now, aren't you, Jack? "

" Well, he *is* Tony's son! "

Sitting down on a sofa, Mrs. Copley stretched her arms out on the cushions and nervously plucked at their embroidery.

" Oh! I can't bear it, Jack! Rose is too good, too pure! "

"My dear Beth, you forget that Eric is utterly unconscious —"

"But the stain is there!"

"I think the stain is where you — we wish to put it."

"Oh! You men! You always stand up for one another! Jack, don't you think it's wrong? You don't approve of it?"

"Of course not, dear. But is that the consideration?"

"I'm thinking of Rose."

"So am I. I'm thinking of her happiness. Ever since Tony died I've been wondering, wondering what it was best to do."

"Tell her!"

"No — no." Mr. Copley came and sat beside his wife on the sofa. "How can we? She would have to tell Eric, and then he would feel that he could not marry her."

"That would be best."

"Why, Beth! You like Eric."

"I do — I do. I'm so sorry for the poor boy. But Rose is our daughter! If she marries him, it will be an open countenancing of such behaviour as Tony's. I don't believe in it, Jack. It's rotten — yes, exactly so! — rotten!" Mr. Copley made a deprecatory gesture with his hand. "No — no, Jack! It's all very well to say Tony's in the family, and *nil nisi*, and all that, but I'd as soon — I'd as soon have Rosalind marry a drunkard!"

"Oh, come, dear, you can't mean that!"

Mrs. Copley shook her head firmly. To her sin was inexcusable, though she was neither rigorous nor catholic in her religion. She occupied a pew in Trinity Church, because she believed that it set a good example, and she abhorred revivalists, because they were insulting; but none of her concepts were built upon reason or faith. Faultlessly pure in her own morals, she could not condone the sins of another. From her birth she had lived in a high-walled garden, shielded from east winds, basking in untroubled sunshine; for those people out upon the moor in the full blast of temptation she had neither cognisance nor understanding. She could not pardon: to pardon one first must sin.

"I think you are wrong, Beth." Mr. Copley's brown eyes were prominent with anxiety.

"There are some things, Jack, a woman can decide about better than a man. I will tell Rosalind the truth."

"I could not."

"It is for a mother to do. I will not break her heart, Jack dear — she's a woman."

"And if she still wants him when she knows?"

Mrs. Copley twirled the great sapphire about on her finger.

"I shall at least have done my duty as a mother," she replied.

Morning broadened into Rosalind's bedroom. Elfin rays of sunshine stole across the floor and danced upon her coverlet, patterning its blue with lakes of gold. There was a great calmness in the pretty room which was neither the placid quiet of afternoon nor yet the languishing hush of summer nights, but a cleaner, cooler peacefulness. As Rosalind awoke, and she awoke early from pure happiness of heart, she felt this calmness steeping her nerves in rest. Yet she could not rest. As the memories of the night before fluttered back in a radiant flight,

there was so much else in life that rest had no place
in it.   She ran to the window.   Morning had flushed
and bubbled over the rim of darkness and the clear
notes of birds struck upon the air, robins cheerily
carolling on the lawn, and below her window a blue-
bird, lost in a cloud of syringa blossoms.

It was so early that no one was stirring through
the great house when she flew down the noiseless
stairs and out onto the terrace.   As yet Nature had
not mixed her colours, and they were so bright in
their newness that Rosalind wanted to touch everything surrounding her, as one irresistibly feels of the
flamboyant stuffs in a vagrant pedlar's bag.   The desire for action, the zeal for running and singing,
caught hold upon her.   But where should she run?
In a comprehensive glance her eyes fell upon Eric's
opened window.   What was he thinking of?   Did
he dream?   Did he sleep calmly and sweetly, as we
ever picture the sleep of those we love?   In the
plenitude of her happiness she threw a great, impulsive kiss towards the window, and as she did so,
somehow the thought of his letter came to her.
That was it!   She would run to the spot where she
had read his first letter; she would undertake an
early pilgrimage and bring back to him a handful of
the wild narcissus which had made the knoll so
bright.   In a moment she was off with the sun full
on her face and her long shadow dancing behind.

How easy life was at last!   Her road stretched
out now to the crack of the doom, clean and inviting,
a fair road, a free road, a road for walking or
dancing or resting or running, a road bright unto its
very end, a road which she and Eric must always
march — together.   There was indeed fear on the
road, but she was protected; there was sorrow, but

she had one with whom to share it; there was disappointment, but there was courage, too. Together how brave and fearless they would be, how strong in union, how sympathetic in understanding! The world before them was a world to love, to conquer, to create!

Past the tinkling brook she sped, nor listened this time to its murmur. That chapter was dry and dusty now, thrown on a top shelf and disregarded, for there were new songs to sing and new miracles to ponder. She thought how Eric had taken her in his arms the night before and how she had trembled at his touch. Unlike her dreams, the scene had been simple; yet as she remembered the feeling of his crisp curls upon her temples she trembled, and stopped. Before her lay the little knoll with its single tree, the tracery of whose gnarled image made dark patterns on the ground. Mounting the gentle rise, she looked expectantly for the star-white blossoms. An exclamation of dismay broke from her lips: the narcissuses lay in withered ugliness upon the green turf, brown and dead! Keenly disappointed, she turned away; the knoll was not so beautiful now. Thinking to take something back to Eric, she plucked a single dusty stalk, then hesitated. No! Unless it were the best and loveliest, she would not countenance it, she would take nothing back; and the pretty story which she might have made for his delight died before its birth. With downturned face she retraced her steps. Shorter and blacker, before her streamed her shadow.

Eric was not visible when she re-entered the house. Vaguely uneasy, she ran through the rooms. How calmly men take love! With a thrilling heart, she ascended the stairs and tiptoed down the hall-

way to pause outside of Eric's closed door. He
was singing! She caught the sound of his voice,
lightly rising and falling in an old French air:

> *" Ah! je voudrais être mouche,*
> *Pour voleter dessus la bouche,*
> *Sur les cheveux et sur le sein*
> *De ma dame belle et rebelle;*
> *Je picquerais cette cruelle*
> *A peine d'y mourir soudain! "*

The blood seemed alive in her body. This *dame
belle et rebelle* was herself; he was singing of her!
With her ear pressed close to the door, she listened —

> *" A peine d'y mourir soudain! "*

The spirit rose within her like sap in a budding
tree. This voice was hers! It would sing to her
in chill winter nights and in the slumbering noons
of summer, in the rain-soaked fields of April and
in the flaming orchards of October; it would sing
pain out of life and sweetness in, but whatever it
sang, it would sing always to her. Choked with
tenderness, she touched for a moment her lips to
the door — then, unobserved in her worship, fled
down the hallway.

The morning papers were in the drawing-room.
Picking up the *Herald*, Rosalind moved to a sofa
by a window and sat down where the sunlight played
in the gold of her hair. From an alabaster bowl
beside her hand arose the odour of heliotropes, delicate and sensuous. She glanced across the headlines — a murder, a bank cashier missing, a double
victory for the Boston Americans, a train wreck —
and smiled at her inability to comprehend what was

before her. The knowledge that Eric was coming, that his foot might even at this very moment be on the stair, destroyed all interest in past events. This was not her world! Her world lay in the nervous expectation of her heart. Skimming over the page, she acquired none of it, and was about to lay it aside when a name caught her eye. Her fingers were suddenly numb and she felt the colour stream from her face. What was she reading? There! Under the wreck headlines! From the list of those " Probably Fatally Injured " stared up at her: " Benjamin Cary, Boston lawyer, aged 28; residence with Dr. Cary at 244 Beacon Street! "

She clapped her hands to her head. It could not be! Benjamin? She read the paragraph again and again, the awful story jumbling before her eyes. The reporter had spared no words in his description; every adjective that could harrow the heart was impressed, doubly and trebly fulfilling its horrible service. For an unknown cause the flying cars had jumped the rails in the subterranean part of the Back Bay station, creating a veritable carnage. In a moment that which had been a swift-moving train had become a flaming scrap-heap of twisted steel and splintered wood. Rosalind's blood ran sick as she grasped the details. On the second page she found definite news of Benjamin. " Mr. Benjamin Cary of 244 Beacon Street, City, was returning from a business trip to New Orleans. Not a single person in his car escaped serious injury. He was standing in the vestibule at the time of the crash and his body was found there, somewhat burned. He was totally unconscious. Both legs were broken, one at the hip. It is feared that the spine —"

Rosalind flung herself face down on the sofa, unable to read more, tortured by the picture of the wreck in her inward eye. She knew too well the reason of the return from New Orleans: it had been for her answer. While last evening she had been in Eric's arms, Benjamin had been racked in agony. Where? Where was he? Where had they taken him? She turned back to the account in the paper. " Mr. Cary was rushed to the Longwood Hospital, of which his father, the distinguished specialist —" Oh, God! How cruel she had been! How unmeaningly cruel! Had she but known she would have acted otherwise, surely she would have! Tears came and blotted out her thoughts.

Suddenly she felt arms around her, a face close and cool by her hot cheek, a voice caressing in her ear.

" Darling, what is it? Rose! Blessed Rose, what has happened? Tell me."

It was a sin to feel his gentle hands pressing about her and not to resist. She knew that he was kneeling by the sofa, and when she lifted her heavy head, she found his face close beside hers, anxious and grieving. It was a sin that he should kiss her wet lips and her blue eyes, misty with tears, but she had no will to prevent him.

" What is it? Please! Do not cry, love."

She looked into his green eyes, green as the summer sea dancing at dawn; they pierced deep with sympathy. Over her pallor came a vivid flush. Could she tell him? What would he say? A moment later she was angry with herself for the thought; there was nothing between them to be kept silent.

" Eric, look!" she whispered, holding out the

newspaper. " Benjamin, poor Benjamin, he's —"

She could not finish; in her mind she saw a little calendar with ANSWER BEN written opposite June first.

" By Jove! What a smash-up! " Eric's eyes were big with surprise and wonder. " Poor Cary! "

He looked at Rosalind quickly. Raising her eyes to his, she matched his gaze. She hoped he would not ask the question which she saw trembling on his lips.

" I'm sorry for him," she heard him say in a dull voice.

He arose and stood stiffly by the sofa.

" Eric," she murmured. " You don't — you don't —? Don't you trust me, Eric? "

He bent over her in a rush of tenderness, staring through her eyes to her heart.

" I must." His voice was rough in his throat. " I do."

" Trust me for a day, dearest. I cannot explain to you now. I must see Benjamin, but — but — oh! Trust me, Eric! I love you so much."

She caught his hand and pressed it tight between hers. As they stood in the sunshine, gazing deeply into each other's eyes, the scent of heliotrope drifted about them.

Some three hours later Rosalind stepped from her automobile at the Chief's entrance of the Longwood Hospital. The day had become close and hot. In the dazzling of the sun the roses which she carried in her arms withered and hung their heads.

The Chief was alone in his immaculate office. As he came forward to greet her, Rosalind noticed that there was much pain in his face and that his eyes shadowed a surpassing weariness. She tried to say something.

"Doctor, I . . ."

Suddenly she wished she had not come. It flashed through her brain that Dr. Cary felt that his grief was also hers, that she loved his son, that she had come almost as Benjamin's fiancée. When he took her in his arms and kissed her naturally and simply, Rosalind withered like the roses in the hot sunlight. His son she had not loved, did not love, never could love; to-morrow she must refuse to marry him. A horror for the falseness of her position possessing her, she sank down silently on the horsehair sofa, uneasy, ashamed, abashed.

"I am glad you have come," the doctor was saying kindly. "He has spoken your name continuously since the accident."

"My name?" she repeated faintly.

"He has been delirious, of course."

"Does he — does he suffer terribly, Dr. Cary?"

"He is still but half-conscious. He will suffer —" The surgeon bravely shrugged his shoulders. Rosalind could feel that he was struggling to keep his composure, that the struggle was a great one, and she dared not look up. Before such unhappiness she was small and mean.

When Dr. Cary spoke again, his voice was calmer.

"His work in New Orleans was not finished."

"No?"

Rosalind's head bowed pathetically. Then it had all been her fault! Did Dr. Cary know? Did he blame her?

"He wrote me in his last letter that he was returning only for a day. He said that he had an engagement on June first that it was necessary to keep. Poor boy! His letter is still on my desk."

An engagement on June first that it was necessary to keep! Rosalind shivered. To-morrow she must keep that engagement, too. How? As her thoughts whirled in a chaos of past memories an inward voice cried out revolt. It was unfair! She could not jeopardise her own life! It would not be just to give herself to Benjamin.

"And now, Rosalind, now!" The doctor's voice was strained in his throat. "If he does not die, he never can be of use again. Both legs are broken, and he is paralysed, always will be paralysed. My son will always be a cripple. . . . Think of his health and strength, too. God! It's cruel! It's damned cruel!" Rosalind felt tears swimming in her eyes, and would have liked to speak. "Only his mind is left. As soon as he comes from his delirium that will be clear, but his suffering —"

The doctor broke off blankly.

"Do you want me to see him?" she asked faintly.

"Will you?" The voice for a moment seemed brighter, and she thrilled happily. "It will help."

With the flowers still held to her breast she quitted the room with the doctor and they hurried through the silent corridors to the private ward. As they approached the nurses' desk, the figures about it arose.

"He's half-conscious, sir," whispered the head nurse in reply to Dr. Cary's question.

Motioning to Rosalind to wait outside, the surgeon entered his son's room. She looked about vaguely, stunned by the ironical complexity of the situation. Benjamin occupied the last room of the

ward; through the partly opened door she could
see that it was darkened. She wondered how the
air was kept so cool. At the nurses' desk a system
of flashing lights had supplanted the more noisy
bells. It seemed a good system; but what if the
nurses went to sleep? Would the colour awaken
them?

A touch on her arm startled her. Dr. Cary was
making a sign in the doorway. Straining her courage to the utmost, she followed him into the room,
the cool air of which was impregnated with the
odour of antiseptics. A fan whirred wearily in a
corner, ceaselessly moving from one side of its
standard to the other. After the light of the hall
it was impossible to see in the shuttered darkness.
As she moved nearer the bed, a beam of sunshine
falling through the blinds made a warm white line
on her black dress.

The first full view of Benjamin startled her.
Strapped to the bed on his back and swathed in
bandages, he appeared in the half-light enormous.
And then his face! As she gazed on the strong,
clean features twisted in agony, on the working
mouth, and on the tortured brow, the roses fell
from her arms. In that moment her sense of duty
broke its bonds and transfigured her; in that moment she rose to a nobler life, higher than self and
selfish interest. Mercy struggled on her lips; chivalry purified her heart.

"Benjamin!" she murmured.

Bending over the bandaged figure, she softly kissed
its lips.

CHAPTER XXIII

A DECISION TO MAKE ·

LIKE an invisible blanket, heat oppressed the city. From the housetops to the baking earth it deadened the sweet air of Heaven till the city panted in the sultry atmosphere. A billow of suffocation rolled in through the opened windows of the drawing room of 8 Louisburg Square and broke upon the furniture into myriad lesser waves which clung and eddied about the brocade curtains. Foreign voices filled the streets outside. From a window Rosalind could make out shadowy figures, swarmed from the steaming North End in search of air. Flung down at random, these figures sprawled upon the green or leaned against the iron fence, their white shirts barred by its black palings. There was no air for them and they protested in a high, insistent monotone; not for warmth had they sought America. In the hot lamplight the Square had a garish look.

Mrs. Copley sat fanning herself. Magnified by the heat, the voices outside poured through the window in an irritating drone.

" If they would only keep quiet! " she remarked for the tenth time. But neither Rosalind nor Eric observed that she had spoken.

Apart from the physical discomfort caused by the breathless heat, Mrs. Copley was dissatisfied in her

293

mind. In the morning she had put on her cap of virtue; she had determined to speak to Rosalind as a mother should speak to a daughter, to tell the truth about Eric, to give, in short, advice and guidance. This elucidation, a duty both to Rosalind and to the world, the news of Benjamin's accident and the hurried dash to town had postponed from hour to hour, and her maternal wisdom still lay heavily upon a wearied brain. Few parental ailments are as painful as an attack of dyspeptic virtue — and the day long there had been no relief. Since Rosalind's return from the hospital the time had passed in preoccupied silence, with only an occasional message from Dr. Cary to break the sultry monotony. Alternately the news was good and bad, as Benjamin gained or lost advantage in his close and terrible struggle with death.

Bells throughout the city struck nine o'clock. The sound reverberated as if mountainous balls of lead were being rolled on the heavy air. Dropping a magazine which he had been making a feeble pretence to read, Eric stood up and would have liked to stretch.

" Do you want to go out, Rose? " he asked.

" I imagine it is worse out of doors than here," interposed Mrs. Copley.

" It's not possible." There was a shade of petulance in Rosalind's voice. She wished that she and Eric might be alone. Had he felt the consecration of this room? But one little day past she had been in his arms in the very spot where now she stood.

" It's worth trying," Eric persisted.

Rosalind looked gratefully towards him.

" Thanks, Eric, but I can't. Dr. Cary said he'd

call me up himself at nine. I must stay." She
sank into a chair. "And I'm so tired; it seems as if
my head would split."

"I'm sorry, dear."

His voice was but a whisper on the air, audible
to her alone. As it sank into her heart, she forgot
Benjamin and dwelt through Eric's thoughtfulness
and love in a different world. But almost in the
same moment her self-pity seemed mean and base,
and she hated herself.

A bell buzzed distantly in the house.

"That's Dr. Cary."

Rosalind moved to the door.

"You're coming back, dear?" asked Mrs. Copley. She must speak to-night.

But Rosalind was gone. The telephone was in a
dark embrasure at the end of the hall, where the
heat was packed tight, layer on layer of it, deadened
there from morning. For a moment Rosalind was
dizzy, and she found sweat upon her lips as she put
them to the mouth-piece.

"Rosalind?"

"Yes, Dr. Cary?"

"Both legs are set and he is more comfortable.
He has just come out of the ether."

"I am so glad!" Rosalind murmured.

"I was with him as he — I heard a great many
things, Rosalind."

Though faded with weariness, the doctor's voice
was very kind. The receiver trembled in her hand,
and her voice was so unsteady that she dared not
entrust more than a monosyllable to it.

"Yes?"

"I know now what engagement he had to keep.
Poor girl! I am sorry for you!"

He was sorry for her! She leaned against the warm wall.

"Doctor . . ."

"I have always been very — well, never mind! You will come to-morrow morning?"

"What time?" she managed to articulate.

"Early. Ten o'clock. He expects you to come; it means — well, everything!"

Rosalind shut her eyes tight.

"Doctor!" Her voice was small and distant. "Will he — live? Is it —?"

A moment's pause gave her strength.

"I will tell you the truth, Rosalind, because it is well for you to know. We cannot be definite yet. With God's help, yes. I think so. Oh, God! I think so!" His voice rang in momentary despair. "You can help, Rosalind."

She said something — she hoped so, she wished so, she would try to help, she would do her best. The words were not hers.

"Then good-night. To-morrow morning at about ten."

"Ten," she echoed. "Good-night."

He had rung off. As she groped for the table to replace the telephone, a step sounded in the hall-way. She fumbled for her handkerchief with a hand which felt weak and numb, and wiped her forehead and lips.

"Well?" asked a low voice. Eric was beside her in the darkness.

"They do not know. He — he may live."

She felt Eric's fists clench at his side.

"Don't, Eric."

The oppressiveness of the embrasure weighing upon her, she placed her hand on his arm for support. Her brain whirled with the strain and heat of the day; she wanted to break down, to weep, and to be comforted, but the thought of Benjamin reigned above her desire. She must not weaken; she must be firm and clear in her consideration.

" I must go," she said in a breathless voice. " I am exhausted, Eric; I must go."

" Will you leave me like this? "

She felt that she was hurting him, but did not dare trust herself in speech. To preserve a shred of equilibrium it was necessary to quit Eric, to be alone at once. As she took a step from the embrasure, she was caught up in a silent embrace which made the blood beat fiercely through her body and fading stars dance before her closed eyes. In the sudden tumult of her heart all thought of resistance vanished and she raised her hands to Eric's head, mingling her fingers in the dampness of his curls. As their faces burned together, her dishevelled hair, wet about her temples, caught upon his cheek, and her lips, moving as the lips upon them moved, murmured fragments of the lover's litany. She was without strength or motion, without will or wisdom, a weight clinging to his breast. Something of the oblivion of death drifted between them and the weary world; where they stood it was cool and distant from earthly revolution.

A flaming arrow suddenly burned its path into her brain. After the first unrestrained moment she remembered, and wrenched herself from the stifling lock of Eric's arms. Stumbling down the hallway and up the stairs, she reached her room, where she flung herself upon the bed in abandonment. A fire of self-reproach consumed her, and, deep in the pillows, her face was hot with the kiss to which she

had resigned herself — while Benjamin was rising
from the arms of death because he trusted in her
love.   How weak, how unpardonably miserable she
had been!   In one moment she could talk to Dr.
Cary in sympathy for the suffering of Benjamin,
she could allow him to believe that she loved his
son and would marry him; in another, she had permitted, nay, lived in the embrace of his greatest rival.
It was mean, unchivalric, revolting; it poisoned her
sense of justice.

There was some one in her room.   Though in
her self-castigation she had heard no sound of an
opening door, she underwent that curious sensation
of being looked at.   Without raising her head she
held her breath and was in a moment strangling in
the hot pillow.   Could it be Eric?   She was frightened, and a mixture of desire, anger, and shame at
her own weakness possessed her turbulent mind.
Then a cool hand touched her head.   Like a dying
spurt of water the blood receded through her body;
faster and faster it fled away, leaving her shivering
and weak as after an outburst of childish grief.   It
was her mother's hand.

" My dear Rose, what is it?   Tell me, tell your
old mother, Rose.   Let me help, dearest."

Rosalind felt her mother's lips upon the back of
her neck and her pearls brushing over her shoulders.
The cool hand ruffled her warm hair in an effort to
comfort.

" Is it Benjamin, darling?   He is not worse? "

Ashamed of herself and of the tear-stains on her
face, Rosalind sat up.   She did not look at her
mother, but took her hand gratefully.

" No, Mamma.   He will live."

Mrs. Copley wondered at the bleakness in Rosalind's voice, wondered to find her daughter — so controlled and mature that in many ways she seemed an equal — in a passion of tears.

" Can I help? "

" No, Mamma.   I am tired."

" Little wonder, darling.   It has been a long, hard, hot day.   Go to bed and rest: a sleep will do you good.   Shall I have Edouard bring a fan? "

" No, thank you," she answered dully.   Her mother was kind, but Rosalind wished to be alone and think.   To-morrow was June first, and in this night her life must be planned.

" I think I feel a breeze."   Her mother's hand was silhouetted gracefully against the darkness of the opened window.   " It will surely be cooler."

" Yes."

Mrs. Copley looked uneasily into the outer darkness.   Could she speak of Eric now?   Perhaps the best moment for such a relation was one of stress.

" Rose."

" Yes, Mamma? "   Her head throbbed.   Why could she not be left alone?

" I want to tell you something."

Rosalind's silence made the telling seem to her mother much harder now, and her courage wavered.

" You — you — are listening? "

Rosalind nodded and a braid of her dishevelled hair tumbled down her back.   Raising her arms, she allowed the rest to fall.   It was cooler so.

" Your father and I have talked it over and we have felt it our duty, though it may be an unpleasant one, to tell you what we know."   (What was she saying, Rosalind wondered.   Would she not go away?   It was cruel to talk to her when she was so tired and sad.)   " You know that we have al-

ways wanted you to be happy. We have given you
everything that we thought it best for you to have.
And you have realised it; you have been a dear
daughter, Rosalind. Your father and I are proud
of you, and there is nothing which can make a mother
more happy than to be proud of her children."
(How sententious kind mothers can be! One by
one Rosalind felt her nerves wearing, fraying, snap-
ping.) "What I have to say to you is about Eric."

"Please, Mamma! Please don't!" Rosalind
sprang to her feet, her gold hair shadowing down
her back. There was pleading and weariness in her
voice. "I can't stand any more to-night."

"But —"

"Please! If you love me!" Rosalind cried a
little hysterically. It was too much for her to bear!
She could not, would not listen; she would run out
in the street, but of Eric she would hear nothing.

"Why, Rose!"

Mrs. Copley was alarmed. She regarded her
daughter with the air of one who has just discovered
that an innocent hill, crowned with marigolds and
daisies, is volcanic.

"I'm sorry, Mamma, but I'm unstrung with all the
excitement. To-morrow. Any day; but not now."

She put her arms round her mother's neck and
kissed the lovely face. She was proud of her
mother, worshipped her beauty, admired her tact,
adored her with all her love; but no one could help
her now. She must work out her existence by herself.

"My little girl!"

"Good-night, Mumsie!"

"Good-night."

Listening until she heard her mother enter her

own room, Rosalind shut and locked the door. Then she flung herself on her bed and lay for a long time, supine and still.

Gradually thought formed itself in her mind, almost as it does from the chaos of sensations in the child's brain. For a while she had been unable to think; now the thoughts pieced themselves together, here a little and there a little, marshalling themselves into lines of increasing regularity. As she began to understand more clearly the problem before her, the feeling of exhaustion diminished, and she arose from the bed and switched off the lights. It would be easier to think in the dark. Drawing an armchair to the window, she sat down. Through the cloud-haze no stars were visible and she could see only the nearest lights of the Esplanade, mistily shining as if through a veil.

The problem was clear. It was the happiness of her life which she was to decide, and the judgment must fall to either Eric or Benjamin. The former she loved: the latter she did not. Entering her life suddenly and abruptly, Eric had swept her from her feet and had possessed almost in a day her thoughts and her being. One need not necessarily be a fatalist to feel that a certain person fulfils every requirement, is endowed with every desired attribute, and comprehends the sympathy and worth of living in his life. Love is after all a sensation and not a belief. When a woman feels that a certain man is the incarnation of what in the nights of her maidenhood she has dreamed of, when she feels that " even his stubbornness, his checks and frowns have grace and favour in them," then she is dependent on her heart and not on her brain. So Rosalind had felt; so to her heart of hearts she had talked hyper-

boles of Eric. But she was convinced also that her
love was built upon a rock. Had she not tested
her love by an analysis of reason? In every light
she had found him fair; in every position she had
found him worthy; in every minute she had found
him to be desired above all things. How was he
not then the perfect comrade? Intense and pure
had been her adoration. It had burned in her
heart like a white, hot flame which consumes all
opposition, a white, hot flame which grows and
dances whiter and hotter the more it is fed. Even
now it burned within her as she thought of Eric,
and the decorum of two centuries of calmly proper
ancestors suffered an abeyance of control. Having
given her lips to Eric, was she not his? He possessed her heart, her mind, her soul; the promise
of the insignificant casing of her flesh had lain in
their first kiss. Life without love she could not
contemplate; and Eric was love, and therefore life.

It was difficult to turn from this radiant field to
a thorny path, but what of Benjamin? At first, she
recollected that she had liked him; the unconscious
attraction which all women find in big, healthy men
had stirred her. When the edge of that attraction
was dulled, she had found him only a machine, quite
lacking in voluntary response. His eyes, keen in
business, were shallow in art; the depth of his soul
was readily plumbed. Had not fate struck him
down, he would have succeeded; such men, strong,
iron-willed, dogged, determined, such men always
succeed, but the failure of a Blake or a Chatterton
to some ways of thinking is the better success. Not
that Rosalind thought Eric a Blake or a Chatterton; but she knew that whisperings of genius did

stir within him, for she had heard them when her
lips were close to his and she had seen

> The light that never was on sea or land

gleam in his eyes.

This whisper, this light was not in Benjamin.
Taking him in all, he was a man.   But Rosalind had
wanted a great deal more and had found echoes of
it in Eric.   Call this rhapsodising if you will; Rosalind was still young enough to find much truth to
nature in rhapsody.   About her friendship with
Benjamin she could weave no imaginative halo.
Like himself, it was a question of fact, and she had
long ago been forced to pin herself to a day on which
to define her attitude towards him.   To-morrow
was that day; to-morrow she was to answer yes or
no.   Which should it be?   Her part of woman
cried out against the former.   What! give all her
youth, all her life on earth to a cripple, to the wreck
of a man whom she had never loved?   It could not
be thought on!   Marry a paralytic to be his nurse
through a sad existence, when Eric offered her
health, genius, and love?   A thousand times no!

From thinking on Benjamin her mind reverted to
his father.   It was of no use to be brave while his
sad, tired eyes stared at her, and while she felt his
hands upon her shoulders, his paternal lips upon her
cheek.   If she refused Benjamin, how could she
meet those eyes again?   It was her fault that his
son's life had been shattered, all, all her fault, and
despite the doctor's kindness she knew that he held
her responsible. . Aware of their secret, he was
aware also of Benjamin's sacrifice.

A flicker of indignation flared in her heart.   Sac-

rifice? Benjamin need not have come unless he so
desired; surely she had not wanted him. But he
had come, and there lay the bitter truth. The world
would hold her guilty; it would demand a life for a
life, the promise and beauty of hers for the battered
wreck of his. God! What an exchange! It was
right, but was it fair? Was it fair that she fade
the rose of her youth in striving to soften his pain,
in wheeling him, feeding him, tending him, in sitting
beside him during long winter nights when joy seems
asleep, in bringing him flowers in summer when her
heart lay over the golden horizon, in loving him
as best she could, and, when memories streamed
back to damn her choice, in tolerating his love with
lip-smiles? Sure this was a barren counterpart to
what she would have made of life. Yet, however
barren, it was her duty. Duty is indeed a stern
daughter of the voice of God, an inexorable, unre-
lenting, unkind mockery made for the scientific regulation of life. Yet this time it was synonymous
with chivalry. To marry Benjamin would be in the
highest sense of the word chivalric, would be an act
commensurate with what we like to think is noblest
on this pinfold earth. What if no one ever knew
the greatness of her sacrifice? What if the world
thought she was marrying Benjamin, because she
would allow no injury to come between her and her
love? Ah! well! The world is a small, greasy
spot in comparison with eternity. We are not
placed here by Divine Command to lay attentive ears
to earth and regulate our lives by what we hear, but
to rise above ourselves. Cast before her was an opportunity to fulfil the purpose for which a soul had
entered her body. To neglect it would be sin.

By degrees Rosalind found herself rising to a

loftier pitch, which was not happiness, but which so satisfied her conscience that it left her calm. She thought of Dr. Cary again and of his kindness to her godfather, of how for years his skill had prolonged the invalid's life. Would it be gratitude fair in the eyes of Heaven to break his son's heart, when she had already destroyed the body? Her promise might mean life to Benjamin. Had not that lain under Dr. Cary's words? It made her shudder to think that a human life depended on her will; but as the tremor stirred her body, it strengthened her half-formed determination.

Two paths lay before her, the one insufferably beautiful, the other stern and hard; yet she thought the latter might be easier to tread. Conscience, which of old drove Adam into an abyss of fears, is a terrible thing. How relentlessly would it dog her if she chose Eric! No sweetness on this earth could banish it from her pathway. But chivalry is strong, and it would always be her guide and comforter, however bleak and dull the way, if she gave yes to Benjamin.

CHAPTER XXIV

A DECISION MADE

ROSALIND walked slowly down the hall from her room. Morning had come and with the clean, fresh sunshine a kind of strength. It is never so hard to live in the morning; there is a sense of utter revelation and open-heartedness which simplifies existence. For the time being mortal woes, which cling and brutify with the encircling of night, seem superficial: in the splendour of day's rebirth the personal element must appear small and mean.

So Rosalind went out to meet her lover with a courage that deceived herself. On the way to the stairs she passed her mother's room, and, the remembrance of the night before cutting keen into her dutiful mind, she paused with her finger on her lips and her brow wrinkled. What had it been all about? Something in regard to Eric? Quietly she opened the door and stepped inside.

Mrs. Copley was eating iced grapes. In a cloud of lace and silk, the soft, fluttering nothings of fairy web which summer temperatures demand, she reclined in bed like some beautiful and discontented Pompadour. There is not one woman in a million to-day capable of holding a *petit lever;* the feminine art of being beautiful in bed is lost, lost forever in the swirl of suffrage and golf and bridge. Not so with Mrs. Copley: no art of beauty was lost to her.

306

Upon her silver hair a mist — it was no more than
that — a transparent mist of lace, such as Pease-
blossom might have brought to adorn Titania; her
neck and bosom bare and shaped to the gentle intake
of her breath; the silken white coverlet suggesting
grace beneath; the crystal dish of ice and sea-green
grapes; and over these her hand flitting like a sky-
lark winged from the blue deep.

"Oh, Rose, what a terrible night!" A kiss.
"I am sure I scarcely closed my eyes. Grapes?
They're deliciously cool; I couldn't bear anything
else this morning."

Absently Rosalind chose one from a shining
cluster.

"I thought on my way down, Mamma, I'd — I'm
afraid I wasn't very agreeable last night. I was exhausted. What was it you wanted to say?"

A flush crept into Mrs. Copley's cheeks. In the
preoccupying discomfort of the hot night she had forgotten her yesterday's determination. No morality
is a match for temperature. With a great grape
half way to her curved lips, her soft, white hand
paused.

"It was something I — that is, we, your father
and I — wished you to know a-about Eric."

Rosalind was very still. She sat upon the foot
of her mother's bed, her eyes bent upon the myriad
motes of sunlight flickering on the cracked ice.

"I — we think you ought to know," Mrs. Copley
hurried on to get it over with. "He — he is not
Monsieur Rolland's son."

"Well?" Rosalind's voice was even, undis-
turbed.

"He is . . . he is ille —" (No, she could not
bring herself to use that word to her daughter; from

such contamination, even of speech, Rosalind should
be apart.)   " He is your godfather's son, dear."

She swallowed a grape hastily and choked over it
a little; Rosalind's clear gaze was upon her.

" Uncle Sing-Sing's son?   But he wasn't married, Mamma!"   Busied with a ribbon on her night-
gown, Mrs. Copley did not look up.   She could not.
In the experienced eye of her mind she saw bright
colour flood into her daughter's face as realisation
came; and in that moment regretted her presump-
tuous virtue with all her heart.   " Oh, Mamma,
Mamma, you don't mean — yes, you do.   You mean
— that . . ."   Rosalind   twisted   her   hands   together in a passionate confusion of feeling.   " Eric
doesn't know, Mamma.   I'm sure he does not know.
He never —"

She broke off.   It was on her lips to speak of
his love, to declare her faith that he would not have
sought her heart with this secret untold.

" He has never known," returned Mrs. Copley,
glad to bring some comfort.   A sudden ability to do
her task filled her heart: she laid aside the grapes
and took her daughter's hand.   " Darling, I told
you this because I —" her voice sank very low —" I
did not want you to marry any man without knowing
what might later cause regret."

" You think that I shall marry Eric? " Rosalind
lingered over the question.   " No, Mamma, I cannot.   I am going to meet him now and tell him that I
— I cannot."   Her voice trembled.   Across Mrs.
Copley's face fluttered a shade of relief.   " But you
are wrong in thinking that what you have told me
could ever influence my choice.   What does it matter
who a man is, if you love him?   Birth is all an accident.   If I could, I would marry the man I loved a

dozen times over, no matter what the world thought." Rosalind's heart rose within her like a warrior to battle all mankind for the ideal of her love. So is it ever with strong spirits; their lives are but pawns to hazard for those they cherish. "There is no comfort in this, Mamma; it makes my struggle all the harder. Oh, I should like to marry Eric, to dare Boston, dare every one just to show my love. Such a proof would be worth having, such a proof before the world!"

She had moved to the door and stood there, defiant and pure, eager as Abdiel was of old to do battle against the countless enemies of his ideal and Master.

"Yes, dear. You are right."

Her mother took the crystal salver in her lap again and plucked a grape. It was very comforting to know that Rosalind was after all *not* going to marry this foreigner; the rather headlong words she had just uttered were beside the point.

Mrs. Copley looked up with a bright, engaging smile; but her daughter was no longer in the room.

Eric was standing by the window in the library, waiting. The white curtains fluttered idly beside his hand; save for that, it was very still.

When Rosalind entered the room, he went to her with unaffected sympathy and love to take her in his embrace.

"Wait, Eric. I —"

His arms fell to his side. There was something in her voice and eyes that frightened him.

"Rose, what is it? What has happened? There is something, I know. Since yesterday there has been a change. You asked me to wait and to trust

you. So I have, dearest; so I always shall. But I
am human. . . . When will you tell me what it is? "
"Now."
He found Rosalind's lifted eyes suddenly bright
and brave, and wondered.
"Don't tell me, dearest, unless —"
"I must."
A kind of fatalism rang in Rosalind's voice and
she abhorred the sound. Her reserve was but play-
acting, hateful however necessary; yet for a time
she hesitated to break it. These were the last moments of her happiness; she must be firm and not
waver. What she had so recently learned from her
mother fired her mind, flaming athwart her cool decision of the night before and urging her to marry
Eric in a pre-eminent vindication of her love. Yet
he must never know, she whispered to herself, he
must never know. She must bear his burden for
him.
"Eric! " she burst forth. "I will tell you now.
Promise that you will listen."
As he nodded, the sunlight danced upon the top
of his head and a shadow streaked across his face.
"It's about Benjamin. He loved me. You
know what sort he is, Eric, determined and insistent.
He asked me last March and wouldn't take no,
though I told him I didn't love him. I liked him
well enough, and to save his feelings I said I'd try to
love him. Weeks ago we agreed on a day when I
should give an answer, a — a — well, tell him the
result of my trying. To-day is that day — June
first."
Her nervous fingers moved a button of the sofa
on which they sat in endless revolution; her eyes,
which she dared not lift to Eric's face, fell upon his

long-fingered hand, resting on his knee in the sunlight.

"I did try, Eric, until you came. Then it was no
use. I — I loved you always, from the very first,
and it has been rare and sweet, dearest." The feeling of tears was in her eyes and she sought to hold
them back. "Benjamin never quite understood my
heart. He could not. He thought with the assurance of such men that it would all come out right in
the end, that you were only a passing fancy. His
letters from New Orleans showed me that he did not
understand. I tried to let him know. I tried to let
him down gently, but it only made things worse.
Oh! it was hateful! If I had to say no, I should
have done it at once. But I put it off; I was a coward; and then, I was in love." She smiled wistfully. "Benjamin went to New Orleans, you know,
on business. He hoped to finish by June first, but he
didn't and left in the middle of things to come back
for my answer. Dr. Cary told me that. And then
— then the accident."

"But —" Eric murmured. He felt a great stillness in his heart.

"Please, Eric!" she pleaded. "Ben came back
because he expected I was going to say yes. He was
sure of it. If he had only known my mind, there
never would have been this accident. It's my fault,
you see. He was justified in thinking that I would
say yes. It was natural; why not? Yesterday,
when I went to the hospital, Dr. Cary took me in his
arms, and last night over the telephone —" Rosalind broke off, her voice drying in her throat. "I
went into Ben's room yesterday, Eric. They say he
is wrecked, paralysed, crippled for life, ruined! He
was half-conscious and his face — oh! it was knotted

in pain! Dr. Cary was with me. I kissed Benjamin; I had to."

Eric was flung back on the sofa, staring at her as if his eyes would never close.

"You don't — you can't —" he stammered.

"A minute, dear. Last night," she continued wearily, "I thought it out. Don't you see how it is, Eric?" She braced herself, for she felt that as soon as he recovered his amazement she should need great strength. "I cannot marry you," she said in a low, breaking voice. "It must be Benjamin."

Without knowing why, she arose and made as if to move.

"Wait a moment, Rose! What — sit down, please! You can't decide these things like that, dearest. You can't say that!"

"If Ben lives, I must marry him," Rosalind reiterated, as if the repetition gave her firmness. But she sat down again.

Eric ruffled his fingers through his hair.

"Why, Rose, you — you can't mean —! You don't love him?"

"I hate him!" Her voice rang out in momentary agony. Then she felt that she had overstepped. "No, I don't hate him," she corrected in a mild, dead voice. "I don't hate him."

"Could you live with such a man?"

"I must."

"A cripple, Rose? Give all your youth and age to a cripple?"

"I've taken his from him. A life for a life," she repeated from her thoughts of the night before.

"No — no!"

"The world —"

"The world is cruel and unfair! Oh, let us forget the world in ourselves; let's lose its law in a higher law." He put his face near hers, so near that she could feel his breath as he spoke stir over her hair. "There are other lands than America, other peoples, other thoughts, other cares, but there are only two like ourselves. Why, it is nature, dearest, that we should live together. Come! Look in my face, Rose! Look in my face and tell me that you love me! I know you do! I know you want me. You've told me so, and I've kissed your lips, and you're mine, body and soul, you're mine!"

As his arms went round her, Rosalind felt her head swimming.

"Eric! Eric! Please! You're making it impossibly hard! You mustn't talk like this!"

He left her and with hands plunged deep in his pockets strode from the window to the door, to and fro, forward and back, exclaiming to himself.

"You can't mean it! I won't believe it! It's impossible! You can't mean it!"

"I do, Eric. I do, indeed. We must all do our —"

"Duty?" He anticipated bitterly. "Would you put duty before me?"

"If I thought it was right."

Eric realised that his question had been a mistake.

"I am sorry. But is it your duty? If you love me — Why! Rose! Your life will be a mockery, a misery with that man."

"I have thought of my life."

"Have you thought of mine?" he flung out with the inherent selfishness of man.

"You don't mean that!"

"I do! I do!" he hurried on in a last, great

appeal. " It isn't fair to do this. There are two of us in it, Rose. You cannot love me —"

" Oh, Eric, don't be cruel! "

" I want you, Rose. I've got to have you — your gentleness and your strength, your sickness and your health, everything about you! I must have you! "

" What of me? " asked Rosalind, caught by the tumult of his passion. " Do you not think, Eric, that I love you, that I want you as much as you want me? Do you think because women are weak they cannot love? Love is our very being; it's an incident with men. I love you with all my soul."

" Yet you won't marry me? "

Old, far-off memories haunted in his question as he hung over her, his hand upon her bending shoulder.

" It's not a question of that, Eric. I can't! "

" You have finally —"

" If Ben dies, I shall be free."

" God! " Eric sank down on a chair beside her, his head in his hands. One cannot wish for the death of a fellow man!

" He will live," Rosalind said slowly. " He is sure that I will marry him and be a good, loving wife after this flurry of excitement. He will live. You see, it is a question of his life or my happiness."

There was a long pause and the curtain flapped idly on the breeze, now out of the window, now in. When she spoke again, her voice was scarcely audible.

" It must be his life."

Eric remained motionless, his elbows on his knees, his face covered by his hands.

" Eric."

He made a sign that he heard.

" I have rung the bell. Edouard is coming."

Eric arose; his eyes were wet and hot. Going to the window, he stood there with his back to the door, while Edouard silently entered.

"Is the car ready?"

"Yes, Miss Rose."

"I will be down in a moment."

When he had disappeared, Eric turned to her again.

"Where are you going?"

"To the hospital — to him."

A small clock ticked upon the mantelpiece, each moment nearer to Benjamin and farther from Eric; save for that, it was very quiet in the room, very quiet and very much more beautiful than any room might be in their lives again.

Rosalind moved slowly to the door. As she turned and looked back at him, standing in the sunlight with bowed head and clenched hands, a great tenderness ruled her, dominating will, determination, everything.

"Eric, will you kiss me?" she asked in a stifled voice. "It is the last time."

He came to her quickly and silently, and raised her to his lips.

CHAPTER XXV

THE WORLD SET FREE

ROSALIND did not see Eric again. Yet she could not but hear rumours of him — sly, provocative bits of gossip spread by those who knew nothing of her grief, fragmentary conversations abruptly ended on her entrance to a room, a line in some society column, a word in some letter. He had returned to Philadelphia and was plunged in work; he was with friends there; he would remain in America till July.

It was not as if he had died, not as if some swift, unpremeditated fate had torn him from this earth. In death there may be a limitless comfort; in life there is none. Eric was living, breathing this same air of Heaven, pressing this same dust beneath his heel, within reach and call — and yet more separated from her than if the grave were prisoning his young grace and beauty. Rosalind could not think upon it. Her world was suddenly narrowed to herself. So much of circumscribing space had been dedicated to her love and made memorable by its associations that she could not go to the old haunts or sing the old songs. The material world had become vacuous, yawning, unbearable; all living was tangled and confused in her own heart. The flood of feeling oppressed her by day, and her eyes, losing the colour of sight, became mirrors in which she saw the world

she would have made her own; at night her love betrayed determination in her dreams. She and Eric
were continually together — by summer seas, on
sun-crowned mountains, in places that neither had
ever known. And there was perfect happiness between them. To awake from this into the pulsing
silence of a June night with the warm sky pricked
with stars was to be robbed of Paradise.

Yet she knew that there was no other way. She
sought daily to steel herself, to bring in her visits to
the hospital something more than a smile — though
that cost her pain enough, to be sure — something
more than solicitude. Day after day she visited Benjamin, day after day. He grew better rapidly: his
great strength fought off the pain; his great love
purged from his mind the suffering. Beyond all
hopes he mended. Both legs set well. "What a
day," a young interne told Rosalind, " when we can
set the nerves as we can the bones ! " For while the
mind was utterly lucid and untouched, while other
members and organs of the body retained their pris-
tine vigour, Benjamin's legs had lost their ability to
move, helpless, motionless in paralysis.

And then came the day when Benjamin asked to
see Rosalind alone. As yet they had not spoken of
marriage; as yet there had been no intimation of a
decision between them. But to-day Benjamin felt
strong, felt able and equal, like Sir Andrew Barton in
the fine, old ballad, " to rise and fight again." For
love was to him a fight, a good fight, to be sure, but
none the less a physical struggle rather than an emotional phase.

He lay propped up in the bed, his eyes very bright,
his face pale. Beside him sat Rosalind. Through

the hospital window floated that murmuring tran-
quillity which is born on summer afternoons of the
intermingling and softening of many distant sounds.

"Rose," he began slowly, "we are long past the
first of June."

"Yes, Ben." She leaned towards the bed that he
might not have to speak loud; she would make everything easy for him now.

"And I want to say something . . . hard to say.
Do you know that my legs will never get better?
Has Father told you?" She bowed her head. He
laughed to comfort her. "I shall always be — sort
of smashed up like this. And so I wanted to say
. . . I wanted to say that I felt now . . . as I am
now . . . I couldn't ask you to marry me." He
said this very simply and very bravely, his proud
sense of right lending him courage. He could surrender to justice and to nothing else. "I couldn't
ask you to become the wife of — a cripple. I shall
be of use in the world and do good work . . . but
that isn't what a woman wants. So . . . so I
thought I'd just tell you about it," he finished rather
blankly.

His courage helped to strengthen Rosalind. For
a moment she caught at his renunciation and warmed
her poor heart with the beauty which acceptance of
it offered; then she remembered. The truth was too
plain before her; it was her whom every finer feeling
commanded to make the sacrifice.

"I am ready, Ben," she said in low tones.

"Ready? You mean?" In his voice there was
a painfully expectant break.

"I will marry you. I —"

"You — you love me enough to — what! As I
am? As I now am? Do you understand, Rose?

I cannot walk; I shall not be able to walk.   Do you
realise —"

"Don't, Ben!"   She put her hands to her tortured brain.   The picture he drew was too bitterly
faithful of the future she must choose, too uncon-
scionably divergent from the future she had pictured
with Eric.   The clash was unbearable.

"I'm sorry" (in quick regret, misunderstanding
her emotion), "forgive me.   I did not think you —
you cared enough.   There is such suddenness in it."
His mind kept reverting to the physical disability, an
obstacle to him insuperable.   "You will take me this
way?   Oh, Rose, as I am?   You must love me; I
was afraid, terribly afraid that you did not, but now
I think you must."

In his voice there was a kind of awe, an inspired
wonder; he had seen a miracle.   His eyes sought
Rosalind's face with the regard of one transfigured;
his whole spirit seemed to bend before her.   Beneath this worship and this thankfulness Rosalind
trembled.   Acutely conscious of the falseness in her
position, torn with a grief for Eric and a sympathy
for Benjamin, dragged this way by emotion and that
by honour, wearied, anguished, exhausted by the
precedent strain, she felt unequal to the task of living.   To tell Benjamin the truth was necessary;
there must be no deceptions, no half-truths, no confusion between them.   Out of the chaos in her brain
this one thought crystallised, and she began to speak.

"Ben, listen a moment.   I . . . I want you to
know.   Eric —" she found his face very white and
rigid as she spoke the name —"Oh, forgive me, he
is something . . . was something more to me than
you understand.   You never liked him, Ben, you
never made him out.   But he was very dear to me."

She paused; and then, stirred by some impulse foreign to intention, added with wistful simplicity: "I loved him . . . I don't think you ever appreciated the — the depth of it all. You were away, you see, and Eric was very different. It was not fancy, Ben, it was . . . love."

There was long, unstirring silence.

A ray of light from the sloping sun crept upward on the wall. Something in its fading glow tugged at Rosalind's heart; it was less bright now than a moment before; in another moment it would be gone. Gone with her visionary world of happiness and Eric, forever gone.

"There, it's told now . . . over and done with, and we need never, never think more of it." Her voice faltered beyond her control on the repeated word. She sought to change the subject. "It makes no difference . . . to us. Now, let's discuss when you'll be getting up and —"

"No, Rose, please," his voice cut in distinctly. "It does make a difference."

"I think not. I think I know myself."

"It is not a question of that," he said slowly. "I thought . . . you cared for me. And you do not. Only for a moment I thought so. It was strange; I felt it strange then. Only for a moment." Hoping that she would speak, he played with the idea, rephrasing it tenderly, as a father touches with passionate gentleness the cheek of a dying child. But Rosalind could say nothing. There was a great hungriness in his voice, when at last he asked: "Then you do not . . . love me?"

"Not that way," she answered in a whisper.

"And — and you could not learn?"

Rosalind clapped her hands together before her face.

"Not now, Ben, please! While you are suffering, I cannot."

"I shall not suffer so much when I am sure," he said with a pathetic air of reproof.

"I can never learn . . . now." Her voice was gentle, utterly gentle, but something in it brought a cry to Cary's lips.

"Yet you would make this sacrifice for — for me?" he asked timidly.

"Yes, Ben."

Again silence filled the little room. The glow flickered a moment on the ceiling to vanish with the wheel of day; the sun had commenced to shine in another land.

"You have taught me a great lesson, Rose." He broke the quiet first. "You have made me strong; you have made me see things right." That same sense of honour which had prompted him to absolve her from a pledge because of his physical injury, urged him now again to act the nobler part. A fine soul is finest in adversity. "I would not tarnish your life: it is too beautiful, too sacred to me. Marry you? Take advantage of my helpless limbs? Oh, no, no. I can live somehow, but not with your heart sad . . . not with your heart sad."

"But, Ben, you . . ."

"It is better that I lose you — far better. You need never feel that you owe me anything; you need never let what has happened be a cloud. If there is any debtor, it is I."

"But to leave you . . . like this . . ."

"I shall not be lonely," he said painfully with an

air of deep resignation resting on his slow-moving lips. "I shall have your friendship, your understanding."

It was as if a great wind were blowing in Rosalind's heart. At his words she felt her tribulations and grief vanish as the distempered pestilence of day flies before the clean, first breeze of night. She rose to her feet, her heart swelling within her, and looked down upon the stretched figure on the bed.

"Ben, you are making my life, you to whom I thought I must give myself in a bondage. Yes, it was that I thought. May I take your hand? I am not worth the touching of it — and yet, *you* know how it is."

The subtle inflection of her voice stirred a tremor across the white face. It was a heavy hand that Rosalind lifted to her lips, heavy with pain and with surrender.

For a long time she stood thus beside his bed, clasping his great, weary hand and bending slightly in the twilight. Like the falling of a feather darkness had come, as silently and as peacefully. Far in the distant sky she could see a single bright star, new-risen in the arc of night; and its clear, crisp ray shone suddenly deep into her heart, deeper than maidenhood, deeper than dreams, deep to where love labours and forever is reborn.

Footsteps sounded in the corridor. She felt Ben's hand press hers with a fierce tenderness and then relax.

"They are coming. Oh, good-bye . . ."

"Ben," she whispered, "dear, brave friend."

With this she turned and flitted from the room to the world that she had painted, to the world set forever free — and to Eric.

PRINTED IN THE UNITED STATES OF AMERICA

THE following pages contain advertisements of a few
of the Macmillan novels.

ERNEST POOLE'S NEW NOVEL

His Family

The publication of a new novel by the author of *The Harbor* is an event of greatest importance in the literary world. Rarely has an American story met with the success enjoyed by that book and confident have the critics been in their predictions as to Mr. Poole's future work. These predictions would seem to be fully realized in this volume. *His Family* has to do with a father and his three daughters, and their life in the midst of the modern city's conflicting currents. These daughters are very different one from the other in character and the way in which individually they realize earlier ideals or ambitions of their parent, the manner in which he sees himself in them is one of the most interesting qualities of the work, that is tense with emotion, alight with vision and vitally interesting from the very start to the close.

THE MACMILLAN COMPANY

Publishers   64-66 Fifth Avenue   New York

Regiment of Women

BY CLEMENCE DANE

$1.50

This is a story of a clash of wills. How Alwynne Durrand, a sweet-natured, optimistic young girl, comes under the sway of Clare Hartill, clever, attractive, unprincipled, wholly selfish, and how in the end the spell is broken by a man,—this is the author's theme and as she handles it, it is a tremendous theme. Seldom has there been so outstanding a character in fiction as is Miss Hartill. She dominates the entire story, and though the reader cannot like her, nevertheless he will be fascinated by her, much as Alwynne is. And in addition to Miss Hartill there are other clearly drawn people in the book; Alwynne, who is all that a heroine should be; Roger, who saves Alwynne from the unhappiness towards which she seems to be moving, and Elsbeth, Alwynne's aunt, who more than once crosses swords with Clare. The tale is full of incident and variety and cannot but be welcomed by the reader who appreciates a story in which real people move and act.

Lost Endeavour

Another of John Masefield's earlier works is now reprinted. "Lost Endeavour" is a stirring story of adventure, dealing with pirates and buccaneers, and life on the seas in a day when an ocean trip was beset with all kinds of dangers and excitements. Those who have enjoyed "Captain Margaret" and "Multitude and Solitude" will find this tale equally exhilarating.

THE MACMILLAN COMPANY

Publishers   64–66 Fifth Avenue   New York

Gold Must Be Tried by Fire

BY RICHARD AUMERLE MAHER

There are a great many people who regard Mr. Maher's "The Shepherd of the North" as one of the finest stories published last year, a fact which taken in connection with the praise which critics bestowed upon the author for that book makes the announcement of a new story by the same author of distinct importance. "Gold Must Be Tried by Fire" is a vivid and powerful piece of writing, with a central character quite as satisfactory as was the Bishop of the first tale. This character, Daidie Grattan, is a mill hand, who revolts at the monotonous drudgery of her existence. Something closely akin to tragedy touches her and she acquires a new vision. Fortified with this she sets out to alleviate the industrial injustices with which she is familiar from her own personal experience, aiming in the end to uplift and encourage her people. The love story which is woven into this is one of engaging proportions and the happy solution of the problem which has kept the lovers apart brings the volume to a satisfactory close.

THE MACMILLAN COMPANY

Publishers   64-66 Fifth Avenue   New York

Changing Winds

BY ST. JOHN G. ERVINE

$1.60

Wells has pictured the tragedy of war as it falls upon
people looking as it were the other way. Mr. Ervine in
this novel "Changing Winds," shows the same tragic force
falling upon four young men as sparkling and vehemently
alive as ever were, looking directly and intently at life
in all its aspects; and accepting war (all but one of them)
almost blithely when it comes. The title is from the
famous sonnet, "The Dead," by Rupert Brooke, to whose
memory the book is dedicated, by whose spirit it is filled.
And, to use the words of the sonnet, these four lives are
pictured as "blown by changing winds to laughter" winds
of all sorts of interest, the Irish situation (which is frankly
and freshly treated), industrialism, society—"lit by the
rich skies all day." Split, so blown that when the frost
of war does settle upon them there is left for all the pathos
(is it by reason of art or the truth of life?) "a white un-
broken glory," "a shifting peace under the night." The
book is the longest and most ambitious Mr. Ervine has
yet written; it will rank high among the very best novels
written about the war.

THE MACMILLAN COMPANY

Publishers   64-66 Fifth Avenue   New York

Jerry

BY JACK LONDON

There cannot be many more new Jack London books, a fact which will not only be a source of deep regret to the lover of truly American Literature, but which also gives a very deep significance to the announcement of Jerry. It is not at all improbable that in this novel Mr. London has achieved again the wide-sweeping success that was his in the case of "The Call of the Wild." For Jerry is a dog story; a story which in its big essentials recalls the earlier masterpiece, and yet one which is in no way an echo of that work, but quite as original in its theme and quite as satisfying in the way in which that theme is treated.

Benoit Castain

BY MARCEL PREVOST

This story deals with an episode that took place in a little corner of northern France just after the outbreak of the war. It is as well written as the author's reputation would lead one to expect and has been splendidly rendered into English. The theme is handled in a direct and simple way and shows special knowledge of the section of the country where it is laid. It is altogether a most interesting human document in novel form.

THE MACMILLAN COMPANY

Publishers   64-66 Fifth Avenue   New York

CPSIA information can be obtained
at www.ICGtesting.com
Printed in the USA
BVHW040221170420
577798BV00008B/53

9 781298 710017